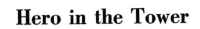

Hero in the Tower

by HANS HELLMUT KIRST

HERO
IN THE
TOWER

Hans Hellmut Kirst

Translated from the
German by
J. MAXWELL BROWNJOHN

COWARD, McCANN & GEOGHEGAN, INC.
New York

It all began in the late summer of 1940, soon after the Germans' spectacularly successful campaign in France, when a heavy antiaircraft battery was stationed on the outskirts of D., a town some fifty miles southwest of Paris. The immediate result was a series of fatalities, all officially recorded as accidental deaths.

They occurred at a time when the national necessity for war had started to gain widespread acceptance, a time when murder itself was considered quite normal and referred to in current parlance by other, more agreeable names. Even today, there are many who even now would describe what happened as "only human," if not legally and morally unobjectionable.

And yet, even at that early stage, there did exist a few individuals who regarded the so-called exigencies of war as a blatant personal challenge. It soon dawned on them that, under prevailing rules, their only course was to murder the murderers—or at least one of them.

Murder was duly done, and "Case D." resulted. This book seeks to reconstruct its background.

Hero in the Tower

1

Death in the Morning

"He's had it," Sergeant Major Krüger said expertly. "Neck's broken—must have snapped like a twig."

With a connoisseur's eye, he examined the body that lay sprawled in front of his immaculate boots. He had seen a number of dead bodies in his time, not only during the triumphant campaigns in Poland and France but at odd intervals before and since. To Krüger, death was all in a day's work.

"It would have to be Schulz," he went on. There was no particular reproach in his voice, more a note of human understanding. Krüger's displays of emotion were familiar to those who knew him well. "Trust the poor bastard to make trouble even as a corpse."

The word "trouble" seemed to galvanize him. Three of Krüger's men were standing there, alert and deferential, registering the precise degree of docility proper to his unit and personal presence.

"You," he said, "what the hell are you gaping at? Anyone'd think you've never seen a dead man before." He pointed to the flagstones. "That's brains, you know, not scrambled egg."

One of the soldiers snickered obediently. The other two strove to look equally amused. Krüger, who had a reputation for wit, sensed there was no need to waste any more time on them.

Suddenly he caught sight of a fourth man standing in the background, a corporal whose face was unfamiliar. Krüger was unimpressed: sloppy stance, pallid cheeks, popping eyes, gaping mouth—in short, a thoroughly unsoldierly apparition. Easy meat for the Krügers of this world.

"Look," he said soothingly, "cream puffs like Schulz are expendable, so why worry when they get what's coming to them? We're fighting a war. This is a tough unit. Anybody see what happened?"

"He fell out of the tower window," one of the soldiers volunteered eagerly. "Sailed through the air like a bat—I saw him with my own eyes. Next thing I knew, he landed. . . ."

"Splat on the flagstones, eh?" It was clear nothing could ruffle Sergeant Major Krüger. "Still, he'd have broken his neck even if it had been gravel, falling from that height."

Krüger stared up at the tower of the ancient château. His gaze traveled up the crumbling façade, past elongated apertures imitative of arrow slits, to where, set in an expanse of pale-gray rain-washed stone threaded with dark fissures by centuries of frost, tiers of windows jostled each other beneath a conical roof. The topmost window was wide open.

The sergeant major smiled. He felt reasonably sure he had glimpsed a face in the shadowy interior of the tower, a pale, intense, clean-cut face which drew back and disappeared like an abruptly extinguished lantern. He nodded to himself.

"Gunner Schulz," he concluded, jerking his thumb at the

corpse, "had been detailed to clean the tower windows—detailed by me personally. The stupid cunt must have lost his balance and fallen. In other words, it was an accident. Got it?"

At least three of the four men appeared to get the message. They stood dutifully with their backs to the crumbling old château whose north tower loomed over them. This was where they had spent the weeks following the great and glorious defeat of France, wonderful weeks of gorging and boozing which all of them were determined to enjoy in peace. Only a fool would stick his neck out and make trouble.

"I asked you dumbbells a question. Did you get me?"

"Yes, Sergeant Major," three voices replied in unison.

Krüger nodded and turned to the fourth man, the corporal whose face he didn't know. He looked amenable enough, not that the sergeant major expected anything else. Individualists had no future in his outfit.

"That's settled, then," Krüger said, legs planted sturdily apart and hands on hips. "It was an accident, and that's what you'll say if you're asked—all four of you. Now get moving, you lazy bastards. Nobody stands around with his thumb in his ass as long as I'm in charge here. Clear up that mess and dump it in the stable."

"What if it wasn't an accident?" It was the fourth man again. His tone was extremely polite, and the diffidence in his voice conveyed regret at having to speak at all. "Seems to me there might be another explanation."

Sergeant Major Krüger turned on him with an air of disbelief. "What's that supposed to be—a joke?"

"I simply took the liberty. . . ."

"You simply what? Listen, you amateur comic, and get this straight. Anyone who takes liberties with me needs his head examined."

"I simply thought. . . ."

"So you thought too, did you? Well, here's another tip. I'm the one who does the thinking around here—or hadn't you heard?"

Sergeant Major Krüger, an adept in the art of barrack-room repartee, was constantly at pains to expand his repertoire. All his men knew this, including the three standing in front of him. Relieved that for once they were not Krüger's target, they smiled to themselves. The stranger seemed finally to have grasped what he was up against, because he shut his mouth and kept it shut.

Krüger promptly construed his reaction as a mark of respect. "All right," he continued magnanimously, "explain yourself, you miserable s.o.b. What the hell do you mean by speaking out of turn?"

"Perhaps I didn't express myself properly, Sergeant Major." The soldier stiffened to attention, not very convincingly. "I didn't mean to take a liberty and I don't often permit myself the luxury of thinking. My remark was ill judged and irrelevant."

Krüger grinned from ear to ear. He peered at the man with amused curiosity. "You really are a comic, aren't you? Is that the way you normally talk, or are you trying to be a wise guy?"

"Only a fool would try that," the corporal replied, sounding almost sincere. "Sergeant Major," he added smartly, after an infinitesimal pause.

"Well, then," Krüger said. "Maybe you aren't so dumb after all."

"I do my best to learn, Sergeant Major."

Krüger's gaze dwelt suspiciously on the corporal's pale face. "You catch on damn fast—almost too fast. Okay, you were mumbling something about the accident a couple of minutes back. What was it?"

"Nothing special, Sergeant Major. Really, nothing worth repeating."

"You let me be the judge of that," snapped Krüger. "Well, what's eating you? Come on, friend, out with it!"

The corporal glanced up at the tower. "It's only a theory," he said cautiously. "The body was already lying there when I arrived."

"Good," observed Krüger, not displeased. "What's this theory of yours?"

"I only heard what was said—that he sailed through the air like a bat."

"So what? Why shouldn't he sail through the air, Professor? What's so strange about that?"

"Nothing much," the corporal conceded. "I only thought, if he sailed through the air he can hardly have fallen like a stone—the way he would have if he'd been cleaning a window and lost his balance."

"Listen to the man!" Krüger said. "He's been thinking again. Okay, what *if* he sailed instead of fell? What would that signify, in your expert opinion?"

"It might mean he committed suicide. On the other hand, he might have been helped on his way—pushed deliberately."

Krüger frowned. "So that's what you think, is it? Or rather, that's what you thought before you heard my opinion. You did hear what I said, I suppose?"

"Yes, Sergeant Major, you said it was an accident."

"Well?"

"In that case, it must have been," the soldier replied meekly. "After all, you should know."

Krüger screwed up his eyes as if trying to identify a target at long range. Still peering, he said with sudden decision: "Don't get any funny ideas, that's all. I don't like idea men in my outfit, let alone snoopers. Everything's run by the book here, so get that into your thick skull. Any questions?"

"No questions, Sergeant Major."

The words hung in the air as though awaiting amplification, but none came. Krüger felt satisfied. Being a thorough man—"Better be safe than sorry" was one of his favorite expressions—he still decided to modify his original order.

"The body stays where it is," he commanded. He leveled a forefinger at each of the other three in turn. "You make sure nobody moves anything. You get hold of a blanket or tarpaulin and cover him up—hurry up about it. And you," he said to the third man without drawing breath, "get me QMS Softer. On the double!"

"Yes, Sergeant Major!" The triple response crackled like a fusilade.

"And keep mum!" snapped Krüger. "If anybody has the nerve to start spreading latrine gossip about this man's death, I'll personally kick his ass. Is that clear?"

It was, pellucidly clear. One of the soldiers stood fast. The other two sprang to life, counterfeiting pure zeal with a skill born of long practice. They were Krüger graduates. Things hummed when Krüger was around. Absolute obedience was his stock-in-trade, and he luxuriated in such demonstrations.

This time he didn't luxuriate for long. The stranger seemed to demand his urgent attention. Drawing a deep breath, he turned to him and said with menacing calm, "All right, you —who the hell are you? How did you get here and what do you think you're doing here?"

"Corporal Bergen," the newcomer replied, trying to click his heels but failing miserably. "Transferred from group headquarters to Battery No. 3. I've been assigned to the signals section."

"So that's who you are!" Krüger heaved a sigh of relief. "God damn it soldier, why didn't you tell me in the first place? That simplifies everything."

A look of comprehension dawned on Bergen's face. "If you say so, Sergeant Major, I suppose it does."

"You bet your sweet life it does." Krüger beamed at him fiercely. "Know what you are, Bergen? You're a pushy young pup. Lucky for you I'm an animal lover, isn't it? As far as I'm concerned, pups can piddle anywhere they like as long as they don't raise a leg near me. Anybody who fouls my doorstep is in trouble. I can take a lot, but that's where I draw the line—understand?"

"Yes, Sergeant Major, I understand."

"Then report to the orderly room on the double," Krüger said sternly, adding with faint amusement, "By the way, any idea why signals needs a replacement? Because your predecessor liked to fool around with things he didn't understand. He went to bed with a hand grenade. They had to scrape him off the mattress with a shovel—nothing left of him but porridge. Let's hope you're more careful."

"What gives around here?" Bergen inquired. One of the soldiers had returned with a tarpaulin and was helping the other drape it, almost reverently, over the corpse. "What goes on in this place?"

"What a damn fool question to ask! You from outer space, or something?" said the tarpaulin-bearer, bending still lower over the body.

The sentry posted by Krüger, a gunner named Wassermann, was a short, wiry youngster with foxy eyes. He sidled over to Bergen. "Sounds as if you don't know much about this outfit."

"I'm all ears," Bergen replied. "Why not let me in on it?"

The first gunner, who was still kneeling beside the corpse, glared at Wassermann. "Keep your big mouth shut. If you want to sound off, don't do it while I'm around."

"Screw off, then," Wassermann retorted, unimpressed. He continued to eye Bergen with interest.

"Okay," Bergen said, "fill me in. What's so special about this outfit?"

Wassermann cackled dryly. "You've just joined the finest and most successful unit in the whole of the glorious German army. We never let up, even when the guns stop firing. Battery No. 3 is fighting its own war."

Bergen indicated the shrouded body. "Is that one of the casualties?"

"Sure."

"I didn't hear that," said the gunner who was kneeling by the corpse.

"Okay, so you're deaf." Wassermann glanced around carefully to see if there was anyone else within earshot. Reassured, he went on, "I suppose you think we're safely in the middle of occupied enemy territory, don't you? Well, we're not—we're right in the front line. That's a big responsibility to some people."

"Who, for instance?"

"I'm leaving," announced the soldier who was tending the corpse. He rose to his feet, frowning, and disappeared quickly through a side entrance into the château.

"What's with him?" asked Bergen. "Is he scared of something?"

"Not scared, just conscientious," Wassermann said. "He likes to toe the line, keep his nose clean, play ball—that type. This is a heavy ack-ack battery on active service—the guns are only four hundred yards away, complete with live ammunition in case enemy planes come visiting. Combat-ready twenty-four hours a day, that's Battery No. 3. Like I said, we're in the front line here."

"What about this château?"

"Battery HQ," explained Wassermann. "Organized to within an inch of its life by Sergeant Major Krüger. Krüger's in cahoots with Captain Hein, and Hein has a direct line to God Almighty. He's got shares in this war."

"Sounds as if you don't like the setup."

"I have to like it. That goes for everybody around here,

including you. The gun position's over there, on the edge of the grounds. This château and the family church are the HQ buildings, where they keep the supplies, transport and so on. It's all part of the same outfit. One big happy family, that's us, and nobody's going to break it up—nobody and nothing." Wassermann paused. "What's on your mind—feel like trying to buck the system?"

"Maybe, with a little help. Yours, for instance."

"So the fag finally copped it, did he?" Quartermaster Sergeant Softer, commonly known as Moon Face, or MF for short, was the NCO responsible for battery supplies. He waddled swiftly up to Krüger and stood there with his spherical head a little on one side. "He didn't get a chance to spill anything, I suppose?"

"Only his brains. By the time I arrived he was lying there like a prefabricated cow turd," Krüger said.

Softer's grin was unabashed. "That's the ticket. One more fairy we don't have to worry about."

Krüger and his current sidekick were standing at the main entrance of the weather-beaten three-storied château. Every guidebook listed the place although most of its architectural merits had long since disappeared.

Château D. had once, together with some dozen other country seats, been owned by the Dukes of Orléans. Its grounds were now dotted with the assorted motorized transport of Battery No. 3: personal utility vehicles, Henschel trucks, gun-towing tractors with caterpillar tracks. The drives, lawns and flower beds had been churned into a mess worthy of twentieth-century warfare.

Sergeant Major Krüger had requisitioned the château and outbuildings on behalf of Battery No. 3 and its headquarters personnel. His allocation of premises displayed a systematic approach. The ground floor housed the kitchens and canteen—hours severely restricted except for senior

NCO's, who had access at all times—together with various storerooms and the orderly room. The first floor provided sleeping quarters for junior NCO's and gunners, who were housed on a strictly segregated basis in vaulted chambers of varying sizes.

The upper floor had, at Krüger's suggestion, been reserved for the battery commander. Captain Hein's quarters consisted of a large banquet hall, a bedroom, and the tower chamber that commanded a panoramic view of the surrounding countryside and overlooked the family church on the edge of the grounds. This church, also timeworn to the point of dilapidation, was crammed with tombs and coffins whose significance had yet to dawn on the members of Battery No. 3.

Softer had a sudden thought. "I hope he was properly dressed—Schulz, I mean."

"Don't worry. Parade-ready. Even his fly was buttoned."

"So we're lucky again? There's no Schulz like a dead Schulz. At least he can't go around dropping hints or making trouble for the unit. Feel like a drink?"

Krüger nodded acquiescence and followed Softer into the quartermaster's stores, which occupied a large proportion of the château's ground floor. The first cavernous chamber contained ordinary supplies. The second was lined from floor to ceiling with shelves bearing bottles, officially listed as "captured enemy equipment." The third housed crates and cartons filled with soap, perfume, cosmetics and silk underwear destined for use as "troops' comforts"—a dramatic demonstration of Germany's armed victory over France.

Krüger and Softer installed themselves in a pair of comfortable leather armchairs in storeroom No. 2. A number of opened bottles stood nearby. Being familiar with Krüger's tastes, the QMS knew that his favorite hair of the dog was a tangy white crème de menthe which absolved the drinker from cleaning his teeth.

Krüger took the brimming tumbler Softer handed him and drained it at a gulp. He shook his head blissfully and exhaled with relish. After an elaborate pause, he said, "All the same, things aren't as quiet as they could be."

"Trouble, you mean?"

"Looks like it."

"Nothing you can't handle," Softer said briskly, and refilled their glasses. "Bottoms up."

France had a magnificent climate, Softer reflected. You could drink around the clock without feeling any ill effects. *Nobody* must be allowed to spoil things, least of all a flaming faggot like the late and unlamented Gunner Schulz. "You've coped with worse things before now," he said. "This kid with the broken neck—he's small game, Krüger. Small game doesn't stink much and it doesn't stink for long."

Softer's voice had a businesslike ring. There was no need for mutual flattery—the two men understood each other too well. They'd been together ever since the Polish campaign. The quartermaster sergeant's suety face crinkled in a reassuring grin. "I can't imagine you getting jumpy, not after all this time."

"Takes a lot to send my blood pressure up, I admit, but I'm just beginning to wonder how long it can go on."

"For as long as it pays us to keep things this way—for the battery's sake, our sake, your outfit's sake—anything you like. Christ, Krüger, we've only just started! The real pickings are yet to come."

Krüger studied the clear but sticky liquid in his glass. "Pickings?" he mused. "With this battery commander?"

"Why not? Hein concentrates on his own hobbies. He doesn't interfere with ours as long as we give him a free hand. You aren't planning to dump him, are you?"

"I could, now, if I wanted to."

"What's the point?" Softer frowned. "You don't know what his replacement would be like. A new man could give us a lot of trouble. Better the devil you know, if you ask me."

Krüger continued to brood. "We can handle anyone in this outfit. It doesn't matter who they send us—we always cut them down to size in the end."

Softer raised his glass with an encouraging air. "We know Captain Hein from top to bottom, especially bottom, and that's money in the bank. My advice is, keep him satisfied."

"It's what he's satisfied by that worries me," growled Krüger. "Today's could be the last straw. I'll have to report Schulz's death whether I like it or not, and that means a court of inquiry. There's no way around it."

"Who cares?" Softer retorted. "Come to think of it, an inquiry mightn't be a bad thing. Let them stir up a bit of mud. It'll give you a chance to sort things out, and that's what counts. The bigger the fuss the more favors Hein'll owe you when it's settled."

"Maybe you're right," Krüger said grudgingly. A thin film of sweat mantled his brow as he drained his third tumbler of crème de menthe. Captain Hein was planning to recommend him for the Iron Cross, or, failing that, the War Service Cross with crossed swords. It would be crazy to cut off his own nose. "We'll have to be damn careful, that's all I know."

"Our battery commander's a war hero, don't forget. He wants to preserve his reputation, but he won't be able to—things being the way they are—without your help. I told you already, Hein's money in the bank. You can count on me."

"How, exactly?"

"Any way I can. Refreshing witnesses' memories with generous doses of cognac or supplying hand-tailored statements by strong-arming a few of the weaker brethren—things like that. I'd go to a lot of trouble and expense for you, Krüger. If push came to shove."

"You're bringing tears to me eyes," Krüger said dryly. "What's in it for you?"

"Nothing!" protested Softer. "Nothing at all. Except for the little matter we discussed already—my battery recreation center."

"Your brothel, you mean."

"Call it what you want. I look at it from the health point of view. My aim is to provide a service—female company plus guaranteed hygiene. If that isn't a morale booster, what is?"

"Try telling that to Captain Hein."

"No problem—not after today." Softer's moon face glowed confidently. "He knows which side his bread's buttered—or he will, once it's pointed out to him. You're just the man to do it, Krüger. Nobody better, and no time like the present."

"Anything wrong, Sergeant Major?" Captain Hein, OC Battery No. 3, demanded. "You seem worried about something. What is it?"

"It's Gunner Schulz, sir."

"What about him?"

"I detailed him for duty as your personal orderly, sir, as usual. First thing this morning."

"He turned up," Captain Hein said casually. Almost absently, with his lean face averted and his eyes fixed on something in the far distance, he added, "Why bother me with such trivialities?"

Sergeant Major Krüger, fresh from the quartermaster's stores, had climbed the broad and crumbling staircase to Hein's suite. "You didn't hear what happened?" Krüger inquired cautiously.

"What is there to hear?" Hein's narrow, angular head, with its thinly incised lips, compelling blue eyes and helmet of metallic fair hair, jerked as if he were sniffing the air.

He reached almost automatically for the glass in front of him.

Ever since the glorious defeat of France, in which he had played a significant part, Captain Hein had made it his custom to drink nothing but champagne. Veuve Clicquot Ponsardin 1933 was his favorite, and he poured it down like mineral water from morning till night—indeed, throughout the night as well.

"Well, Sergeant Major, what *has* happened?"

"So you don't know, sir." Krüger's tone conveyed admiration for such a masterful display of composure.

"What ought I to know—in your opinion?" Hein was actually smiling now, though only faintly: He presented the familiar spectacle of recent days: a lone figure seated at the far end of the long table. The sergeant major was still standing near the door of the banquet hall.

"If you're referring to Schulz, Sergeant Major, I can't say I find him particularly prepossessing—no promise whatsoever. As far as I'm concerned you can reassign him to general duties immediately. You'll find him up in the tower chamber, cleaning windows."

"He isn't there anymore," Krüger announced. "We found him at the foot of the tower, on the flagstones. Dead. Killed instantly, it looked."

"How appalling," said Captain Hein, every inch the imperturbable man of war. He sounded totally unmoved. Death was deplorable, of course, but inevitable. "No guts, that boy. How did he come to do such a thing?"

"Doesn't the captain have a likely explanation?"

"You expect me to provide one?" Hein asked softly, taking delicate sips from his champagne. "What do you take me for, a kindergarten teacher or the commander of a battery whose senior warrant officer you happen to be?"

"Sir," Krüger said, with an undisguised edge to his voice, "this death could raise some awkward questions."

"Could, but needn't necessarily—is that what you mean, Sergeant Major? I hope so."

"Group HQ have to be notified of all deaths—it's routine, sir," Krüger said. "You know what that means—an official inquiry. It's automatic, even if the whole thing *was* an accident."

"And was it an accident—in your opinion?"

"Of course, sir," Krüger said promptly. "That is, as long as the captain thinks it's the most likely explanation. It might be the only one, under the circumstances."

"I see we understand each other as usual," Hein said calmly. "You've obviously hit on the proper way to handle the whole affair. I consider it as yet another proof, if one were needed, that I can rely on you completely."

"I do my best, sir," Krüger replied, straightfaced. Even more solemnly, he added, "There's nothing I wouldn't do for the battery."

"You're a dependable man, Sergeant Major," Hein observed. "No one appreciates your loyalty more than I do, and loyalty deserves its reward—official recognition of some kind."

"Thank you, sir."

"But what form should it take? Don't hesitate to speak up if you've any ideas on the subject."

"A sense of solidarity is its own reward, sir," Krüger assured him. Aphorisms of this kind had been Krüger's trademark ever since he took to following Goebbels' effusions in the *Völkischer Beobachter*. "All the same, I wouldn't say no to an official pat on the back—just as a matter of principle, if you know what I mean."

"I think I do." Hein gave a thin smile. "The battery has been allocated some decorations and you're applying for one—correct?"

"Personally, sir, I'd be happy to pass it up. I wouldn't begrudge it to anyone else with a fair claim to it. On the other hand, if you're looking for someone who really deserves a medal, you could do worse than pick me. After all, I did help bring out a couple of casualties under enemy fire."

"The Iron Cross is yours, Sergeant Major. You've earned it."

"Thank you, sir," Krüger said again. "And as far as this accident goes. . . ."

"You'll produce some convincing evidence to support the facts—I know I can rely on you to protect the battery's good name. You can do it, Sergeant Major. You've always coped with our little problems in the past. I'm sure you won't disappoint me this time."

Noon the same day saw the arrival of two warrant officers, Konz and Kator, from the provost marshal's department, their broad chests adorned with the silver plaques that identified them as members of the German military police. They behaved in a bluff and hearty manner, like a pair of animated teddy bears.

Alert to the unerring voice of instinct, they made their way into the château and headed straight for the quartermaster's stores. Here they stood lost in admiration of Softer's loot.

"Not bad!" said one of them—Konz or Kator.

"Not bad at all!" said the other—Kator or Konz.

"Troops' comforts," Softer hastened to explain, gesturing to one of his minions to find Krüger. "All reserved for military personnel."

"We're military personnel too," mused one of the MP's.

Softer's antennae vibrated. "Of course," he agreed amiably, "but I can't issue any of this stuff without Krüger's say-so."

Krüger appeared promptly in response to Softer's SOS. Summing up the situation at a glance, he launched into his all-pals-together routine. The MP's were allowed to sample the best that France—and Softer—could provide. The quartermaster sergeant even dug out some Franziskaner Spatenbräu, straight from Munich.

"Nice place you have here," said Konz—or Kator—appreciatively. "Well organized, too—a real home away from home."

His companion sank back into an armchair. "A man could really put his feet up and relax here. Pity we're on duty."

"Who cares why you're here?" Krüger cried jovially. "The main thing is, you're enjoying yourselves."

"We are that," declared Kator—or Konz. "Can't remember when I enjoyed myself more."

They drank Armagnac with Spaten beer chasers and plowed through ham and eggs followed by loaves of fresh-baked white bread and Camembert. Harmony descended on the gathering like a gentle dew.

"Fact remains," said one of the MP's, belching vigorously while the other yawned, "we're here on business."

"What's it about?" Krüger inquired. "I'm sure we can settle it between us if we tackle it head on. Let's hear the worst."

Konz—or Kator—turned to the sergeant major and lowered his voice confidentially. "Charges have been made against a member of your battery, a sergeant name of Ronge or Range."

"What's he supposed to have done?"

"Started a riot in town. He cleared the Hôtel de France and seriously injured at least three people while he was at it—an infantryman, a French civilian and a member of the town commandant's staff. They're all in the hospital."

"Quite an achievement," Krüger said, stroking his jaw. "Worked them over thoroughly, did he?"

"You can say that again," one of the MP's confirmed.

"Shame he had to pick on somebody who works in the town commandant's office, that's all."

"So it was the town commandant who made the complaint, was it?"

"May have been," Konz—or Kator—conceded reluctantly. "We aren't permitted to divulge the name of an informant during the preliminary stages of an investigation."

"The town commandant's a big fat zero," declared Krüger. "Speaking as a man with front-line experience, he's all hot air—a goddamned civilian in uniform."

"All the same, it doesn't change the fact that we have to follow up information received. We've no authority to drop a case unless someone proves we're barking up the wrong tree. The evidence has to be watertight. Any ideas?"

Ideas were Krüger's specialty. He suggested his guests might care for something sweet, and Softer materialized with some canned pineapple rings steeped in kirsch. While the MP's were devouring them, Krüger thought hard. He knew exactly who they were after. It was Senior Gunnery Sergeant Runge, Hein's golden-haired boy and a universal credit to the battery.

"Ronge, you said, or Range?" drawled Krüger. "We don't have a sergeant here by that name."

"You mean it?" said Konz—or Kator. Whichever it was, he seemed genuinely delighted.

"No Ronge, no Range."

"That wraps it up, then. Your statement has been officially noted. Now we can get down to some serious drinking. If your quartermaster has got another crate or two of that Spatenbräu tucked away, I wouldn't be averse. There's nothing that can't be cured by a couple of beers between friends, that's what I always say. Friendship's a great thing, Sergeant Major. Let's drink to it!"

* * *

"There's a funny smell around here," Gunner Wassermann declared loudly, fixing his immediate neighbors with a challenging stare. "Anybody else notice it?"

He had taken his place at one of the three canteen tables allotted to the rank and file. In front of him stood a brimming bowl of pea soup flavored with smoked ham. The ham itself reposed in a dish on the fourth table, which was covered with a white paper cloth and reserved for senior NCO's.

There, in solitary state, sat Sergeant Arm, battery transport officer. Deliberately, Arm carved himself a large slice of ham. He sat there with it poised on his fork, apparently lost in thought but really alert to what was being said in the bare, lofty, whitewashed room that served as a canteen.

A dozen or more men were eagerly spooning up their soup in silence. They too appeared to be digesting the significance of Wassermann's query. One of them, a corporal whose face was unfamiliar to Arm, broke the silence.

"A smell?" said Bergen, edging closer to Wassermann. "Of what?"

"Shit, my friend, pure and unadulterated shit." Wassermann treated his table companions to another provocative stare. "What's more, it stinks to high heaven. I should know —I'm a connoisseur."

Bergen eyed the others hopefully. They might be feigning indifference but they were certainly tuned in. One or two of them went so far as to give Wassermann an encouraging wink.

"Take corpses," Bergen said thoughtfully. "They stink too. Not much to begin with, but it's only a question of time before everybody notices."

"Not everybody," Wassermann remarked with undiminished volume. "A lot of people in this place seem to have lost their sense of smell. They couldn't tell the difference between pea soup and a dead body."

"Do you mind?" Sergeant Arm's powerful baritone reverberated through the room. A net of wrinkles appeared on his lean and weather-beaten ski-instructor face as it broke into the semblance of a grin. "I came here to eat, Wassermann, not vomit."

"When I said it stunk around here," Wassermann pursued relentlessly, "I didn't mean the food."

"I don't give a fuck what you meant." Sergeant Arm looked annoyed. "I've got a healthy appetite and I don't plan to have it spoiled by you or anybody else, understand?"

"Perhaps Gunner Wassermann ought to explain in more detail," Bergen suggested politely. "Speaking for myself, I'd be interested to hear what he's driving at."

"You, whatever your name is, take your plate and get lost." Arm didn't raise his voice. "That goes for all of you— all except Wassermann. You can finish your pig swill outside. If you don't like it, blame the corporal with the big mouth. All right move!"

The gunners needed no second bidding. They picked up their bowls and filed out looking relieved. Bergen seemed inclined to linger but was hurriedly propelled outside. A minute later the canteen was empty except for Arm and Wassermann, who sat facing each other two tables apart.

"Are you crazy?" Arm demanded. His good humor still hadn't deserted him. "Somebody must have been putting ideas into your head, Wassermann, or you wouldn't be looking for trouble this way. Who put you up to it?"

Wassermann looked doggedly determined. "This setup would make anybody sick sooner or later."

"This setup?" said Arm, stiffening. Very slowly, his goodwill started evaporating. "You're not by any chance referring to Battery No. 3?"

"No, Sergeant, I'm talking about the war."

A grin reappeared on Arm's face. So the big-mouthed bastard didn't dare question the unit's sacred name after all. Alfons Arm—or "Hot Lips," as he admitted to having been christened by ladies of exalted social rank—promptly reverted to amiability.

"While we're on the subject, Wassermann, I've been getting pretty sick of *you* these past few weeks."

"I didn't know you cared, Sergeant," Wassermann said. "To what do I owe the honor?"

Arm shook his head with subdued melancholy. To those who knew him, this was a danger signal.

"You poor bewildered little bastard," he said, apparently more in sorrow than anger. "I suppose you think you can sound off whenever you feel like it because you happen to be one of my best mechanics. Just because you can repair a gun tractor better than anybody around here, you figure you're fireproof—is that it?"

"I was only trying to. . . ."

"Stir things up—that's what you were trying to do, sonny boy, and not for the first time. Well, if you think you can make trouble in front of me you'd better think again."

"I sometimes get the feeling, Sergeant. . . ."

"So do I, but only with women." Arm paused to enjoy his own joke. "Look, Wassermann, *nobody* makes the same mistake twice, not with me or Krüger. You stick your neck out just one more time and I'll wring it. People will start saying: 'Wassermann belongs to the transportation section, and that's Arm's department. Arm's responsible for him'—and where will that leave me?"

"But things have been happening lately. . . ."

"Bullshit! It's none of your business or anybody else's in my section. And don't think you're indispensable, Wassermann, because you aren't."

"In that case, Sergeant, I'd like to put in my third application for a transfer."

"I bet you would, you miserable s.o.b.!" Arm bellowed with laughter but his eyes regarded Wassermann coldly. "What are you planning to do, sabotage the transportation section? All right, I admit you're a good mechanic. You're needed here and I'm going to hang onto you one way or another, so make up your mind to it. There are ways."

"For instance?"

"Well, stopping your special allowances, to start with. Then there's extra guard duty, no leave passes and a season ticket to my circus. How does that sound?"

"Not that," said Wassermann. "Anything but that." Arm's "circus" was a weekly parade for special offenders. Almost everybody who had tasted its delights wished he'd never stepped out of line in the first place. "Okay, I'll keep my mouth shut."

"No reason why you shouldn't use it for eating," Arm said encouragingly. "Or drinking—not to mention a few other things. Surprising what you can do with a girl if you use your ingenuity—take it from me, I'm an expert." "Hot Lips" smote the table delightedly. "All right, come over here and sit down. Make yourself at home."

Gunner Wassermann obeyed the summons. He took his bowl and sat down beside Arm, who promptly sawed off a hunk of smoked ham the size of his fist and dropped it in Wassermann's pea soup. "Chin up," he reassured him. "We aren't a bad bunch—in fact we're too softhearted for our own good. It's all a question of toeing the line."

"Taken any statements yet?" inquired the officer from the Judge Advocate General's department, a major named Born. "Any witnesses?"

Sergeant Major Krüger looked ingenuous. "What sort of witnesses?"

"Well, people who actually saw the deceased fall to his death."

"Nobody did," Krüger replied flatly. "Someone heard a thump, went to look, and found him lying there on the flagstones. That's the whole story, sir, just the way we put it in our report. In other words it was an accident. Why, does anyone say different?"

"Any reason why they should, Sergeant Major?" Major Born's eyes twinkled amiably behind rimless glasses. He was a short, slight, dapper man with a spark of gaiety which he took care to conceal beneath his uniform in the interests of military discipline. "Seriously, though, I'm here to investigate the accident and confirm your report. Just for the record."

Krüger frowned. "It isn't standard procedure, sir."

"You mean a phone call would have done? You report the incident, we rubber-stamp your report and file it away—is that what you mean?"

"More or less." Krüger, himself an expert manipulator of red tape, spoke with airy condescension. "Anyway, this sort of accident usually comes under Group HQ, not Regiment."

"Don't jump to any conclusions, Sergeant Major—they could be the wrong ones." Major Born's eyes twinkled again. "We of the JAG's department are simply here to uphold the rule of law. And that, I trust, is a subject as close to your heart as mine."

Born was attached to Regimental HQ. In Krüger's estimation he was one of the egghead desk warriors who were employed to make life more difficult for honest-to-God soldiers —a civilian who had been incongruously stuffed into uniform and was determined to make the most of his petty authority. Krüger quickly sensed that it might be inadvisable to rub him the wrong way.

"I'm sure Captain Hein will welcome your visit, sir."

"You really think so?" Born asked eagerly. He was aware of the war hero's record and glowed at the idea of meeting Captain Hein in person.

"In the meantime, sir, I'll round up all the witnesses I can find."

"You do that, Sergeant Major." Major Born smiled at Krüger, man to man. "And try to consider the whole thing as a matter of form—pure routine. After all, we have plenty of time on our hands at present, between one campaign and the next. We can afford to spend more time on things than usual."

Krüger was familiar with every aspect of desk warfare. Group HQ, and the Group commander's adjutant in particular, was obviously anxious to cover itself by passing the buck to Regiment. Major Born, who had undoubtedly been sitting around twiddling his thumbs, was the ideal man for the job. He could picture the reaction at Regimental HQ. "Handle it, Born. . . ."

Well, that was precisely what Born must be allowed to do. He was promptly conducted to the spacious banquet hall, where Captain Hein greeted him with consummate courtesy and pressed him to accept a glass of champagne. War hero and upholder of the rule of law toasted each other ceremoniously.

Meanwhile, Krüger was procuring the witnesses Born had asked for. He sent for the three men he had found in the vicinity of Schulz's body. The trio, Wassermann included, eyed Krüger apprehensively.

"Now hear this, you village idiots," he said cheerfully. "Some desk warrior has just turned up from Regiment. He wants to have a word with you—yes, you, believe it or not. But don't start pissing yourselves, not yet. I'll make sure you do that afterward, if you don't say the right things. Got me?"

"Yes, Sergeant Major!" came the triple response.

"The truth, the whole truth and nothing but the truth, that's what I want. Speak up and don't be shy. Don't lay it on too thick, either. No need to shed tears over Schulz. Any trained soldier ought to be able to tell the difference between a man and an asshole. That's what they call a sense of discrimination."

Krüger went on to subpoena an expert witness in the person of Corporal Neumann, the ever reliable NCO in charge of the battery medical section. Neumann had a pear-shaped body mounted on legs that looked spindly even in their clumsy boots. His rosy face wore a perpetual smile and he tended, in offhand moments, to wring his hands like a funeral director offering condolences.

"I know what I know," he assured Krüger, "—all I need to know, that is. I'm an expert, Sergeant Major. I've been trained to recognize any kind of corpse and how it got that way."

Krüger looked moderately amused. "Well, help us to get this one buried double-quick, unless you want to become your own best customer."

The stage was set for an on-the-spot inquiry beneath the tower itself. Time: 1600 hours. Weather: sunny and cloudless. Temperature: approximately 70° Fahrenheit. Those present: Battery Sergeant Major Krüger, his three witnesses and medical adviser. Major Born turned up last, lurching slightly, suggesting that the captain's champagne had not been wasted.

"This," said Krüger, indicating some chalk marks applied by Corporal Neumann, "is where the body was found."

"I've got it on ice," Neumann announced professionally, "down in the cellar next to our temporary sick bay. The man must have died instantly."

"You're certain?" asked Major Born.

"Positive," Neumann assured him. "Schulz smashed his skull, broke his neck, and sustained two spinal fractures. He never had a chance to cry out, sir, take my word for it. Take pigs, for example. You stun them with the butt end of an ax so they pass out and bleed to death quietly. Land on these flagstones from a height of sixty feet, sir, and you'll do a lot more than stun yourself. Nobody survives a smashed skull, man or pig."

"Thank you, Corporal," said Major Born, not unimpressed. "Now, Sergeant Major, may we have the witnesses who found the body?"

Krüger jerked his head at witness number one, Wassermann. He was standing there with his shoulders slightly hunched, looking at no one. "All right, soldier, we're listening!"

Wassermann stepped forward hesitantly and said, "I only heard the thud when he landed. I was in the grounds, working on a gun tractor which had been causing trouble. . . ."

"Stick to the point," Krüger said briskly. "He made a thud, did he?"

"And how—I mean, yes, Sergeant Major. As you so aptly put it, he landed like a cow turd hitting cement. Except that, in this case, the cow would have had to be a pretty tall one."

Krüger turned a deprecating smile on Major Born. "I didn't actually use the word 'cow turd' in that connection, sir. If I remember right, I applied it to the men who were standing around with their mouths open, doing nothing. I expect you misunderstood me, Wassermann, isn't that right?"

"Yes, Sergeant Major," Wassermann confirmed hastily, "I must have. Anyway, it struck me as abnormal, the sight of him lying there."

"Not that Schulz was ever what you'd call normal," Krüger amplified. "He was a bit queer. Isn't that right, Wassermann?"

"In a manner of speaking."

"Immaterial and irrelevant," declared Major Born. "Suitable for corroborative purposes only. This won't get us very far, Sergeant Major."

Krüger hastily produced his second witness, a starved-looking gunner who belonged to Quartermaster Softer's supply section and was responsible for the distribution of cooked meats and preserves. Several hundred pounds of sausage and cheese had passed, unaccounted for, through his hands in the previous three weeks alone, but little good it had done him personally. It was widely rumored that he had a tapeworm.

"Schulz was hopeless," he said mournfully. "He didn't fit in—hadn't the guts to try, I figure. Not a bad kid in some ways, but too much of a mother's darling. I was just on my way to the canteen when it happened. I heard somebody scream, ran over and saw Schulz. He was lying there like a burst sack of potatoes. Well, I said to myself, it had to happen sometime, the way he was inclined."

"Oh?" said Major Born. "What way was that?"

"Well, like I said, he never had the makings of a soldier. A lazy bastard—always trying to feather his own nest. I suppose he thought he would get away with murder just because he had a pretty face. I know I shouldn't speak ill of the dead, sir, but it's the gospel truth."

Krüger gave the emaciated storeman an approving nod and signaled to his next witness, a paunchy gunner. He only confirmed what had already been said. "Put it this way, sir. Schulz didn't fit in with the rest of the guys. Two beers and he'd puke his guts up, and as for appreciating a barrack-room joke. . . . He used to blush like a virgin. No head for heights either, as you can see."

"I see," observed Major Born. He turned to Krüger. "I gather Gunner Schulz wasn't the most stable or soldierly of individuals."

"He was an unfortunate case," Krüger said promptly, "no guts, no initiative, no team spirit. There's one in every unit, sir. You just have to make the best of a bad job. Schulz saved us all a lot of trouble, writing himself off like that."

"You may be right, Sergeant Major." Born toyed with his glasses. "From my point of view, however, it's essential to form as full and factual a picture of the incident as possible. I trust you understand. Don't you by any chance have another witness?"

"Not that I know of, sir."

"A corporal named Bergen, for instance?"

Krüger, who was pretending to thumb through a sheaf of papers on his clipboard, glanced up in surprise. He eyed the military lawyer suspiciously. "My I ask who gave you his name, sir?"

"I can't tell you, I'm afraid—I don't recall." Born's smile was bland. "I only know someone mentioned him—during a phone conversation, I believe."

"A phone conversation with whom, sir?"

"It's slipped my mind. Anyway, the suggestion must have come from someone."

"The adjutant at Group HQ?" asked Krüger. More to himself than anyone else, he added, "It sounds like him."

"It may have been—on the other hand, it may not," Major Born said evasively. After all, internal rivalries were no concern of his. His duty was to maintain contemporary standards of justice and serve the nation, if only at regimental level. "This man Bergen—would you be good enough to send for him?"

"He won't know anything," Krüger said, point-blank. "He only got here this morning."

"Nevertheless," Born persisted urbanely, "I'd like a word with him."

Krüger shrugged. "It's a waste of time. Still, if you insist. . . ."

"I don't insist. I'm merely expressing a wish."

The sergeant major nodded, this time to Neumann, who scuttled off toward the château and disappeared inside like a weasel.

Major Born devoted the interval to an examination of the building. It made an indestructible impression despite its symptoms of decay. So did the church in the background, an equally dilapidated but majestic-looking building surrounded by huge trees. It seemed to Born that history hung heavy in the air.

Bergen appeared ten minutes later. He saluted Major Born but kept his eyes fixed on the battery sergeant major, who stared back.

"It's about the death of Gunner Schulz," Born said. "What can you tell us?"

"He doesn't know a thing," Krüger interrupted.

"Please let him answer for himself," Born said. For the first time, he sounded slightly nettled.

"I don't know a thing about it," said Bergen, still looking at Krüger.

"You see, sir!" Krüger exclaimed triumphantly. "It's like I said. By the time Bergen showed up, Schulz was lying there with his brains scrambled. Isn't that right?"

"That's right," Bergen said, "Sergeant Major."

Cross-examined, Bergen went on to confirm this statement in detail. The body was laying on the flagstones, one of the tower windows was open. Schulz appeared to have been killed instantly. Anything to add? No, nothing to add.

Krüger gave a succession of approving nods. The military lawyer abandoned the struggle with an air of exhaustion. Metaphorically closing the file, he said, "My findings are as follows: no signs of foul play, no sufficient grounds for suspecting suicide. Everything points to accidental death. I formally confirm that Gunner Schulz was the victim of an unfortunate accident."

"It wasn't so easy this time," Krüger informed his battery commander, "but I managed it."

"I knew I could rely on you, Sergeant Major."

Captain Hein was standing in the middle of the banquet chamber, poised and alert. He was in full uniform, belted and holstered, his hands encased in one of six pairs of dove-gray deerskin gloves. His luminous eyes rested on the peaked cap that lay beside him on the table. Presumably, he was about to visit the gun position.

"These difficulties we've been having," Krüger said discreetly, "—Group HQ seems to be at the bottom of them."

"Group HQ?" sneered Hein. "They can't hurt us. Every

headquarters is a hotbed of envy and intrigue, Sergeant Major. To quote an old gunner's maxim: Once you've identified a target, open fire immediately; if your field of fire is obstructed, clear it! Act on that principle and you won't go wrong."

"The adjutant at Group thought he'd throw a monkey wrench in the works by sending us a replacement for that signals NCO we lost—a troublemaker named Bergen. Luckily, I got his number in two minutes flat. He seems to be toeing the line all right, now I've defused him."

"Good work, Sergeant Major." Captain Hein sounded a trifle impatient. He had probably devised some new evolutions for the gun crews to perform and was lusting to try them out. "I have the fullest confidence in you, certainly when it comes to garbage disposal."

"I'm getting plenty of practice, sir," Krüger confided. "Earlier today I had to dispose of two MP's who came to question Sergeant Runge."

"Runge? My senior gunnery sergeant?" Captain Hein's nostrils flared in outrage. "A trumped-up charge, obviously. Who was responsible for it?"

"The town commandant, from what I could gather."

"Damned impertinence! Who does that uniformed civilian think he is!"

"As I said, sir, I managed to sidetrack them. Runge's in the clear."

"Excellent, Sergeant Major. I appreciate your efforts. Always tackle the enemy head on. Attack is the best method of defense—Moltke says so and so do I. You've done more than enough to earn your Iron Cross. Anything else to report?"

"Not exactly, sir," replied Krüger, exercising the tact which any interview with Hein demanded. "It's more a suggestion, really. A little rearrangement of accommodation— purely an internal matter."

The captain's lips curved in a thin smile as he surveyed the town of D. through the spacious windows set in the east wall. Krüger imagined that he was looking in the direction of the town commandant's office, not that the view appeared to interest him. Just as indifferently, he allowed his gaze to travel along the ancestral portraits on the west wall—a row of fleshy, effete and powdered faces—until it came to rest on Krüger.

"Very well," he said. "Who's the target this time?"

"The custodian, or whatever he's called. The one who looks after the church and grounds. He's redundant."

"Then get rid of him."

"You mean I can requisition his quarters, sir?"

"Why not? If you're convinced of the necessity, I approve. You have my permission to evict the custodian and that scrawny, slatternly-looking wife of his. Serve them right for never greeting me properly when we pass on the stairs. They can consider themselves lucky I don't have them arrested on suspicion of sabotage. By all means get rid of them."

"Their apartment, sir—can I find a use for it?"

"As you please." Captain Hein's tone conveyed a mixture of magnanimity and impatience. Briskly, he reached for his cap. "As a matter of interest, what do you intend to do with the vacant rooms?"

"Battery recreation center," announced Krüger. "The quartermaster's been planning it for weeks. Somewhere for the men to relax when they're off duty."

Hein's lips twisted in a mockery of mirth. "You're a cunning devil, Krüger. You propose to establish a brothel here—correct?"

Sergeant Major Krüger shrewdly echoed his commander's bantering tone. "Not for my own benefit, sir," he said with a chuckle. "One or two of the others seem to be in urgent need."

"And you approve?"

"I disapprove on principle, sir, but I've given the matter a lot of thought. The way I see it, most men get the itch from time to time, so we might as well keep tabs on them while they scratch."

Hein's mirthless smile persisted. "Plausible enough. However, what do you envisage in practical terms? Be brief but precise, please."

"Well, sir, the emphasis would be on personal hygiene. If you can't abolish sexual intercourse you might as well organize it properly. It's the best way to keep the battery up to strength and avoid losses from VD."

"Filth!" exclaimed Hein. His acid amusement was almost uncontrollable now. "Nothing but filth wherever one looks. I suppose it makes them feel like men, eh, Sergeant Major? Well, it may be their way of life but it isn't mine."

"I appreciate that, sir, as I hope I've shown—more than once."

"Very well, permission granted." The captain smoothed some invisible creases from his tunic, deftly tweaking it into position. "One more thing, though. I need a replacement for that man—what was his name?"

"Schulz, sir. Certainly, sir. Has the captain any personal preference?"

"What about Gunner Schubert—Johannes Schubert? He looks as if he might suit me."

Krüger did not have to weigh the implications. He knew what they were, just as he knew that if you scratched a man's back there was every likelihood he would return the compliment. Krüger not only accepted the principle of reciprocity but lived by it.

With characteristic thoroughness, he asked, "Does the captain mean Gunner Schubert of the signals section?"

"Precisely, Sergeant Major. Any objections? Anything worrying you?"

If he had any worries, Krüger knew he could not afford

to voice them at this stage. It was a perfect piece of give-and-take. He had delivered the goods and coupled their delivery with a request. His request had been granted, which meant that he had to offer a *quid pro quo*. A vicious circle, hard to escape but profitable to be in the middle of.

"Schubert it is, sir," he said briskly. "I'll see he reports to you right away. Let's hope everything goes smoothly this time. We can't afford another inquiry like today's."

"You're a tower of strength, Krüger," Hein said, putting his cap on. "Never feel tempted to let me down—you might regret it. However, knowing you as I do, I feel confident you won't. In fact I'm banking on it."

Interim Report No. 1

Case D., which the present book seeks to reconstruct, has aroused fierce but largely unpublicized controversy since it first came to light in recent years.

Some of the more typical and informative comments, expert opinions, conjectures, statements and items of documentary evidence are presented here in an edited form which preserves their essentials intact. They all originated almost exactly thirty years after the events in question.

Here, to begin with, is the result of a preliminary interview with ex-Major Born, now a retired county court judge residing in Lower Saxony.

"My conscience—if that's what you mean—is clear. Crystal clear. I simply did my duty, as I always have done. Very few people can imagine what that entailed at the time.

"As one of my senior law lecturers, Professor Heidenstamm, for whom I always cherished the greatest admiration, used to tell us: 'Laws currently in force may be a practical criterion of behavior but they are not sacrosanct or inviolable.' The professor was, I might add, executed for anti-Nazi activities, but I always tried to uphold his principles. It wasn't easy, certainly not in those days.

"I was then attached, in my capacity as a military lawyer, to an antiaircraft regiment serving in France. Its constituent batteries were deployed southwest of Paris, the four comprising Group No. 1 being stationed in the vicinity of D. The weather was sublime in the late summer of 1940—I recall that distinctly—but various matters were preying on my mind even then.

" 'It'll end badly!' I remember confiding to a close friend, and I can recall his reply, also uttered in confidence. 'It will indeed,' he said. 'Whom God would destroy he first sends mad —and our fellow countrymen are too drunk with victory to realize it.' That shows you how farsighted we were, even at that early stage. Among ourselves, of course.

"We knew what was going on, or thought we did. The impressive victories in Poland and France never blinded us to the truth, never prevented us from doing our duty—unflinchingly, though I say it myself.

"Most of the offenses that came our way were routine. Unpremeditated crimes committed under the influence of alcohol, self-inflicted wounds, desertion. Some, of course, turned out to be accidents.

" 'I want a thorough job done. Be as objective as you possibly can.' Those were my instructions from the regimental CO, Colonel Rheinemann-Bergen. An admirable man, the colonel—I should like to stress that. He was suspected of high treason in connection with the bomb plot of July 20, 1944, but managed to clear himself. We got on extremely well.

"I must, for all that, confess that Battery No. 3 of Group No. 1 did present me with a few knotty problems. Two, if I remember rightly—or was it three? One of them, the last to arise, concerned the battery commander personally and had all the elements of a Greek tragedy.

"Everything was thoroughly investigated, however, investigated with painstaking precision, if I may say so. Any wild conjectures that may have arisen later should be dismissed out of hand. I can give you the following categorical assurance:

"By prevailing standards, the situation was entirely normal."

Personal views
of M. Jean-Pierre Dupont,
custodian
of the château and family church,
now retired but still residing in D.

"I have nothing against the Germans, monsieur, not in principle. I am, or was, a loyal supporter of General de Gaulle. As such, I was an early advocate of Franco-German friendship.

"Not, of course, that this prevented me from facing certain facts and drawing my own conclusions. I bear the Germans little malice. Even so, circumstances weighed heavily on me at the time, just as they did on my beloved wife, who shared my cup of sorrow.

"On the other hand, I did develop some understanding of the Germans' problems, human and military. I myself am a veteran—I fought in the Great War as a young man.

"Being an old soldier rich in front-line experience, I accepted the necessity for certain things—the gun position on the grounds, for example. As for the parking of vehicles, this was understandable on account of the need for camouflage against Anglo-Saxon air attack. And if the Germans' trucks and tractors did do a certain amount of damage to the gardens, well, one had to take it in good spirit. As an old soldier, I certainly did.

"That the victorious troops should have requisitioned the château itself was unsurprising, though not entirely necessary. Being members of a tough and seasoned unit, they could just as well have bivouacked in the open, especially at that time of year.

"Be that as it may, they installed themselves in the château. I gladly offered advice, but only to minimize the possibility of interior damage. The château—humorously referred to by its German occupants as The Egg Box—would have provided more than enough accommodation for us all.

"They were good, efficient soldiers who knew their job, I can swear to it, monsieur. The battery sergeant major—Krüger, I think his name was—saw to that. He kept his men on a tight rein but managed to be human at the same time. Many a bottle of good red wine came my way thanks to him.

"But my poor wife was tortured with anxiety, especially at night. When the singing became raucous, for example, or when music blared from the tower where the captain had his quarters. The noise often continued into the small hours. It wasn't pleasant, I grant you, but as I used to tell my wife, to console her—soldiers are the same everywhere.

"Then came the sad day when Sergeant Major Krüger told me—with evident regret—that we had to vacate our apartment immediately.

" 'Why?' I asked, and he replied, 'Captain Hein's orders. I'm afraid nothing can be done.'

"My poor wife wept. Krüger, generous as ever, provided us with a truck to remove our belongings. Captain Hein happened to pass by as we were leaving and I requested an interview, but he waved me aside. A very imperious man, Captain Hein.

"We had just loaded the truck with a few essentials and were preparing to leave as instructed when I caught sight of the captain standing at one of the tower windows, laughing loudly. Why should he have done that? I can still hear his laughter today, but there was little joy in it. I remember thinking so at the time.

"Down in D. I reported to the town commandant, a captain by the name of Schmidt, Christian name Karl. The townspeople sometimes called him Monsieur Charles, an affectionate nickname that pleased him greatly. He could not have been more sympathetic when I explained our predicament. 'They can't treat people like that!' was his reaction—or words to that effect.

"This Karl or Charles—in any case, Schmidt—was the finest possible type, but he carried little weight with Captain Hein. That soon became apparent, monsieur. Things went from bad to worse, until—finally—a disaster struck."

Excerpts
from an interview with Frau Magdalena Hein,
mother of the late Captain Hein.

FRAU HEIN: I find it presumptuous, though typical of the modern age, that I should be required to answer questions about my beloved son whose sole purpose may well be to besmirch him and his memory.

INTERVIEWER: No one, Frau Hein, is presuming to do anything but try to establish the full truth about him. We are simply clearing up a few points.

FRAU HEIN: On past experience, I am bound to regard any such inquiry as superfluous. My only motive in submitting to your questions at all is a wish to refute various allegations which have been irresponsibly publicized by certain organs of the press.

INTERVIEWER: In that case, let us concentrate on facts alone. On the person of Karl Ludwig Hein—was he a good son?

FRAU HEIN: The best a mother could have had.

INTERVIEWER: You were very attached to him, you and your husband?

FRAU HEIN: That goes without saying. Our love for him did not, however, blind us to our duty. Utterly devoted to him though we were, we planned his upbringing with extreme care. You might say that he was predestined to a boyhood which combined parental protection with the free development of manly virtues. It was not simply that his father insisted on this. Karl was reared in the family tradition—if that conveys anything to you.

INTERVIEWER: It conveys a good deal. If I follow you, Frau Hein, your son was instructed from an early stage in what are generally known as traditional values.

FRAU HEIN: Quite so, though I suspect that my full meaning escapes you. No one can manufacture heroes, as you and those who share your political bias seem to imagine. We merely tried to prepare the soil in which heroism could flourish.

INTERVIEWER: And succeeded, by all accounts.

FRAU HEIN: Karl was a unique person. We were all extremely proud of him, my husband and I and his seven brothers and sisters. We still cherish his memory. The dear boy was awarded the Iron Cross Second Class during the Polish campaign, when he destroyed three enemy tanks. The Iron Cross First Class followed soon afterward, during the early weeks of the French campaign. He accounted for two more tanks and three aircraft—possibly five.

INTERVIEWER: There seems to be some doubt about that. Statements have been made to the effect that enemy losses were deliberately exaggerated.

FRAU HEIN: I beg your pardon! The figures in question were checked and double-checked, not only by his regimental commander but also by the general in command of the division to which he was attached. Are you casting doubt on the integrity of two experienced military leaders, men who have since held high appointments in the Federal German Army?

INTERVIEWER: Forgive me. It's just that I distrust heroism on principle.

FRAU HEIN: That's your affair. Personally, I have no time for such an attitude. I only know this: Karl was never anything but a loving, attentive and affectionate son. Numerous letters, testimonials and spontaneous expressions of sympathy from his friends and comrades bear witness to his nobility of character and conduct. I wholeheartedly reject any unfounded insinuations to the contrary. To me and those who knew him, my beloved son still symbolizes the undying courage of the German soldier. What are you trying to do—wantonly blacken his memory, just when the authorities are considering whether a new Federal Army barracks should be privileged to bear his name?

2

Prussian Roulette: Phase One

"All set to go at last, men!" Quartermaster Sergeant Softer grinned broadly. "No point in having a tail if you don't wag it, is there? Well, the same goes for another part of your anatomy."

After due consultation with Krüger, the quartermaster had convened those NCO's who seemed to him to carry the most weight at Battery HQ. There were five of them apart from himself and Krüger.

"The drinks are on the house."

Softer's guests had assembled in his inner storeroom. Bottles of German beer and schnapps stood ready and waiting—Franziskaner Spaten from Munich and grain spirit from the north.

Krüger cleared his throat. "Well, at last we can let our hair down when we feel like it and not worry about interruptions. There aren't any more spies on the premises."

"The custodian's gone," Softer explained. "Serves him right, the nosy French bastard. Captain Hein gave him his marching orders at last."

"Great!" exclaimed Sergeant Arm. His tanned face re-

47

mained as impassive as ever. "If his quarters are vacant I can move my transportation supplies in there."

"No you don't," Softer told him amiably. "I'm the one who says what gets moved in there, and it won't be spare tires and axle grease. My kind of supplies come in bra and pants, in case you ever feel like requisitioning some."

Sergeant Arm's mouth hung open for a moment. "Well, I'll be damned! You mean you're planning to install a brothel in there?"

"A what?" Sergeant Forstmann, slim, blond-haired and zealous, drew himself up indignantly. Forstmann, who presided over the orderly room, considered himself additionally responsible for the battery's political orthodoxy and moral tone. In relinquishing him to the army, the Hitler Youth had lost a budding champion of German cultural values. "I must have misunderstood."

"You understood me all right, Forstmann." Softer's eyes twinkled as he glanced at the others to reassure himself they were in the right mood. "You're welcome to call it a brothel if you like. What's in a name, anyway? You might just as well call it a recreation center."

"You should be ashamed of yourself!" Forstmann's voice was shrill now. He glared imperiously at his fellow NCO's but discovered their thoughts were elsewhere. Some had unbuttoned their tunics and were sweating slightly as they contemplated the laden bottle racks that lined the walls. "You should be ashamed," Forstmann persisted. "Imagine even suggesting such an idea!"

"Why not?" retorted Softer, settling himself deeper in his chair. "Anyway, who are you to object? I saw you down at the Hôtel de France two nights ago, moving in on some little French. . . ."

"Shut up!" Forstmann snapped. "That was different. I was trying to establish contact with a member of the French civilian population—cementing international relations, as far as present circumstances allow."

"Come off it!" Softer said. "Cementing international relations—is that what they call it these days? Well, in the future you can cement them on the spot, any way and any time you fancy. Added to that, it'll be cheaper, more comfortable and guaranteed hygienic."

"Any time, you said?" Sergeant Arm grinned. "Does that include odd times of day—like right after lunch? I like a quick dip after lunch."

"Don't worry," Softer assured him. "Regular customers will get preferential treatment, and as far as I'm concerned everybody here qualifies for preferential treatment and special terms."

"Count me in." Corporal Kaminski, Captain Hein's personal driver, spoke decisively. "If it's all right with Hein, of course."

Krüger assured them that the battery commander had actually given the scheme his personal blessing. Sergeant Moll, the sheeplike chief clerk, said cautiously, "It all sounds great in theory, but would we get away with it in practice?"

"Some people get away with murder," remarked the seventh member of the party, a reserve NCO named Hiller. Hiller, commonly known as Tino, was a cheerful little mouse of a man—clearly recognizable as a civilian in uniform but invaluable because of his engineering qualifications. Like Wassermann, Tino Hiller could repair any vehicle in trouble. This made him indispensable to Sergeant Arm and a small but vital cog in the works of Battery No. 3. Sometimes, though not often, he seemed to grasp this.

"You're a good mechanic, Tino," Arm told him reprovingly, "but don't stick your nose in."

"All right, Sergeant, I'll save it for Softer's recreation center."

"You can't do this!" Forstmann insisted, his blue eyes ablaze with righteous indignation. The more he drank, the more flamboyant his Germanic ideals became. "It's undignified, the whole idea."

"Don't be a wet blanket, Forstmann." Softer flourished his tankard of foaming Munich beer. "What the hell does dignity have to do with it? You can either screw or be dignified. It's a matter of choice—you can't do both at the same time."

"Let's stop parading our principles, shall we?" urged Krüger. "This brothel—or whatever you want to call it— can't hurt anybody, especially since the captain isn't against the idea."

"Of course he isn't," Softer said swiftly. "He may not be that way inclined himself, but he knows the score. Fucking isn't just human—it comes under the heading of troops' welfare. Battery No. 3 leads the field in everything else, so why not that too?"

"There's the question of personal hygiene, too," said Krüger. "I look at it this way: A man's got a right to a decent sex life, especially when he's fighting for his country. He may have a loving wife or girlfriend tucked away at home, but she can't do him much good when he's stationed on the other side of Europe. That makes it the army's job to supervise the women he goes with. We can't afford troop reduction from VD so we'd better take precautions before it's too late."

"Look at Regimental HQ," Softer put in. "The place is lousy with amateur whores in uniform, all officially listed as secretarial staff, but they're reserved for the officers. Our place would be a lot more democratic."

"What about overhead?" inquired Sergeant Moll, an accountant in civilian life. "I don't deny it's a good idea, but it'll have to pay."

"Our prices will be reasonable," Softer assured him. "You'll all get a discount, too. Finding the right location was our only problem, but that's solved. There are four rooms vacant now that the custodian's gone. Three'll be reserved for the ladies of the establishment and the fourth can double as a waiting room and manager's office."

"These three girls of yours," Moll asked, "will they be enough to cope with the whole battery?"

"For the moment." Softer had the figures at his fingertips. "I've worked it out as follows: total battery strength, a hundred and fifty; prospective customers, a hundred and twenty. Daily performance rate, five customers per girl—and that's a conservative estimate. Three times five are fifteen, fifteen customers multiplied by six, allowing one rest day per week, makes ninety. In other words, everybody in the unit can have it once every ten days. That ought to do to start."

"What about us?" inquired Sergeant Arm. "Do we get extra turns in addition to the discount?"

"As many as you can fit in."

Forstmann persisted in his disapproval, egged on by Tino Hiller.

"I'm sorry, but I just don't think your scheme is in line with the Führer's thinking."

"Come again?" Softer's jellylike frame quivered with mirth. "Are you telling us the Führer never fucks?"

"Stop it!" Forstmann demanded. "That's an outrageous thing to say."

"It'd be worse if I said the opposite. You're suggesting the Führer isn't a man, which he is. That means he enjoys the occasional fuck—it stands to reason."

"This is the end!" snarled Forstmann. "You're debasing the finest living specimen of German manhood—dragging him down to your own filthy level."

Softer was unmoved. "God Almighty, Forstmann, even the Führer drops his pants occasionally. We all do, including the divisional commander."

"I refuse," Forstmann said stubbornly, "to hear his name mentioned in connection with a brothel. Some people might call your remarks subversive."

"That's a matter of opinion," Krüger decreed. "The battery commander's decisions are all that concern us. I already told you—Captain Hein has approved the estab-

lishment of a battery recreation center. Hands up anybody
who disagrees."

Not a hand twitched.

"They're at it again," remarked Gunner Wassermann,
more to himself than anyone else. His attention seemed
focused on a bottle of wine that stood beside him, glinting
in the moonlight. "No quality but plenty of volume."

"German folk songs," said Corporal Bergen, joining
Wassermann on a stone bench near the wall enclosing the
château grounds. "All good, solid traditional stuff—part of
our cultural heritage, as Goebbels would say."

The senior NCO's choir, now located in the canteen,
continued to rend the night air. Wassermann listened in
silence for a while. "Their repertoire's limited. 'Tannenbaum'
is Krüger's stock item. They usually sing it four or five
times in the course of a single binge. It takes them several
hours to get around to the really refined numbers like 'Up in
the Hayloft' and 'What the Farmer Saw.' "

"You're a connoisseur." Bergen reached for the bottle. He
took an experimental swig, emitted a grunt of approval and
swigged again, more vigorously this time. "You know something about wine too," he said, drawing a deep breath.
"What is it?"

"Chablis," Wassermann replied. He peered at Bergen's
face in the moonlight but the shadows blurred its contours.
"None of the others likes white wine, so I reserved some
cases for my personal consumption. I keep them between
a couple of tombs in the church. You're welcome to share
them."

"Why so generous?"

"Because you appreciate the stuff, like me. Besides, I
enjoy talking to you, Bergen. There's something different
about you, even if you are just another name on the battery roll."

"What does that make you?"

Wassermann grinned. "I don't rightly know, yet. Not that it worries me. They give you plenty of choices in this outfit. You can either be a bug to be squashed, or a dog that whines with gratitude when it's kicked, or a cow that obediently gives milk and ends up in the stewpot anyway. I tell you, Bergen, the possibilities are endless!"

They stared into the deepening gloom. The château's bulk stood out dark against the night sky. Its windows were blacked out, but slivers of light showed through slits in the curtains at ground level, where the canteen was located, and in Hein's quarters at the top of the tower.

"What goes on here?" Bergen demanded.

Wassermann gave a suppressed chuckle. "Why ask me? I like a quiet life. I don't speak out of turn."

"You do sometimes. I haven't been here long but I know that much. There's a funny smell around here—that's what you said in the canteen today."

"Sure I did," Wassermann agreed cheerfully. "That was just tactics, though. It doesn't really matter whether I think the setup stinks or not. The main thing is, they try and shut me up by making concessions—granting me little privileges."

"Isn't it risky?"

"Not if I don't push my luck. I'm a qualified mechanic, which makes me as good as indispensable. With your knowledge of radio and signals equipment, you could carve yourself a nice little niche like mine. We could have a lot of fun if we cooperated. How about it?"

Bergen did not reply. He peered into the darkness where, on the other side of the grounds, the church stood in lonely isolation. He pictured the serried ranks of tombs inside and the cases of Chablis hidden among them.

"Come on," Wassermann said suddenly, "let's go downtown. I know an easy route over the wall. We'll pay a visit to the Hôtel de France. The food's good, and we can amuse ourselves by gossiping about Battery No. 3 to the town commandant's chief clerk—he passes everything on to his boss. It's no skin off our nose, and it could be useful if we play our cards right."

"They've stopped singing," Bergen said. "But there's music coming from the tower now, can you hear it?"

Wassermann nodded. "The captain's playing records. He always turns the volume up full. Sounds like a whole regiment farting in unison."

"It's Wagner."

"If you say so. Whatever it is, something's brewing in that great brain of his. He must be dreaming up some nasty surprise for the gun crews, God help them."

"Air alert," said Captain Hein. He uttered the words calmly, as though to himself. His composure was unassailable. Hein could—when he wanted, and he usually did—display the chill impassivity of a fish, the adamantine hardness of granite or marble.

He glanced at his stopwatch as he spoke, then stood poised on the balls of his feet, legs slightly braced like a matador's, and studied his surroundings: Battery No. 3's gun position. Battery No. 3 was a kingdom over which Captain Hein held absolute sway. All his subjects rendered the implicit and unquestioning obedience proper to their station in life.

Without a moment's hesitation, the gunner who happened to be nearest him yelled, "Air alert!" And again, "Air alert!"

Every man in the gun position was permanently prepared for Captain Hein's arbitrary behavior. His soldiers had been given every opportunity to adapt themselves. Their reactions were almost automatic. More voices took up the cry until they were drowned by the whine of three hand sirens.

Within a few seconds the area had become a human ant heap.

Near the château but separated from it by a road known as the Rue Napoléon lay a sports field. This was where Hein had sited four heavy antiaircraft guns, two dual-purpose guns of smaller calibre, and a predictor. None of the battery's equipment was permitted to lie idle. Hein made sure of that, ably and unwaveringly assisted by his star subordinate, Senior Gunnery Sergeant Siegfried Runge.

Turning to Runge, Hein told him in a confidential voice of great carrying power, "Make them hop to it, Sergeant. Anyone who busts a gut in the process gets scheduled for additional training. I want this unit fully operational, and I'll decide when it is."

The latest performance took its course with exemplary speed and precision. The gun crews rushed from their tents, poured out of the nearby canteen hut and cut short their activities in the two field latrines. They turned out just as they were, in their underpants, stripped to the waist or fully dressed, but all with the regulation steel helmet rammed down over their ears.

"Move, you lousy bunch of cripples!" bellowed Sergeant Runge, who seemed to have an infallible nose for practice alerts and was always one jump ahead of everyone else. "Move, unless you want some help from the toe of my boot!"

It was an unnecessary threat. The men redoubled their efforts. Runge glanced at Hein, who rewarded him with an almost imperceptible nod. Hein and Runge understood each other and always had. Battery No. 3, which had accounted for such an impressive tally of enemy aircraft, owed its exceptional record primarily to their joint efforts —of that they were certain.

The men of Hein's battery scrambled to their stations. Obediently, according to the emergency procedures laid

down by Battery HQ, the gun barrels swung westward to
face the likely source of an air attack. Lateral direction 270
degrees, angle of elevation 45 degrees, live ammunition
ready, the first shells inserted in their fuse-setting devices.

"Predictor crew ready!" reported Sergeant Runge, far in
advance of everyone else—which was only to be expected.

The next announcement—"Guns ready!"—did not follow
for several seconds. It was made, prematurely but with
martial fervor, by Reserve Second Lieutenant Helmreich,
whose shrill voice almost cracked under the strain. Helmreich gazed at his battery commander, craving approbation,
but Hein never so much as glanced at him.

"Battery No. 3 ready!" Lieutenant Minder barked loudly
and confidently but failed to carry conviction. Minder's
words seldom carried conviction with anyone, least of all his
battery commander.

Captain Hein studied his stopwatch intently, then
stared into space with an air of sorrowful surprise. As
impassively as ever, but in a voice with the edge of a cut-
throat razor, he said, "One hundred seconds plus."

His announcement was clearly audible over a wide area
because everyone around him was listening with bated
breath. They all realized what that plus meant.

A hundred seconds was the maximum time limit Hein set
for practice alerts. Anything slightly under it he termed
"satisfactory." Sixty seconds rated as "good." Less than sixty
seconds would have been "excellent," but the battery had
never yet bettered a minute. Today's pitiful performance
meant trouble.

"Practice makes perfect," Hein said tersely.

With that, the gun crews were assured of employment for
hours to come. Hein continued to stand, motionless and
unapproachable, beside the predictor in the center of the
gun position—though the battery's focal point was, by defi-
nition, wherever he happened to be at any given moment.

Sergeant Runge was privileged to stand next to him, while the two gunnery officers, Minder and Helmreich, took station three places to the rear. Three paces precisely, or three times 30 inches—no more, no less. More would have been tantamount to dissociation, less would have seemed obtrusive. The gun crews had frozen into immobility, like frightened hares.

Hein gave Runge a meaningful nod and the sergeant sprang to life. "Take cover!" he roared.

At lightning speed, the gun crews vanished into the nearest tents, into folds in the ground and slit trenches. The two officers stood fast, waiting for special instructions which seldom if ever came. The captain shifted his weight from one leg to the other but preserved his matador's stance.

"Air alert!" yelled Runge.

Rodentlike, the soldiers popped out of their holes and flung themselves at the guns and equipment, manned them, checked their firing data, placed ammunition ready. Minder and Helmreich avoided each other's eyes. They stared straight ahead at the ramrod back of their commander, who might have been a statue.

The future sequence of events was universally familiar. It took the form of an ever swifter transition from "Take cover!" to "Air alert!" and "All clear!" The process had been known to continue into the night. Runge issued the orders while Hein supervised and the two gunnery officers, totally ignored, stood there like wax dummies.

Sergeant Runge harangued the gun crews incessantly. All the men were streaming sweat, and some of them could barely stand. "Move, you lazy bastards!" screamed Runge. "Pull your fingers out or I'll have you at it all night! There's no room for deadbeats in this outfit, so shift your asses!"

The captain and his favorite sergeant made a perfectly balanced team. Almost everyone in the battery felt its effects daily. When Hein was awarded the Iron Cross First

Class, Runge promptly got the Iron Cross Second Class, and Runge would no doubt receive the Iron Cross First Class as soon as Hein was invested with the Knight's Cross, for which he had already been recommended. The sky was the limit.

"Take cover, you fat-assed jerk-offs!" roared Runge. "Dig in! The old slit trenches are out, so dig yourselves some new ones—deeper ones. If any part of your anatomy shows over the top, I'll blow it off!"

Runge's eloquence was cut short by the untimely arrival of a staff car, an Opel Olympia sedan converted into a military vehicle by the addition of some gray-green camouflage paint. It stopped in the center of the gun position and an officer jumped out, a well-fed and cherubic-looking specimen whose stomach bulged like a rubber ball. He bore down on Hein.

"Schmidt, town commandant," he said politely. "Are you Captain Hein?"

"I am." Hein's tone was cold and dismissive. "I don't recall that we had an appointment."

"I tried to reach you by phone several times. Without success, I'm afraid. Sorry to descend on you like this."

Captain Hein inclined his head in the merest suggestion of a bow. "You may not realize it, Captain, but my battery is on active service. We're at war."

"I appreciate that, of course." The town commandant did his best to sound urbane, but he was sweating profusely. His lunchtime bottle of Burgundy had taken effect. Moreover, the battery commander's tone annoyed him. Hein might be a brother officer, but his manner was far from fraternal. "I hesitate to intrude, Captain, but it's about the custodian."

"What about him?"

"You've evicted him. I wouldn't presume to fathom your motives, but I know this much—his eviction has caused great offense."

"To whom, may I inquire?" Captain Hein asked the question with provocative calm. "Why should I cater to the personal wishes of a few insignificant French civilians? A war was fought here, Captain Schmidt, a war which we won and the French lost. The inference is inescapable. All that matters is to consolidate our gains. To relax our grip now would be the height of irresponsibility—or hasn't that dawned on you?"

"I merely wanted to point out. . . ." Captain Schmidt's voice trailed off as he fought to preserve what was left of his dignity—in vain, as he quickly realized. "I was going to suggest some form of compromise. . . ."

Captain Hein regarded his visitor with mounting disdain—a potbellied, big-buttocked civilian incongruously attired in the uniform of a German officer. Nothing could have offended his sense of propriety more.

"Military requirements," he said with finality, "take precedence over personal considerations. Kindly make a note of that."

"But I beg you also to remember, Captain, that we've been instructed to respect the interests of the French civil population as far as possible. . . ."

"Who has been so instructed, Captain Schmidt? You, perhaps, not I. My battery is on active service. Enemy aircraft could appear at any moment. We must prepare for that eventuality. What are you trying to do—sabotage our combat readiness?"

"God forbid!"

"In that case, Captain, I must ask you to withdraw. In plain language, stop pestering me. What is more, kindly refrain from doing so again."

"Well, you barracks-room lawyer, how are you settling in?" Sergeant Major Krüger sounded jovial but wary. "Getting used to the way we run things around here?"

"Trying to," replied Bergen. "There's plenty to get used to."

"So it doesn't come easy?"

Bergen shrugged in a decidedly civilian fashion. He found himself growing less military in manner rather than more, these days, but he took it as a sign of progress. "I learn something new every day, Sergeant Major."

"Let's hope you get your lessons right. Know why I hope so, Bergen? Because you're no fool. You're a smart boy who catches on quick. I can use somebody like you. When you have to put up with an assortment of morons like most of the men in this battery, someone like you makes a welcome change. You scratch my back and I'll scratch yours—that's my motto. My family are farm people. I was brought up to believe that almost any kind of shit makes decent manure."

Krüger had summoned Bergen to the orderly room. Sergeant Forstmann was temporarily absent, checking the liquor supply on Krüger's orders. Another senior NCO's get-together—the second that week—was on the schedule.

"What can I do for you, Sergeant Major?"

"You were transferred here direct from Group HQ, right?" He told Bergen to stand at ease. This was an ominous sign. Outward familiarities on Krüger's part were almost always a prelude to unwelcome requests. "And what did you do at Group HQ?"

"Make trouble, so they said."

Krüger, perched on the edge of his desk, looked up. His face muscles twitched slightly, indicating amusement. "Why so determined to convince me you're a hard case, Bergen?"

"I'm not, Sergeant Major. Just the same, I figure my assignment to Battery No. 3 was a sort of punishment. The adjutant had it in for me."

Krüger gave a snort of irritation and slid off the desk. He grabbed his fly, did a quick knee bend to loosen his crotch, and straightened up again. His movements had the ponderous grace of a dancing elephant. "Christ," he said, "either you're as dumb as they come or you're a swindler. I'd bet on the last."

"They may have got rid of me because I overheard a couple of phone conversations," Bergen volunteered. "I couldn't help it, Sergeant Major. I was on switchboard duty at the time."

"That supposed to be a hint? You mean you've a pretty good idea of what's been going on—like the little differences of opinion between the adjutant and Battery No. 3, and the battery commander in particular."

"There was a little difference of opinion between the adjutant and me, that's all I know. It wasn't my fault—we just didn't operate on the same wavelength. He got rid of me as soon as he could. That's why I was transferred here, of all places."

"You can cut the 'of all places,' friend." Krüger's expression didn't alter, but his voice rose a decibel. "So you made a nuisance of yourself at Group HQ? All right, you've had your fun, but don't think you can play the same game with us. Group HQ is comic opera compared to Battery No. 3. Wagner's more our style."

"So I've noticed—that radio in the tower can really belt it out. The captain's got some record collection—just about everything Wagner wrote and a touch of *The Merry Widow*. Quite a mixture."

"So you're a music critic as well, are you?" Krüger grinned savagely. "I take it you've got nothing against Wagner?"

"Who could object to the Führer's favorite composer?"

"You're wasted on the army, Bergen. You ought to be a diplomat." Krüger feigned amusement. "You're putting on an act, aren't you—pretending to fit in here, playing along with us. What's the big idea?"

"Just this, Sergeant Major," Bergen replied. "I don't like

trouble and I don't go looking for it—I enjoy life too much. I know my stuff when it comes to radio and telephone circuits, as you'll probably discover in due course. What's more, I've already found out that a man can get on very nicely in this unit as long as he switches to the right frequency in time. Hard work when you're on duty and a quiet life when you're off—what more could anybody want?"

"Stay in line, that's all." Krüger's eye rested almost benevolently on his latest acquisition. He had a soft spot for realists. "Sounds like you've caught on at last. Keep me happy and you won't regret it."

Krüger sat down behind the desk. He spread his legs, automatically fingering his fly to check that it was closed. "You must have made friends with the members of your section by now. What do you make of Gunner Schubert?"

"What should I make of him, Sergeant Major?"

"Bergen," Krüger said in an alarmingly muted voice, "I don't expect back talk when I ask a question—I expect an answer, right? I'll try again. This Schubert—how does he strike you?"

"He's a little immature, in my mind."

"I told you before, Bergen, leave your mind alone—thinking's my job, not yours." Then, from one moment to the next, Krüger's tone changed. "Still, you may be right. The boy's face looks like a baby's backside and he's probably got brains to match. In other words, his balls haven't dropped."

"He tries hard, though—in fact he's quite a promising signaler. But otherwise he's as green as he looks. He's too young for this outfit, I'd say—much too young."

"A virgin, you figure?"

"Could be," Bergen conceded cautiously. Krüger's interest, especially in this point, did not escape him, not that he had any idea what it meant. "Knee pants would suit him better than uniform. He's a retarded Boy Scout—still believes in traditional virtues like loyalty, honor, decency, justice and so on."

Krüger was visibly gratified. "He'll need all those where he's going—drum that into his head, Bergen."

"May I ask why, Sergeant Major?"

"Because he's taking over as Captain Hein's personal orderly effective immediately, and you're going to coach him."

"How?"

"That's a stupid question, Bergen. What are you planning to do, pump me? I'll bet ten beers to a pinch of shit you already understand the situation. A pretty face and a mind like a blank check—that's what's required, and that's what friend Schubert has. He's all yours, Bergen. Give him a wash-and-brushup, and above all give him a lecture on the subject of personal hygiene. The captain's got a thing about personal hygiene."

"May I draw your attention to one minor detail, Sergeant Major? This signals section I've been put in charge of—it isn't up to strength. I can't spare a single man."

Krüger's meaty face darkened. "Don't play the old soldier with me, Bergen, I've been in the service too long. You're trying to sidestep me."

"Not at all, Sergeant Major. I was merely thinking of operational efficiency. I was only trying. . . ."

"Trying to what? Meddle in things that don't concern you? Nudge me into bribing you? You've got a nerve, considering you've only just joined the battery. Damn well do as you're told and shut up."

"By all means, Sergeant Major," Bergen replied hastily. "Gunner Schubert will be relieved of his duties with the signals section and trained for his new job. Main qualification: personal cleanliness from head to toe and all intermediate stations."

"Good," growled Krüger. "Why didn't you say so in the first place? Either you cooperate in this unit or you'll wish you'd never been born. And don't expect any special privileges at this stage. You've got a hell of a long way to go."

QMS Softer eyed Sergeant Forstmann with smug satisfaction. "There isn't a better organized supply system in the whole goddamned army. Impressive, isn't it? Go on, be honest."

"Well, yes." Forstmann's tone was slightly grudging. "I'll give you one thing—you take good care of the battery."

"And all in the interests of combat readiness," Softer explained modestly. "I take my cue from the battery commander."

"But what about all those bottles?" asked Forstmann. "Our boys can't possibly drink them all."

"They don't have to. They can buy them and send them home to their nearest and dearest. Call it my contribution to home-front morale."

A frown settled on the orderly-room sergeant's Nordic brow. "I'm not sure I approve of that. It sounds suspiciously like profiteering to me."

"Profiteering?" Softer pretended astonishment. "You're a hundred and eighty degrees off target, Forstmann. I've got the interests of the fatherland at heart. After all, what could be more important than morale? A full belly, a few beers and a piece of ass now and again—that's what wins wars. My recreation center is all part of the same scheme, don't you see?"

"It's a matter of principle," Forstmann said doggedly.

Softer shook his head. "There are times when I almost feel sorry for you, friend." He knew very well why Krüger had sent Forstmann along. The champion of Germanic ideals must be made to see sense or he might upset the applecart. "You can't have anything against brothels—they're a historical fact."

"It's a question of morality, not history, Softer."

"Morality's a matter of luck, as the mouse said when it

failed to fuck the elephant." Softer smiled ingratiatingly but without success. "Joking apart, though, what can a fine, upstanding young man like you have against a roll in the hay? You won't miss out, I promise you."

"Leave me out of it," Forstmann said primly. "It isn't that I don't sympathize, Softer. Even the ancient Greeks and Romans. . . ."

"There you are! It's like I said—brothels are a sign of civilization."

"But here, in this particular case, there might be trouble."

"Not under my system." Softer warmed to his subject. "I've got it all worked out. The gun crews never get more than eight hours off out of twenty-four, and what do they do with their spare time? Get drunk, of course. They feel the urge but they can't satisfy it. Frustration makes them aggressive. Brawls, rape, desertion—that's how it'll end, my boy, and it's our patriotic duty to do something about it."

"The situation isn't as simple as that, I'm afraid."

Softer drew a deep breath and prayed for patience. It was no use trying to browbeat the man.

"Listen," Softer said, "you're a patriotic type, Forstmann —we all realize that." His moon face took on an even rosier hue. "You've got principles. We respect them and we're ready to make allowances for them. Believe me, there's nothing about this recreation center of ours that need worry you."

"How do you mean?" Forstmann demanded, not without interest. "How can you reconcile patriotic principles with non-Aryan sensuality?"

"You don't know women," Softer said. "They'll do anything for money. If we brief them the right way, they'll lay the members of this battery and give them a dose of political indoctrination at the same time. It could be a real breakthrough in ideological training."

"You think so?" Forstmann sounded faintly impressed.

"Maybe your scheme *does* have its merits after all. A shame it's out unless you can find the right accommodation."

"No problem there. The captain has allocated us the bailiff's apartment."

"That was yesterday."

"Well?"

"Today," Forstmann explained, "just over an hour ago—Sergeant Major Krüger hasn't heard yet—the orderly room received advance warning of some new arrivals. A research team."

"A what?" Softer looked faintly surprised. "What kind of research team?"

"Three people—professors, experts on something or other, sent here by some government department. What's more, they've been personally entrusted with a special assignment by Reich Marshal Goering. Our instructions are to provide them with accommodation. The bailiff's apartment is the logical place."

Softer was sweating now. "It's a double cross! Who's idea was it, saddling us with a bunch of eggheads?"

"Could have been one of two people," Forstmann confided. "There's the town commandant. . . ."

"Never!" Softer said firmly. "Schmidt may have it in for Captain Hein, but he'd never dare. I know his kind."

"In that case it must have been Group HQ—probably the adjutant."

"Seifert-Blanker? I wouldn't put it past him, the scheming bastard." Softer was outraged. "He's always on the lookout for new ways of spiking the captain's guns, just because Hein's got a chestful of medals and he hasn't. He'd begrudge Hein the dirt under his fingernails. They're like cat and dog, those two, and we suffer for it."

"I don't think we ought to jump to conclusions," Forstmann said sternly. "All I know is, three civilians have been billeted on us for the duration of their special assignment

—something to do with the church on the grounds, I believe. Phoned orders today, written confirmation tomorrow. I'm afraid we're stuck with them."

Softer gave a low moan. "They can't do this to me—us, I mean—not now, just when things were shaping up. I tell you, Forstmann, I'm going to have that brothel come hell or high water."

"Close the door," Captain Hein said sharply. "No, stay where you are, but make sure the door is closed."

Gunner Schubert checked that it was, then stood stiffly at attention. His battery commander was bathed in a pool of flickering light. Two gleaming candelabra, presumably of silver, flanked him as he presided at the head of the great refectory table, six feet wide and twenty-four long, which dominated the banquet chamber.

Johannes Schubert, radio operator and field telephonist, gazed meekly at Captain Hein. His lily-white face was crowned by a mop of dark wavy hair—almost black, with a bluish sheen—which fell gracefully from his fine temples to the nape of his slightly inclined neck. He seemed anxious to present a picture of eager devotion, like a gentle page attending his sovereign with mingled awe and trust.

"Do you know why you're here?" Captain Hein's voice sounded disconcertingly mild. The muscles in his angular face seemed to twitch as the candlelight played over it in the gloom. The surrounding walls were hung with dusty paintings and tattered tapestries of the seventeenth and eighteenth centuries. "Were you told what was expected of you?"

Gunner Schubert sensed that a prompt and unequivocal reply was called for. "Yes, sir," he said.

"Well, what did they tell you?"

"That I've been detailed to attend to the captain's personal requirements."

"Meaning what?"

Johannes Schubert gulped audibly. His palms were moist but he did not dare wipe them on his trousers. As though transfixed, he stared at the flickering candles and avoided his commander's eye. He heard himself say, briskly, "Cleaning the captain's quarters, uniforms, personal equipment. . . ."

"Not good enough!" An almost brusque note had entered Hein's voice. "You've missed the essential point." Several seconds passed in spellbound silence. Then, disconcertingly mild once more, he said, "What matters here, first and foremost, is something quite different and far more important. I refer to mutual trust."

"Yes, sir."

"Do you know what that means, Schubert? I bestow my trust on you—my unbounded trust. In return, I expect the same. Are you prepared to trust me?"

"Yes, sir."

"I expected no less of you, Schubert." Hein raised his right hand in a gesture of invitation. It was a slender but powerful hand. "Come closer."

Gunner Schubert stepped forward, jerkily, like a man on parade. Three paces short of his battery commander, he halted. He now saw that Hein was resplendent in his number ones, a spotless uniform of gray-blue serge, perfectly tailored. He wore the Iron Cross First Class, the ribbon of the Iron Cross Second Class, and the silver badge awarded to those wounded in action. There was still ample room at his throat for the Knight's Cross.

"Closer!" Hein commanded. "Approach to within one pace, but refrain from breathing on me—I permit no one to breathe on me. Now hold out your hands."

Schubert did so. His outstretched hands neared the captain's face. Inclining his head a couple of inches, Hein submitted the backs of Schubert's hands to a thorough and prolonged inspection. He could detect nothing, from wrist to fingertip, but rosy flesh superimposed on a tracery of fine bones—not a speck of dirt.

"And the other side!" Hein said curtly.

He scrutinized the palms of the outstretched hands perserveringly and with dawning satisfaction. "A man's hands," he said at last, "are a reflection of his personality. Hands become soiled—one can acknowledge this without tolerating it. Hands can be washed. They can be kept clean if their owner so desires. You appear to cherish such a desire, Schubert."

"Yes, sir," said Schubert, looking mystified.

"Cleanliness!" Hein uttered the word like a profession of faith. He rose to his feet and stood erect, eyes and decorations glinting in the candlelight. "That is the prime requirement. I have attached supreme importance to cleanliness all my life—cleanliness of body, mind, soul. A holy and harmonious trinity, Schubert."

Hein began to pace the room, never leaving the glow cast by the candles. His body remained rigid but his hands fluttered like moths around a flame. Eyes fixed on something unseen in the far distance, he said, "I owned a dog once, a dachshund. Brown, smooth-haired, short legs, perfectly bred. My parents gave it to me as a present when I was a boy. I looked after it for years. Five years, to be exact. I used to feed the animal, take it for walks, play with it, fondle it. Then, one day, it took to vomiting. Outside at first, then indoors. It began by ruining the carpets and ended by fouling my bed. Obviously, it had to go. With a heavy heart, I drowned it. I cried my eyes out, of course, but it was borne in on me that life is like that. One has to make decisions—a never-ending series of decisions. In favor of cleanliness in all its forms."

The words tumbled over each other as Hein spoke into the gloom. Listening deferentially, Schubert sensed that the captain was addressing himself alone. The flow ceased as suddenly as it had begun, with the finality of an extinguished light.

Captain Hein drew a hand across his brow and temples. He stood motionless for some moments and then resumed his seat. The affable note returned to his voice.

"Cleanliness, Schubert! While we're on the subject, how often do you change your underpants?"

"As often as possible, sir."

"How often, exactly?"

"Every three days, sir, if I can. Sometimes I have to go a week without changing them, but it isn't my fault. We're short of soap and spare underwears."

"I shall attend to that. In future, you will change your personal linen daily. I don't wish you to smell of anything—anything!—when you're in my presence."

"Very good, sir. Underwear to be changed daily, sir."

"What about your teeth, Schubert? Let's have a look at them. Bend forward and open your mouth—but don't breathe on me! Bare your teeth—roll back your lip with your finger. Top first, then bottom."

This maneuver was duly carried out. The results were gratifying: every tooth intact and well tended, no artificial restorations or additions; gums firm and healthy-looking; tongue unfurred and fresh in color.

"Good," said Hein. "You maintain a high standard of oral hygiene. An extremely important point, Schubert. Noble sentiments never issue from a foul mouth, or if they do, never with conviction. Are you familiar with the works of Hölderlin?"

"I've read some of his poems based on Greek tragedies, sir."

"Excellent, but more of that later. I shall also question you on the music of Richard Wagner at the first opportunity—I advise you to do your homework well." Hein said all this with an absent air which conveyed that he was intent on other things. "I assume I have no need to tell you that you must clean your teeth every time before reporting to me for duty?"

"Yes, sir, teeth to be cleaned every time, sir!" Schubert confirmed, all the more zealously because of his growing bewilderment. He was ready to promise anything if only he could leave the captain's presence.

"Rest your head on the table in front of me—here, where my glass has been standing. You hesitate? No? Very well. I wish to inspect your neck, Schubert—your hairline, the transitional areas between head and neck, neck and shoulders. Cleanliness is my sole concern. In a person permitted to enter my immediate vicinity, it must be beyond reproach. In other words, it must equal my own."

This check, too, appeared to meet the captain's requirements, but with one or two reservations.

"Your hair gives a well-tended impression, Schubert, but its length is excessive. From now on you will visit a civilian barber once a week at my expense. But no hair oil, no scented sprays or pungent hair lotions!"

"Very good, sir."

"And now, Schubert, remove one of your shoes—the left one let's say. The sock too, of course. Place your foot on a chair so that it catches the light. Now spread your little toe sideways. Nothing must be neglected, however trivial it may seem."

"You can count me out!" Sergeant Arm stormed into the orderly room and bore down on Sergeant Forstmann. "I'm not going to be put upon, not by anybody!"

"What are you so steamed up about?"

"You, among other things. I'm surprised at you, Forstmann, getting mixed up in this brothel business after all your fine talk."

"I'm not mixed up in it," Forstmann protested. "I decided to withdraw my opposition, that's all." Sensing a challenge to his integrity, he sought refuge in an official manner. "To the best of my knowledge, Sergeant, you raised no objection to the scheme yourself."

"Well, now they can stuff it." Arm adopted a defiant stance, legs apart and arms akimbo, as though he intended to relieve himself on the orderly-room floor. "I'm responsible for every last damned vehicle this battery has. I'm not going to play second fiddle to a fat pig like Softer."

"I appreciate your point of view," Forstmann assured him. He could afford to say this because they were alone. "To be honest, I'm completely against the idea of organized copulation. Just between you and me, though, it doesn't look as if it's going to happen. The premises Softer had in mind are needed for something else—a civilian research team."

"I know that, Forstmann, and so does Softer." Arm was so furious he could hardly speak. "The double-crossing bastard's come up with another idea—one that'll leave me out in the cold."

"Sounds like him."

"You bet your sweet ass it does," growled Arm. "He has his eye on that glass house in the grounds, the conservatory I use as a repair shop—that's where he proposes to billet these civilians. In other words, I'm supposed to vacate. How about that?"

"I'm very sorry, of course."

"Is that all you can say?" Arm snorted with fury. "Well, I'm not having it, and that's that. He'll get that place over my dead body."

"I can imagine how you feel," Forstmann said diplomatically.

At that moment Softer appeared, drawn to the scene by a nose that scented trouble a mile off. He greeted Arm and Forstmann with a complacent grin.

"What's up, men, a little difference of opinion?"

"You keep your cotton-picking hands off my transportation section!" shouted Arm, determined to do battle. "Those vehicles of mine are vital to the war effort. Your brothel gets zero priority compared to them."

"Come off your high horse, Arm," Softer said smoothly. "Nobody's got any designs on your vehicles. We've all got a job to do, and mine is to keep this battery happy."

"Yes, but not at my expense."

Sergeant Major Krüger was the next to turn up, attracted by the shouting. He appeared without his uniform tunic, face pink and puffy from the effects of his afternoon nap. His eyes were alert, however, and his voice had the usual edge to it.

"I do the shouting around here," he announced. "Anybody else has to get my permission first. What's it all about?"

"It's this bastard here," Arm said in a more subdued voice, leveling his forefinger at Softer. "He's trying to stab me in the back."

"Oh, come now," Softer protested with an air of injured innocence, "you mustn't take it that way. I'm simply giving you a chance to show how public-spirited you are."

"Public piss!" snarled Arm.

"Listen," said Krüger, "I don't expect my NCO's to bill and coo the whole time, but I won't have this adolescent brawling either. In the first place it disturbs my well-earned rest, and in the second it's a waste of time. What I say goes."

Krüger had taken charge as usual. "Okay, let's hear what you have to say—one at a time."

Softer was first. Arm and Forstmann were told to get a breath of fresh air, leaving Krüger alone with the QMS. The two men exchanged grins.

"So you want to take over Arm's workshop, do you?" Krüger began.

"Yes, as quarters for this so-called research team. That'll leave the other rooms free for our recreation center. I know what Arm's after—he wants to cash in. The only reason he's making trouble is to squeeze a higher price out of me. Well, let him. I'm not tight-fisted."

Krüger nodded judicially. "Of course, you've hit the nail on the head. What are you prepared to offer him?"

"A few cases of liquor—half a dozen, let's say, and a barrel of Munich beer thrown in, plus three weeks' supplementary rations. We might even cut him in on the brothel profits. Five percent ought to do."

"You might be right," Krüger replied thoughtfully. "All the same, you're forgetting something. Arm's in a stronger position than you, and he knows it. His transportation section runs like clockwork. If it came to the pinch, Hein would decide in his favor."

"Why should it reach that stage?" demanded Softer. "You could persuade him—and if I know you, that's just what you're going to do."

"You know me," Krüger said with a wink, "and I know you. That being the case, I take it that booze and extra rations are just a preliminary offer."

"Well, yes, if you say so."

"I do. They won't be enough on their own. If Arm gives up that greenhouse of his, you'll have to supply him with a tent of the same size. Also, you'll have to do a lightning conversion job on the conservatory and split it into three or four rooms. That should be right up your alley."

"Krüger," Softer said admiringly, "you're a goddamn genius. You could sell snowballs to Eskimos and make a profit. Leave the rest to me."

Sergeant Arm, who was next in line for treatment, proved a more difficult patient. As Krüger suspected, he had a pretty accurate idea of the strength of his position. He began by making allusions to the military efficiency of Battery No. 3, and ended by invoking the name of Captain Hein, who would—he said—undoubtedly take his part.

"Let's cut out the crap and be practical," Krüger said

briskly. He conveyed Softer's terms in full detail. "Not bad, right?"

"Not bad for a start," Arm conceded, trying to conceal his surprise at the unexpected magnitude of the offer. Then resentment bubbled up again. "I wouldn't call it generous, though. That double-crossing profiteer can afford it, with his connections. He'll end up a millionaire, the way he's going, and where does that leave us? I mean, where do we come in?"

"What are you driving at, Arm?"

"Well, what's a brothel compared to a transporation section? Which is more important—three whores opening their legs for money or a fully mobile ack-ack battery? Every vehicle in this outfit is operational, thanks to me—if it's got four wheels it's ready to roll. I figure that's worth something."

"I get it. It's time you cashed in on all your hard work, right? Well, why not, as long as the battery benefits one way or another. What did you have in mind?"

"Car rental and haulage," Arm said, lowering his voice confidentially. "Something to spark morale, like Softer's brothel—something to help the boys make the most of their spare time."

"I don't see why not, as long as it pays." Krüger left the words "me" and "my battery" unspoken.

"It's like this," Arm went on, even more confidentially. "We've had an assortment of foreign cars on our hands ever since Dunkirk and Calais. There's a Bentley, a Panhard and an American Ford, all kept in perfect running order by me— or rather, by Hiller and Wassermann under my supervision —but never officially tested. In other words, we can use them any time."

"You mean you want to set up a car rental business financed by the members of the battery?"

"You got it, Sergeant Major." Arm was enthusiastic. "I'd contribute three first-class vehicles, work out the rental and mileage charges, and supply any amount of gasoline. The boys ought to get to know France, especially gay Paree. There'd be ten percent in it for you."

"Not for me," Krüger amended sharply, "—for battery funds, which I look after. Nobody buys me, Sergeant—I'm a pearl beyond price." He laughed at his own joke, but only briefly. "Not ten percent, either," he added. "Twenty-five."

"Done!" said Arm. "Is it a deal?"

"It's a deal." Krüger thrust a hand inside the gaping neck of his shirt and scratched pleasurably. "Just for the record, what sort of category would you put this organization into? Troops' welfare?"

"You took the words out of my mouth." Arm beamed with delight. "Nobody could accuse us of not having the battery's interests at heart, could they?"

"I wouldn't think so."

"And if they did?"

"I'd leave my boot up their ass."

Considering the matter carefully, neither Arm nor Krüger could think of anyone who was likely to make such an accusation.

Lieutenant Minder addressed himself to Corporal Bergen with a frank familiarity which transcended their difference in rank.

"Well, what're we in for this time?"

Minder slapped Bergen on the back. He was a great believer in the common touch, especially when applied to subordinates in key positions. As NCO in charge of signals section, Bergen qualified.

"Tell me," Minder continued out of the corner of his mouth, "why should the battery commander be attending muster parade in person? Krüger usually handles it. Also, why all this insistence on a full turnout?"

"I wouldn't know, sir," Bergen replied politely. "I only came to repair the field telephone."

He had, in his capacity as a battery signalman, received instructions to report to the officers' quarters overlooking the gun position. Obviously, the new arrival was to be given the once-over.

At the requisitioned villa beside the sports field, he had been greeted by a smiling Lieutenant Minder and his sidekick, Second Lieutenant Helmreich. A round-shouldered little man whose pathetic aspirations to zeal and efficiency had earned him the nickname Hein's Watchdog, Helmreich possessed a harsh, froglike voice but used it blessedly seldom. He seemed to realize that in Battery No. 3 his words carried even less weight than Minder's.

"So you don't know a thing?" Lieutenant Minder eyed Bergen with quizzical amusement. "I suppose you never listened in on a phone conversation in your life?"

"It's strictly against regulations, sir."

Minder's chuckle became a laugh. He winked at Helmreich. "Did you hear that? This man not only knows the regulations—he actually obeys them. And he expects us to believe him. Shows how little he knows us, doesn't it?"

Second Lieutenant Helmreich did not look at Bergen. He never looked straight at anyone he was addressing except Captain Hein, and Hein had been compelled to issue him with an express order to that effect. "It must occasionally happen," he said, as though conducting a monologue, "that signals personnel overhear an occasional telephone conversation—inadvertently, of course."

"Even if they do, sir, they're forbidden to discuss what they overhear."

"Naturally," said Helmreich, studying his incongruously large red hands. "On the other hand, Corporal, it might be pointed out that we are your direct and immediate superiors."

"Even then, sir, passing information about conversations we accidentally overhear is strictly forbidden."

"So that's your game!" exclaimed Lieutenant Minder, still

striving to sound amused. "You're taking out insurance, eh? I know your kind." His tone conveyed that he was familiar and capable of dealing efficiently with all types. "Ever heard of cooperation?" he asked amiably.

"Yes, sir, but how does it apply here?"

"Your predecessor knew. He could have given you a few tips on the subject if he hadn't met with that regrettable accident. What I mean is, don't hesitate to inform us immediately if you hear something that might interest us."

"Only for the sake of improved efficiency, of course," Helmreich put in. "We ought to know in advance what we're in for—it's only fair."

"Exactly," said Minder. "In other words, keep us abreast of the latest developments at headquarters."

"Very well, sir, if you order me to."

"Nonsense, man, don't give me that! We're not ordering you to do anything, merely suggesting. Just a tip on successful teamwork. You don't have to take it if you don't want to."

Bergen was spared the need to reply, for the moment at least, by the sudden appearance of Runge. Without deigning to knock, Hein's favorite stormed into the officers' living quarters, once an elegant room but now reduced to a shambles.

Runge, a stocky and self-important man with a powerful presence, reported briskly, "Gun crews ready for muster parade, sir. Battery commander sighted."

Minder and Helmreich were galvanized into action. They grabbed their uniform caps and clapped them on their heads, buckled their belts, smoothed the creases from their tunics, cast a last superfluous glance at their mirrorlike boots.

They hurried out with Runge at their heels. Bergen, whose existence seemed to have been forgotten, decided that the prospect of a free show was too good to miss. He strolled outside.

The gun crews had, as usual, paraded in the immediate

vicinity of the predictor. Every man had turned out with the exception of four aircraft spotters, one for each of the four cardinal points, who were scanning the sky some distance away but within earshot.

Captain Hein approached his gun position escorted by Sergeant Major Krüger. In practical terms, this meant he was driven there by Corporal Kaminski in his command car, a jeep-style Mercedes which covered the four hundred yards between château and gun position at a sedate, almost ceremonial pace and stopped at the edge of the sports field.

Hein vaulted gracefully from the open car. Krüger tried to emulate him but spoiled the effect by landing heavily. The late summer sun illumined the scene with harsh clarity.

The gun crews snapped to attention. Sergeant Runge reported them present and correct to Second Lieutenant Helmreich. Helmreich croaked at Lieutenant Minder, and Minder reported to Captain Hein.

Hein returned Minder's salute with a dismissive wave of his gloved hand. "Have the men stand at ease," he commanded. At Minder's order the gun crews stood at ease but maintained their mute rigidity. They presented a highly disciplined spectacle which Hein took for granted.

"Sergeant Major," he said, "read the regimental order."

Krüger raised his clipboard and began to read in a loud but unemotional voice. "Regimental Order No. 153/40 of the 18th instant," he announced. "Subject: latest intelligence reports and action to be taken in respect to defense and security measures. The latter to be devised and tested in view of possible attacks by hostile or subversive elements, spies, saboteurs and fifth columnists."

This, as it laboriously emerged from a continued reading of the regimental order, meant in practice that "groups of saboteurs, operating in the most insidious manner" had for the first time engaged units of the all-conquering German army. There had only been sporadic incidents so far, but their local effects could not be ignored.

Further details were given. In one instance, shots had been fired under cover of darkness at German troops on the march. In another, an attempt had been made to tamper with a signal box. The culprits were presumed to be British army stragglers, dissident and incorrigible members of the French population, or infiltrated saboteurs.

"Initial losses," read Krüger, thankfully reaching the final paragraph, "have been far from heavy, thanks to the vigilance of all ranks. They do, however, make it necessary to institute precautionary measures. Much as we regret this, we have no choice. We have, in open battle, defeated the armies of countries which declared war on us. We are here to preserve peace, defend freedom and maintain order. Nothing and no one will deflect us from this endeavor. I expect every man under my command to do his duty. Signed: Rheinemann-Bergen, colonel and regimental commander."

"That's all we needed," Lieutenant Minder muttered apprehensively.

Second Lieutenant Helmreich remained steadfastly silent, gazing at his battery commander as though praying for a miracle.

"Saboteurs, eh?" growled Runge. "Let them come—we'll cut the bastards to ribbons. We ought to begin by demolishing that water tower. It spoils our field of fire."

"Preliminary measures," said Hein, glancing at Krüger.

Krüger cleared his throat. "Sentries will be doubled and checkpoints reinforced. All personnel leaving the battery area will carry small arms. Effective immediately, all ranks visiting the town will do so in pairs or larger parties. All suspicious incidents are to be reported immediately. All conversations with outsiders are to be avoided. All ranks will report in and out to the gun-position guard commander, who will enter their names in writing."

Captain Hein nodded. "Men," he drawled, "those are just incidentals. What matters most is the fighting efficiency of this battery. Well, we've already taken care of that. Every gun crew has been instructed in hand-to-hand combat and infantry tactics. All that remains is to brush up on what we've learned. Is that clear?"

"Yes, sir," replied Lieutenant Minder, on behalf of the assembled gun crews.

"Our base of operations must be effectively secured against enemy attack—kept in a state of even greater combat readiness. Anything that could obstruct or hinder us in the execution of our duty must be removed immediately. Is that equally clear?"

The eyes of every man on parade were focused on the target of these remarks, Lieutenant Minder, who immediately grasped what the captain was driving at. Common experience of battle in Poland and France had attuned Minder's ears to every nuance in Hein's voice. It was no coincidence that Minder had been awarded the Iron Cross, even if it was a class lower than Hein's.

"I take it, sir," said Minder, "that all civilians resident in the immediate neighborhood ought to be evacuated—certainly those whose homes give them an unimpeded view of our gun emplacements."

"Excellent," commented Hein. "An admirable suggestion, Lieutenant. Act on it at once."

Minder realized that Hein had railroaded him into another decision. He still found it hard to accept the process but was careful not to reveal it. "That means clearing all the houses around the gun position. Certainly, sir. The only thing is, what do we do with their occupants?"

"Drop them in the town commandant's lap," Hein decreed, "with my compliments. And tell him this: Security takes priority over personal convenience. It's time he got used to the idea."

* * *

Battery Sergeant Major Krüger surveyed his assembled NCO's complacently. "Someone's got to suffer," he said. "We can kick out as many French civilians as we like, on tactical grounds."

"But what's it got to do with tactics, Sergeant Major?" It was Tino Hiller who asked the question, ingenuous and unsoldierly-looking as ever. "The regimental order didn't say anything about evicting civilians from the houses around the gun position."

"No, but it implied it." Sergeant Forstmann spoke with a certain disdain for his fellow NCO's humanitarian leanings. "It's all a matter of interpretation."

"Not just a way of getting back at the town commandant?"

"Interpretation depends on circumstances, and circumstances vary. It's up to each unit commander how he assesses them."

"You mean he can do what he wants?"

Forstmann nodded. "Inside his own sphere of command."

"These French civilians," persisted Tino Hiller. "Do they come into Captain Hein's sphere of command?"

"Not any longer. They've gone."

"What the hell are you worrying about?" Krüger interrupted. "Look at it this way: It's the farmer who decides when to slaughter his pigs. The pigs don't even know when they're due for the ax."

"But they squeal," said Hiller.

"So will you if you don't shut up," Krüger told him sternly.

A subdued chuckle ran around the circle of NCO's. Krüger had invited them to join him for a few friendly drinks in the canteen. The liquid refreshment, of which there was plenty, had been provided by Sergeant Softer.

"In this outfit," declared Krüger, "you have to be able to

spot the difference between guts and hot air. If in doubt, consult me." Krüger's eye came to rest on the newcomer to the group. Signalman Bergen was frowning.

Krüger's eyes narrowed. "Anything puzzling you, Bergen?"

"No, Sergeant Major," Bergen assured him politely.

"Fine. In that case, perhaps you'd give us the situation in a nutshell."

"As I see it," Bergen said, "the sequence goes like this. The custodian had to vacate his apartment. The town commandant groused but got nowhere, so he retaliated by foisting a party of civilians on us, probably in collusion with the adjutant at Group HQ. As a result, the town commandant now finds himself saddled with a bunch of homeless French refugees from the houses around the gun position—about two dozen I gather."

"Thirty, to be exact." Krüger peered at him expectantly. "A nice round number. Any objections?"

"Should I have?"

Krüger gave a hoarse chuckle. "You're a sharp one, Bergen, I spotted that the first time I set eyes on you. Well, nothing wrong with being sharp. I can use a few brains in my collection." He nodded to Softer, and a dozen bottles materialized. Krüger had made it clear to the regular members of the NCO's social club that Bergen needed thawing out. "We've got to find out what we're dealing with," was his final injunction before the party started.

Krüger never took his eyes off Bergen. "In case you didn't know, son, this outfit is one big happy family. We've been through some tough times together but we've had good ones, too. And, we like to be friendly."

"So do I, when I can."

"There you are then—you're going to fit in nicely. What I mean is, you can join the club if you want to. It's an honor, you know. You aren't even a bombardier, let alone a sergeant, but you do a sergeant's job as head of the signals section. Being a broad-minded and generous crew, we'll stretch a point." Krüger paused. "Of course, there's no obligation to join if you have any objections to the idea."

"I wouldn't say that, Sergeant Major."

"You mean you'd like to?"

"Well, yes . . . if you really think. . . ."

"Full membership and all that goes with it?"

"I don't know exactly what it entails, but. . . ."

"You're in! Congratulations." Krüger turned to the rest. "Hear that, men? We've got a new member." He applied his lips to an almost-full bottle of schnapps, measuring the swig with his thumb—a remarkably broad one. Then he passed the bottle to Bergen. "All right, friend, let's see if you're worth your membership."

Bergen drank without hesitation. A full thumb's breadth.

The bottle made the round. It was almost empty by the time it reached the last member of the gathering. Nobody gagged, not even Tino Hiller. Forstmann, who rapidly became sick-drunk on hard liquor, poured the stupefying schnapps down his throat with heroic self-control.

"And now," said Krüger, rubbing his hands briskly, "the initiation ceremony. All our newly elected members have to pass it. Are you game?" Krüger's piggy eyes twinkled with ominous glee. "It's a test of courage—our way of finding out if a man's got guts or if he'll shit his pants in an emergency. Watch this!"

Almost simultaneously, Krüger and Sergeants Arm and Moll each produced an 8-mm automatic. They slammed them down on the rough wooden table and propelled Bergen toward them. Three more pistols came to light, a Walther 7.65 and two Mauser 6.35's belonging to Softer, Kaminski and Forstmann, respectively.

Bergen registered the proceedings with numb astonishment. He noticed that Hiller and Neumann took no part in them, perhaps because they were considered unworthy. As for the six pistol suppliers, they seemed to have been overcome, from one moment to the next, by the mood of grave solemnity proper to celebrants in a ritual act of supreme importance.

"Six pistols," explained Krüger. "All six cocked, safety catches off. The magazines are empty, but one of them contains a live round. All you have to do is choose. Then put the muzzle to your head and pull the trigger. That, Bergen my friend, is our own special party game—Prussian roulette. All right, take your pick."

"Why Prussian roulette?" Bergen asked, playing for time.

"Because it's a sort of variation on Russian roulette," Krüger told him. There was a note of urgency in his voice now. "In Russian roulette they use a single revolver with one of the six chambers loaded. Our game's an improvement —six guns instead of one. Okay, go ahead and choose." There was a momentary pause. "You don't have to, of course, not if you've changed your mind about joining. Some men lose their nerve—they don't appreciate our little traditions. Don't worry, everything's voluntary with us."

Bergen stared at the pistols lying in front of him. Then he glanced up and saw eight pairs of eyes fixed on him, appraising, watchful, amused, challenging, concerned, alarmed, suspicious, contemptuous. Swiftly, as though on impulse, he reached for one of the three 8-mm automatics—the one that belonged to Krüger.

Bergen raised the pistol and put it to his forehead, immediately between the eyes. He hesitated for a split second, then pulled the trigger.

There was a sharp metallic click.

"That's it," said Krüger, happy in his awareness of universal agreement. "From now on, Bergen, you're one of us."

Interim Report No. 2

Assurances
given by Herr Karl Schmidt,
town commandant of D. during the German occupation of
*   France,*
formerly a captain in the German army,
now a ministry official
in one of the southern provinces of West Germany.
Special field of responsibility: Franco-German youth
*   exchanges.*

"Surely it's clear by now that innuendoes and accusations of
this sort are aimed not only at the German soldier of those days,
who genuinely had nothing in common with that monster Hitler, but equally at the German soldier of today and, through
him, at the freedom-loving people of the Western world and
their will to defend themselves.

". . . Although I did not volunteer for duty as town commandant of D., I tackled the job with high hopes of mitigating
the burdens of occupation and assisting the victims of war—a
self-imposed task which I fulfilled with a large measure of
success. Testimonials to that effect are available for inspection.

". . . I must begin by expressing my appreciation of the
understanding shown me by a wide section of the French population, not only private individuals but also local government
officials. We always strove to work together in an atmosphere
of mutual trust.

"Furthermore, the commander of the antiaircraft regiment
of which the inestimable Captain Hein's battery formed part,
a Colonel Rheinemann-Bergen, wrote me a letter containing
the following: 'I am delighted by your consistently sympathetic
approach to the interests of the French population whose welfare it is our duty to promote.' Here is a photostat of the
document in question.

"I can also assure you, in confidence, that I cherished a very
special regard for Captain Hein—a regard which was, I am
sure, reciprocated in full. I certainly had the highest admiration for his exceptional organizing skill, his vigorous and resolute personality and his merits as a military tactician. If for no

other reason, I was deeply affected by the shocking news of his death.

"Certainly, I shall never forget his saying to me, one day when we were chatting as old friends do: 'My dear Karl, it may seem as if we're facing two different ways, but—believe you me—we're in the same boat.'

". . . I'm also convinced that he—Captain Hein, that is—had a very special brand of humor that eluded the majority of those who came into contact with him. As, for instance, when he said to me: 'What do you mean, the war in France is over? I *am* the war around here!' There was little doubt of the subtle irony underlying this remark."

Excerpts
from an interview with Madame M.,
Christian name Marie-Antoinette,
once an occupant of the bailiff's apartment at D.,
now resident in Bordeaux.

". . . I've always yearned for security and a quiet life. I'm married now, to a winegrower. Yes, blissfully happy, thank you. Two children, a boy and a girl. Pierre will inherit his father's vineyards and Hortense is engaged to a local landowner. All very satisfactory, *n'est-ce pas?* Idyllic, some people might call it.

"What are you trying to do, ruin my life? No? In that case, what *do* you want? The truth? *Cher monsieur*, the truth depends on your point of view. All right, you can have it as far as I'm concerned. On condition you don't give my real name and address, of course. Promise? *Eh bien.*

"It all started when I bumped into a German NCO named Softer. He's a wholesale vintner now—does business with my husband and our future son-in-law. Monsieur Softer has done a lot to bring the Germans and French together—he's even on some important Franco-German friendship committee. That's the kind of man he is, *dieu merci.*

"Our first meeting took place in D., quite by chance. He happened to be spending the night at the same hotel as me. That's when our friendship dates from.

"*Eh bien*, to cut a long story short, Softer offered to find me a room—somewhere safe, because things were difficult under the occupation. He managed to clear a couple of rooms in the decrepit old château where he was stationed and I stayed there for several weeks, doing part-time work.

"Just so I wouldn't get too lonely, *mon cher* Softer found two other girls to move in with me. Young ladies from upper-class homes, they were, very well brought up but full of fun. One was the daughter of a senior civil servant from Nancy and the other came from Alsace—the daughter of a staff officer, I think. Their names were Margot and Suzanne.

"Why look at me like that, monsieur? I can guess what you're thinking. I suppose they've talked you into believing that the three of us were—well, not too particular about the company we kept. If that's what you're driving at, words fail me! I've had enough of these spiteful, dirty-minded insinuations. All they amount to is sour grapes.

"If you really want the truth, here it is: We spent most of the time shut up like nuns. What if *nôtre cher* Softer did visit us from time to time—nothing wrong with that, is there? And what if he did sometimes bring a friend along—*pourquoi pas?* We even had some pleasant evenings together, as far as circumstances permitted in those dark days.

"But that was all. Innocent social gatherings attended by young people thrown together by the fortunes of war, monsieur. There was no more to it than that, I assure you."

Extracts
from an article contributed to the Preussische Zeitung
by the then war correspondent Konrad W.,
together with comments
by Konrad W., now editor of a leading West German news-
    paper.

Original article:
"Captain Hein, hero of Mlawa and Warsaw, of the Maginot Line and Dunkirk. . . . Six tanks, five aircraft, numerous road-blocks, the clearing of a passage over the Saône, the bombardment of various infantry positions and the destruction of at

least three reinforced concrete bunkers—all these to his credit. A proud record indeed!

"Yet the man responsible for all these triumphs is distinguished by his extreme modesty. His own words testify for him: 'The chance was there and I grabbed it!'; or, when being decorated with his Iron Cross First Class—soon, it is rumored, to be followed by the Knight's Cross—this gem of self-effacement: 'I shall wear it for my men!'

"Captain Hein is a man of medium height but looks taller because of his slim, athletic build. He has the litheness of a greyhound and the toughness of tempered steel—Krupp steel. His blue eyes, clear as a mountain stream, seem to be permanently focused on the probable source of an enemy attack. 'Preparedness is all,' he says simply."

Today's comment:

"Only those who lived through that period can fully understand and correctly interpret the tone of my article. They alone will be able to judge what it *really* entailed, this compulsion to wage secret resistance, consciously and deliberately—conscious of the merits of the German soldier, who was utterly guiltless, but in deliberate opposition to Hitler and his ideology, which we so early came to recognize and despise.

"Who can still gauge what it meant in those days to write as we dared write? Almost every line put our lives in jeopardy because every word was noted.

"Nazi press tycoons threatened us daily with investigations, disciplinary proceedings and trials. Many of my colleagues were hauled before the people's courts, where the shadow of the gallows loomed over all. . . .

"Not even that could deter us, though we recognized the need for caution. Those of us who possessed a gift for it, as I did, tended to seek refuge in a refined form of satire. My article is full of it. You have only to read between the lines."

Original article:

" 'Your men,' I said to Captain Hein, after his battery had carried out a practice alert with extreme precision, 'would follow you to hell and back.'

" 'That's the way it should be,' he replied, as if it were the most natural thing in the world."

Today's comment:

"Note the various shades of meaning, especially in the phrase 'follow to hell and back.' Although I say it myself, it took some courage to brand war as hell in an age of fanatical militarism! Outwardly, of course, it might appear to be just another cheap cliché, but such were the only weapons available to us.

"And then, to cap it all, 'the hero'—another piece of irony, by the way—declares: 'That's the way it should be.' What an indictment of absolutism and blind obedience, and how we all laughed when I read the galleys aloud to the few friends and colleagues I could still trust!"

Original article:

"Grandfather Hein, a successful platoon commander during the Boxer Rebellion. 'Send for the Germans!' came the despairing cry, and a Hein was there! His son, a brave and conscientious chaplain at Verdun. Many a man died, comforted, in his arms. And now, this unique grandson!

"As his distinguished regimental commander, Colonel Rheinemann-Bergen, remarked to me over a drink in the officers' mess: 'Men like Hein don't grow on trees.'

"A final verdict by the general commanding his division: 'If any man can do the impossible, he can.' "

Today's comment:

"These remarks scarcely require amplification—they speak for themselves. The well-aimed sarcasm that underlies the whole piece is unmistakable.

"I need hardly add, I suppose, that we always strove to safeguard the interests of the German soldier himself. He was a clean fighter, staunch and true—a representative of all that is finest in our Western way of life. No, our dogged and resolute opposition was reserved for Nazi excesses and Fascist beasts in human guise.

"I cannot pretend to have been entirely aware that Hein himself belonged to the last category, but I instinctively sensed he did. This is quite apparent from the tone of my article—at least to those who, as I have said, are capable of reading between the lines."

Recollections
of a Madame Daumier,
still resident in the town of D.

"It gives me no pleasure to look back on those days, monsieur. However, since you are so eager to delve into things that happened long ago, I will do my best for you. Not that I feel you will relish the story when you hear it—after all, monsieur, you are a German. But then, I like to think that some of you have learned a little in the past thirty years. One should never abandon hope, *n'est-ce pas?*

"The facts are as follows. We lived in a small house overlooking the sports field, I and my children—three girls, then aged eight, five and three. Their father, my husband, was missing, presumed killed. I later heard that he had managed to escape to England, but we never saw him again because he was killed during the liberation, only a few miles from this very town.

"This lay in the future, of course. All I knew at the time was that we must somehow try to survive the war. One day, however, German soldiers forced their way into our little house —four or five of them led by a sergeant named Runge. 'Madame,' the sergeant said, very politely, 'I'm afraid we must ask you to leave at once.'

"I know I started to cry—what else could I do? The children cried too, clinging tightly to me, but Sergeant Runge said, 'I'm sorry, but you must be out of here in half an hour at the latest.'

" 'But why, why?' I pleaded.

" 'Orders, madame.' That was all he said, although he still spoke kindly. 'You may take as much as you can carry, so be sensible and don't make trouble.'

"I was like a madwoman—no other word can describe my state of mind at the time. Then I saw the commander of these

Germans, a captain—probably the Hein you mentioned earlier. I rushed up to him and fell on my knees. 'Help me!' I cried. 'For the love of God, help me!'

"But all he said was, '*C'est la guerre, madame.*'

"He said it with great regret—I'm almost certain of that. There was nothing he could do, and his sergeant added, 'Orders from the top.'

"Today, in the light of all I have learned since, I know what he meant. It was that man Hitler! Hitler was to blame for everything. He compelled even the most decent of his soldiers to do ruthless things. I and my three little children were simply the innocent victims of men who could not help themselves. And all because of Hitler!"

3

Fate Takes a Running Jump

"Here we are at last! It's just as I imagined it."

The powerful female voice issued from an Opel Olympia sedan daubed with gray-green camouflage paint. The car pulled up outside the château. The door was flung open and the owner of the voice climbed out—a middle-aged, formidable-looking woman.

"Hey, you!" called a sentry, emerging from behind an ornamental shrub and trotting over to the car. "This is a restricted area. No unauthorized persons admitted."

"We," the woman retorted, "are authorized."

The sentry grinned. "You don't say."

"Stop being obstructive, young man." The speaker wore a shapeless but serviceable linen suit. She had a stern face and a center part which might have been incised with a scalpel. "We're expected."

"Not by me you aren't." The sentry scrutinized the woman and the car, both of them coated with a thick layer of dust.

A man got out. He was gray-haired and bent, with a pink face and a matching pair of pinkish rabbit eyes. He turned and tipped the front seat forward, then reached inside and helped another female passenger out. The first thing that emerged was a tangled mass of brown hair framing a pale, inquisitive young face. Next came slender shoulders and two well-rounded breasts clearly visible beneath a tight blouse. A pair of mobile hips completed the picture.

"I'm simply dying to wash my hands," she said brightly.

"But of course," said the old gentleman with the pink eyes. "It's been a long and tiring trip."

The sentry, still reveling in the whole bizarre situation, said, "If you have to, you have to, but not on the grass—it's strictly against orders. Come over into the bushes with me and I'll show you where you can do it in private."

"Kindly keep your obscene suggestions to yourself!" snapped the elder of the two women. "As for you, Fräulein Erdmann, I advise you to phrase your remarks with greater care—certainly in the presence of an uncouth, ill-educated lout like our friend here."

The elderly man was unconscious of what was going on around him. He gazed spellbound at the church on the edge of the grounds, advanced a few steps as though it held some magical attraction for him, and then halted. At last he said, "It's beautiful, breathtakingly beautiful, but smaller than I'd imagined."

Fräulein Erdmann smiled. "I'm often disappointed by the size of things when I finally get to see them."

The elder woman looked around at the wide assortment of vehicles, most of them half camouflaged by trees and bushes: trucks, personnel carriers, half-tracks, gun tractors. There was no sign of life apart from the sentry, and he—she clearly implied—was not a member of the human race. "Is everyone asleep," she persisted, "at this hour, in broad daylight?"

"Nobody's asleep," the sentry assured her. "This is just the midday break. We're up half the night sometimes. We deserve some time off."

In fact, slumber reigned over Battery No. 3. Captain Hein had retired to recoup his energies and given notice that he did not wish to be disturbed for three hours. Sergeant Major Krüger had promptly and predictably announced that he was off to do some important paperwork in his personal quarters. Everyone knew what that meant, and the word soon spread.

"Where's the commandant?" demanded the energetic lady. "Bring him here at once, sentry. I wish to speak to him."

"We don't have a commandant," the sentry said, a trifle uneasily. She was beginning to get on his nerves. "This is a combat unit, lady, not a leave center. We have a battery commander."

"Then get him, and kindly refrain from boring us with any more of your pleasantries." She surveyed the sentry with contempt. "If you must know, we're here on official business. This," she pursued, indicating the pigeon-chested old man lost in contemplation of the church, "is Professor Magnus. I am his administrative assistant, Dr. Werner-Weilheim. The third member of the party is our secretary."

The sentry's brow cleared. "You're the eggheads! Why didn't you say so in the first place? We were expecting you but we didn't know what to expect." He sprang to life and vanished into the château.

Frau Dr. Werner-Weilheim stared after him with irritation. "This place is run like a pigsty," she said. "Never mind, we'll soon straighten it out. This isn't the first time we've encountered such treatment. Leave everything to me, Professor."

The professor nodded mechanically. As a scholar and historian, he was only too happy to delegate the more mundane problems to his assistant. She cleared all manner of obstacles from their common path, not only so that he could work in peace but because it satisfied one of her congenital urges. He tried to concentrate exclusively on the church while

Elizabeth Erdmann slipped off into the nearest undergrowth.

Quartermaster Sergeant Softer emerged from a side entrance and waddled toward them. "Good afternoon!" he called while still some distance away, extending his plump hands with all the unctuous charm of a Levantine carpet dealer. "Welcome to Battery No. 3, Professor! Delighted to make your acquaintance, *Frau Doktor!* We were expecting you, of course, but not quite as early as this."

"Well, here we are." Frau Dr. Werner-Weilheim gave Softer a curt nod. "Suitable accommodation has been prepared for us, I trust?"

"But of course, *Frau Doktor.*" Softer allowed himself to be diverted by the sight of the lovely Fräulein Erdmann as she emerged from the bushes, looking relieved.

Softer licked his fat lips. His expert verdict on Fräulein Erdmann was that she had class.

"And who do we have here?"

"Our secretary," the *Frau Doktor* told him dismissively. "And now, kindly conduct us to our quarters—the bailiff's apartment, as arranged."

"Ah," Softer said quickly, "that's been requisitioned for another purpose. Just as well, too—it was a rat's nest. We can offer you something far better—the palm court. I've had it specially converted to suit your requirements." He pointed to a clump of fir trees some distance from the main building. The tip of a rust-marred iron and glass-domed structure could just be discerned in their midst. "A home away from home, I assure you. Shall I lead the way?"

Giving Professor Magnus and Fräulein Erdmann a skeptical glance, she marched off. The professor edged a little closer to the church while his secretary paid a second visit to the bushes. Meanwhile, Frau Dr. Werner-Weilheim inspected what Softer had to offer, namely, four rooms separated by wallboard partitions and an outside lavatory. She pulled the chain but nothing happened.

"Impossible!" she snapped. "You can't expect us to sleep in this slum. I would remind you that we are representatives of a cultural institute, not vagabonds."

"Of course, *Frau Doktor*, but I assure you. . . ."

"We're only wasting valuable time, Sergeant. Go and get your superior officer—on the double!"

Softer wrested Krüger from his well-earned midday repose. "Jesus, Sergeant Major," he groaned, "they've really saddled us this time. An old battle-ax, with hair on her chest and a voice like a foghorn. She actually told me to bring you on the double."

"Sounds promising," Krüger said with evident amusement. "Kicks like a mule, does she? Well, you can do a lot with mules if you handle them right. A short sharp clout and they eat out of your hand."

Krüger sought out the research team and curtly introduced himself. "Just to get things straight from the start, ladies and gentlemen, you haven't been directly assigned to me or my unit. We were asked to be of assistance and we will be, but only as far as we can."

Frau Dr. Werner-Weilheim was unimpressed. "Nonsense, man. Stop beating around the bush. We've been posted here by our ministerial chief acting in consultation with Reich Marshal Goering. We demand and expect every possible assistance, and that includes the provision of adequate accommodation."

"The bailiff's apartment," the professor said politely, "was set aside for us, according to written instructions from our department. Your regimental headquarters confirmed this."

"No government department gives orders to the army," said Krüger. "Also, instructions issued by a regimental headquarters one day can be superseded the next. This battery is on active service—we're fighting a war."

"Really?" The professor raised his eyebrows. "It all looks very peaceful to me."

"Of course," Krüger said, "we do have a few peacetime pleasures, too. Just to prove it, let me send you over a case of wine. Which do you prefer, Burgundy or claret?"

"Claret—personally." The professor's reaction was worthy of a connoisseur. "Some 1933, if possible, though '35 would be equally welcome. All appearances to the contrary, '33 was an extremely commendable year—for wine, of course."

"You obviously know your stuff, Professor." Krüger smiled for the first time. "I'll have a dozen sent over to you this afternoon. We're a friendly bunch in Battery No. 3 as long as people meet us halfway."

Professor Magnus regarded Krüger with a gleam of anticipation in his little pink eyes. "Speaking for myself, Sergeant Major, I find your attitude extremely gratifying. I'm sure we shall all get along like a house afire."

"If we don't," Krüger said, "it won't be my fault, I assure you."

"For my part," Frau Dr. Werner-Weilheim said tartly, "I insist that the original agreement be honored in full." She tweaked her skirt down over her substantial haunches. Krüger eyed them with an involuntary flicker of interest.

"We'll do our best for you," he said. "I've detailed someone to act as a sort of liaison officer—an NCO by the name of Bergen. He'll look after you all right."

"This is where you step in," Krüger told Bergen a few minutes later. "It'll give you a chance to show what you're made of."

"How, Sergeant Major?"

"Just bear one thing in mind—always saddle horses from the ass end, mares included. And don't be too impressed by the fact that you're dealing with a bunch of eggheads. Every great mind has an asshole to match."

"And that's the end you want me to concentrate on?"

"Remember it exists, that's all. In other words, professors are human. They're welcome to root around in the dust of ages as long as they don't get in my hair, right?"

"Right, Sergeant Major." Bergen's voice rang with devotion to duty, but the sound, like so much else within the orbit of Battery No. 3, was deceptive.

"Don't stare at me." Uttered in a voice as soft as silk, these words were addressed by Captain Hein to his current orderly, Gunner Schubert. "I dislike being stared at."

"Yes, sir!" Schubert had closed the door of the banquet chamber and was standing just inside. He gazed at Hein with puzzled humility, hoping for some sign of goodwill. Nothing could dispel the grisly sensation that alternate torrents of hot and cold water were chasing each other down his spine.

"I don't wish you to loiter by the door like a flunky, Schubert. I abhor domestic servants. I see you as something quite different—a modern version of the medieval page, perhaps. Are you so lacking in confidence that you hesitate to approach me?"

"I didn't want to intrude, sir. I was waiting for further orders."

Hein shook his angular head. His glacial eyes regarded Schubert searchingly. "You can hardly be intruding since I requested your presence. Consider that, Schubert—I did not order you to come, I merely requested. You note the subtle distinction?"

"I shall in future, sir," Schubert assured him.

"And I shall expect you to. I demand no blind obedience to orders in your particular case. I wish to be able to trust you implicitly. May I do that?"

"I hope so, sir."

"Not good enough, Schubert. You must be absolutely positive."

"I . . . I am, sir."

"Very good. We're making progress. What are orders, after all? I can give orders to any one of a hundred and fifty men, orders which must be obeyed to the letter regardless of content. For instance, what would you do if I told you to jump out that window?"

"I don't know. . . ."

"All right, Schubert—you don't know, not yet." Captain Hein smiled to himself. "On the other hand, ninety-nine percent of my men would jump if I ordered them to. And why? Because they're absolutely devoted to me—in other words, they trust me implicitly. They would assume I had set up nets or other safety devices. What about you? Doesn't your imagination extend that far?"

"I'm not sure, sir."

"I understand. This is all virgin territory from your point of view. You're an idealist by nature but you've yet to grasp the true meaning of idealism. You trust me but you've yet to learn what trust ultimately entails. It's only a question of time. Meanwhile, you may count on my patience and understanding. Do you smoke?"

"No, sir."

"Good, excellent—another point in your favor. Kindly ensure that no one else smokes in my personal quarters while I am absent."

The captain was sitting in his favorite place at the head of the long refectory table. Candles were again burning in the silver candlesticks on either side of him. Clearly, Hein was fond of semidarkness.

He wore a glistening jet-black robe of Japanese silk—the gift, so it was rumored, of a female admirer who had made it for the war hero with her own hands. Hein had thrown it on with the nonchalance peculiar to him, exposing a portion of his handsomely hirsute chest. Dangling on a slender chain was a cross, evidently of gold.

"Deep and boundless trust is the essential basis of all human, all masculine relationships," he said. "Why hesitate to acknowledge it? Come over here, Schubert, and stand beside me. Unless, of course, you decline to."

Schubert came closer. He felt simultaneously attracted and repelled but could not have explained why. It was as if his equilibrium had deserted him. He moved uncertainly in the captain's direction. Beneath its mop of soft wavy hair, his beautiful, sensitive face burned with a nameless fever.

Even in his confusion, he noticed that a glass stood in front of Hein, empty. Beside it, draped in a white damask napkin, was a bottle of champagne; also, covered by Hein's own napkin, a mysterious object the size of a man's hand. Instinctively, Schubert halted at an appropriate distance.

Hein watched his progress with an unwavering smile. "Tell me," he said, "do you know how to serve champagne?"

"I think so, sir." Schubert tried desperately to remember his lessons. His face shone with sweat and his armpits felt sticky beneath his tunic. Breathing hard, he said, "You start by removing the bottle from the liquid in which it has been chilled. The temperature should be approximately seven degrees Centigrade."

"For my taste, not more than ten nor less then five degrees. What next?"

"Before being opened," recited Schubert, "the bottle should be wrapped in a white napkin, almost to the neck. The wire fastener is removed by twisting the loop counterclockwise. The cork is then loosened with the thumb and forefinger of the right hand. No undue noise should result. It is also advisable to tilt the bottle slightly to prevent any of the contents from overflowing."

Hein nodded approvingly. "Correct. That, to the best of my knowledge, accords with traditional practice in the best restaurants—Maxim's, for example. Who instructed you or saw to it that you underwent instruction? The sergeant major?"

"Yes, sir."

Krüger had taken the precaution of sending Schubert to Softer, who had passed him on to Bergen. Bergen promptly requisitioned three bottles of champagne "to practice on" and reserved two of them for his personal consumption. Vital particulars about the serving of champagne had been provided, at Wassermann's instigation, by the headwaiter at the Hôtel de France, who had done his training in Paris.

"And now, Schubert, describe the position of the hands."

"Champagne is served with the right hand only. The left hand should be held behind the back at hip level."

"Excellent." Hein sat up, baring even more of his chest. The cross gleamed gold in the candlelight. "So much for theory, Schubert—now to business. Pour me some champagne, but read the label first. Impress the name and year on your memory. That is the mark I prefer, the one reserved for me alone. Quartermaster Sergeant Softer is responsible for supplying it."

Schubert picked up the opened bottle, which was already half empty. He read the label and rewound the napkin. Gingerly, holding his breath, he poured. No headwaiter could have performed the operation with greater care.

"Not bad," pronounced Hein. "You have steady hands, Schubert. What is more, you evidently take trouble over their appearance. I approve of that. Now put down the bottle and rest your hands on the table beside it. No, nearer, just to the right of my glass."

Johannes Schubert pressed his moist palms hard against the smooth cold wood of the table to disguise how much they were trembling. The captain inclined his head to examine them with a grave and meditative expression. His own hands moved upward and outward in a shallow arc and then, like gulls coming in to land, swooped with gentle assurance onto Schubert's.

Schubert gave a convulsive start, knocking over the captain's champagne glass. It broke, and the contents flowed across the table toward Hein, who leaped to his feet and stood there with his chest heaving. He had gone very pale.

'I'm sorry, sir," Schubert stammered.

"You!" The word sounded like a strangled cry. "You actually dared to touch me?"

"It was a mistake, sir—a sudden start."

"I permit no one to touch me." Hein's voice had regained some of its crispness and there was a predatory gleam in his eye. "Never do that again!" He bowed his blond, close-cropped head and stared at the spreading pool of champagne. His hands sought and found each other in a viselike grip which turned the knuckles white. When he next spoke, it might have been to himself.

"I touch what I wish to touch, but nobody touches me unless I wish it. I detest hands that reach and grope in my direction. I have always abominated the touch of others— slimy, sweaty paws, chapped skin ingrained with filth, horny palms, grimy fingers, black-rimmed nails. . . .

"I can still see one outstretched hand, the hand of a boy— not raised in greeting but leveled in accusation. It happened in Poland, in some village we passed through. It was a loathsome, grubby child's hand, encrusted with earth, brown and sticky. The face above it was pinched, contorted, filled with hatred. The mouth pursed as I watched, then spat. At me!

"I wrenched my driver's wheel around and we drove full tilt at the slobbering face, knocked it down and buried it beneath our wheels, but that foul and stinking hand seemed to reach up in a last gesture of defiance. It thudded against the bodywork several times—drummed, you might say, as if it were beating a tattoo of detestation. Then the drumming grew fainter and stopped."

Silence fell, but the captain continued to stand there like a statue. Schubert did not dare move a muscle.

A full minute passed before Hein straightened up and

looked around with an air of surprise. He gave an unconvincing laugh and shook his head. "Ever since then," he said, "I have made it a rule to wear gloves in public. Physical contact is unavoidable sometimes. They help me endure it."

He sat down again in the high-backed, heavily upholstered leather chair which he had thrust back in his hurry to escape the spilt champagne. "Just now," he said, watching Schubert closely, "you were agitated—excited, even. Why?"

"I don't know, sir."

"But you were. Was I the cause of your . . . your excitement?" Hein continued to scrutinize his bewildered orderly through the candles' glow. "I strongly recommend you to practice self-control, Schubert, even under the most extreme pressure—in fact I insist on it. I have a well-developed aesthetic sense, especially where hands are concerned. I loathe to see them tremble like jelly."

Hein extended both arms at shoulder level and looked at his fingers. Not a tremor could be detected. Then, with a single swift movement of his right hand which left the other wholly motionless, he reached for the napkin on the table and flung it aside to reveal an automatic pistol.

He raised the pistol and held it at eye level, manipulating the safety catch with his thumb. "Can you guess what I'm aiming at?" he asked.

Schubert shook his head, although he had the inescapable sensation that the muzzle was pointing straight at him. If not at the center of his forehead, perhaps at his right ear. He stood stock still.

"Immediately behind you," Hein went on, "hangs a picture representing death and one of its victims. An allegorical absurdity by some undistinguished eighteenth-century dauber, with every detail slavishly painted in. It offends me."

Hein fired twice. Schubert seemed to hear the bullets hiss past his head, only millimeters away. He scarcely heard the double detonation of the shots themselves.

"Now look around."

A little unsteadily, Schubert turned. He saw a carefully, almost pedantically painted personification of death, a skeleton in a flowing black gown with its skull pitilessly denuded of flesh. Two bullet holes had transformed its eye sockets into dark and bottomless pits.

"That," Hein said with a relaxed smile, "was symbolically intended, so to speak. You follow my meaning, Schubert? Try to understand—I advise you to, most earnestly. You may count on my help."

"Thank you, sir. I'll do my best."

"You're perspiring," Hein observed. "Sweat is running down your face—your palms must be wet with it. The thought displeases me. Kindly go to my bathroom at once. You may use my soap and take it with you when you go, as a gift. From now on, use the same brand at my expense. I have a well-developed sense of smell, too. Remember that."

"Having trouble? May I help you?" Tino Hiller spoke with exquisite courtesy.

Bergen eyed him warily. "I'm always in trouble. I'm getting used to it."

"It's the best policy," Hiller said. "After all, you've just joined a crack unit. According to the battery sergeant major —and he got it from the battery commander—members of a crack unit take problems in stride. They actually welcome them because they're a challenge."

"Maybe, but who creates the problems?"

"Why not send a questionnaire around the battery?"

Tino Hiller bent expertly over the engine of the radio truck. Bergen had been vainly tinkering with it for over an hour during the midday break. The engine was dead and he was responsible for it. It was all part of the system—someone was always responsible for something.

Hiller deftly checked some leads, then laughed. "I knew it! Somebody put the distributor head out of commission."

"Come again?"

"The leads have been cut with a pocketknife."

Bergen stared at Hiller incredulously. "You mean it's common practice around here?"

Tino Hiller nodded. There was a look of infinite patience in his dark eyes, also a gleam of amusement—not an emotion he often ventured to display. "Monkey business, my friend. It happens all the time. You're new here, so they naturally want to put you through your paces—see how far they can push you."

"I get it," Bergen said thoughtfully. "Or rather, I'm beginning to. If I'd gone to the transportation sergeant and reported the truck out of action, he'd have laughed in my face and told me I was a fool who couldn't fix his grandmother's sewing machine. Was that the idea?"

"More or less."

"And everybody would have shared the joke. A welcome topic of conversation at the next NCO's beer party?"

"Don't take it too hard. This is pretty refined humor by Battery No. 3's standards. There are cruder kinds—but I guess you've already noticed that."

Bergen looked at Hiller with dawning interest. With his tunic enveloping him like a sack and the crotch of his trousers hanging two feet from the ground, he presented a far from imposing picture. More than that, his boots were not only two sizes too big but conspicuously scuffed.

"What about you?" Bergen said. "Do they play the same tricks on you?"

"Now and then." Grinning, Hiller added, "Not exactly the same, though—I happen to know something about the internal combustion engine."

"So they all say. I take it you can repair anything on four wheels. That leaves Sergeant Arm free to organize things his own way—spare parts, gasoline, complete vehicles. They tell me he even raids neighboring units."

"Forget it," Hiller said gravely. "Or, if you can't forget it, never mention it in front of witnesses. Better get one thing straight: Arm's an administrative genius—even Captain Hein thinks his activities are vital to the war effort."

"But without your expert knowledge the battery would be up the creek."

"Maybe," Hiller conceded. He sat down on the grass, lay back and stretched his legs pleasurably. "I'm like Wassermann. They think I'm indispensable, which has its advantages."

"But they don't take you seriously, do they?"

"Can't say they do, not when it comes to beer busts or NCO get-togethers, but why should I care?"

Bergen joined Hiller on the grass. "What exactly *do* you care about?"

"A quiet life," Hiller said. "They leave me more or less alone, which is saying a lot when you consider the setup."

"Meaning what?"

"This unit is part of an army which knocked out the Poles in a matter of weeks and cut the French to ribbons a few months later. It's hardly surprising if some of these guys throw their weight around. Hitler always told them they were supermen and now events have proved him right. You'd better resign yourself to the fact."

"Think so?"

"Yes, if you want to stay healthy."

Bergen shrugged. "All I know is, there's a fishy smell to everything that happens around here."

"Crap! Everything's a hundred percent normal, certainly by present standards. This battery is a tribute to German drive and efficiency—a vintage assortment of skilled organizers, reliable technicians, experts in fighting wars and making the most of them. On top of that, they're commanded by an acknowledged war hero who takes his cue from one of the most successful militarists in the history of the world. And that's the outfit you're planning to take on single-handed."

"Who says I am?"

"It sticks out a mile," Hiller said dryly. "You're itching to throw a monkey wrench in the works. I know, I've seen you operate."

"During that ridiculous gunplay, you mean—Prussian roulette, or whatever they call it?"

"Yes, then in particular." Hiller sounded almost commiserating. "That was when you first made an impression on me. You also impressed the battery sergeant major, and that could be dangerous."

"Krüger sat up and took notice the first time he laid eyes on me. We were standing beside a dead body. Maybe that's what made me stick in his mind."

"Whatever you do, don't underestimate Krüger. You wouldn't be the first to sell him short, but I can't think of anyone who didn't live to regret it. Krüger can be the soul of patience and understanding for as long as it pays him. Then he comes down on you like a tone of bricks. He's much smarter than most people think."

"More dangerous than he looks, you mean?"

"Yes, but I'm afraid you'll catch on too late—most people do." Hiller shrugged. "Krüger's timeless, somehow. He isn't half as concerned with the Führer and fatherland as you'd imagine. All he cares about is Battery No. 3. That's Krüger's world. He's been tending it like a garden for three years or more. Anything that reflects on the battery reflects on him. He'd do *anything* to protect its reputation, and he isn't choosy about his methods."

"The Prussian roulette idea—is that one of them?"

"Of course." Tino Hiller chuckled. "Krüger thinks unqualified cooperation by subordinates is a surefire guarantee of their reliability. Anyone who complies with outrageous demands on him will automatically obey outrageous orders at a later stage. You passed the test with flying colors. How come you didn't hesitate?"

"Because I knew it was a bluff. It was, wasn't it?"

Hiller frowned. "I wouldn't count on it. Apart from that, I don't feel qualified to give an opinion. I wasn't invited to play, as you probably noticed."

"Because you don't belong to the inner circle, I suppose."

"Exactly," said Hiller. "Me, I don't even own a pistol. It's a privilege to own a pistol in Krüger's outfit. He dishes them out like medals, mostly from captured stock, but he's the one who decides what people do with them. Personally, I think it's very possible that one of the six was loaded."

"What if somebody blew his brains out—me, for instance?"

"It would probably be written off as a fatal accident. Involuntary suicide while cleaning a gun, with six witnesses to confirm the story. Doesn't that make you go weak at the knees?"

Bergen looked unimpressed. "There's one small point you may have missed. The gun I grabbed so unhesitatingly was the sergeant major's. If anyone was going to run a risk, it wouldn't be Krüger. You follow my train of thought?"

"Christ Almighty, Bergen, don't put your faith in logic—not in this place. You're surrounded by members of the master race, drunk with victory and blind to reason. They're still as high as kites and they won't sober up until it suits them."

"Or until someone douses them with cold water. Anyway, who do you call members of the master race—Arm and Softer?"

"They think they are. Captain Hein certainly qualifies, but even he thinks twice before tangling with a man like Krüger."

"I'm in no hurry to commit suicide, if that's what you're afraid of. Anyway, thanks for the warning."

"I don't know what you're talking about," Hiller retorted with a grin. "I never warned you about anything or anyone. I didn't give you any information or advice, either, not about distributor heads and not about Prussian roulette. I was simply passing the time of day. Incidentally, do you play chess?"

"I'll learn," Bergen promised.

"Do that, but don't take too long. Who knows how much time you have left?"

"I came to apologize," said Lieutenant Seifert-Blanker, adjutant to the commander of the antiaircraft group stationed in and around the town of D.

"Don't give it another thought," replied Captain Schmidt. The town commandant spoke cordially. He seemed to be on the verge of embracing his visitor. "I simply do my duty here, hard as it sometimes is."

They had met for lunch at the Hôtel de France. The town commandant's offices were accommodated in the local *mairie*, where he and his staff had taken over the ground floor, but the restaurant of the adjacent hotel was his favorite venue for meetings with visitors who merited preferential treatment.

"You must be absolutely inundated with demands and requests," the adjutant said sympathetically, "—some of them extremely unreasonable, no doubt. I can't think how you handle them all, especially with a local commander like Captain Hein."

Captain Schmidt did not blink. "What a man!" he exclaimed. "A distinguished and influential young officer, wouldn't you agree?"

"So it seems," said Seifert-Blanker, appreciatively eyeing the preliminaries that had just been served: stewed snails, grilled scampi and gossamer-thin slices of smoked salmon accompanied by a bottle of Anjou Rosé. "However, appearances can be deceptive."

"Does that apply to Captain Hein?" the town commandant demanded avidly. "Nobody has ever hinted to me that our idol may have feet of clay. Isn't he to be awarded his Knight's Cross in the next few days?"

"They're still talking about it. No final decision has been made." The adjutant lowered his voice confidentially as he leaned forward and selected some more snails. "Medals and orders are superficial marks of distinction, my dear Captain Schmidt. They have their part to play, but they aren't relevant to every situation."

Captain Schmidt leaned forward. "You mean that the focus of official attention has shifted, if only temporarily?"

The adjutant nodded, chewing. He was a spruce little man with the beady eyes of a watchful sparrow. "Put it this way," he said. "It isn't enough to have won a brilliant military victory—we have to consolidate our gains and exploit them with a proper sense of purpose."

"How true!" Captain Schmidt exclaimed. "What you say is entirely in line with my personal estimate of the situation." His voice trembled a little. "Hence the high hopes with which I took up my present appointment, arduous and challenging though it is."

"We all realize what good work you're doing—I and the Group commander, not to mention a number of other unit commanders in this area. In fact, one of my main reasons for visiting you was to express our appreciation."

"I'm delighted to hear it." Captain Schmidt hurriedly refilled his guest's glass until it overflowed, but Seifert-Blanker did not appear to notice. "Pacification is my motto, Lieutenant—pacification in a dual sense. I try to reconcile the requirements of the units stationed in my area with those of the civil population. In short, I try to foster mutual trust—a sentiment which will, in the not too distant future, promote international harmony. It's bound to prove mutually beneficial in the long term."

"Excellently put." Lieutenant Seifert-Blanker radiated enthusiastic approval. "Between you and me, the CO commented on your admirable work in glowing terms only the other day. I congratulate you, Captain."

"Thank you, thank you. It hasn't been easy, though I say

it myself. There were bastions of prejudice to storm, if you'll pardon the metaphor, but I persevered. Success springs from small beginnings. For instance, I already work very closely with the local mayor. I give lectures in schools. I've installed a German wing in the local hospital, and I've even seen to it that French and Germans receive equal treatment in restaurants and licensed premises generally. I also attend religious services regularly on Sundays."

"Remarkable!" exclaimed the adjutant, draining his glass. "I think you should know, Captain, that we not only appreciate your work but are ready to give it our wholehearted support. In other words, we're prepared to assist you with any snags you meet."

"I trust that includes Captain Hein and his high-handed measures, which have, I regret to say, caused considerable unrest here and hampered my efforts to. . . ."

"Quite, quite. You already gave me a pretty clear indication of your difficulties on the phone, Captain—that was one of the reasons for this meeting. Let me be absolutely frank. You and I, like all responsible officers, are aware of our duty to the army at large. No single unit can be allowed to build up an isolated personality cult. Its sole objective must be to form part of a unified and integrated fighting force."

"This is an extremely delicate situation," Schmidt said. "Am I to understand that you're ready to give me direct backing?"

Seifert-Blanker nodded portentously. "Let's say we're determined to keep things on an even keel. We won't hesitate to step in as soon as we're in possession of some solid evidence—in other words, as soon as someone submits some."

"Evidence?"

"Yes, of course. Telephoned complaints are no good by themselves—nor, unfortunately, are personal discussions, however cordial and informative. Any differences that may have arisen between you and Captain Hein are your concern alone. We at Group Headquarters cannot take official action until we receive a detailed report relating to some definite abuse of authority."

"From me?"

"Or from Captain Hein himself—not that we need worry about that eventuality, I imagine."

"It's an extremely awkward business," Schmidt said, his brow clouding, "—really, most awkward. Extremely ticklish. It needs careful thought."

"Think about it by all means, but don't take too long. Another few days and it may be too late. My advice is, strike while the iron is hot."

"Physical fitness promotes combat readiness!" Captain Hein not only enunciated this maxim but ensured that it was acted on. He laid particular stress on what he termed "sport," both as an aid to training and as a leisure activity.

Standing orders required headquarters personnel to indulge in fifteen minutes' early morning physical training every day, Sundays and holidays included. Shrewdly and as a matter of course, Hein left all the details to Krüger. Considering that his own physical condition left no room for further improvement, Krüger entrusted the supervision of PT to one of his NCO's, usually Forstmann or Arm, with instructions to make as much noise as possible so that the sound of their matutinal yells would carry easily to the top of the château tower.

Where the physical toughening of his gun crews was concerned, Hein himself took a hand. In this respect, as in others, he favored surprise. He used to appear at the most diverse times of day, look around coolly, and announce, "A little sport, I think."

Once again, he wielded his stopwatch, and in little more than a minute—seventy-three seconds on this particular occasion—his fighting men were transformed into teams of athletes. The relatively gratifying speed with which this occurred was attributable to the "Runge system." Runge had ordained that the gun crews should wear fatigues instead of underwear. This meant that they had only to strip off their uniforms and change their footwear, a lightninglike process which never failed to excite admiration during tours of inspection by senior officers.

"All hands on deck!" Runge shouted briskly. He was privileged to take command on such occasions, the two gunnery officers, Minder and Helmreich, being once again relegated to the background. "Preliminary training session, begin! Time allowed: ten minutes. We'll start at intermediate level."

Everything was brilliantly organized. In the center of the gun position, between the predictor and the guns, were various installations and items of sports equipment—a broadjump pit, a high-jump pit, some parallel bars, a horse, and a horizontal bar.

"Target for today: the high jump," proclaimed Captain Hein. This came as no surprise. High jumping had recently been made the focus of Battery No. 3's athletic endeavors, and not by chance.

"Put the bar at one meter thirty-five!" decreed Sergeant Runge. Captain Hein nodded approvingly. This was the height required for aspirants to the Reich Badge of Sport and, consequently, the standard to be attained by a unit which aspired to universal excellence.

Hein stationed himself in front of the bar, booted and in full uniform. Having removed his cap and belt, he flexed his knees, ran up, launched himself into the air, and easily cleared the bar.

"Right, men," Runge adjured them, "let's see you do the same, every last one of you!" And woe to the man who hobbled around with flabby knees, fluttering arms or a hollow back! Hein reserved his approval for absolutely impeccable performances only, and Runge saw that he got them.

"Make a note of individual results," Hein commanded.

"Put your backs into it!" yelled Runge. "Keep it going smoothly, one after the other. I want to see those fat asses sail through the air!" Anyone who failed to clear the requisite one meter thirty-five he singled out with a bellow of "Lazy Cunt!" or "Clumsy Mother!"

After all five teams had gone through their paces at the high-jump pit, Runge shouted "thirty-four." That meant thirty-four failures. As if to underline this gross decline in performance, he added, "Two more than yesterday."

"The whole battery is confined to barracks," said Hein. He appeared personally insulted. "At least until the number of failures drops below thirty."

Runge had herded the unsuccessful high jumpers together. Hein surveyed them in meaningful silence, his eyes lingering on features that particularly displeased him—superfluous fat in the abdominal region, faces the color of cream cheese, pendulous and oversized buttocks.

"Appalling," he said, "simply appalling." Still in the same contemptuous but indifferent tone, he went on, "And now, air alert."

"Air alert!" echoed Sergeant Runge.

Once more, in a matter of seconds, the scene changed. The men raced to their guns, grabbing the steel helmets that lay ready at their action stations in accordance with standing orders. They also climbed into their boots, no additional items of dress being necessary on such occasions.

"One damned thing after another," Lieutenant Minder muttered to his brother officer, Second Lieutenant Helmreich. They had also donned their steel helmets. "Couldn't he spare us his bright ideas, just this once?"

"Oh, come on!" Helmreich protested uneasily. With his helmet pulled down low over his face, the squat little subaltern looked like a worried tortoise. "After all, everybody admits we're the best battery in the army. If the battery commander gets his Knight's Cross, there'll probably be an Iron Cross First Class for you. That means I'll finally get my Class Two."

Minder looked skeptical. "All well and good, but according to my information they've only allotted one Knight's Cross to the regiment, and the CO has designs on it himself. Looks as if Hein's outranked, doesn't it?"

"I'd like him to get it," Helmreich said, successfully feigning loyalty. "It would boost the battery's prestige."

"So what? It all adds up to the same thing—we're sunk, whatever happens. If they don't give him his Knight's Cross all hell breaks loose. If they do, he may go right around the bend. One way or another, my friend, we're in for it."

"Guns cleared for action, sir," announced Runge.

Hein stared straight ahead, apparently deep in thought. Total silence reigned, as though it would have been sacrilege even to breathe in his presence.

Clearly enjoying this breathless hush, Hein gazed across the gun position and the Rue Napoléon to the park which almost oppressively encircled the burial place of the château's dukes. His eyes took in the château itself and the glass dome of the conservatory, and everything they rested on seemed to be part of a unified and indivisible whole—all ruled by himself alone.

"What," he asked searchingly, "if at the same time—while the battery is engaging enemy aircraft—our position is attacked by infiltrators—by saboteurs? What then?"

He glanced with no particular confidence at his two gunnery officers, who said nothing, then turned to Sergeant Runge.

"If the battery is required to engage high-flying aircraft," Runge recited promptly, "guns of lighter caliber will assume a ground-defense role supported by signals personnel, aircraft spotters and sentries. During low-level air attacks, the crews of the heavy guns and predictor will join in operations against infiltrators and saboteurs."

Captain Hein nodded. Runge was a member of the old school—his school. Like his battery commander, Runge knew what it meant to be a real fighting soldier. He was a tower of strength.

"Let's practice that," said Hein.

It was an announcement calculated to occupy the next few hours. The gun crews resumed their antlike activities.

"Telephone call for the battery commander!" came a yell from the edge of the sports field. "They say it's important."

"Who is it?" asked Hein.

"The town commandant, sir."

"Tell him," Hein proclaimed in a chilly voice that carried to the farthest extremities of the gun position, "to tie a knot in it. Pass that on, word for word."

"This place is an absolute shambles," declared Frau Dr. Werner-Weilheim. Her bosom heaved. "It's outrageous, the conditions we're expected to work under."

Sergeant Forstmann felt increasingly like a cornered animal. "I'm sorry, madam," he said, "I'm afraid you've come to the wrong place. It's no use complaining to me."

Frau Dr. Werner-Weilheim had bulldozed her way into the orderly room with crimson cheeks and hair in disarray. Sweat ringed her armpits. "How dare you treat us like this!" she insisted.

Forstmann defended himself manfully. "You surely can't mean me, madam. I'm not responsible for you and neither is my department."

"I've put up with some shoddy treatment in my time," she pursued relentlessly, "but this takes the cake. It isn't that I'm spoiled, young man. As I always tell myself, we live in a great and historic age—an age that demands sacrifices from all of us."

"Exactly, madam. Everyone has to put up with a little discomfort from time to time."

"Discomfort be damned! Sacrifices, I said—but meaningful ones! Anyway, why are you staring at me like that? If anyone in this place is capable of understanding me and my motives, it's you."

"Why me?"

"Because, party member Forstmann, rumor has it that you were a Hitler Youth leader. If so, you ought to be proud of the fact."

Forstmann drew himself up. "I am."

"In that case, you're my man."

"Your what, madam?"

"My man . . . the man for me. I mean that metaphorically, of course," she explained, moving in on Forstmann so that he was pinned, panting, against a filing cabinet. "I'm appealing to your sense of patriotism."

"I don't understand."

"It's quite simple," she assured him. "As you're no doubt aware, the professor and I are engaged on an assignment of the utmost cultural importance—one which owes its direct inspiration to the party. If we are to carry it out satisfactorily, we must insist on adequate accommodation—in other words, the bailiff's apartment. Even you must admit that we have a right to a lavatory that functions properly."

"Of course."

"Then *do* something about it! It's your duty as a party member. Surely you, of all people, wouldn't wish to be suspected of supporting the establishment of a brothel?"

"God forbid . . . I mean," Forstmann amended swiftly, "it would conflict with my principles as a good National Socialist." A sudden thought struck him. "Who told you all this? It wasn't that man Bergen, was it?"

"Corporal Bergen, who has been detailed to assist us, does not enjoy my wholehearted approval. He's better at gossip than action—like most men. I hope I'm not wrong in assuming that there are a few exceptions, even here. You, for example."

"I'll do my best."

"I sincerely hope so, party member Forstmann. I'm relying on you. Don't let me down!"

"Girls," Sergeant Softer announced briskly, "we're in business. This battery is one of the finest units in the German army—ready for anything. Now's your chance to be the same."

In front of him, elbow to elbow on a wine-red brocade sofa, sat the three newly engaged members of his staff. They eyed Softer attentively. Business, after all, was business.

In the center: Marie-Antoinette, superbly proportioned, sitting there as though killing time—in a first-class waiting room—before the next train. On her right: Margot, bovine and willing, with the dreamy expression and alluring simplicity of a child. On her left: Suzanne, whose lush, Renoirish figure was coupled with the sharp and appraising stare of a Parisian concierge.

Behind Softer stood Neumann, the corporal in charge of the medical section, whose present function was that of a major-domo. "All set," he said. "The ladies' health couldn't be better. I checked it out an hour ago, personally. By hand."

"Neumann is a dirty beast," Marie-Antoinette stated calmly. "But why not, as long as it pays?"

Neumann never took umbrage at anyone or anything. "I was only doing my duty," he said mildly. "That includes swabs and so on. After all, I know what a Wassermann test is."

"Save it," Softer told him with a grin. "All I care about is performance. Do your stuff, girls, and you won't regret it. I'm a generous man."

Marie-Antoinette stared at him with polite interest. "Are we allowed to accept what are vulgarly known as tips?"

Margot, looking slightly shamefaced, said, "Sometimes, monsieur, with a particularly sympathetic client, I get carried away. Surely you wouldn't begrudge me a little bonus now and then?"

"A contract is a contract," Suzanne said briskly. "The fees you offer are for good, solid performances. We have made an agreement and I, for one, am ready to abide by it at no extra charge. I happen to have German Alsatian blood in my veins. *That* imposes a certain obligation—at least on me."

"I can see we're going to get on splendidly, girls," Softer said. "You won't have any complaints about the way you're treated. After all, you're dealing with the members of a victorious army. If I know anything about you, you'll do your best to meet our requirements."

"I look forward to it," Margot said softly.

"I'm quite certain," Suzanne said, "that our efforts will be suitably rewarded."

"Which brings us back to the matter of tips," Marie-Antoinette persisted. "What about them?"

"Normally," Softer told her soothingly, "every client will come equipped with a voucher issued by me, countersigned by Corporal Neumann and redeemable by Sergeant Moll within twenty-four hours. Standard performance per voucher: thirty minutes of your time, including one completion. Any additional marks of favor from satisfied customers, whether in cash or kind, will be regarded as private income."

Marie-Antoinette spontaneously blew Softer a kiss. Margot smiled contentedly and Suzanne gave a vigorous nod of approval.

"The laborer is worthy of his hire," Softer declared. "Which reminds me, girls. I'd like a special effort from you all this evening. Apart from the fact that I'm footing the bill for once, our establishment is making a sort of trial offer to build up trade. So put your backs into it and give them a real run for their money—my money, rather."

"Will any officers be coming—your captain, for example?"

Softer grinned. "Stranger things have happened. I want things to go off smoothly, though, so let's not meet our troubles halfway. All the same, girls, bear one thing in mind: In our outfit, anything's possible."

Captain Hein strode into the orderly room, slim and erect. Pausing on the threshold, he surveyed the cowering Forstmann and his Wagnerian tormentress.

"Nothing special to report, sir," Forstmann announced, snapping to attention. His voice cracked with the effort to sound brisk and efficient. "This is Frau Dr. Werner-Weilheim of the research team. She came to discuss a few administrative details."

The captain's right hand, encased as usual in dove-gray leather, twitched slightly in a curt gesture which clearly told Forstmann to hold his tongue. He turned to the *Frau Doktor* and submitted her to an indifferent stare.

"Am I addressing Captain Hein?" she asked.

Hein responded with an almost imperceptible bow. His face remained entirely motionless, but his eyes glinted like sunlight falling on snow crystals.

"Captain," the *Frau Doktor* said stiffly, "I feel it my duty to set the record straight. My conversation with this man has not been concerned with administrative details alone. We have been discussing more fundamental questions—questions relating to moral standards, among other things. We of the research team have a special assignment to fulfill, and decent quarters are the very least we expect. I trust the sergeant has seen the force of my arguments."

"In principle, certainly," Forstmann agreed, "but only as far as our own particular circumstances allow—as I already told the lady, sir. It seems the toilet facilities in the conservatory leave a lot to be desired."

Forstmann fell silent under the gimlet gaze of his battery commander. Slowly, never taking his eyes off the sergeant,

Hein removed his dove-gray deerskin gloves and slapped them in a rhythmical and loose-wristed way against his riding breeches. Then, still unspeaking, he devoted his attention to the *Frau Doktor*.

Her bosom rose and fell. "Captain," she said, doing her best to meet his eye, "it isn't just a question of toilet facilities. We don't demand preferential treatment—on the contrary, we accept the hardships of war and are happy to share them with our gallant German soldiers. What we refuse to accept is unfair discrimination. To be absolutely blunt, Captain, we resent being ousted by a gaggle of French whores!"

A hint of a smile appeared on Hein's face. "Madam," he drawled, "I'm honored to make your acquaintance. May I take the liberty of inviting you and your colleagues to dinner? At eight this evening, if it suits you."

"Let's hope nobody gums up the works at the last minute," Softer said anxiously. "I'd hate anything to go wrong."

Krüger wagged his head. "Don't worry, it's all going like clockwork. We may tackle things indirectly but we get there in the end."

"I envy your nerve," Softer said. "You certainly know how to handle people, but what about Forstmann? He worries me."

"Forstmann's got the brains of an ox," Krüger said complacently. "If he was fat enough we could slaughter him. Since he isn't, we might as well feed him up."

"Then there's Bergen. He strikes me as a lot more dangerous. Who let that crazy bitch in on my pet scheme? Bergen, of course! I tell you, Krüger, that sly son of a bitch is trying to torpedo my brothel. God knows what would happen if he rustled up some outside support—Lieutenant Minder, for example."

"Minder'll think twice before he challenges me," Krüger said with sovereign calm. "I know too much about him. Forstmann's nothing but an overgrown schoolboy. A touch of the cane and he soon comes to heel. Bergen's different, though. He needs special treatment—I've known that from the start. What's more, I'm going to see he gets it."

"Thanks," Softer said. "I've put too much time and money into this business to have it loused up now."

Krüger's raucous laugh reverberated from the storeroom walls. "Come off it, Softer, you're bringing tears to my eyes. That brothel of yours is ninety-nine percent in the bag. Hein's having dinner with Professor Magnus and his lady friends, so you can rest easy—the captain's an expert when it comes to outflanking people. As for Forstmann, he's only making a fuss because he thinks he'll get his oats quicker that way. If you take my advice you'll make sure he does."

Softer was well prepared for this and other eventualities. He summoned the half dozen NCO's of the inner circle and greeted them warmly over a table groaning with open bottles.

"Friends," he said, "today is a great day in the annals of Battery No. 3—or, rather, a great night—and one I'm sure you'll be proud and happy to remember in years to come."

"Thanks to my generous help," interrupted Sergeant Arm. "If I hadn't moved out of the conservatory, that Wagnerian cow would be sleeping in Softer's brothel tonight and every night."

"God and the Führer preserve us!" Softer exclaimed. "We all know what you've done for the battery, Arm, old pal. That's why I'm calling on you to perform the official opening ceremony. The finest filly in the stable—Marie-Antoinette—is ready and waiting, not to say champing at the bit."

"Thanks a lot," said Arm, visibly flattered. He bowed and raised his hands to silence a smattering of applause. "It wouldn't be right, though. Krüger ought to get first crack."

Krüger gave Arm a comradely slap on the back. "Arm, my son," he said with every appearance of gratitude, "it's a kind thought but quite unnecessary. I'm more or less the landlord of this establishment—you're the guest of honor."

"If that's the way you look at it," Arm said, rising, "I gratefully accept the invitation to open the bazaar."

"I now take pleasure," Softer intoned like a toastmaster, "in announcing the names of the other two clients who will be taking part in the inaugural ceremony. First, Corporal Kaminski, deputizing for Captain Hein in his capacity as the battery commander's personal driver. Mademoiselle Margot has been reserved for him."

"My pleasure," said Kaminski, terse as ever.

"And, last but not least, party member Forstmann, riding Suzanne for the honor of the Third Reich."

"Thanks," Forstmann said, "but I don't care to—for ideological reasons."

"Oh, come on," Softer exclaimed. "You're not going to be a wet blanket, are you?"

"Anyone would think he was planning to resign from the club." Sergeant Moll, ex-accountant and brothel bookkeeper, spoke with gloomy reproach. "It won't cost him a mark, either. I call that looking a gift horse in the mouth—in other words, downright un-German."

"It's downright idiotic, if you ask me," Arm said contemptuously. "But maybe he hasn't got what it takes. I've often wondered."

"You keep your obscene insinuations to yourself!" snapped Forstmann.

"Then prove me wrong. You couldn't have a finer opportunity."

"It's a matter of principle."

"In my unit," Krüger said smoothly, "I decide on matters of principle. You wouldn't want to be accused of lack of cooperation, would you? You wouldn't want to be kicked out of the club? After all, man, we take turns with the same orderly-room chair. Surely something must have rubbed off on you?"

"Well, all right," stammered Forstmann. "If you really insist. . . ."

"Voluntarily or not at all. It's now or never."

"In that case, I volunteer for duty."

"Congratulations!" Softer clapped and the others grinned. "Now you've got that off your chest, go to it."

"Welcome, ladies. Welcome, Professor," Captain Hein mouthed mechanically, as if he had learned the greeting by rote. His grave face shone archangelically in the candlelight. "I'm delighted that you have consented to share this meal with me. I trust you enjoy it." Without raising his voice, he added, "Kindly serve the first course."

Hein was sitting in his usual place at the head of the long table. Two seven-branched candlesticks stood on either side of him and one in front of each of his guests. The captain had put on his full-dress uniform, midnight-blue with scarlet gorgets and a strip of snow-white shirt visible at the throat. He wore a fixed smile.

Privileged to sit on his right, albeit at a distance of ten feet, was Frau Dr. Werner-Weilheim. The *Frau Doktor* wore a dark-brown silk dress trimmed with off-white lace which adorned her bosom as an antimacassar might have adorned a well-padded armchair. She was still breathing heavily. The captain had steeled himself sufficiently to kiss her hand on arrival, an act which robbed her of speech for a considerable period. Opposite her, on Hein's left, sat Elizabeth Erdmann, sporting a poppy-red summer dress which barely covered her nipples. Professor Magnus, a small, bent figure in raven black, occupied the lower end of the table. He seemed ready to doze off at any moment.

"My friends," Hein said suddenly in a gentle, almost singsong voice, "you see me in an unfamiliar role. Entertaining is not my forte. During the fighting in Poland I shared plain black bread with my men. That was far more to my taste. However, it is a soldier's duty to rise to any occasion. . . ." He stopped as abruptly as he had begun.

Caviar formed one of the preliminaries, also lobster, crawfish and snails. These were served on silver dishes of oval design. Gunner Schubert waited exclusively on his captain and stood behind his high-backed chair during interludes. The three guests were served with quiet and watchful efficiency by Corporal Bergen, who had been recommended for the job by Schubert. Softer & Co. had filled the dumbwaiter to overflowing with an assortment of choice French specialities, the product of many hours' strenuous work by the head chef of the Hôtel de France, borrowed for the occasion.

After the preliminaries came a fish course consisting of pike in a cream-and-mushroom sauce. Then, as a culinary *pièce de résistance*, the main course or courses, according to choice: duck in orange sauce, capon in Burgundy, or pigeons in cognac. The guests chose with care and dined with something akin to reverence, watched in silence by Hein, who ate little.

Elizabeth Erdmann eyed Hein's handsome personal orderly with burgeoning interest. Frau Dr. Werner-Weilheim, her hand still aglow with the kiss which had convinced her that Hein was worthy of her admiration, kept her gaze fixed on him. Meanwhile, Professor Magnus appeared to be waking from his state of semislumber.

"A truly regal repast, Captain, and wholly appropriate to our present surroundings."

Hein raised his eyebrows. "Our present surroundings?"

"Of course. Several centuries of French history lie buried in the family church."

"Really?" said Hein. "In that dilapidated ruin?"

"I'm absolutely positive—hence our presence here. For centuries, the members of an elite military caste came here to die and be interred."

"We, too," Hein declared, "are an elite."

"This one wrote a glorious page in the book of history."

"And we," said Hein, "have written the final chapter."

"Bravo, well said!" Frau Dr. Werner-Weilheim exclaimed

impulsively. "You and your men, Captain, have shared in a historic event which has earned us the European supremacy that has been our due for centuries past."

"My dear *Frau Doktor*," Hein said solemnly, raising his glass to her, "I see we understand each other. To our future collaboration, and may it bear fruit."

Elizabeth gave an unabashed yawn and stretched so voluptuously that her breasts threatened to pop out of her dress, eyeing Gunner Schubert, who was stationed behind the captain, as if he were a luscious item of dessert. She raised her hand and beckoned him, but he remained stiffly at his post and ignored her.

Instead, the attentive Bergen materialized with a bottle of champagne. He refilled her glass, bending low over her cleavage. Elizabeth winked at him but said nothing. Captain Hein was sitting stiffly erect and seemed once more to be gazing intently into the far distance, and Frau Dr. Werner-Weilheim was staring at him with the look of one undergoing a profound religious experience.

Hein said, "Centuries of French *gloire*, here within these walls? You mean it?"

"Within these walls," Professor Magnus assured him, his silver hair gleaming in the candlelight. "Human tragedy, triumph and disaster, victory and death, glory and mortality —these walls have witnessed them all. The men in question withdrew to this very building to die as soon as they realized that their last hour was at hand—would-be monarchs, mighty dukes, revered princes of the church, military leaders long accustomed to the palms of victory."

"Military leaders too?" inquired the captain. "Heroic figures?"

Professor Magnus nodded. A noted authority on seventeenth- and eighteenth-century French history, his reputation in twentieth-century Germany was that of a scholar with suspiciously liberal views. It had not been his good fortune to recognize, early enough, the overwhelming and irresistible superiority of National Socialist values. That was why, instead of being posted to Paris, Orléans or Fontainebleau, he had been shunted onto this siding at D. His strong but secret penchant for academic shenanigans had not, however, suffered in the process.

"As a matter of fact," the professor added, expertly sniffing the cheese board Bergen had just proffered, "this château witnessed the death of at least one unique military genius— Charles Louis, Duke of Orléans."

"Charles Louis—Karl Ludwig . . . ," Captain Hein echoed the words in a subdued voice. Then, with quiet intensity, he said, "My own Christian names!"

"What a happy coincidence!" cried Frau Dr. Werner-Weilheim.

Professor Magnus stroked his jaw. "It could be more than mere coincidence."

The *Frau Doktor* was even swifter to chime in: "It could! History has a strange way of repeating itself."

Hein treated her to another lingering and appreciative stare which sent the blood surging to her leathery cheeks. Schubert hurriedly refilled Hein's glass while Bergen again bent—even lower this time—over Elizabeth's cleavage.

Professor Magnus thoughtfully dissected his cheese, smiling to himself. "Charles Louis, Duke of Orléans," he observed, "was one of the most dazzling figures to emerge in Europe during the Hundred Years' War against England. He feared neither God nor the devil, so it was said. He flung himself at the enemy, heedless of personal danger and numerical odds, and continued to do so until the last."

"Did he die a hero's death?" Hein asked reverently.

"A coffin bearing his monogram reposes in the family church," replied Magnus, savoring his cheese. "It is reputed to be empty, but popular legend has it that the duke will someday return to found the greatest empire the West has ever seen."

"I can understand that," breathed Hein, "—yes, I can understand that. The myth of the immortal hero. . . ."

"You have an unerring grasp of essentials," the *Frau Doktor* told him warmly. "In an age like our own, what could be more important?"

The captain rose and walked around the table. He stood looking down at the professor's assistant with an appreciative expression, then took her hand and kissed it once more.

"As long as there are still German women such as you, *Frau Doktor*, no form of self-sacrifice is in vain. Thank you for your kind words."

"No, no, Captain, the debt is all on our side," she assured him fervently. "History imposes an enormous obligation on us. You obviously accept that principle."

"And act on it every day of my life. So do the men under my command—I see to that. If it weren't so, life would be unendurable. For them and me."

"I'm Suzanne," the girl said. "How would you like it?"

"Like what?" Forstmann asked politely.

"What you came for, of course."

Sergeant Forstmann was in the back room of the bailiff's apartment, where he had been briskly conducted by Corporal Neumann. He saw a comfortable bed and, hovering beside it, the voluptuous female who had introduced herself as Suzanne.

He tried not to look at her. Swerving away, he noticed several items of decor: a washstand bearing a china bowl filled with water, two freshly laundered hand towels carefully draped over the back of a chair, and two cakes of soap, one pale blue, the other pink. The room was a tribute to Softer's genius for organization.

"We don't have to go through with this," Forstmann said. Suzanne looked surprised and hurt. "Don't you like me, monsieur?"

"It isn't that." The sergeant spoke with deep sincerity. On a stool by the bed lay a dress, a slip, a bra. Forstmann concluded the girl could only be wearing panties. A swift glance confirmed his suspicions. "You're—you're very beautiful," he said. "Of course you appeal to me."

"In that case," Suzanne said in a businesslike tone, "why not come here? You appeal to me too."

"Really?" Forstmann sounded gratified but did not budge. "I wouldn't want to bother you, though . . . on principle."

"I don't understand."

Forstmann was finding it hard to retain his composure, especially now that the girl had lain down in front of him, in the middle of the big bed. She smiled but kept her legs demurely closed. "It's my convictions," he blurted out. "I'm a patriotic German . . . a good German."

"I understand," Suzanne assured him. "Come here and I'll show you just how understanding I can be."

"No!" Forstmann cried desperately. "It isn't as simple as that, not for me. Don't worry, you won't lose. You'll get your money and a special bonus on the side. We did it . . . that's all you have to tell them."

"Then why not do it properly?" Suzanne gave him another smile. "Because your heart isn't in it? Why not? Deep down, I'm just like you. I feel the same way . . . try me and see."

Forstmann moved toward her like a man bewitched. He bent over the bed. "With me," he announced, "everything has to be proper and aboveboard—Germanic, if you know what I mean."

"Of course I do!" Suzanne cried, pulling him down to her. She clamped her arms and legs around him. "We have a lot in common, Sergeant. I was born in Alsace."

"So that's why you speak such good German! That

makes things much easier. You really meant what you said just now?"

"Let me prove it!"

Forstmann, who was already on his knees, bent still lower over her, breathing heavily. "You have German blood, and yet you do this? Aren't you ashamed?"

"Why should I be ashamed to do it with you?"

"And others."

"But they're Germans too, like you and me." Suzanne smiled and hugged him tighter. "These are great times, Sergeant. Why shouldn't they also be good times—good times for people like us? The main thing is for each of us to do our duty in our own way."

"Yes, yes!" cried Forstmann, moving inside her.

Minutes went by.

"Now," moaned Suzanne, "I could shout '*Heil Hitler!*'"

"Do that!" he groaned. "Do that!"

And, as he came, she did.

Which thrilled him to the core of his being. Utterly spent, Forstmann collapsed on top of her and lay quietly. Then, with his lips between her breasts, he murmured, "You've—you've convinced me!"

"If history teaches us anything," said Captain Hein as the dessert stage approached, "it is surely this: that we must carve ourselves a meaningful place in the age in which we live."

"Just as you are doing here," Professor Magnus said brazenly. He accepted some pineapple rings in kirsch and asked for a cognac with his coffee. "This château—this whole town—is peopled with the spirit of the past," he went on, pursuing his favorite theme. "What better breeding ground for a rapprochement between Germany and France, the pillars of the Frankish Empire?"

The *Frau Doktor* smiled at Hein to neutralize the possible

ill effects of this last remark. "Yes, but even if great things did happen here—which remains to be proved in every detail —I still wonder if they were truly meaningful. Were they meaningful in comparison with all that has happened in our own day?"

"A fair question," said Hein. "After all, we have now reached what is probably the greatest watershed in the history of the world to date."

He gestured to Schubert to refill his glass. Elizabeth was studying her surroundings with a predatory air. She looked first at Schubert and then, much more cursorily, at Bergen. Professor Magnus, Captain Hein and Frau Dr. Werner-Weilheim claimed none of her attention. With slightly narrowed eyes, she peered at the picture that hung on the back wall of the banquet chamber—the allegorical figure of death with two bullet holes in lieu of eye sockets.

Bergen, who was pouring coffee, whispered, "Don't waste your time on that. It's blood that counts in this place, not paint."

Elizabeth stared at him. "How would you know what interests a girl like me?" she retorted with a cryptic smile, also whispering.

At that moment—spurred on, no doubt, by the thirty-year-old cognac of which she had already accepted four glasses—Frau Dr. Werner-Weilheim rose to her feet.

"I drink," she said, flourishing her glass at Captain Hein, "to the existence of men like you!"

Hein rose, a little unsteadily but with dignity, and bowed to her. "I am a man," he said, "and I exist."

"I give thanks for the fact!" she cried reverently.

"And so do I," said Professor Magnus. He also rose. "You, Captain, have grasped the true meaning of history. The past has no substance or value unless we gauge its effects upon the present."

"What is happening here in Europe," Hein said, "must and will be the crowning glory and consummation of a historical process that has been going on for thousands of years."

"We are living in a crucible," said Professor Magnus, "a crucible filled with the most resplendent manifestations of Western culture: Arminius of the Cherusci, Charlemagne, Goethe—Hitler, of course—and, last but not least, that Duke of Orléans who bore the names Charles Louis."

"A toast!" said Captain Karl Ludwig Hein. He swayed for a fraction of a second, but the hand that raised his glass to Professor Magnus and the *Frau Doktor* was as steady as a rock. "We are born," he declared, "to prove our worth!"

Magnus resumed his seat, smiling to himself like a contented cat. "My friends," he said happily, "this is a time of boundless opportunities. Let us make the most of them. My God, how it could pay!"

"Well, did she do all right?" Krüger asked confidently. "Were we exaggerating when we said you'd get your money's worth?"

Krüger and his intimate circle had made themselves at home in the bailiff's living room. Softer had provided a barrel of Munich beer, so the mood was mellow and growing more so. Krüger's question was directed at Arm, the first client to make his mark with the ladies of the establishment. "No complaints about the service?"

"Lovely bodywork," replied the transportation sergeant, reaching for a tankard of beer. "Nothing wrong with her engine either—plenty of go. I could have carried on all night without changing gear. I recommend the lady. She's custom-built."

The second satisfied customer to appear was Corporal Kaminski. He stretched silently and nodded to himself. Accepting a bottle from Softer, he fortified himself with three fingers of cognac and flushed them down with beer. Only after diligent questioning on the subject of Margot's performance did he reply, laconically, "Not bad. . . . Not bad at all."

Which, for Kaminski, was saying a mouthful.

Finally, Sergeant Forstmann appeared. His fellow NCO's raised their glasses in congratulation. Their good wishes were timely, judging by his slight pallor and the weary way he slumped into the nearest chair.

"So little Suzanne did her stuff, did she?" Softer leered.

"You can say that again," groaned Forstmann. "Man, is she something! I'd never have dreamed it, not in a thousand years. Know what she hollered, just as we came to a boil? '*Heil Hitler!*' "

Softer shook his head wonderingly. "Hear that, boys? It's fantastic!"

And Forstmann, strong in the faith, said, "It's the dawn of a new age, that's what it is."

Interim Report No. 3

Declarations
made by Frau Dr. Werner-Weilheim,
currently employed by a West German cultural institute.
Special field of responsibility: the care and
maintenance of public monuments.

"How dare you! I never 'gushed' over Captain Hein, whatever some evil-minded people may say, nor was I in any way 'under his spell.' No familiarities, let alone intimacies, ever occurred between us.

"Should the impression have arisen that I felt drawn to Captain Hein, I can assure you that my sentiments were not directed at him as a man. I attempted to view him in a broad historical context. He struck me as a worthwhile sign of the times, and continued to do so until tragedy overtook him.

"While it is not my intention to state categorically that Professor Magnus, my erstwhile superior, played an immediate part in the events leading to Captain Hein's death, I would not exclude that possibility.

"From the outset, I entertained the profoundest reservations about the alleged authenticity of historical events connected with Charles Louis, Duke of Orléans—not that I immediately detected the falsity of a hypothesis which was to have such fateful consequences. Professor Magnus was, after all, an internationally acclaimed authority in this specialized field. I could not have guessed that he would abuse his reputation.

"Having had ample opportunity to study Captain Hein, I can state without hesitation that he was a perfect gentleman in the truest sense, reserved by nature but extremely courteous, certainly toward me. Apart from that, he radiated an almost majestic aura of solitude. Hence, perhaps, the positively classic nature of his demise—a heroic figure viciously hounded by evil, insidious, slavering jackals.

"It does not surprise me that something of this kind should be wholly misunderstood, nowadays, by irresponsible scribblers whose minds are full of the effusions of Freud and his cronies. We are living in an age pitiably devoid of tradition—one of which it may be said that for every monument there is a vandal eager to despoil it. Thus it is with the memory of Captain Hein and all he stood for."

In place of more recent information,
excerpts from old field post office letters,
the following written by Senior Gunnery Sergeant Runge
  (dec.).

Letter 1:
  " '. . . Runge,' the captain said to me, 'self-confidence comes first—self-confidence based on personal performance. There's no limit to the demands you can make on your men once you've got that. That's the secret of leadership. . . . Apart from that,' he said, 'I demand absolute trust. We realize the value of trust, experienced soldiers like you and me, because we've seen what it means in practice.' . . . Cooperation certainly pays off. As soon as the captain got his Iron Cross First Class, my Class

Two was in the bag. Now he's been recommended for the Knight's Cross."

Letter 2:

". . . Nobody could deny we've done wonders already, but there's never any harm in setting your sights even higher. 'Runge,' the captain said to me the other day, 'always be prepared—preparedness is the most important thing in life.' It means a load of chores from my angle, but a good NCO takes the rough with the smooth. . . . We have to deal with a lot of deadwood in this outfit. You can't expect cattle to see they're destined to write an important page in world history—that's what Captain Hein says, and he's right. I've never known him be wrong. . . . Take it from me, all these boys want to do is stuff their bellies and sleep. You have to lean on them or they'd lie back and warm their fat asses in the French sun. They're a lazy bunch. Now that we're on top in Europe, they think they can relax. That applies to some of the officers too, unfortunately, especially the ones who've been called up for the duration. They're no better than civilians in uniform. . . ."

Letter 3:

". . . It's a question of setting standards and sticking to them. It's all right being softhearted, but these French civilians do their level best to take advantage. They don't appreciate our generosity. They grin at us and whisper behind our backs. I wouldn't put anything past them, sabotage included. One, who was sneering at us, got my fist in his throat. Lieutenant Minder complained, but he soon changed his tune when we ran a Frenchman to earth in his home and found a rifle and some boxes of ammunition stashed away in the attic. I shot him in self-defense before he had a chance to fire back. We can't afford to take everything they hand out.

"Even Lieutenant Minder had to admit that, once he'd been worked on by Krüger and me. We don't have to worry about Second Lieutenant Helmreich. He tries, the poor bastard, but he's useless. He spends the whole time looking for an ass to crawl up. The captain knows it, too, and despises him for it. He doesn't have any time for ass-kissers. Neither do I. That's another reason we get on so well, him and me. . . ."

Preliminary comments
made by Tino Hiller,
then a junior NCO in Battery No. 3's transportation section,
now chief engineer of an automobile factory in Bavaria.

"Did it really happen? I sometimes wonder if nightmares aren't an essential part of everyday reality.

"At this distance in time, everything that happened or may have happened seems shrouded in a sort of red mist.

"Maybe it's simply that I don't want to remember. You could call it a Freudian block, I suppose, though I can't say we thought much about Freud in those days.

"You want me to be as objective as possible? How would you define objectivity, my friend? Let's take Sergeant Arm, regarded objectively: skillful at organizing people, a diamond in the rough, a man with a touching streak of sentimentality—depending on circumstances. An admirable NCO with his heart in the right place and his nose pointing in the right direction. In short, a gem.

"Now to be subjective. Subjectively, I'd say that Arm was a ruthless opportunist with his eye glued to the main chance, a brute capable of pissing his pants with emotion as long as the object of his emotions was himself. And he was a bully. He abused his position by administering regular doses of undeserved punishment at his weekly 'circuses.' In other words, he was a lousy bastard.

"Again, was Krüger just a wheeler dealer, or was his prime concern to safeguard the interests of Battery No. 3—'his' battery?

"And what about Softer? Just an unscrupulous profiteer, or somebody who deserved credit for keeping the men well fed and satisfying their recreational needs?

"Then there was Forstmann. Just a Nazi fanatic, or a lamentably misguided idealist?

"My dear fellow, how can you possibly expect me to give you a balanced opinion after all this time?

"Bergen? Oh, no, not him too! What am I supposed to tell you about Bergen? Was he shrewd or stupid, an outsider suffering from bouts of depression or a frustrated do-gooder? Objectively speaking, he was a dark horse—you couldn't get to the bottom of him.

"All right, if you want a personal opinion, I'd say that Bergen had a pretty fair idea of what he wanted from the outset. He was disgusted with things in general—fed to the back teeth—and he tried to fight back. It almost finished him, but not quite.

"Is that what you wanted? It doesn't amount to much. What do you hope to achieve at this stage? The Germans have stopped trying to rise above the past—they bury it instead. Out of sight, out of mind, that's the rule these days.

"Long live Germany, all the same. The mass graves still stink to high heaven, but what of it? We can always hold our noses."

4

Trials and Tribulations

"I've been thinking," said Frau Dr. Werner-Weilheim.

"You have?" Sergeant Forstmann regarded her warily. "Well, thinking never does any harm as long as it's along the right lines."

He had just been summoned to the conservatory, whose walls were already adorned with the first fruits of research: architectural drawings, mostly of the church—cross sections, side elevation north, side elevation south, front view, rear view—all the work of Professor Magnus. In their midst, tinted reddish-purple, ermine-white and metallic gold, the drawing of a robe vignetted in cloudy blue.

Forstmann stared. "What's that?"

The *Frau Doktor* seemed positively mild this fine summer morning. "Magnificent, isn't it, Sergeant? One might be forgiven for imagining that it formed part of a king's coronation regalia. In fact, it's merely the house robe of one of the Dukes of Orléans, a certain Charles Louis. I myself produced the drawing from data supplied by Professor Magnus."

"It's great," Forstmann conceded. "Really impressive." His enthusiasm failed to disguise his anxiety. "Is that why you sent for me, to show me the drawing, or is there something else? You said you'd been thinking."

"Yes, Sergeant, I have. About your battery commander."

Forstmann sat down on the nearest of the packing cases and eyed the *Frau Doktor* as if confronted by a sacred cow. All he knew was that Krüger had, only the night before, issued a standing order to the effect that all three members of the research team were to be handled with kid gloves.

"Fine," he said cautiously. "So you've been thinking about Captain Hein. Did you reach any conclusion?"

"Yes, an extremely favorable one, needless to say." The *Frau Doktor* sat down close to Forstmann. He sensed the warmth of her massive thigh and shoulder, but did not recoil. He couldn't, or he would have fallen off the packing case. "Captain Hein," he heard her say, "is the complete gentleman, lofty in his ideas and noble by nature."

"He certainly is."

The *Frau Doktor* nodded vigorously, so vigorously that the packing case gave an ominous lurch. They both edged closer. Forstmann had started to perspire.

"The captain is far too high-minded," she went on, "to concern himself with trivialities—in other words, with minor blemishes in his sphere of command. It's our duty to relieve him of such burdens."

"Our duty?"

"Of course, party member Forstmann." They were both perspiring now. "As patriotic Germans, we have certain overriding responsibilities. I'm sure you wouldn't wish to evade them."

"Of course not, but could you be a bit more specific?"

"The captain can't be expected to deal with every little problem that arises. If he is to be fully effective, he must have helpers and associates—people he can trust to act for him on their own initiative. And that, party member Forstmann, is where we come in."

"Maybe, but what were you thinking of in particular?"

"Why, this brothel, of course—this sink of iniquity some of your friends have been so quick to establish. My own inescapable impression is that Captain Hein has kept silent merely because it would be beneath his dignity to utter a single word on such an embarrassing subject."

"With respect, madam," Forstmann said politely, "you're wrong. The plan was submitted for Captain Hein's approval well in advance, and he raised no objection."

"Only because he had no wish to soil his lips. Instead, he delegated the task, confident that there are some Germans who have not been utterly depraved—Germans like ourselves."

"The captain never delegates anything," Forstmann insisted. "He always either tells us what to do himself or gets Sergeant Major Krüger to relay the word."

"Party member Forstmann," said the *Frau Doktor*, raising her voice, "from what you say, I might almost believe that you've been talked into supporting this . . . this bawdy house!"

"Not exactly." Forstmann squirmed. "On the other hand, I don't have anything against it in principle. I mean, a recreation center does have its uses if you look at it from the morale point of view."

"I'd never have expected such a thing, not from you," she exclaimed. "Anyone else in this place, yes, but not you! And you, Forstmann, tell me you were a Hitler Youth leader?"

She rose abruptly, disturbing their equilibrium. The sergeant fell to the floor and lay staring up at a broad expanse of thigh and balconylike breasts.

"You can even be patriotic in a brothel," he said furiously, "if you try!"

"I see," she snapped. "So I'm right. You're just another lecher like all the rest. Aren't you ashamed of yourself?"

"Why should I be?" Forstmann demanded, scrambling to his feet.

"Because you're utterly incapable of appreciating your captain's visionary qualities, his lofty ideas and constant readiness to act in the interests of the nation. Even you, a member of our great party, would betray this unique man without compunction."

Forstmann glared at her. "Cool off, you won't get the bailiff's rooms now—they're booked."

"As if that were all I cared about! I'm concerned with the great German nation—with the world in which Captain Hein and other members of the elite occupy so special a place. Their world must be purged of impurity, and I intend to see that it is."

Krüger was lolling out of a first-floor window in the château, on the lookout for profitable diversions. Below him in the grounds, Bergen was tinkering with a radio set. Krüger's eye lighted on him and lingered.

"Hey!" he called. "Want to come up here a minute, or do you want a written invitation?"

"Right away, Sergeant Major!" Bergen called back. He paused to wipe his hands on a rag. Thirty seconds later Bergen was standing stiffly at attention in front of him. Krüger was in the so-called great hall of the château, a large and entirely unfurnished room which housed the rank and file of Battery HQ. Ranged across the floor were sleeping bags and bunks with their owners' duffle bags close beside them. In the center of this bloodless battlefield stood Krüger.

"Nice of you to come and keep me company. No cattle enjoy being alone, you know—the herd instinct. You may not be a farmer's son like me, Bergen, but I figure you know something about livestock. There's all kinds, cows, oxen, heifers, steers. . . ."

"And bulls. Yes, I know."

"Is that what you think I am?" Krüger's eyes narrowed. "I hope you don't have ambitions to be a matador."

"I thought I'd made that clear the other day, Sergeant Major, when we were being questioned by that officer from the JAG's office. I don't stick my neck out if I can help it."

"That was the other day." Krüger returned to the window and leaned back against the sill. He took his time.

Bergen stood there tensely. He had no idea what Krüger was driving at, but he knew that it was his policy to keep men guessing. Shock tactics were his specialty.

"You have fun here, don't you? Never miss an opportunity to enjoy yourself, eh?"

"Like when, Sergeant Major?"

"Like in the Hôtel de France, gossiping like an old lady with that pal of yours, Wassermann. What's more, I hear you gossip with those creeps from the town commandant's office. What's the big idea?"

"No harm intended, Sergeant Major," Bergen assured him hastily. "You know how it is when you've had a few—you say things without stopping to think. It doesn't matter much, does it?"

Krüger lowered his voice confidentially. "Tell me, Bergen, where do you keep your personal belongings?"

Bergen pointed to a duffle bag and suitcase.

"I see," Krüger said. His broad butcher's face exuded benevolence. "Everything looks just fine, at first sight. What if I take a closer look, though? Isn't it possible I might find a few things to complain about—piss stains on your underwear, say, or mud on the soles of your boots, or bits of dried egg on your mess tins? Well, what're the odds?"

Bergen swallowed hard and said deliberately: "Look, you only have to tell me what to do and I'll do it."

Krüger wagged his head admiringly. "I like your nerve, Bergen. Trying to get around me, are you—trying to cut our little interview short because I might dig up something nasty?"

"I don't mind cutting it short if you don't, Sergeant Major."

"That'd be too easy, you double-crossing bastard—much too easy on both of us. When I do a job I do it thoroughly. In my outfit, every backside fits the pants I choose." Without a pause, Krüger went on, "There must be some letters in your kit bag, Bergen—from girlfriends. Give them here."

Bergen hesitated a fraction of a second too long. Almost to himself, he said, "Isn't that my personal business? Even army regulations allow you a little privacy."

"Shut up!" snapped Krüger. "I don't like barracks-room lawyers. Hand them over."

Bergen gave the bundle to Krüger, who weighed it in his palm. "I could read what's in them if I wanted," he said, "but why should I bother? I've read this sort of crap before. On the other hand, I could call them obscene and prejudicial to military discipline and tear them up—or order you to tear them up. Alternatively, I could say you'd torn them up of your own free will. Follow me?"

"All the way, Sergeant Major."

"I thought you would," Krüger said complacently. He tossed the letters back with a flourish. "Another thing, Bergen. Do you take notes? I mean, do you keep a diary?"

"Why should I, Sergeant Major? I'm not that stupid."

"You bob up like a cork, don't you?" Krüger shook his head reprovingly. "Take it from me, Berger, don't get over-confident—not unless you're looking for a session in Sergeant Arm's circus. You don't know what it's like, do you? Well, we can soon cure that. Arm's circus gives one performance a week—more if necessary. You're going to star in the next one, just to give you an idea of what we can do if we set our minds to it."

Bergen strove to look ingenuous. He didn't know exactly what the "circus" entailed, but he had enough experience of Battery No. 3 to guess that it was some form of parade ground sadism modified to suit wartime conditions.

"I still don't know what's expected of me," he said plaintively. "After all, I kept my mouth shut when that army lawyer. . . ."

"Don't play the innocent with me, Bergen—you couldn't have said anything or I'd have skinned you alive."

"You could still, if you wanted to—I realize that. Just the same, Sergeant Major, I'm ready to cooperate any way I can. I thought I'd made that clear."

Krüger's brows darkened. "You don't cooperate with me, Bergen—you obey my orders. Why the hell do you think I detailed you to look after the professor and his team? So you could get poor old Forstmann in trouble with that bitch? What did you hope to gain by that?"

"I apologize, Sergeant Major. The brothel business just slipped out by accident."

"Oh, yeah, and what if I accidentally break your neck for stepping out of line?"

"May I point out that my duties were never clearly defined?"

"Why the hell should they be? Your job was to see that nobody breaks up the happy home. It still is. I don't want any frustrated old cows charging the orderly room, especially when I'm around. In other words, stop stirring things up."

Krüger reached for Bergen's duffle bag. He pulled out various articles of underwear, sniffed them, and tossed them aside disgustedly. The spare boots were inspected, found to have traces of dirt on the heels, and dropped. Bergen's dress uniform received a thorough going-over. Stains were detected on the collar. The cuffs were pronounced frayed and the trousers as creased as a concertina. Bergen dodged as each item was flung in his face.

"That's just a sample," Krüger said amiably. "Know why I'm doing all this?"

"I think so."

"You only think? You mean you still don't know which way the wind blows around here?"

"I suppose," Bergen hazarded, "my first job is to sidetrack the *Frau Doktor*—give her something else to think about. The question is, what?"

"That, shit-face, is your problem."

"I'll do my best."

"Your best had better be good."

"Champagne, as usual," said Captain Hein. "And this time try to avoid unnecessary froth."

Schubert tried to improve on past performance by tilting the glass as he poured. He held it gingerly with a look of intense concentration on his boyish face.

"Wrong in one respect," Hein said gently, leaning back in his chair, "right in another. Wrong because one must never touch the glass while pouring. Right—in this particular instance—because it was an agreeable gesture, a mark of intimacy. I appreciate such things when we're alone together."

"Yes, sir," said Schubert.

He gazed at Hein in the flickering candlelight. This time the captain had swathed his trim body in a snow-white bathrobe. Although dusk had not yet fallen outside, heavy brocade curtains covered the windows in the east wall of the banquet chamber. The air was thick and sweet, as though sprayed with perfume.

Hein, returning from some remote and private world of of his own, said, "My suggestions regarding personal hygiene—have you acted on them?"

"Yes, sir."

"When did you last change your underwear?"

"This morning, sir. I change every morning now, as you instructed."

"Excellent. However, on occasions when you are detailed for evening duty in my personal quarters, kindly change your underwear yet again—immediately before reporting, to be precise. When did you last wash?"

"A few minutes ago, sir."

"Your hands?"

"Hands, face, neck and armpits, sir."

"With the soap I gave you?"

"Yes, sir."

"I may wish, a little later on, to assure myself of that."

Hein gave Schubert a nod which seemed to convey encouragement. Raising his left hand in a gentle movement, he described a semicircle in the air. "You may sit beside me, Johannes. Take a chair and place it on my left, about one meter away. But first, please, refill my glass."

Whether this was a request or an order, Gunner Schubert complied at once. Then he sat down. There was something childish about the way in which he laid his hands flat on the table in front of him, as though he guessed that Hein would wish to see them and be satisfied of their cleanliness. Hein's wish was fulfilled.

"You try hard, Johannes—I appreciate your efforts. You notice that I have not offered you a drink. I need hardly tell you that there is a very special reason for this. I do not wish you to lose control of yourself under the influence of alcohol. My first intention is to get to know you better."

For some seconds, the captain stared at Schubert intently. Then he smote his forehead with his left hand and let it slide downward, clamped hard against his face, until it covered his mouth, which had dropped open. With an air of utter exhaustion, he sank back in his chair and closed his eyes. It was a minute before he spoke again.

"Tell me," he said, very casually, "do you have any friends in the battery?"

"Not exactly friends, sir."

"Anyone you're on particularly close terms with?"

"No sir, no one."

"What about this signalman—Bergen, isn't it—the one who was detailed to look after the professor and his party? Not an unintelligent man, though his appearance and manner leave much to be desired. For reasons I can't quite grasp, you seem to find him a kindred spirit—or am I wrong?"

"Corporal Bergen is a likable person, sir. I belong to his section. Also, he happens to sleep next to me. I enjoy talking to him."

"What about, Johannes?"

"Oh, things in general, sir."

"About me—about our talks together?"

"Never, sir!" Schubert assured him fervently. "That wouldn't be right. I'd never dream of such a thing."

"I hope not, my dear boy." The captain seemed to sink still deeper into his chair. "The entire world is at liberty to know everything that passes between us, Johannes, every last little thing. On the other hand, would the world understand? How many people have the vaguest inkling of what human harmony can mean? Human harmony in all its classical freshness and spontaneity—Greece, Hölderlin, Kleist, and, above all, Wagner!"

Hein rose. He drew himself up to his full height, took his glass and drained it with an abrupt jerk of his head. "You and I," he said passionately, "are witnessing the dawn of a new age, an age that will be marked by the restoration of true values, the formation of a new elite, the development of a higher human awareness. We must show ourselves worthy of it—worthy beyond any shadow of a doubt!"

Schubert gazed at Hein, filled with awe. He was overwhelmed by such wide-ranging ideas. His boyhood dreams seemed to be coming true in a way that surpassed his wildest imaginings. He felt as if he had been privileged to meet Achilles or Siegfried in person. He clasped his hands in gratitude and bowed his head as though baring his neck to an unseen sword.

"Stay like that!" said Hein. "Stay just like that!"

Schubert froze. Not a muscle of his body moved. He seemed to have stopped breathing. The only outward sign of life was a whitening of the knuckles as he clasped his hands still tighter.

Hein bent over the bowed head and laid both hands on Schubert's shoulders, pressing down hard. Schubert could feel the captain's breath hot on his neck.

Suddenly, Hein seemed to recoil. Without daring to look, Schubert heard him reel across the room and collide with the wall. Hein stared fixedly into the candlelight.

"Good," he said in a toneless voice. "A good smell, almost imperceptible but pure and wholesome, like a breath of spring. The scent of youth, which is immortal even in death. Not the stench of fat old men who exude putrefaction. Old men have mouths like sewers and groping hands greasy with repulsive sweat. . . . My father was like that."

Hein edged sideways into the gloom, keeping his back to the wall. The candlelight, which barely reached him, transformed his body into a slender, flickering shadow, but his voice was clear and distinct.

"And then there is the smell that clings to women—the sickening, stupefying smell that seems to issue from their erogenous zones. The penetrating aroma of sour milk, the musky scent that seeps from their armpits, their nipples, their heaving loins. . . . Not even my mother, who was systematically defiled by my father, could spare me that—fine woman though she is. I revere her in spite of everything."

Hein thrust himself away from the wall and darted into the light. His shadow dissolved as though it had never been. He came to rest in front of Schubert, who stared up at him, bewildered but docile. Hein covered the young orderly's hands with his own.

"And what of the smell born of blood which spurts,

pulses, and finally oozes, which smacks of shells and shrapnel, shattered limbs, riddled bodies, smashed skulls—all the dark symphony of heroic self-sacrifice? Blood is part of war—it has the numbing but redeeming scent of battle. Have you ever smelled it, Johannes? No? Not consciously, perhaps—you have much to learn. But I tell you this: Anyone who has breathed the scent of soldiers' blood as it gushes forth, pumped from their veins by the fear of death but purified and refined, transfigured by heroic self-denial —anyone who breathes that scent has savored life to the full. The world is sublime in its savagery, but any man who allows it to overwhelm him is lost. He must face the ultimate demands of existence with open eyes and be prepared to live with them. I can do so, and I shall teach you to do so too, Johannes, because there is an affinity between us."

Schubert nodded mechanically. He did not want to show how lost he felt at that moment—almost robbed of personal identity.

"I know what you mean," he murmured. "I see it all!"

Hein drew a deep breath. "I rejoice to hear you say that. It encourages me to hope that you will, in the not too distant future, learn to comprehend this world of mine."

After standing there stiffly for a moment, he said: "Light me!" and strode off without waiting for an answer.

Schubert picked up one of the candlesticks, raised it to head height, and followed him. With the rhythmical tread of an automaton, Hein traversed the banquet chamber and his bedroom, heading for the tower. This lay at the end of a narrow passage, just high enough to admit a man of average build. It ascended slowly and terminated in three steps.

Reaching the tower chamber, Hein advanced on one of the four windows—the one facing east—and flung it open. The night air flowed in, soft as silk.

Still wearing his white bathrobe, Hein stepped onto the sill, which was little more than eighteen inches from the floor. Balancing with supreme self-assurance, he spread his arms as though in benediction or an all-encompassing embrace.

"It is night," he said. "I stand here like a man on a cliff top, poised above the abyss. You know the feeling, Johannes?"

"I can imagine it."

"But I ignore the drop. Instead, I look far out over a sea of darkness, far beyond Paris and France to where Germany seems to glow on the horizon. I have a vision of the Reich, Johannes, bathed in distant flames which leap to heaven in a blaze bright enough to warm my heart, even here. Ah, my dear boy, the glorious experiences that lie in store for you!"

"Is this a personal visit," Elizabeth Erdmann asked, "or are you supposed to be here on official business?"

"Which do you prefer?" Bergen retorted. "You only have to say—I'm always happy to oblige a lady."

The girl laughed. It didn't seem hard to amuse her. Studying her with interest, Bergen saw two soft brown eyes which held an agreeable hint of doelike naïveté and a rather overgenerous mouth topped by a dainty nose. Framing all this was a silky curtain of hair falling in a series of soft undulations to her shoulders.

"You're a sight for sore eyes," Bergen told her. "Pity you have to cast your pearls before a lot of swine like the members of Battery No. 3.

"Looks are relative," she replied, matching his tone. "It all depends on the competition. There isn't much around here."

"Granted, but it doesn't alter the fact that you're a smart chick."

She grinned. "Quite a bird fancier, aren't you? What's all this leading up to, anyway, a lecture in ornithology? If so, count me out."

"Maybe I've got you classified wrong. Maybe you're a member of the cat family. Don't worry, I've got a thing about cats too."

Elizabeth was working at a massive table in the conservatory. She had apparently been typing out the notes that were the products of Professor Magnus' research to date. It was clear she didn't resent the interruption.

"Listen," she said, "why beat around the bush? Either you came to flirt or you're here on business. If it's me you're after you picked the wrong time—I'm busy. If it's official business, Frau Dr. Werner-Weilheim's the person you want. She's over at the church with Professor Magnus."

"As far as I'm concerned she can creep into the crypt and stay there." Bergen sat on the edge of the girl's desk. "Suppose it's you I'm interested in. Would it annoy you?"

"Not at all," she replied calmly. "Are you planning to go to bed with me?"

"Why not?" Bergen heard himself say. He had no time to be surprised at the question or his own reply—his reaction was instinctive. "Any time."

"You plan to save money, I suppose."

"I what?" Bergen looked bewildered.

"Well, from what I hear you've set up a brothel. Attractive girls—I've seen them around—and all available to the battery at any time. The only thing is, they're in it for the money. What do you want from me, a free ride?"

"I beg your pardon!" Bergen struggled to retain his composure. "No one would put a price on a girl like you."

"Which amounts to the same thing. Burn a little incense at my shrine, say a few kind words, and I'll lie down like a lamb—is that it?" Elizabeth chuckled with a mixture of childish glee and impish satisfaction. "What do you take me for? More to the point, what are you really after?"

"You attract me."

"Thanks, I've heard that one before, but what's really behind it all?"

"I was going to suggest a partnership—one that could pay off for us both."

"That's more like it. So you want us to team up. Why?"

"Any number of reasons," Bergen said. "I'm mainly thinking of the *Frau Doktor*."

"Why, does she attract you too?"

"You're joking! I want to stay one jump ahead of her, that's all. She's a troublemaker, and the more trouble she makes the harder it is for me. I've been put in charge of her, you see. Direct orders from Battery HQ."

Elizabeth laughed aloud. "You honestly expect me to play games with a woman of her caliber? I've got more sense. Other people have tried it and failed. In case you didn't know, the *Frau Doktor* is a pillar of the Berlin cultural establishment. She's a nickel-plated copper-bottomed institution, if only because Reichsleiter Rosenberg is reputed to have slept with her a few times. I don't know what he sees in her, but he's welcome. More than welcome."

"Look," Bergen said gravely, "I can see why you don't want to commit yourself, but you won't lose by it."

"What are you offering?"

"Me, for a start."

She smiled. "I'll bear that in mind. What else?"

"Anything you like. Stacks of pure silk lingerie in the colors of your choice. Finest-quality French perfume—one bottle of every leading make. Softer's already had orders to supply the necessary. Well?"

"So that's how you value me." Elizabeth stretched gracefully, like a cat.

Bergen watched with a connoisseur's eye. He edged closer. "Don't get me wrong, sweetheart. It'd give me pleasure to make you happy, especially since the benefits would be mutual."

"Tell me something," she said suddenly. "Is Captain Hein nearsighted?"

"Why, because he didn't pay enough attention to you at his dinner the other night?"

"Nonsense, you're way off target. My guess is, Hein's as cold as ice, at least with women. Well, that's his privilege. All that interests me is whether he's got a photographic memory."

"He certainly has from one point of view," Bergen said, looking mystified. "He's a demon for detail. Once he gets a thing into his head he can juggle with it forever. Distances, ranges, ammunition expenditure, fuel consumption, casualty figures—he can reel them off months after the event. It's all part of his so-called military genius."

"I wasn't thinking of that. My point is this: Would Hein have an exact recollection of the curtains or carpets in his quarters? Would he remember every detail of a picture hanging on the wall?"

"What on earth are you driving at?" Bergen looked still more mystified. "Never mind, I figure you'll tell me in due course. As far as paintings go, he expresses his love of art in a way that suits his personality—he pops off at them with an automatic. Rembrandt or pinup calendar, it wouldn't matter what it was."

She smiled to herself. "I'm thinking of the painting on the inside wall of the banquet chamber. It's a Fragonard."

"You could have fooled me. Are you interested in it?"

"Let's say I don't want it used for something inappropriate—like target practice. That would be a shame. It's much too valuable."

"You mean you want the picture? For yourself? All right, if you've got a yen for a piece of old canvas, why not?" A sudden thought struck him. "Hey, has this got anything to do with Marshal Goering?"

"You're getting overexcited," she said coolly. "I don't

want anything. I'm simply trying to gauge the state of the market. Trade seems to be brisk around here."

"Could be," Bergen replied. He had grown thoughtful. "We'll have to see what we can do. I may even be able to quote you a bargain price. It could pay, in the long run."

"Air alert!" bellowed Sergeant Runge. Simultaneously, Captain Hein's Mercedes field car left the grounds of the château, crossed the Rue Napoléon and bore down on the gun position. In front beside the driver, elegantly braced against the windshield, stood Hein.

"Air alert!" Sergeant Runge continued to bellow. "Air alert!"

He peered confidently in the probable direction of his battery commander. Hein was punctual to the second. Corporal Kaminski's foot rested lightly on the accelerator, keeping the vehicle rolling at a steady twenty miles an hour.

The gunnery sergeant had no more need to shout "Air alert!" The cry had already been taken up by others, among them the aircraft spotters, predictor crew and anyone else who felt inclined. The output of pure sound was staggering and burst over the town of D. like successive claps of thunder.

Runge stood waiting to greet the battery commander at his preordained place beside the predictor. Only there, at the very hub of all this concentrated firepower, was it proper to acquaint Hein with the vital information that his guns were ready to open fire. The ritual words were not, however, spoken by Sergeant Runge. Before he could open his mouth, Lieutenant Minder elbowed Second Lieutenant Helmreich aside and stepped swiftly forward.

"Battery cleared for action!" he announced.

Hein did not twitch an eyebrow, nor did Runge. The battery commander merely nodded at his second-in-command, who had turned out in full uniform with a speed so unusual as to excite suspicion.

"What about small arms?" Hein asked. The question was directed solely at Sergeant Runge, who took perceptible pleasure in the fact. His rugged face came to life again—or rather, betrayed signs of unqualified devotion to duty.

"Small arms loaded and ready, sir," Runge reported briskly. "Live ammunition issued, fifteen rounds per rifle, two magazines per submachine gun."

"Grenades?" asked Hein.

"Already distributed, sir—three per man. Another five per man in reserve at the battery dump."

"Excellent," said Hein. Pitching his voice so as to reach every member of his unit, he went on: "Assignment for today: infantry training. Defense against surprise ground attack, also hand-to-hand combat. Tactical training with live ammunition."

This, as every member of the gun crews realized, meant a bloody afternoon complete with sweat, grime, strained muscles and minor injuries. Hein's men stared gloomily into space.

"First, however," ordained the battery commander, "a little something to tone you up. Ammunition handling."

The gun crews looked, if possible, even gloomier. The NCO's name for one of the numerous specialties peculiar to Battery No. 3 was "pass-the-baby."

The babies in question were 88-mm shells, a little over twenty-five pounds and as long as an average man's arm. These were used as an adjunct to elaborate obstacle races in which competitors chased each other in and out of foxholes, over sandbag barriers and around the gun emplacements.

The high spot was signaled by the order "Change babies!" This maneuver could be carried out in file, in echelon, or between two teams facing each other. There was also a form of leapfrog involving two or three men at a time. The shells were not live, so nothing very serious could happen apart from the occasional physical collapse, crushed foot or dislocated shoulder.

Hein magnanimously left the supervision of his battery's routine afternoon activities to Lieutenants Minder and Helmrich. Drawing Runge aside, Hein walked him up and down, deaf to the swift succession of barked orders.

"I need hardly say," Hein told Runge, "that I have the fullest confidence in you. I scheduled the alert for fourteen-fifteen hours," Hein pursued, "and notified you in advance. My two gunnery officers turned out in full battle order. Who tipped them off?"

"Not me, sir."

"Of course not." Hein's tone was positively cordial. "But who did?"

"Sir, if you ask me, there's a leak in our communications center."

"Precisely my own diagnosis. We must do something about it, Sergeant—that and other things. I get the impression that our combat readiness has declined. There must be an effective way of pepping the men up. Give it some thought—I'm relying on you."

Runge stared into space, his face flushed with pride and mental exertion. "I'll think of something, sir."

Abruptly, the battery commander swung around and addressed his sweating "nursemaids." "Take cover!" he called. "Ground attack from nine o'clock. Predictor under mortar fire. Guns Nos. 1 and 2 under machine-gun fire. Adopt Contingency Plan 3."

The gun crews took cover, not forgetting to dispose of their babies, which were passed from man to man at top speed until safely stowed away in the ammunition store.

Gun crews Nos. 3 and 4 crawled methodically across the gun position to help repel the imaginary attack on their hard-pressed comrades.

"Not very convincing," was Hein's professional verdict. "A tired performance."

"No zip," Runge amplified. "Move it, men, and keep those fat asses close to the ground!"

"Give me your gun," Hein demanded. Runge put his submachine gun in the outstretched hand.

Flipping the safety catch, Hein clamped the weapon to his hip and, with glacial self-assurance, pulled the trigger. The gun danced convulsively. A long burst ripped into the ground just ahead of the foremost gunners, sending little mushrooms of dust spurting into the air.

"Crawl, you lazy bastards!" Runge screamed. "Crawl like the devil, unless you want to end up with two assholes apiece!"

The men wriggled across the grass on their bellies like terrified seals, gasping and sweating. A telltale stench announced that one of them had fouled his pants.

Lieutenant Minder, who had hurried over, stood rooted to the spot like a pillar of salt. Second Lieutenant Helmreich withdrew, wrinkling his nose in disgust, but Sergeant Runge almost exploded with delight. Captain Hein stared with vague satisfaction at the whisp of smoke issuing from the muzzle of his borrowed submachine gun.

"Not bad," he said finally. "To begin with."

"To begin?" echoed Lieutenant Minder, whose jaw had dropped. "What else did you have in mind?"

Hein looked through him, not at him. "Entirely novel methods of training, Minder, methods designed to maintain and increase the striking power of this unit. Having laid the foundations of this new program, we must immediately build on them. Unless, of course, someone can produce an alternative suggestion?"

No one could.

Minor escalation

Captain Hein and Sergeant Major Krüger.
Place: the banquet hall of the château.
Time: 1700 hours.

HEIN: (*Abruptly laying aside his cap and belt with barely suppressed impatience*): Early this afternoon, when I visited the gun position for a practice alert, the two gunnery officers had already turned out in full battle dress. How did they manage it?

KRÜGER (*discreet but businesslike*): Well, sir, I suppose they must have been notified in advance.

HEIN: Exactly, Sergeant Major. I not only suppose so, I regard it as self-evident. Notified by whom, though? Not by me. Not by you either, I'm sure. I simply spoke to Runge on the phone and mentioned the time I wanted the alert to start. Runge's trustworthy enough, isn't he?

KRÜGER: A hundred percent, sir.

HEIN: But who else could have thwarted my plans in this underhand way? This is the first time such a thing has happened in my sphere of command—in other words, Sergeant Major, your sphere of command. Kindly locate the leak and stop it—for good.

Battery Sergeant Major Krüger and Corporal Bergen.
Place: the orderly room.
Time: 1715 hours, same day.

KRÜGER (*entrenched behind his desk, but crouched like a beast about to pounce*): What's the matter with you, you idiot? Have you gone completely out of your mind?

BERGEN: What makes you think it was me, Sergeant Major?

KRÜGER: You must be a lot dumber than I took you for, or you wouldn't have taken it into your head to shit on the battery commander's doorstep. I don't miss much,

Bergen. Nobody ever double-crossed me without being spotted, get it?

BERGEN: Got it, Sergeant Major.

KRÜGER: About midday today you listened in on a phone conversation between Captain Hein and Sergeant Runge. By accident, of course. No need to look innocent, you conniving s.o.b. So you listened in. Fair enough, except that you promptly went and spilled the beans to Lieutenant Minder. What on earth for? Trying to butter him up?

BERGEN: Lieutenant Minder asked me to keep him informed of anything affecting the combat readiness of the battery —especially practice alerts. I acted in the interests of greater efficiency, Sergeant Major.

KRÜGER: The truth is, you saw a chance to crawl up Minder's backside and you grabbed it. But why Minder, of all people? What the hell did you hope to get out of it? Whatever it was, stay away from his asshole from now on. No more information to unauthorized persons, no tips about confidential matters—not even a prearranged code signal on the phone bell to say there's a practice alert in the offing. Otherwise, I'll have your ass.

BERGEN: I understand, Sergeant Major.

KRÜGER: I should goddamn well hope you do, you miserable little bastard. Just so you don't forget, I'm going to ask Sergeant Arm to run through his circus tomorrow for your special benefit. Looking forward to it? No? Well, I certainly am.

Corporal Bergen and Gunner Schubert.
Place: the junior ranks' quarters on the second floor
    of the château.
Time: approximately 1800 hours.

    Enter Bergen. The room is almost empty at this hour, most of the men being outside or in the canteen. Bergen

*looks around carefully, then walks over to a bunk, sits down
and flops on his back. He heaves a sigh of relief.*
Gunner Schubert is lying on the next mattress.

SCHUBERT (*companionably*): Had a hard day?

BERGEN (*after a long pause, staring at the ceiling with its
wealth of crumbling plaster festoons*): Depends on what
you call hard. I'm so sick of this place I could puke.
Still, they may kick me around but I'd rather have my
job than yours.

SCHUBERT: I don't blame you. My duties are far from simple
—in fact they're a lot more difficult than the others
imagine. You do understand, though, don't you? I'm
sure you know how I feel. It isn't that I'm unhappy or
anything like that. It's just that I'm mixed up. You're
the only person here I can talk to like a friend.

BERGEN (*sharply, raising his head*): Cut it out! I'm not
your father confessor—your spiritual problems are none
of my business. All I know is, I don't like to see you
playing shoeshine boy to Hein. You're worth more than
that.

SCHUBERT (*with a touch of eagerness*): You don't know
him, Bert. You misjudge him, like a lot of other people.
I know it isn't easy to read his mind, but he lives by different standards, or tries to—much higher standards
than most people are accustomed to. You can't help
admiring him once you get to know him.

BERGEN: A man ought to reserve his admiration for the
opposite sex and show it whenever he gets the chance.
Which reminds me, how about a few drinks at the
Hôtel de France tonight? We could take the Erdmann
girl along. She's woman enough for two.

SCHUBERT (*all gratitude and sincerity*): Thanks for the
invitation. I'd have liked to, but the captain hasn't told
me if he needs me or not. Besides, I've got some homework to do. He lent me a volume of Hölderlin so we

could discuss it next time. That's the way he is, Bert—
tremendously cultured. I've never met anybody like
him.

BERGEN (*turning on his side and studying Schubert's face*):
He really has impressed you, hasn't he? Anybody would
think you were drunk with hero worship. What do you
plan to do, found a personality cult? I don't like the
sound of it, pal, not one little bit. Something'll have to
be done about you. The question is, what?

Lieutenant Minder and Sergeant Major Krüger.
Place: the Rue Napoléon, between battery headquarters
and the gun position.
Time: approximately 1800 hours.

MINDER (*brusquely accosting Krüger*): I really must pro-
test, Sergeant Major.

KRÜGER (*adopting a defensive stance*): What's the trouble
this time?

MINDER: Somebody in this unit is deliberately attempting to
play off the interests of certain people against the rights
of others.

KRÜGER: Not me, sir.

MINDER: No, but you do nothing to prevent it. You make no
effort to check such disgraceful behavior—which means,
in practice, that you encourage it.

KRÜGER (*politely*): Does the lieutenant suggest that I'm
guilty of disgraceful behavior myself?

MINDER (*hastily*): I simply meant, Sergeant Major, that I'm
astonished at the way you've short-circuited our existing
chain of command. For instance, there's a tacit but long-
standing arrangement between Battery HQ and the gun
position that gunnery officers should receive prior
notification of all practice alerts. That arrangement has
been abolished.

KRÜGER: Not by me, sir. Battery commander's orders. If the

lieutenant has any complaint, I suggest he consult the captain.

MINDER (*intensely*): Sergeant Major, which side are you on? We've always hit it off pretty well. I advise you to think twice before you tangle with me. I *could* be your next battery commander.

KRÜGER: Captain Hein's my present battery commander and he'll probably stay that way for some time to come. As for me personally, Lieutenant, my loyalty is to Battery No. 3, not to individuals who may be here one day and gone the next. Live and let live—that's my motto, and I stick to it as long as other people do the same.

MINDER (*raising his voice*): What the hell is that supposed to mean?

KRÜGER: Sir, Battery No. 3 is all I'm interested in. The fact that you showed a personal interest in some paintings in a villa in a Warsaw suburb just after the Polish campaign —one a Renoir—well, that's no business of mine. Not as long as I'm allowed to do my duty as I see it. I'm no painting, Lieutenant. Nobody cuts me out of my frame.

MINDER (*dully, falling back a pace*): Is that a threat?

KRÜGER (*dispassionately*): Not a threat, Lieutenant, just a statement. One I can prove, too, if the occasion arises. I doubt if it ever will. I can't imagine anyone letting it come to that.

Frau Dr. Werner-Weilheim and Second Lieutenant Helmreich.
Place: the officers' billet, a villa on the edge of the gun position.
Time: approximately 1800 hours.

FRAU DR. W-W (*striding in briskly*): *Heil Hitler*, Herr Helmreich! Delighted to meet you. Just to set your mind at rest, I'm fully authorized to be here.

She is indeed. Both she and the other members of Profes-sor Magnus' research team have been granted access to the gun position. The reason: ancient chronicles, surveyors' re-ports and scholarly guesswork all suggest—according to Magnus—that a large burial place underlies the sports field. Stewards and equerries, grooms and wagoners, guards and body servants of the Dukes of Orléans are presumed—by Magnus—to be interred beneath the sod.

Frau Dr. Werner-Weilheim introduces herself and is cordially greeted by Second Lieutenant Helmreich. He offers her coffee, wine or cognac, all of which are politely but firmly declined. Visitor and host stand facing each other with an expectant air.

FRAU DR. W-W: I don't propose to take up more of your valuable time than is necessary, Herr Helmreich. May I quickly say, however, how delighted I am to hear from the junior NCO assigned to our party that you're noted for your patriotism and devotion to duty? Permit me to ask you a question: Are you for or against the establish-ment of military brothels?

HELMREICH (*evasively, but striving to convey the amiabil-ity and charm so clearly expected*): Speaking for my-self, *Frau Doktor*, I can assure you that I would never avail myself of such an amenity.

FRAU DR. W-W (*after a brief appraising glance*): That, Herr Helmreich, is not the point. A man in your posi-tion could, if he insisted on so doing, satisfy his baser urges elsewhere. All that interests me is this: Are you agreeable to the installation of a brothel within the offi-cial confines of this battery? Yes or no?

HELMREICH: No, of course not. On the other hand, I must admit that, circumstances being what they are. . . .

FRAU DR. W-W: So you're against the idea on principle. I wanted to get that straight. It only remains for me to thank you.

HELMREICH (*more than a little bemused*): Don't mention it, *Frau Doktor.*

FRAU DR. W-W: So I can count on you to support our campaign—"Operation Cleanup," as I have christened it. I expected no less of you, Herr Helmreich. Rest assured you will be serving a worthy cause. The brothel must go. *Heil Hitler!*

*Telephone conversations
conducted during the evening of the same day
between Group Headquarters and Battery No. 3.*

Conversation 1:

*Group switchboard to Battery No. 3 switchboard.
Message as follows:*
"Corporal Bergen to report to Group Headquarters tomorrow for check on personal documentation. Report to Orderly-Room Quartermaster Sergeant Rothe."

The immediate recipient of this directive was Sergeant Forstmann, who promptly passed it to Krüger. Krüger stared at the slip of paper with dawning suspicion. "It stinks," he said finally. "They send for Bergen—fair enough, they've a right to—but then they go on to tell us why. That's fishy. Besides, I know Rothe from way back. He doesn't have a thing to do with personal documentation."

Krüger picked up the phone.

Conversation 2:

KRÜGER: This isn't your pigeon, Rothe. What's the game and where do you come into it?

ROTHE: Who said anything about a game? Anyway, I don't know what you're carrying on about.

KRÜGER: Save your breath, buddy boy. What are you trying to do, take me for a ride? You tried something like this last year, remember? Don't tell me you've got an itch to try again. You must be a glutton for punishment.

ROTHE: For God's sake, Krüger, you know the position I'm in.

You're the last person I'd double-cross, considering how
well we've worked together in the past.

KRÜGER: So I'm right. It's the adjutant who's sticking his nose
into our business, as usual.

ROTHE: Please, Krüger, I never said anything of the kind. I
never so much as whispered it, understand?

KRÜGER: Sure, sure, you can stop pissing yourself. I don't know
a thing, you don't know a thing—we never exchanged a
single word on the subject. Any idea what the adjutant
wants with him?

ROTHE: Not a clue, believe me. All Lieutenant Seifert-Blanker
said was: "Send for the man but don't make a fuss. Have
him report to you and pass him on to me as soon as he
shows up." They plan to pick his brains, I figure, but don't
ask me how or why.

KRÜGER: Try and find out. Remember what you said about
cooperating in the past?

"Welcome, Professor!" Hein's sweeping gesture of invitation was matched by an almost jovial tone of voice. "Delighted to have you here."

"Delighted to be here, Captain." The professor deposited a
scroll of paper on the extreme edge of the vast table and sat
down in one of the high-backed chairs, some twenty-five
feet from Hein. "I must confess your champagne is an added
incentive. It's superb."

"One point on which we're in full agreement—and not the
only one, I trust." Hein did his best to convey goodwill.
"May I inquire if your work is progressing satisfactorily?"

"Quite satisfactorily, all things considered."

Hein nodded, trying to gauge the exact significance of
this halfhearted affirmative. Affably, he asked, "No worries
or complaints of any kind? No friction with members of my
unit? I should regret that intensely—and deal with it at
once, I need hardly add. Please don't hesitate to tell me if
I can assist you in any way."

"Many thanks, Captain. My personal responsibility is limited to fulfilling a specific research assignment—at least, that's what I'm trying to do. Administrative matters are outside my province, fortunately. The *Frau Doktor* handles those. She has an almost masculine approach to such things."

Hein laughed, then gestured to Schubert, who was awaiting his signal to fill the champagne glasses. Magnus eyed the boy curiously.

Hein raised his glass. "To history," he said gravely, "and the heroes of the past."

Magnus made no reply but imitated Hein's gesture and drank with relish, staring meditatively into the candlelight. A sly smile appeared on his face and lingered there.

"What about the duke?" Hein asked suddenly. "Charles Louis of Orléans—have you discovered anything further?"

"A great deal," said Magnus.

"Please tell me."

"With pleasure, if it won't bore you."

"On the contrary, Professor, I take a keen interest in history. Besides, the duke's career exerts a peculiar fascination on me. Unless my instincts are at fault, he deserves to be classed as one of the great trailblazers of the Western world."

"He might indeed be regarded in that light, Captain. First, allow me to present you with this scroll as a small token of my regard. I penned it myself."

"What is it?"

"The Orléans genealogical table, modified in a way that gives due prominence to Charles Louis."

The professor handed the scroll to Gunner Schubert, who ceremoniously conveyed it forward. Hein unrolled the strip of heavy cartridge and bent over it. He peered closely at the contents without arriving at any immediate conclusion.

"Very intricate," he declared at last. "Hard to grasp *in toto*, but beautifully done. If I start with Charles Louis and work outward, making him my focal point, all the various ramifications seem to fall into place."

"You're on the right track, Captain."

Professor Magnus leaned back in the big chair and inspected his surroundings with a leisurely eye. On the wall behind him, creased and grimy, marred by craquelure and bullet holes but retaining its ethereal charm, a small-scale allegorical trifle attributed to Fragonard.

The Fragonard was, in fact, the main reason for Magnus' present assignment. Reich Marshal Goering had heard rumors that Château D harbored the painting and wanted it for his collection. Reluctant to complete his mission too soon, Magnus pretended not to have found it yet. He was just beginning to enjoy his sojourn with Captain Hein.

Everything here stimulated his imagination, from paintings to sarcophagi. More than that, he was surrounded by people who excited his interest. Magnus was an avid spectator of the great circus of life and often felt an urge to join in.

A hero in the modern style, this captain, Magnus thought. He might have been modeled by Arno Breker, with his muscular frame, low brow and nutcracker jaw. The aura that surrounded him had the fascinating unsophistication of the eternal child, probably coupled with its playful cruelty. Behind him, like a pale and patient shadow, stood his thin-faced, dark-haired, doe-eyed orderly—just another lamb destined for slaughter on the altar of a putative hero. Finally, Magnus himself, little more than sixty but already a weary, humiliated old man, a frustrated sensualist, repeatedly exploited by superiors of various denominations, happy to take refuge in scholarship but ready to sally forth from time to time when lured by the prospect of perverse or malicious enjoyment.

"I'm listening, Professor," Hein said impatiently. "You had something to tell me, I believe."

"Ah, yes, a few details relating to Charles Louis of

Orléans. First and foremost, Captain, discounting his numerous other attainments, he was a great, indeed, a brilliant soldier, alert to the dictates of military expediency, to the merits of innovation—in short, to progress in the art of war."

Hein nodded. "A prime requirement at every stage in history. The soldier in his role as creative thinker, Professor, as the all-deciding man of action, as the legitimate agent of historical change. . . ."

The captain leaned forward, doubtless to ensure that Magnus caught every word. The professor had excellent hearing, however, and his sense of mischief was equally well developed.

"The duke won high praise from no less a person than Prince Eugene of Savoy. Eugene called him a light to lighten Europe in her darkest hour. Schiller described him as a man without equal, and Frederick the Great is said to have exclaimed, after losing a battle: 'With Charles Louis in our ranks, we should have carried the day!' "

Hein did not alter his position. Still leaning forward with his hands flat on the table, he asked, "How would you define his major contributions to history and the art of war?"

"Well," Magnus said quickly, "in the first place, Charles Louis took great pains to ensure that his men received combat training under realistic conditions. He kept them on their toes night and day, drew up a regular training schedule which included forced marches of supreme severity, made them practice their skill at arms on straw dummies. He doubled his stocks of horses and even tried to treble them in the interests of mobility and efficiency, his avowed aim being to increase the speed and endurance of his cavalry by providing three mounts per man. He also taught his troops the most effective methods of combating snow and freezing temperatures—in fact, he could be called the originator of the winter campaign."

"Splendid," breathed Hein, "simply splendid." He straightened up and beckoned to Schubert to refill the glasses.

"Tell me," he went on, "have you located the duke's tomb?"

Magnus nodded. "It's in the family church, just in front of the main altar. The coffin bears a Latin inscription."

"So that's where the great man lies. . . ."

"Officially, yes. A number of documents take it for granted, but not all. Personally, I remain unconvinced. There has always been a suspicion, persistent though studiously suppressed, that the sarcophagus is empty. My preliminary findings seem to confirm this."

"So it's empty?"

"Yes, as far as I can judge at this early stage." Magnus paused for effect. "Of course, it would fit the legend very neatly."

"Legend? What legend?"

"It bears a resemblance to the one about Emperor Frederick Barbarossa, who is reputed to be sitting asleep in the Kyffhäuserberg with his beard curled around a marble table, waiting to be recalled. The events surrounding this duke of ours are equally nebulous. According to several accounts, he mounted his charger and rose toward the horizon as though ascending into the sky. He was never seen again."

"Do you plan to open the coffin?"

Magnus smiled regretfully. "My assignment doesn't extend that far, I'm afraid. My team is merely one of many which have been commissioned by Reichsleiter Rosenberg to list items of cultural or historical merit, preserve them from damage or decay, catalog them as accurately as possible, and report their existence to higher authority. I am not empowered to do more."

"Would you show it to me?"

"The duke's sarcophagus? By all means."

"And would you open it if I managed to persuade you it was essential to do so?"

"Why, which do you distrust—legend or the official version?"

"Neither, necessarily, but I must know more. I want the whole truth."

"Truth is relative, Captain. All we can say for certain is that he must be dead by this time."

"But where did he die and how? Under what circumstances?"

"Why not here in this very room?"

"This very chair, you mean?"

"Perhaps, perhaps not. He needn't necessarily have died in the chair you're occupying at this moment. It's more than possible that his death occurred in the room where you sleep. It's also conceivable that he died in the tower chamber, gazing in the direction of Paris, where a royal degenerate squatted on his gilded *chaise percée* amid wanton women, servile courtiers and all the vapid gossip of a decadent court. Anything is conceivable, Captain. The possibilities are legion."

"But I want to know the true facts, Professor. Don't you see? I feel like a man entering upon an inheritance charged with sacred obligations, obligations which he cannot and will not evade." Hein placed both hands flat on the tabletop and pushed himself erect. With clockwork precision he strode down one side of the long room, turned, retraced his steps, and finally started pacing to and fro.

"I want to know . . . I must know," Hein said, still pacing. "Did he really die in this building, and if so where? On the spot where my bed stands, in the very bed where I sleep? And if he did die in the château, where are his remains? If they aren't in his coffin, why aren't they there and where else could they be? It must be possible to find out."

"I shall do my best," said the professor, his straight face concealing a puckish delight. "Since it means so much to you, I shall endeavor to produce the necessary evidence."

"Please do, as quickly as you can."

"A worthy object of research, Captain, and one which holds promise of great things—certainly from my point of view."

Interim Report No. 4

Extracts
from a subsequent account
provided by Frau F. (as in Fortsmann),
formerly Mademoiselle Suzanne,
one of the three female occupants
of the bailiff's apartment in Château D.

". . . not that there were any problems of that kind in my case. I found the whole atmosphere quite natural, mainly because I was born and brought up in Alsace.

"Few people can have any idea of what that meant at the time. Our beautiful little province used to be part of Charlemagne's empire. The French ruled it for many years, then the Germans, then the French again. . . . We spoke both languages at home, which paid off—that's to say, my knowledge of German came in handy.

"In any case, why should I have had anything against German soldiers? My father served with the German army in World War One. On the other hand, one of my brothers escaped to England and joined the Free French. My God, who can blame me for doing my little bit toward bringing our two countries together?

"The war caught me by surprise and left me marooned in D. I was sorry at first, but it wasn't long before my enforced stay turned out to be a blessing in disguise. After all, that was where I met my future husband, bless him.

"Yes, I can honestly say it was love at first sight. . . ."

Extracts
from field post office letters
written at the time
by members of Battery No. 3.

Sergeant Major Krüger to his family, consisting
of his parents, a sister, and five younger brothers:

"The war goes on here without letup, more or less. We can't wait to notch up some more enemy planes. The battery's in peak condition and ready for action twenty-four hours a day. It makes me proud, especially as I can now tell you that I've been recommended for the Iron Cross. Needless to say, the captain had to twist my arm before I'd accept. . . ."

Quartermaster Sergeant Softer to a friend:

". . . any quantity you like at rock-bottom prices, generous discounts on bulk orders, full containers postage-free subject to cash on delivery. Items currently available include. . . ."

(There followed a two-page list.)

Sergeant Moll, ex-accountant, to his latest girlfriend:

". . . Of course I'm being faithful—I shouldn't have to tell you that. . . . You'd hardly believe how isolated we are here. It's positively Spartan, the way we live. . . . I haven't even set eyes on a woman for weeks. As for the French girls, everybody knows they only smother themselves in scent to drown the smell of their underwear. . . . Why should I feel the slightest urge, when I've got you?"

Corporal Neumann of the medical section, to a friend
stationed in Germany:

". . . three of them on tap—day and night, what's more. Sometimes I flip a coin to see which of them I'll lay. We may be getting another one soon, for variety's sake. Business is booming, thanks to yours truly. Wish you were here, old pal, so I could introduce them to you personally. I tell you, there's something to be said for a war."

Gunner Schubert to his mother:

"Dear Mother, I'm fine. They give us plenty to eat and don't work us too hard. The other men are very decent to me. The

weather is gorgeous. We're billeted in an old château. Please
don't worry about me. All my love, ever your devoted son
Johannes."

Statement
by ex-Reserve Second Lieutenant Helmreich,
now senior executive of a municipal savings bank
in Styria, Austria,
also chairman of the local veterans' association.

"Very well, as a man who believes in speaking his mind, I
admit it. Mistakes were made—very grave mistakes, not that I
had any personal share in them.

". . . never an avowed National Socialist but always a loyal
citizen of Greater Germany. That meant, among other things,
that I was constantly alert to the menace of international Com-
munism.

"From that point of view—but no other—I even felt tempted
to welcome the emergence of a man like Hitler. Unfortunately,
both he and a large number of his supporters failed to appreciate the situation correctly and draw the proper conclusions.

"The war should, of course, have been fought on an all-out
basis from the very first. Instead, due to a series of crass
blunders and neglected opportunities, it ground to a halt. Mental apathy was partly to blame.

" 'You mark my words,' I told Lieutenant Minder, but he
paid no heed. My warnings fell on deaf ears, even at that
stage.

"I was quick to recognize the rapid decline in morale. 'All
these victories are too much of a good thing,' I remarked to
Minder, a brother officer of mine, who clearly failed to grasp
my implication.

"Ah, yes, there was a widespread lack of clear-eyed, firm-
jawed military professionalism—even, when all is said and done,
in men like Captain Hein. The deplorable manner of his passing
proved that conclusively. He may have been a good soldier
and an excellent tactician, but to my critical eye he lacked

foresight. Far from looking ahead, he focused his attention on the past.

"My awareness of these shortcomings distressed me deeply. There were numerous others I could mention. For instance, our regimental commander, Colonel Rheinemann-Bergen, had a penchant for philosophical discussion. He enjoyed spouting Kant and Hegel, and his staff—including Major Born of the JAG's office—imitated him like a bunch of parrots.

"Then there was the group commander, a human wine barrel who lived in a state of permanent inebriation. His adjutant, Lieutenant Seifert-Blanker, was an unscrupulous schemer. He seized on every opportunity to make trouble, but only to claim credit for resolving problems which he himself had caused.

" 'Don't say I didn't warn you!' I told Minder, but fate continued to take its inexorable course."

5

Every Hero Needs a Medal to Prove It

It was an impressive spectacle. The men of Battery No. 3 stood there, to quote one of Krüger's more colorful similes, "like turds shat along a tape measure and left to dry." Krüger himself, acting in concert with Runge, had bullied and bellowed them into the proper formation for a ceremonial parade.

Even Quartermaster Sergeant Softer, who habitually tended his stores like a hamster, had scuttled to the scene. After all, a great event was imminent. The divisional commander had announced his intention of gracing the parade with his presence.

To give the general as fitting and sizable a reception as possible, headquarters personnel and gun crews had been drawn up together in three ranks—a comparatively rare phenomenon. Battery Sergeant Major Krüger stood relishing the sight of his entire outfit massed in a single body.

"I've got a length of string," Runge informed Krüger in a chummy undertone, "—a hundred meters of it. We could use it to check their dressing."

Krüger amiably dismissed the suggestion. "My eyesight's good enough."

He lowered his voice as he spoke to avoid possible misunderstanding among the junior ranks. Krüger and Runge were staunch members of the NCO's trade union. They knew the meaning of loyalty and allegiance long before Hitler became commander in chief and took care to present a united front to superiors and subordinates alike.

Captain Hein appeared, this time on foot and walking with the measured tread of one approaching the communion rail. Krüger reported to him direct, blatantly bypassing the two gunnery officers, who stood at one side like lay figures, their salutes ignored.

The captain appeared to see, or want to see, nothing and nobody. Not a word escaped his lips, not even the customary "Thank you." He simply raised his right hand, disclosing that it was encased in an entirely new type of deerskin glove, so silver-gray as to seem almost white. His face was masklike in its rigidity.

Hein did not move, merely stood there in the gentle sunlight, facing his battery. One of the men emitted a resounding fart which was quickly emulated by a near neighbor in the ranks. Unlike the battery sergeant major, who winced at the sound, Hein gave no sign of having heard.

"Divisional commander now approaching the gun position, sir!" Lieutenant Minder called zealously.

"With a large escort," added Second Lieutenant Helmreich, no less zealously.

"I," announced Hein, "shall report to the general direct."

Krüger, who seldom failed to interpret his battery commander's wishes correctly, thundered, "Parade! Parade—'shun! Eyes—left!"

A hundred and fifty heads snapped to the right, precisely in the direction from which the general was bound to come. When a unit had been as admirably trained as Battery No. 3

it was quite unnecessary for an order to be correctly phrased
—what mattered was that it should be correctly executed.
Krüger had taken the precaution of practicing this innumer-
able times.

At a funeral pace, three vehicles bore down on the gun
position. Patches of color were visible from afar: general
officer's white, field officer's red, and, immediately behind,
the field-gray uniforms and mottled camouflage jackets of
the escorting troops. A pennant stiffened with wire jutted
counter to the direction in which the cars were traveling.

First to alight from the leading car was the general, an almost alarmingly frail-looking man with a tendency to skip
and caper. He gazed around rather helplessly, then drew
himself erect—standing, so it seemed, on tiptoe.

The second car disgorged Colonel Rheinemann-Bergen,
imposingly built—he was well over six feet tall—and studiously paternal. After him came the tubby figure of the
alcoholic group commander, who appeared to roll rather
than walk. He was not accompanied by his adjutant, Lieutenant Seifert-Blanker, a circumstance certain well-informed
observers found disquieting.

The third car proved to contain several men equipped with
still and movie cameras, clearly members of an army propaganda unit, who swiftly surrounded Battery No. 3 like a flock
of vultures.

Captain Hein reported to the general. A vigorous bout of
handshaking ensued—first Hein and the general, then Hein
and Colonel Rheinemann-Bergen, then Hein and the group
commander. There was much clicking and whirring from the
propaganda unit, and one of their number rapidly sketched
some heroic artist's impressions for the benefit of the home
front.

Next, the general desired to inspect the battery. "Follow
me, gentlemen!" he called to his entourage, and set off with
Hein at his heels. They passed along the motionless ranks in a

series of ornamental clusters, the general and his staff, the colonel and his escorting officers, the major and his assistant adjutant.

"Know what I'm doing?" Gunner Wassermann whispered to Bergen, who was next to him. "Trying to picture the general wiping his ass—it helps."

Drilled in advance by Krüger and Runge, the men kept their eyes fixed on the general—with some interest, too, because they seldom had a chance to observe so exalted a species of military animal at close quarters.

Quite a few of them strove hard to see him as an eagle-eyed god of war, but isolated individuals felt more as if they had just witnessed the rapid progress of a gaily colored parrot. On the whole, they were disillusioned.

"Men!" exclaimed the general, striking a pose. He had a startlingly high-pitched voice, squeaky but penetrating. "Men, it is your privilege to belong to an elite unit. You have not only contributed, like so many, to the winning of some decisive victories—you have played a crucial part in them. This battery boasts a success rate which can truly be described as second to none. I am here to pay tribute to your achievements."

The general drew a deep breath. "Captain Hein," he called, "be so good as to step forward, not only on your own behalf but also as a representative of your admirable subordinates—of every member of your splendid unit."

Captain Hein marched up to the divisional commander and halted, deathly pale, stiff as a ramrod, sea-blue eyes totally devoid of expression. The general smiled and extended his right arm sideways as the regimental commander handed him a leather case of soup-plate dimensions together with a pigskin folder which evidently contained a citation.

The colonel was smiling too, now, as if to demonstrate his nobility of character. Were it not for Hein, he himself would have been experiencing this moment of ultimate distinction: the bestowal of a Knight's Cross.

"Captain Karl Ludwig Hein," said the general, opening the case and removing a broad black-white-and-red ribbon with a metal order dangling from it, "in recognition of your meritorious conduct, the Führer, Chancellor and Supreme Commander of the Armed Forces, Adolf Hitler, has seen fit to present you with our highest military award. It is my pleasure and privilege to invest you with the Knight's Cross of the Iron Cross."

The general took the ribbon and put it over the captain's slightly inclined head. The order negotiated Hein's cap and came to rest below his collar. It dangled askew, was swiftly tweaked into position and given a light pat with the flat of the general's hand.

"Well," the general said jocularly, officer to officer, "you've made it at last." Which sounded all the more ironical because the general had still to acquire a Knight's Cross himself.

Hein stood there stiffly, dispensing handshakes with mechanical vigor, unspeaking, being filmed, snapped, sketched.

"Always the same old stuff," muttered an army cameraman who was standing near Krüger and Runge. "Couldn't you provide something different for a change? How about some blood and guts? That always goes down well with the public."

"Give it time," Runge told him. "We could be in for a few fireworks before long."

"Let me know in advance, then, but don't bother unless it's something really big. Plenty of noise, smoke, action—know what I mean? You could even wind up in a newsreel."

"Carry on, please," said the general, sounding a trifle impatient. He was an aesthete, and the proximity of this mass of malodorous soldiery had a disquieting effect on him. Besides, he was due back in Paris that evening to dine with some fellow generals at Maxim's. "Shall we proceed?"

"Senior Gunnery Sergeant Runge," the regimental commander announced hurriedly, "you are awarded the Iron

Cross First Class for consistent gallantry in the face of the enemy."

Medal, handshake, dismiss.

"Sergeant Major Krüger," said the group commander, "to you goes the Iron Cross Second Class for recovering wounded under enemy fire."

"And who," murmured Quartermaster Sergeant Softer, "is going to lick my ass for me?" Not many people heard the question.

Three more decorations—also Iron Crosses Second Class— were bestowed in quick succession on men belonging to the gun crews. With a genial nod to all and sundry, the general climbed into his staff car and drove off, followed by the rest of the cortege. A minute later Battery No. 3 had the place to itself again.

Lieutenant Minder advanced on Hein, who looked more like a statue than ever. "Congratulations," he said, then amended this to: "Permit me to congratulate you, sir."

"Thanks," Hein replied frigidly, not moving a muscle.

"Could we persuade you to visit our quarters, sir? We'd like to feel that your award reflected credit on us all. A few drinks. . . ."

"Thank you, no," said Hein. "There's a time and a place for everything. First we have a training schedule to fulfill. In this unit, duty takes precedence over all else. Awards are simply a spur to greater effort. Carry on!"

Sergeant Arm looked peevish. "Does this mean I won't be able to hold my circus today?"

"What ever gave you that idea?" Krüger's tone was reassuring. "Why shouldn't you put your monkeys through the hoop if it amuses you?"

"I thought today was a sort of holiday. On account of the medals."

"You don't have to worry about that. Didn't you hear

what the captain said? It's the same with us farm people. If a bull wins a prize we make damn sure he does his stuff with the cows afterward."

"Nobody gave me any medals," growled Arm.

"Keep your shirt on. If it was up to me, friend, you could have my Iron Cross and welcome to it—bottle tops don't mean much to me. I'm only wearing it for the boys of the battery—they've earned it. Anyway, just between ourselves, you've already been put in for the War Service Cross with swords, and that's more than I've done for anybody else around here."

"You mean it?" Arm slapped Krüger on the back as they strolled back together from the gun position to Battery HQ. "In that case the circus is on. I'll really go to town. Who's due for the center ring this time?"

"Bergen," Krüger replied, deliberately offhand. "Concentrate on him. He's got to be taught which side his bread's buttered."

"I'll teach him all right," Arm promised, rubbing his hands. "I'd have been really pissed off if the show had been canceled. Trust the captain, though. It's business before pleasure with him, no matter what. Still, no reason why we shouldn't raise our elbows this evening to celebrate your great day. How about it?"

Krüger nodded. "I owe it to you and the rest of the gang. Softer will set it up."

"Including a visit to the girls?"

"I don't see why not. All the same, first things first."

Arm's circus generally gave an afternoon performance at the end of each week. It was jointly staged by Battery HQ and the gun position, tacitly sanctioned by Hein, organized by Krüger and Runge, and supervised by Arm.

Sergeant Arm, still remembered from his prewar days at gunnery school as a parade-ground and field-training bully of considerable ingenuity, was anxious that his special talents should not fall into disuse.

"I'll need a second-in-command," Arm said. "Who do you recommend?"

"Kaminski," said Krüger, after a moment's reflection.

Corporal Kaminski, another NCO who had still to be decorated, was in urgent need of encouragement. Anyone privileged to act as assistant ringmaster in Arm's circus could consider his merits had not gone unnoticed. It amounted to an unofficial diploma of excellence.

"Fair enough, Kaminski it is. Who's on parade along with Bergen?"

There had to be at least six performers to make the circus worthwhile. Nine was the maximum because a higher attendance made individual supervision impossible.

On this occasion there were seven victims: Bergen, nominated by the battery sergeant major, four gun-crew members whose inconsistent showing as high jumpers had annoyed Runge, and two storemen adjudged untrustworthy by Softer because, when ordered to fill some packing cases, they had used up more items than the containers would hold.

"Parade at thirteen hundred hours sharp," Arm told them. "Full marching order but leave your packs empty. I'll supply the contents."

This wrapped it up, at least as far as Krüger was concerned. His next duty was to arrange an NCO's party, the second that week. He sent word to Softer to report to him in the orderly room. When Softer appeared there was a trace of resentment on his fat face.

"Oh, Christ," said Krüger, "don't tell me you're another one who's pissed off because he didn't get a medal. Don't worry, it won't be long. You've been put in for the War Service Cross with swords, and that's more than anyone else around here."

"You mean it?" said Softer, snapping at the bait. His face

assumed its customary grin. "That changes the whole picture."

"Good. So what about a party tonight, with a visit to the recreation center thrown in?"

"Done!" promised Softer. "I'll provide the booze. We can close the brothel to ordinary customers any time, say from eleven on. After that it'll be special customers only, and no time limit. The medal merchants from the gun position can have a quick dip just after working hours. That'll leave the place free for us later on. Reduced prices, of course, since we'll have it to ourselves."

Confident that he could rely on Softer's administrative ability, Krüger could now devote himself to more refined pleasures. He seldom missed a performance of Arm's circus and was determined to enjoy this one to the full.

Quartermaster Sergeant Softer slunk, with the stealthy movements of an Indian scout, toward the far end of the château grounds. Skirting the family church, he peered around a buttress at a stone bench near the wall.

A short, skinny man in railwayman's uniform was sitting there with his tunic unbuttoned, and not only because of the heat. He had his arm around the shoulders of a little girl who could not have been much more than ten years old and was clasping her tightly to his chest.

Softer wagged his head at the sight. His persistent grin faded. He cleared his throat and said: "Hope I'm not butting in on anything."

The railwayman pushed the girl away and jumped up, hurriedly tweaking her skirt down over her knees.

"Oh, it's you," he said, recognizing Softer. "You gave me a start, sneaking up behind me like that. Of course you're not butting in. Always glad to see you."

"What's up here?" Softer inquired. "Brushing up your French?"

"We went for a walk—isn't that right, Simone?" The little
girl nodded eagerly. "You see, Softer, just a little nature
ramble. . . ."

"Save it, you dirty old man," Softer told him amiably.
"No need to put on an act with me. You like them under age
—that's it and all about it."

"Do you mind!" The railwayman protested. "Simone is
the mayor's niece. It was him who asked me to look after her.
She's been showing me around."

"The mayor's niece?" Softer eyed the ill-assorted pair uneasily. "All right, that's your gamble. Me, I don't know a
thing—I never even saw you. All I do know is, you promised to shift some stuff back to Germany for me—last week,
when I caught you looking after that widow's daughter. Several wagonloads, you said."

"Any time," said the railwayman, discreetly buttoning his
tunic. "Just tell me when, how many and where to—you
only have to say. I'll do the rest."

"Great!" Softer gave a contented smirk. "That's what I
call service. I'm going to return the favor by breaking up
your little party. In other words, go lech somewhere else.
This place will be hopping with soldiers in ten minutes' time
and the officers in charge aren't as broad-minded as I am."

"Thanks for the tip." The railwayman rose and beckoned
to Simone, who trustingly placed her hand in his. "I'd like
to get one thing straight first, Softer. You're wrong about—
well, what you said just now. There wasn't anything like
that. It's pure affection. I love Simone like a father."

"Oh, sure," Softer said. "Those underpants under the
bench—tell her to put them on quick. Then get lost, the
pair of you. I want that transportation schedule first thing
tomorrow, and keep the price down."

Sergeant Runge was another devotee of Arm's circus. Today, freshly decorated and in high good humor, he joined
Krüger on a bench in the château grounds and helped him-

self to a bottle of beer from the ammunition box which stood beside it. The bench afforded a good view of the entire proceedings.

Corporal Kaminski kicked off by doubling the seven-man squad toward a heap of old stone roof tiles. Sergeant Arm trotted up behind him. "Three apiece," he decreed casually. "To start with," he added.

"Move!" barked Kaminski. "One, two, three!"

The seven men moved, not sluggishly but without undue haste, anxious to conserve their energies as much as possible. Each of them loaded his pack with three large rectangular tiles weighing approximately seven pounds each. Arm surveyed his victims happily, then nodded to Kaminski and strolled off.

"Whistle signals!" Kaminski proclaimed in a near scream. "One blast means halt, two blasts move off on the double, three blasts crawl. If I clap my hands, change places. Thumbs down, hit the deck. Thumbs up, on your feet. That goes for the next half hour."

"You can't beat the old-style methods," commented Sergeant Runge, opening another bottle of beer. "Those blokes are out on their feet already. Either they're a bunch of cream puffs or they're malingering."

"Of course they're malingering," Krüger said expertly. "An act, that's all it is. They learn fast, but they'll never put one over on Arm." He chuckled and clinked bottles with Runge. "The man isn't born who can take us for a ride."

Sergeant Arm's voice rang through the grounds. "Right, I'll take over now." He flexed his knees and drew several deep breaths. "Good," he said, nodding to Kaminski. "You've given the bastards a nice little warm-up." Arm could have bestowed no higher accolade.

Stationing himself in front of the seven wheezing soldiers, he proclaimed, "Double your loads. Six tiles, then we'll do some tree climbing."

This heralded the start of the circus proper. The tree-climbing act was a brilliant inspiration known to initiates as "Arm's monkey tricks."

"All right, you monkeys, get climbing!"

The doubly encumbered members of Arm's squad wormed their way upward, led by those who aleady knew the rules of the game. Reacting swiftly and skillfully, Bergen followed suit but did his best to escape attention by keeping to the center of the bunch.

"Freeze!" yelled Arm.

They all stretched out on whichever branch they had been climbing, chests and bellies flattened against it, arms and legs wound around. Some clung convulsively, in particular those who had buckled on their forty-pound pack so loosely that it slipped sideways and threatened to upset their equilibrium. Two or three faces were clamped fearfully against the bark in tremulous anticipation of Arm's next move.

"Corporal Kaminski," he said, "your sidearm, if you please."

Kaminski drew his sidearm, a heavy steel NCO's dirk, from its scabbard. Arm took it and walked over to one of the squad who had been unwise enough to select a perch near the ground. He slapped the man's boot soles hard with the flat of the blade. "Higher, cunt-face, or I'll give you a spare asshole!"

This was a general warning. Several of the men promptly inched their way higher. Arm got Kaminski to plant his sidearm on the end of a rifle, transforming it into a bayonet and extending the sergeant's reach by several feet. Those who had not already done so scrambled to safety.

"Hanging, commence!" he called.

The high spot of the proceedings had come at last. The seven were now obliged to hang by their arms alone. Weighed down by the ballast in their packs, they dangled from their respective branches, their faces quickly turning green.

"No cheating!" Arm bellowed. "I want to see you hang

there like Christmas tree decorations. Keep a tight asshole, too, because God help the man who shits himself. Piss yourselves if you like—I'm an easygoing man—but anyone who lets go too soon gets a bayonet up his backside. If he doesn't break his neck first."

They soon started to drop, more like rotten fruit than Christmas decorations. One man after another hit the ground with a dull thump and lay there, panting, gasping, retching, whimpering. Arm smiled complacently to himself.

Bergen was the last to fall, as Krüger, who had been enjoying the spectacle, was careful to note. "Look at that," he said thoughtfully. "He's got stamina as well as brains, the stubborn s.o.b."

"Beginner's luck," observed Runge. "It needn't last." The main attraction was over. He rose from the bench and swiftly drained his third bottle of beer. I'm due back at the guns in ten minutes. Hein's got an extra-special exercise planned for this afternoon—a real humdinger to celebrate the occasion."

"See you tonight," Krüger said. "We've got some party games of our own lined up." He winked.

Runge nodded. "I'll be there, but first I'm going to put my boys through their paces. Just so they don't get rusty."

"That's the ticket," Krüger said. "Keep 'em up to scratch."

"Know what's on my mind?" Gunner Wassermann asked with a glint in his eye. "That brothel. I've got a thing about it. What say we put it out of action?"

"Sure, but not right now," Bergen said, yawning. "I've had enough excitement for one day."

"You mean you're giving up?" Wassermann eyed him anxiously. "Did Arm knock the stuffing out of you?"

"For the moment."

Bergen bent wearily over the engine of his signals truck, which again refused to start.

Wassermann grinned at Bergen. "I could fix it in two min-

utes flat if I wanted to, but why should I? I sabotaged the
truck myself during Arm's circus, so I could keep you company afterward. As far as I'm concerned we can spend hours
over it—the whole afternoon if you want. I feel like a nice
long chat."

"What's the point?"

Wassermann shrugged. "It all depends on our lords and
masters. It all depends how smug they're feeling and whether
we don't mind them feeling that way—whether we can do
something to shake them. Just for fun, of course."

"What, for instance?"

"Any number of things. It only takes a little ingenuity,
and we've both got plenty of ideas. How about this one? A
brothel is a health hazard, so we could drop a hint to the
regimental MO and see what happens. Here's another. There
are three girls employed there. That means the town major's
responsible for checking them out. He could at least take a
look at their papers."

Bergen frowned. "What's the point? He might get as far
as Krüger, but that's all. He'd never set foot inside Hein's
office, let alone the brothel."

"Well, what about the group adjutant—Seifert-Blanker,
isn't that his name? He's itching to pin something on Hein."

"I'm supposed to be seeing him tomorrow. Sounds as if
he's planning to pump me."

"There you are, then. It's a perfect opportunity."

Bergen shook his head. "There's nothing perfect about it.
The adjutant may be gunning for Hein—in fact I know he
is—but he hasn't a chance of nailing him unless he can come
up with something solid. The trouble is, anybody who helps
him will be in hot water, and not just with Krüger and his
pals."

"So you won't?"

"Would you, Wassermann? Be honest."

"Maybe not," Wassermann conceded. "It's a crying shame,
though."

"Don't worry," Bergen said thoughtfully. "I'll even the score with Arm soon enough. That's the least I can do."

"Keep going," Hein called to his driver. "Straight ahead!" The Knight's Cross graced Hein's throat as if it had always been there—as if he were fully dressed for the first time. Characteristically, his mind was intent on higher things.

The captain was standing in his open field car, gloved hands resting lightly on the top of the windshield. Seated beside him at the wheel, Corporal Kaminski guided the vehicle skillfully along rutted tracks that had once been well-kept drives. Shortly before they reached the Rue Napoléon the corporal spoke up.

"Exit blocked, sir!"

A black hearselike car had halted at the gates. In front of it—potbellied and port-visaged, with pouchy eyes and bandy legs—stood Captain Karl Schmidt, town commandant of D. He produced a sort of salute.

"Kindly stand aside," said Hein. "Unless, of course, you wish me to run you down."

"Please, please!" cried Schmidt, flapping his hands. "I had no intention of obstructing you. My only wish was to congratulate you on your decoration."

"Thank you. Now may I ask you to clear the road?"

"By all means." Captain Schmidt attempted a smile. "May I, in turn, seize this favorable opportunity to solicit your sympathetic understanding of my special status in this town? Fundamentally, our problems are similar. It's a matter of mutual obligation."

"Is it?" said Hein. "I wasn't aware I owed you any obligation whatsoever. You may send me a written memorandum on the subject if you really think it's worthwhile. Personally, I have more important things to attend to—notably the combat readiness of my unit."

"My main concern," Captain Schmidt declared with ponderous insistence, "is Franco-German reconciliation. We must eliminate potential sources of conflict, dispel the misunderstandings that have dogged our two countries for so many years—indeed, centuries. If that doesn't interest you, it should."

"I have only one interest, Captain, and that is my battery —its military role and fighting efficiency, nothing else. Good day to you."

"What about these incessant disturbances," persisted Schmidt, "disturbances which emanate from your sphere of command alone? I refer, for instance, to the arbitrary eviction of French citizens from the edge of the sports field. Then there's all this sniping at pets—cats, cage birds, and so forth—in the area of the château. One of your men even fired at the mayor's dog—and missed, fortunately. Last but not least, I've received a report that you intend to blow up the municipal water tower on the pretext that it obstructs your field of fire. Well, Captain, what does it all mean?"

"Merely that you have no conception—not the slightest— of the functions of a unit on active service." With sovereign calm, Hein stared through and beyond Schmidt, his chiseled lips curved in a faint grimace of distaste. "Now get out of my way."

"Not before you've heard me out!"

"What are you trying to do, commit suicide? Very well, you leave me no choice. Drive on, Kaminski."

Kaminski discreetly signaled that Sergeant Runge was approaching from the gun position, resolved as ever to prove himself in the eyes of his battery commander. The sun glinted on Runge's Iron Cross First Class.

"Having trouble, sir?" he inquired, jerking his thumb at Schmidt.

Hein nodded and was gratified to note that he had no need to do more. Runge handled the situation with accomplished ease. He began by requesting the other captain, quite pleasantly, to remove himself. "Otherwise your vehicle may come under fire from one of our guns, which wouldn't do it much good. . . ."

"I came here with the most peaceful of intentions," Schmidt complained, "and what happens? I'm threatened—grossly threatened!"

"Who's threatening you? Nobody!" retorted Runge, fortified by an approving glance from Hein. "We're fighting soldiers, sir. You must pardon us if our language isn't as refined as yours." He turned to Hein. "Gun position cleared for action, sir. The men are waiting."

"In that case," Hein told Kaminski, "drive on."

Promptly, Hein's field car advanced on Schmidt's black limousine. The gap between them closed yard by yard.

Captain Schmidt uttered a squawk of alarm. "Back up!" he called to his driver. "Reverse! I refuse to be provoked by you or anyone," he added in a choking voice.

"Good," Hein observed calmly. "Why didn't you say so in the first place?"

Sergeant Runge vaulted into the back of the field car. "I enjoy that, sir. There's nothing like mowing down the opposition if you have to."

Hein inclined his head. "Exactly, Sergeant. I'm delighted to see how competently you deal with ticklish situations. It only confirms how right I was to recommend you for the Iron Cross First Class.

"Very grateful to you, sir," Runge assured him. "I hope there'll be plenty more chances to prove it."

"Sergeant," Hein said, lowering his voice confidentially, "you're officer material—you've got what it takes. I shall put your name forward."

Deep emotion robbed Runge of the power of speech, but not for long. "What matters is the battery's fighting efficiency, sir. It mustn't be allowed to slide—in fact, we've got to boost it."

"Precisely," said Hein. "You're thinking along the right lines."

"I can't help recalling our times in Poland, sir. Take that village near Mlawa, just beyond the frontier—we blasted our way through, shit or bust, and we lost two or three men. If we hadn't had the guts to neutralize the opposition first, we'd have lost a dozen or more."

"You have an excellent memory, Runge. What's more, you know how to learn from past experience—another officer quality. Applying our experiences in Poland to the present setup, how do you suggest we make the most effective use of them?"

"That's just what I've been wondering, sir." The highly decorated sergeant whose sights were now set on a commission knit his brow. "I've given the subject a lot of thought, and there's a chance I may have the answer. If you've got live ammo in the chamber, pull the trigger—that's my principle."

"Good. Let me know as soon as you come up with some usable ideas, and by usable I mean workable. But I don't need to tell you that."

"Anyone there?" came a powerful voice from the threshold of the bailiff's apartment. The door had been brusquely flung open. "I suppose you're all asleep, even at this hour!"

The voice belonged to Frau Dr. Werner-Weilheim, who was determined to inspect the premises from which she and her party were still barred. Bent on collecting evidence of their misuse, she had overcome her natural repugnance sufficiently to penetrate the sink of iniquity in person.

"Anyone there?" she repeated, striding into the salon-*cum*-manager's office. "Or are you ashamed to show your faces?"

Even before her voice had died away, a side door opened and the rosy, slightly porcine face of Corporal Neumann peered around it. His eyes widened in disbelief.

"Well, I'll be. . . ." He paused. "What are you doing here?

This isn't your kind of place. You must have come to the wrong door by mistake. Never mind, to err is human, as they say."

The *Frau Doktor* glared at him. "We'll soon see who's erred!"

Neumann met her glare with an impudent grin. "Don't get any queer ideas—these premises are reserved for men only."

"You unspeakable pig!" she thundered. "Keep your suggestive remarks to yourself! You must have a mind like a sewer, which is just one more proof of the decadence and depravity that reigns in this place. I wish to inspect every room in the establishment—at once!"

"Over my dead body," said Neumann.

"By all means, if you continue to get in my way, you . . . you pimp!"

"Madam!" Neumann protested, drawing himself up to his full but inconsiderable height. "You can't talk to me like that. If I wasn't so easygoing I might take it as an insult."

"I'm addressing you as you deserve. What's your business here? Do you have a specific function in this brothel? Is your presence here fortuitous, or are you performing some kind of official duty? Do you pay, or are you paid?"

"This is too much," Neumann said furiously. "You've no business in here. This is a private establishment."

"It's a hellhole, and one I intend to abolish." Frau Dr. Werner-Weilheim thrust Neumann vigorously aside. He cannoned against the inner door, which burst open.

Marie-Antoinette stood revealed in her negligee. She looked slightly the worse for wear, having already played hostess to the three newly decorated junior NCO's from the gun position, also Softer and Arm.

"Who's this?" she exclaimed, indicating the visitor with a mixture of surprise and professional interest. "I hope you're not a prospective client, madame. I've already had my quota for one day."

The *Frau Doktor* threw out her bosom and submitted

Marie-Antoinette to a gorgon stare. "So you're one of these creatures!"

"Why, are you planning to join us? You look equal to the demands of the job, madame, but appearances can be deceptive. A strong physique isn't enough—you must have experience. Do you qualify?"

Marie-Antoinette's negligee fell open as she slumped onto the sofa.

"So it's true!" gasped the *Frau Doktor*. "This *is* a brothel. I've seen it for myself at last!"

"It's all aboveboard," Neumann ventured from the door. "These premises are rented privately, so they don't come under direct military supervision."

Frau Dr. Werner-Weilheim turned on him. "Hold your tongue, you unutterable little man!"

"*Va-t'en, mon petit Neumann*," Marie-Antoinette told him kindly. "Go and take a look at Margot. The poor girl is having sanitary problems. She approaches her work with a little too much enthusiasm—something which might be said of this entire battery."

The corporal vanished, and Marie-Antoinette bent a coaxing eye on the *Frau Doktor*. "We women should never allow ourselves to become overemotional, madame. Worry spoils a girl's looks, and no man is worth that." She patted the sofa. "Why not sit down? I should be happy to enlighten you on a few things if you like."

The *Frau Doktor* stood rooted to the spot. "So you admit it?"

"Admit what?" asked Marie-Antoinette, smiling.

"That you . . . that you do what you do?"

"*Mon Dieu, madame*, I'm only a woman who does her duty. Can you say the same?"

"I," the *Frau Doktor* said ponderously, "am a representative of German womanhood."

"*Eh bien?* Are you telling me that things are different in

Germany? What could be more international than the job I do, whether free-lance or under contract?"

"I'm concerned with moral principles."

"Ah! There my comprehension fails me—is that bad?"

A bombardier adorned with the Iron Cross Second Class emerged from the rear of the premises and crossed the room. Just inside the door he paused, checked his fly, and saluted. "That was terrific!" he announced.

"*Pas de quoi*," Marie-Antoinette said amiably. "You're welcome. Till next time."

"Aren't you ashamed?" demanded the *Frau Doktor*.

"Should I be?" Marie-Antoinette gave a tinkling laugh. "Are you ashamed afterward? If so, madame, you have my profoundest sympathy."

Frau Dr. Werner-Weilheim fought to preserve her remaining shreds of composure. "The situation is infinitely worse than I thought—a mounting tide of debauchery. Nothing could be more un-German!"

At that moment Sergeant Forstmann, too, appeared from the back, looking unusually relaxed and cheerful. He did not seem in the least surprised to see Frau Dr. Werner-Weilheim on the premises. Instead, he gave her a friendly nod and said brightly, "You see, *Frau Doktor?* This place *is* a tremendous morale booster."

Forstmann bent over Marie-Antoinette and kissed her on both cheeks. "You're all wonderful, especially my little Suzanne. I can't thank you enough."

He turned to the *Frau Doktor* and raised his right arm. "*Heil Hitler!*"

The self-appointed inspector of brothels shook her head when he had gone. "Even Forstmann," she said sadly, "even he. . . ."

Marie-Antoinette gave a Gallic shrug. "He's only a man, madame."

"But don't you ever think of higher things?"

"On the job, you mean?"

Frau Dr. Werner-Weilheim turned away and stared out of the window. "How I pity him," she said, "—not Forstmann, but *him*, surrounded on all sides by abject creatures incapable of grasping his lofty ideas. Only I, perhaps. . . ." She paused. "I shall do whatever is in my power to help him. He deserves it, now more than ever."

Captain Hein stood leaning against the north wall of the great banquet chamber. He was in full uniform except for his cap, belt and silver-gray gloves, which he had removed. His pistol lay nearby on the table, once again covered by a white damask napkin.

He addressed himself to Schubert, who was standing in the center of the room. "Most people would say that today has been a great day for me." He toyed with his Knight's Cross. "And yet, Johannes, I can't help regarding the whole thing as a matter of course. I didn't work for it—I lived for it. You see the difference?"

"I'm trying to, sir."

"You're a willing lad, Johannes, but you've much to learn. You realize that, I suppose?"

"Of course, sir."

"There's method in everything I do. If there weren't, I should automatically deny my right to exist. Why do you think I balance on the sill of the tower chamber and stand there ignoring the drop beneath me, gazing into the far distance—into a future so close I can almost touch it?"

"I don't know, sir, but I'm sure I will soon."

"I hope so." Still with his back to the wall, Hein sidled into the shadows. "Every man who's worth his salt must be able to control himself in any given situation, whatever the outward difficulties. For instance, take the officers' mess of which I was privileged to be a member as a young subaltern. After a heavy night the CO used to draw a chalk line across the carpet and make us walk along it without missing a step. I could pass the test with my eyes shut because, however much I drank, I never lost my self-control. This is the same thing, fundamentally. I can stand poised on a windowsill, ninety or a hundred feet above the ground, without moving a muscle. It's symbolic of the unshakable self-control with which I confront the world—the world we live for."

Gunner Schubert gazed at Hein wide-eyed with admiration. The captain was a great man, strong, handsome and godlike, yet tormented by some nameless melancholy. Again he sought to escape the flickering candlelight by edging into a corner and standing pressed against the wall, a figure demanding sympathy and veneration at the same time. Schubert was ready to give him both.

Hein said to himself, "I had a nursemaid once. She was hired to look after me, teach me the rudiments of writing, do sums with me, sing songs to me, even pray with me. And what did she do instead? She played with me—touched me between the legs. I screamed and pushed her away, shouted at her, denounced her. She was thrown out, sacked. They even charged her with indecently assaulting a minor."

Still wedged in his dark corner at the far end of the room, Hein went on, "Then there was a schoolmistress whose job it was to teach me languages, mainly English. She never liked me, even though I was a good pupil. She treated me like a guttersnipe and had the effrontery to criticize everything I said or wrote. One day I got up from my bench and advanced on her. 'I'm going to kill you,' I shouted, walking slowly and steadily toward her. She fled."

Hein drew a deep breath. "You might interpret that as a youthful will to power—an unquenchable urge to assert myself in the face of all obstacles, an indomitable desire to resist injustice, uphold things of value and tread the path of duty. Note that, Johannes."

"Yes, sir."

"And so I asserted myself," Hein proclaimed.

Schubert knit his brow. "I'm trying to understand, sir, really I am."

"Do you patronize this brothel?" Hein asked suddenly. "Certainly not, sir."

"Are you repelled by things of that sort? Well, are you?" "Yes, yes!"

"Good," said Hein, drawing another deep breath. "Your reaction satisfies me that you're aware of your special qualities, or at least have an instinctive grasp of them. Keep it up, Johannes. Personal cleanliness, personal endeavor, self-control and unbounded faith in those who share the same convictions. Above all, though, a belief that, to exceptional mortals like ourselves, everything in life must have a purpose. Otherwise, my dear boy, why else should we exist?"

Then, in a quiet but incisive voice, he said, "Stand at attention! Turn about! Now touch your toes. Try to rest your palms flat on the floor. That's right. Relax as much as possible. Hold that position until you receive orders to the contrary."

The battery commander regarded his orderly with a smile. There was a hint of relief and liberation in it, even though all that confronted him was the sight of an obediently proffered backside.

"Johannes, my dear boy," Hein said, "we seem to be drawing closer. I wonder if you appreciate how much that means to me."

"Now, you conniving s.o.b., show me just how smart you really are." Krüger had summoned Corporal Bergen for an interview, this time in Softer's storeroom. "The Werner-Weilheim woman has been raising hell—and don't pretend it's news to you."

"Of course not, Sergeant Major." Bergen proved to be remarkably well informed. "The *Frau Doktor* inspected the brothel in person, presumably to collect evidence. Afterward she made notes. It looks like she plans to submit a report—put in a complaint to higher authority."

"And you're tickled pink about it, aren't you?" Krüger eyed Bergen with grim amusement. "Everything's turning out the way you hoped? God Almighty, either you're plain stupid or you're a glutton for punishment."

"I'm neither, Sergeant Major," Bergen assured him. "Being a sheep doesn't appeal to me much, but neither does the prospect of sudden death—especially not when there's so much to live for." He gazed meaningfully at the crates and cartons lining the walls.

"You were over at HQ seeing Lieutenant Seifert-Blanker. What did you tell him?"

"Nothing he wanted to hear."

"You didn't grab the chance to make trouble for us . . . me and the battery commander, I mean?"

"I could have tried but I'm not in the mood for suicide."

"Know something?" Krüger said slowly. "You're a smart bastard—almost in my league. Let's just hope you aren't too smart."

"I'm only trying to fit in. That's the rule around here, isn't it?"

"You catch on quick, Bergen. For instance, it didn't take you long to spot that I had a special reason for seeing you here. I've got something in mind and so have you. When I'm through with you, you're dismissed with my blessing and you can take a few cartons with you. Pick what you like, but don't think you'll get something for nothing—not from me."

"This woman," Bergen said. "She's itching for a show-down. If she submits a report it'll be dynamite. On the other hand, I can make sure it drops in your lap and stays there."

"You're a clown," Krüger said dryly. "At least, you act like one sometimes. I can guess what you've done. You've worked on the Erdmann girl and got her to hand over the professor's mail for forwarding via you. You really think you can lose a written complaint, just like that?"

"It's better than nothing, isn't it?"

"It's idiotic—you ought to know that without being told. I want this problem *settled*, not postponed. Don't waste time on that little secretary, concentrate on the *Frau Doktor*. Have you tried?"

"Yes, but it wasn't any good. I'm not her type."

Krüger's eyes narrowed. "Has she got one?"

"Seems like it," Bergen said cautiously. "One of the girls in the custodian's apartment had a long chat with her. No two ways about it, according to Marie-Antoinette. The *Frau Doktor*'s dying for it, but not with me."

"Who with, then?"

"Well," Bergen said, "I'd put it this way. The lady in question is suffering from a bad case of hero worship—we all know who for. In addition, she seems to be equipped with what some people refer to as baser instincts. From what I've heard, they're focused on somebody else. . . ."

"If you know who it is, for Christ's sake tell me!"

"It's Arm—Sergeant Arm."

Krüger started as if he had been stung. He rose from the cases of cognac on which he had been sitting—they contained some precious bottles of well-matured Salignac—and backed away until brought up short by a stack of cased champagne —Veuve Clicquot Ponsardin 1933, the captain's special reserve. He stared at Bergen with the makings of an astonished grin on his broad face.

"Man!" he said at length. "That's a hot tip—a really hot tip!"

Bergen said nothing. There was nothing more to say. He knew from Tino Hiller that Krüger had gone sour on Arm, apparently because Arm had failed to declare the full takings from his taxi-*cum*-haulage business to Sergeant Moll of the accounts department. What was more, Arm had made a private deal with Softer behind Krüger's back by providing him with a truck for the clandestine transportation of goods to Germany. Still worse, he was suspected of negotiating secretly with German State Railways. No one in Krüger's circle could escape the consequences of such behavior forever.

"So it's Arm," Krüger said promptly, "according to you, that is." Anxious for reassurance, he added, "You really think the *Frau Doktor* will go for him?"

"She'll swallow him whole," Bergen declared. "It isn't as illogical as it seems, Sergeant Major. Nature boys like Sergeant Arm have their own brand of sex appeal, especially for so-called ladies. It's an old old story."

Krüger knew a trump card when he saw one, but he was too shrewd to rush blindly into an alliance with someone like Bergen. He realized Bergen was making an understandable and not ineffective attempt to get revenge. The memory of Arm's circus clearly rankled.

"All right, why not?" Krüger said. "If Arm's in demand he'd better do his duty for the sake of the club. You, Bergen —with my help—are going to show him where it lies. All the same, you'd better come up with some more bright ideas if you don't want to find yourself peeling spuds. Nobody gets free handouts in this outfit—not from me, anyway."

Lieutenant Minder adopted a wheedling tone. "Runge, old pal," he said, "what's the latest?"

Sergeant Runge had been invited—not ordered—to the officers' billet for a private chat, man to man. It opened with a few words of commendation on the subject of Runge's Iron Cross First Class and developed into an appeal for closer cooperation.

"We must get together more often. After all, we both represent the most important end of the battery—the sharp end, so to speak—you on the predictor and me on the guns. I think we ought to work together more closely."

"Against Captain Hein?" Runge demanded stiffly.

"Of course not, what put that idea into your head?" Lieutenant Minder waved an inviting hand at one of the scuffed and drink-stained leather armchairs. "That would be absurd."

"Absurd," Runge agreed. He did not sit down.

"On the other hand," Minder pursued, "we've got to look ahead—consider future developments which can't, in the nature of things, be very far off. Nobody could be more delighted than I am at Captain Hein's latest honor, but it could well mean swift promotion to a higher sphere of responsibility. He'll probably take command of a group somewhere, leaving me to succeed him."

"That could be," said Runge. His tone was uncompromisingly hostile. "Personally, I take my cue from what goes on here and now. From that angle, the setup stinks."

"I don't quite follow."

Runge gazed around him with a look of disdain, fully appreciative of his own merits. He wore the Iron Cross First Class and would soon, Hein had assured him, become an officer. To him, Minder was just another civilian in uniform.

"It stinks of women in here."

"Surely you don't object to women?"

"Not in general. Only when official matters are being discussed. Then I do."

"But my dear chap!" Minder tried a comradely wink. "It can't have escaped you that I occasionally entertain female visitors. I'm only human."

"There's a time and a place for everything," Runge said loftily. "Speaking for myself, I refuse to discuss official matters in the presence of a whore. If Captain Hein knew, he'd blow a gasket."

"My dear Runge, try to see the thing in perspective." Minder looked worried now . . . any reference to Hein was disquieting. "It's only the girl who's been visiting me for the past few weeks—a hairdresser's assistant. I was going to have a short back and sides, if you know what I mean." Another comradely wink. "I've got her cooped up in the bathroom."

"But she can hear us."

"She only speaks French."

"So she says."

"The girl's completely harmless, Runge, believe me. Medium-priced but good at her job. There's no harm in a girl like that, surely?"

"Who can say for certain?" Runge stood in the center of the room, legs planted sturdily apart. "I can't think of a better place for espionage than a house on the edge of a gun position. Someone may be planning an act of sabotage. Walls have ears, Lieutenant. Better get rid of the girl before she overhears something she shouldn't."

"But I can vouch for her, my dear Runge. Quite apart from that, I still haven't. . . . Well, let's say she hasn't quite finished cutting my hair. Why should I pay full price for a job half done?"

"That's your problem, Lieutenant." Runge's lip curled. "Sorry," he said. "Either the girl goes or I do."

"Very well," said Minder, slightly pained but eager to be accommodating. "You're costing me fifty marks."

"Give Softer forty. He'll get you a girl of the same quality and still make twenty marks' commission. He may be a fat slob but he's a good organizer."

Minder did his best to seem amused. He vanished into the room next door. Five minutes later he returned with an ingratiating smile. "I fixed it," he announced.

"Fine," Runge said contentedly. "In that case we can get down to business. You asked me what the latest was. Why bother, when you know the captain as well as I do? There's only one thing he worries about, and that's how to keep us up to scratch."

"But I thought the battery was a hundred percent combat-ready. Isn't it?"

"Two hundred percent," Runge amended. "There's only one thing missing in the captain's opinion, and that's a real solid dose of determination."

"To do what, Sergeant?"

"Something positive."

"Like what?"

"You mean you can't guess?"

"Am I expected to demolish the water tower—is that what you're driving at?"

"Lieutenant," said Runge, "that's a brilliant idea. The water tower blocks our field of fire, so let's flatten it."

"Is that what Captain Hein expects me to do?" Even as he asked the question, Minder knew that he couldn't expect a straight answer. Quickly, he went on, "We'd have to have a pretty plausible reason for doing a thing like that."

"Being prepared is the main thing."

"Prepared for what?"

"Well, for the time when a plausible reason comes along."

"You really think it might?"

"Look, Lieutenant," he said patiently, "just suppose the balloon goes up one of these nights—suppose some saboteurs or subversives shower the gun position with hand grenades or spray it with machine-gun fire. Where would they do it from? Well? You can be pretty certain they'd pick the spot which gave them the best view of the gun position, and that's the water tower. It goes without saying, doesn't it?"

"So you think. . . ."

"I'm not thinking, Lieutenant, I'm simply wondering what I'd do in your place if. . . ."

"But, Sergeant! Are you really suggesting that Captain Hein expects me to destroy the water tower at the first opportunity, irrespective of civilian casualties and regardless of the fact that it's more or less essential to the life of the town?"

"So the town means more to you than the battery's fire-power. . . . Take my advice, Lieutenant. Don't let the captain hear you make a remark like that or you'll be out on your ear. Then you'll never get his job."

* * *

"A private tour of inspection, Professor—with your permission." Captain Hein made this announcement in his best off-duty tone. "A belated visit, if you like. Am I disturbing you?"

"Please consider yourself welcome at any time." Magnus was sitting at his desk surrounded by drawings, plans and models. "It's a pleasure to see you, Captain, even if I'm not in a position to offer you anything remotely comparable with your favorite champagne."

"I took the liberty of solving that problem in advance."

Hein clapped his hands. The door behind him opened and Gunner Schubert entered bearing a tray laden with two glasses and an ice bucket containing a brace of champagne bottles. He deposited it carefully on the professor's desk.

"Splendid!" exclaimed Magnus. His eyes sparkled. "You certainly know how to gladden my heart, Captain. In more ways than one."

Schubert poured some champagne and then, at a nod from Hein which rendered the professor's sanction unnecessary, withdrew to a post near the door.

Karl Ludwig Hein solemnly raised his glass and gazed at Magnus through the pearling bubbles. "To your invaluable work," he intoned, "to the leader of our great nation, and, last but not least, to Charles Louis of Orléans—our duke!"

Magnus drank with evident pleasure, then said softly, "Not so much our duke, Captain, as yours."

Hein's face clouded. "You mean you take exception to some facet of the man's character? Have you unearthed something disagreeable about him?"

"No, no, nothing of that kind—the greatness of Charles Louis as a soldier, a captain of war, is beyond dispute. It's merely that my own research is less concerned with broad historical perspectives, battles and so on, than with detail. I list items, decipher inscriptions, elucidate documents. . . ."

"Professor," Hein said with a trace of indulgence, "we

all have our specific function to fulfill, each in our own sphere. The soldier fights wars, the scholar—among other things—assembles and preserves historical relics, the farmer and industrial worker supply the fighting soldier with food and equipment. Even the executioner has his part to play."

"How true!" Magnus agreed. "You have an unerring grasp of essentials, Captain, that's why I say that the duke, as a military leader, belongs far more to your world than mine."

"But he also represents a link between us, isn't that so?"

"Yes, except that my own function, as I've already said, is restricted to assembling factual material."

"What factual material? Have you shed some new light on the subject?"

The professor beckoned to Hein to join him at his desk, where he pointed to an unrolled drawing. "You know what this sketch represents?"

Hein identified it with ease. "A battle plan." He indicated a number of features with his right forefinger. "An expanse of almost level terrain bisected by a river twenty or thirty feet wide. In the northeast, an isolated hill surmounted by a windmill. Near the latter, a few houses—a small village or hamlet."

"What an eye!" exclaimed Magnus. "You haven't omitted a single detail of importance. This sketch is, in fact, a reconstruction of the Battle of Boursin, otherwise known as the Battle of the Red Mill. The mill and its neighboring houses in the northeast were occupied by the enemy. The duke's forces were deployed to the southwest. Putting yourself in Charles Louis' place for a moment, how would you have attacked?"

"Frontally—head on."

Magnus did not even blink. "Remarkable! Precisely the duke's response. And what would have prompted you to adopt such a course?"

"The defender of that building," Hein said, "a mill di-

rectly overlooking a river, would consider his position unassailable from the southwest. He would take steps to counter an outflanking movement from the north, but only if he
were a trained tactician as opposed to a common or garden
soldier."

"Brilliant!" said the professor. He drained his glass, which
was immediately refilled. "Your thought processes, Captain,
are exactly those of Charles Louis. He acted just as you
would have done in his place."

"That," Hein said simply, "goes without saying."

Magnus fitted his fingertips together. "So the duke attacked with all the troops he could muster, early on the
morning of May 15. He attacked head on without maintain-
ing any form of reserve. He threw in every available man—
staked everything on a single card."

"Naturally. No half measures!"

"By noon he had lost half his force but the crossing was
accomplished. The river ran red with blood, so they say, but
the mounting pile of corpses acted as a bridge. When evening
came, only a few hundred of the duke's men were left alive
—scarcely more than three or four hundred, if we are to believe the chroniclers.

"With the sun setting on his left, Charles Louis rallied his
surviving troops for the last decisive assault. His final in-
spiring call to arms is said to have included the historic
words: 'We all have to go sooner or later—why not now?'
Then his men flung themselves at the mill and the houses,
set them ablaze, and—shortly before midnight—carried the
hill. The remnants of the enemy fled, demoralized and
panic-stricken, stumbling over their own dead in the darkness."

"The old story," Hein observed gravely. "Wounded, dead
and dying, shattered limbs, blood and tears, pain and torment
—the eternal and inevitable price of victory. It never
changes, except that we have the unique good fortune to

know what we're fighting for—even if we die in the process."

"Look over there," called the professor, pointing to a stand in the far corner of the workroom. It was man-sized, draped in a gray dust sheet. Toddling over to it, Magnus grasped the sheet and pulled it off to disclose a voluminous cloak, predominantly purple, with heavy silver embroidery and ermine trimmings.

"The duke's robe," he announced.

"Magnificent!" said Hein, gazing at it spellbound. "Majestic—worthy of the man himself."

"A reconstruction based on old engravings—I had it made for research purposes. The cloth resembles that which was used at the time. The size, cut and color are identical. Unless I'm much mistaken, Captain, the garment would fit you."

"Possibly," Hein replied in a flat voice. He advanced on the cloak with measured tread, stretched out his hands to it, fondled it like a diffident lover, seemed on the verge of burying his enraptured face in its folds.

"I should esteem myself very honored, Captain, if you would consent to accept this robe as a gift to celebrate your acquisition of the Knight's Cross."

"Thank you," said Hein, and it was as if he had clasped the ducal robe in a joyous embrace. "Your generosity warms my heart."

Interim Report No. 5

Information
volunteered by the head of the current affairs department
of a West German television company,
formerly with an army propaganda unit in France.
Name: Frederick Jenserichen.

"They were pretty peculiar times, take it from me, but we tried to make the best of a bad job. You couldn't help seeing the funny side, sometimes, though it was bad policy to laugh in public.

"No, of course we weren't Nazis. We got wise to those jokers early on. We never put out any propaganda, either, even if we did belong to a propaganda company. That was just a name. It didn't mean much, certainly not to us.

"Getting wise to people was a talent you developed in our job —nobody ever conned us! We worked as a team—cameraman, sound technician and driver, with me acting as a sort of director. We shot everything that came in range. Our stuff wasn't bad, either. A lot of people actually raved about it, up to and including the top brass at the Ministry of Propaganda and Public Enlightenment. We produced something like fifty newsreel reports inside five years. That's a record.

"Oh, no, we were too smart to get mixed up in the real thing —crawl along behind tanks or squeeze into fighter cockpits. We were quite happy to leave that to other people. Some of our chaps actually died 'for the fatherland,' but what we wanted to know was, why? For what fatherland, if you please? Hitler's?

"Some assignments were so routine we could have done them blindfolded. Take Captain Hein's investiture. I wouldn't even remember it if there hadn't been a sequel—and, oh boy, what a sequel!

"There was something different about Battery No. 3. What struck me more than anything else was the personality of some of the NCO's—Sergeant Major Krüger, for instance, and a sergeant by the name of Range or Ronge. He put on a show that even brought tears to my eyes, and that's saying something.

"Was I present at the time? What do you mean by perfect authenticity? Authenticity's relative, like everything else, my friend. They told us what they wanted and we delivered the goods. That was our job.

"You can produce anything on film. A battle casualty, for instance. Borrow a man from his unit, roll him in the dust, smear him with engine oil—which looks like congealed blood in black-and-white—and get him to lie down with his legs and

arms doubled up. You want to see a tank blow up? An old
wreck and a can of gasoline will do the trick. A war hero? Just
a matter of pose, background and lighting. You can make a
cow look heroic if you know how."

Explanations
provided by ex-Corporal Neumann
in answer to questions
on the subject of his special sanitary duties.

"It wasn't a brothel or whorehouse at all, gentlemen. There
wasn't a single such establishment in the whole of the German
army—not officially—and that went for Battery No. 3 too.

"It just so happened that we found ourselves burdened with
three French civilians, female. Ladies, mark you, not whores.
They weren't prostitutes but they certainly weren't amateurs
either. It was their contribution to the war effort, and they
made a pretty good job of it.

"Being in charge of the medical section, I handled the whole
operation. Business was strictly controlled. I worked out the
regulations myself and submitted them to Krüger and Softer.
They approved the plan, except that Krüger dressed up the
language a bit. I've taken the liberty of bringing a copy along.

Standing Orders Relating to Private Recreational Activities:
   1. *Premises.* Bailiff's apartment.
   2. *Hours.* 1500 hours to lights out, daily, Sundays
excepted.
   3. *Duration.* Thirty minutes to one hour. Charges vary
accordingly. Extensions may sometimes be obtained by
prior arrangement with the club secretary.
   4. *Bookings.* At least twenty-four hours' notice required,
exceptions by arrangement. Applications must be made
direct to the club secretary, either individually or in groups
not exceeding six. The club secretary will maintain an
appointments book listing time, duration and object of
visit, personal preferences being taken into account where
possible. This list is to be made in duplicate, one copy for

filing at the recreation center, the other for forwarding to the accounts department.

5. *Charges.* The normal tariff is RM10 for thirty minutes, RM20 per full hour. This charge does not cover special activities, which must be prearranged with the hostess on duty and paid for in advance. No complaints can be considered subsequent to the termination of such activities. The total sum due for payment will be noted in duplicate by the club secretary.

6. *Payment.* Payment will normally, though not invariably, be made in cash. Sums outstanding in respect of services rendered will be deducted from next week's pay and remitted direct to the management of the recreation center.

7. *Dispatching procedure.* The visitor, his application having been entered in the appointments book and confirmed by the issue of a voucher, will report to the recreation center not less than five nor more than fifteen minutes before the appointed time.

He will then, in the interests of personal hygiene, be issued with a cake of soap and a clean towel to facilitate the ablution of his private parts. These will undergo further ablution upon completion, when any complaints may be submitted to the club secretary. . . .

"And so on and so forth—pages of the stuff. There was also a set of internal directives for the benefit of club hostesses and their qualified supervisor—*i.e.*, me.

"Regular douching, physical checkups carried out by yours truly, analysis of smears and swabs by a pal of mine at the local field hospital. We didn't overlook a thing. What more could anyone want?

"As for special requests, group activities, et cetera, you had to be flexible. That's just what I was, friend, and Battery No. 3 gave me plenty of scope."

6

To Every Bullet Its Billet

"You're needed," said Krüger, "—urgently."

Sergeant Arm entered the orderly room apprehensively. Krüger waved him into the well-upholstered visitor's chair. Corporal Bergen was standing in the far corner, smiling.

"What's that s.o.b. doing here?" Arm demanded. He was alarmed to note that Krüger looked unwontedly mild, Bergen suspiciously amiable. "I didn't know you employed sewer rats in your orderly room."

Krüger's expression was almost pitying. "If you think I'm losing my grip, Sergeant, forget it. No louse makes his home in my fur for long, whatever his rank. Bergen's only here to act as a sort of witness."

"Against me?" Arm's voice rose a couple of decibels. "Because of my car rental business? He doesn't know a thing—I mean, about accounts and so on. Don't be so suspicious, Krüger. I'll let Sergeant Moll have a complete set of figures —say tomorrow or the day after. Then you'll change your tune!"

"For the moment, Arm, I'm concentrating on something

215

quite different—something just as fishy, but not the way you
think. Better get ready for a shock."

Krüger placed a tumbler in front of the transportation
sergeant and beside it an open but untouched bottle of
brandy. He poured a hefty slug. "Top-quality cognac,
guaranteed fifty years old. The pick of Softer's collection."

"Why do I qualify?"

"Because you'll need courage when you hear what's coming to you."

Krüger held out the tumbler, then nodded to Bergen.

"I've been acting as contact man with the research team,"
Bergen said. "The sergeant major detailed me to keep tabs
on them. Not unnaturally, my main problem has been the
Frau Doktor. She's mad at not being billeted in the bailiff's
apartment—so mad she's about to make real trouble. The
sergeant major says we've got to stop her at all costs."

Arm frowned. "Where do I come into it?"

"You'll soon find out," Krüger told him with a trace of
commiseration. "First, though, I'd get some of that cognac
inside you. Bottoms up!"

Sergeant Arm poured the magnificent old brandy down
his throat without enjoyment. "Christ Almighty," he said,
"what're you driving at?"

Encouraged by a wink from Krüger, Bergen continued.
"The *Frau Doktor* is planning to upset the applecart. In
accordance with Sergeant Major Krüger's instructions, I've
been trying to sidetrack her. For instance, I offered her special rations. Nothing doing. Then I tried to mobilize the professor. Nothing doing there either. I was even prepared, at
Sergeant Major Krüger's suggestion, to offer her my personal services in an intimate capacity."

"Don't make me laugh!" There was relief and amusement
in Arm's hearty guffaw. "Christ, talk about the flea and the
elephant!"

Krüger gave an affirmative nod. "Right first time. You've
put your finger on it."

"Have I?" said Arm. His misgivings flooded back. Refilling his tumbler, he asked, "What's that supposed to mean?" Krüger gave Bergen another nod. "When you get down to basics," Bergen pursued, "the *Frau Doktor*'s more of a woman than most. She's choosy, though. It would take someone pretty exceptional to satisfy her high standards—someone quite out of the ordinary."

"Let me spell it out for you," Krüger cut in. "The *Frau Doktor* can make real trouble for us—each and every one of us. If she ever manages to torpedo what's going on in the bailiff's apartment it'll automatically lead to other big changes in the present setup. Softer's wholesale business could be affected and so could your trucking activities. That's why it's time for the best available man to go into action. Now do you see?"

Arm's expression was a blend of horror and disbelief. "You don't mean me? Not *me*, for Christ's sake?"

"You and nobody else," Krüger assured him warmly. "You're the only man for the job. Isn't that right, Bergen?"

"Definitely," said Bergen.

"You conniving bastard!" Arm turned on Bergen. "What are you aiming to do, shit on me from a height? Try it and I'll scramble your balls with the toe of my boot!"

"Keep your shirt on," Krüger recommended. "Bergen wouldn't be fool enough to shit on either of us—he knows what the upshot would be. I've heard the whole story, Arm, and there's a lot in what he says. Go on, Bergen, tell him the rest."

"I'm only reporting the facts and trying to pick the bones out of them . . . ," Bergen said.

"All right," urged Krüger, "get picking. Don't keep the sergeant in suspense."

Bergen squinted into the middle distance. "Well, the *Frau Doktor* is always pumping me about Battery No. 3 and various people in it. Most of them are worthless, according to her."

"Does that include me?" Krüger was impulsive enough to ask.

"She didn't actually mention you by name," Bergen replied blandly. "On the other hand, she didn't rule you out." He carefully avoided Krüger's angry glare and concentrated on Arm. "I finally discovered that there are only two men in this outfit who rate with the *Frau Doktor*—two men she really admires. One is Captain Hein, her hero. The other is you, Sergeant. You're her idea of a real he-man."

"A he-man, eh?" said Arm, not unflattered. He reached instinctively for his glass, found that it was empty, and refilled it. "Well, why not?" he said, taking a swig and leaning back in his chair. "I've always been a success in bed, specially with the upper classes. I had an honest-to-God countess drooling over me in Poland. Man, did I take care of her little problem! She never wanted the war to end! Then there was this parson's daughter in Trèves, before the French campaign—hovered around me like a bitch in heat. I figure I must have something."

"You have for the *Frau Doktor*," Bergen assured him.

Abruptly, Arm's face fell. "But not her—not that battle-ax!"

"You're underestimating her," Bergen said eagerly. "Don't be put off by appearances. The *Frau Doktor* scorns makeup —at least, she does for the moment. Even the way she speaks is a form of camouflage. I should know—I happened to see her under the shower. Gentlemen, is she well stacked! She's got everything, and all in the right places. Good solid stuff, believe me."

"No kidding?" said Arm. Krüger smiled at him. "And you say she's got a thing about me?"

"She's crazy about you." Unhesitatingly, Bergen went whole hog. He had nothing to lose. If his plan failed he was done for. An encouraging wink from Krüger strengthened his resolve.

"I first got suspicious when she started asking questions

about you, Sergeant—apparently casually, but she didn't fool me. Then I caught her hovering by the window, watching you inspect some vehicles. Soon afterward she asked me for a picture, and I got her a copy of the latest NCO's group photograph. She snipped you out with a pair of scissors. Your picture is in a briefcase right next to her bed, where she can take it out and look at it."

"Fair enough," said Arm, draining another tumblerful of brandy. His expression was almost transfigured. "If that's the case, why should I be backward in coming forward? I'd better take a closer look at her."

"No one's stopping you," Krüger prompted him. "You'll probably get your money's worth," he added quickly. "My guess is, mature ladies with ministerial experience can give quite a performance in the right hands. Besides, you'll be doing the battery a favor and enjoying yourself at the same time."

"No time like the present," Bergen put in, throwing caution to the winds. "Professor Magnus is having dinner with Captain Schmidt in town and I've got a date with his secretary at the Hôtel de France. That leaves the *Frau Doktor* on her lonesome in the conservatory."

"Into battle!" boomed Krüger.

"One little suggestion, Sergeant," Bergen said. "Don't rush things. The *Frau Doktor*'s bound to play hard to get—that's the way it is with her kind. Otherwise they feel humiliated."

"Here goes, then." Arm rose, rather unsteadily. He reached for the almost empty bottle on the desk and Krüger pushed another across to him. Arm stuffed it in his capacious hip pocket.

"Don't say I'm not willing," he mumbled. "But if anyone's playing games with me I'll settle his hash for good."

"Johannes, my dear boy," Captain Hein called in a soft, plaintive voice, "come here. I'm feeling unwell."

Hein was lying on his bed in the rectangular room between

the banquet hall and the tower chamber. He was clad in his underwear only—short pants and a sleeveless vest, both of them as white as a snow drop. Black socks encased his feet. He looked exhausted. His arms lay limp at his sides and his eyes stared fixedly at the crumbling plaster ceiling.

"What can I do for you, sir?"

"Your presence is enough, dear boy." Hein twitched his fingers slightly. "Place your hand on mine."

Schubert did so.

"Not like that!" The captain's voice rang out with sudden, knifelike clarity, but he did not change his position. "Don't squeeze! I won't permit you to do that—not yet. Lightness of touch, sensitivity, delicacy—aim for those."

"I'm trying, sir."

"Without success!" Hein jerked his hand away and was gratified to note the brusque gesture had cut Schubert to the quick. The boy stood there looking pale and unnerved. "Your name is Johannes, isn't it?"

Schubert could only nod.

"I was christened Karl Ludwig, but my mother's pet name for me was Charles." The captain smiled to himself. "My mother has a fondness for France, possibly because she has never been here. For instance, she's totally unaware of the appalling lack of sanitation, even in the castles and palaces of the great. Have you noticed it too, Johannes?"

"No," Schubert said helplessly.

"Some weeks ago I visited that monstrous piece of architectural bombast known as the palace of Versailles. Walking along the corridors, I was struck by some yellowish-green stains on the marble walls. Any idea what they were? No? It's simple! The courtiers used to relieve themselves there because they had nowhere else to go. Just imagine!"

"Couldn't they have gone outside?"

"The corridors of Versailles are long, Johannes, and they would never have dared use the windows. Being drunk, they could have lost their balance and fallen."

Schubert made no comment—nor, seemingly, was he required to do so. The captain had slightly raised his head from
the silk cushion and was staring along the short passage that
led to the tower chamber. The windows were wide open,
revealing a dark-blue curtain of night sky spangled with stars.
"Windows . . . ," murmured Karl Ludwig Hein. "I have a
love of windows—open windows, high windows, gaping
windows like portals of infinity that defy the man of courage
to step through them."

Johannes Schubert gazed at his battery commander with
awe and devotion.

"At cadet school," Hein said, "we had a commandant who
expected us to show unswerving faith in him whatever the
circumstances. One day, for example, we were ordered to
file through every room in the administration building, starting at ground level and ending on the top floor—the second
floor. Kindly note that, Johannes."

"I have, sir."

"In each of the rooms sat an officer who questioned us
individually on some subject or other—personal particulars,
knowledge of regulations, tactics, and so on. One question
only, short, sharp and to the point. In the last room on the
second floor we were confronted by the commandant himself. All he said was: 'Jump out the window.' Well, what
would you have done?"

"I don't know, sir."

"Put it another way, Johannes: What would you have
done if I had been the commandant and you the cadet?
Would you have jumped as instructed?"

"For you, sir? Yes, I think so."

"Bravo, Johannes! Excellent!" Karl Ludwig Hein sank
back on his white silk cushion. "That's how it should be. I
acted just as you would have done. My decision was based on
trust, and on the following line of thought: Either he would
countermand his order in time, or he had provided for my
safety by means of a net or a heap of mattresses. So I jumped

without a moment's hesitation and fell thirty feet—into a net. Faith is all that matters, Johannes. Do you have faith?"
"In you, sir? Yes, absolute faith."
Hein closed his eyes. "Your assurance holds promise of great things." Almost inaudibly, he murmured, "I may have occasion to raise the subject again—soon. You understand?"
"Yes, sir."
"Then come here. Closer—closer still! Put out your right hand and hold it over my heart. As close as you can without actually touching my chest."
This, too, Schubert tried to do. He did so as instructed—lightly, sensitively, tenderly. The captain's heart pulsed regularly, like that of a man whose sleep is free from disturbing dreams.
"This war," Hein continued as if to himself, "—war in general—compels men of my caliber to do things which may appear harsh and exacting to those who don't know us, who lack the smallest inkling of our true nature. Such is the cross I have to bear. I can bear it as long as there is at least one person who understands me, or tries to. You could be that person, Johannes."
"I'm trying, sir. I think I understand already. . . ."
"Keep your hand over my heart—protectively, Johannes. It must seem as if you are stroking the air that vibrates above it. No pressure, no hint of possessiveness—not with me!"
"Of course not, sir."
"As a child," said Hein, "I embraced a pet rabbit and crushed it to death. Later on, a girl almost died in my arms—it was as though I had wanted to assimilate her, absorb her into my own body. Only a few weeks ago, before you joined this unit, I had my arms around a gravely wounded man whose entrails were adhering to my uniform. I clamped my hand over his nose and mouth—this hand, Johannes—until he died. In other words, I suffocated him. I couldn't endure to hear his cries or watch him suffer. It sometimes happens that a man must kill the thing he loves. You understand?"

"Yes!"

"Good." Captain Karl Ludwig Hein rose from his couch like an uncoiled spring and stood erect in his underwear and black socks. "Gunner Schubert," he said, "I promote you to Corporal!"

"*Bon appétit!*" Gunner Wassermann fixed Bergen with a quizzical stare. "Don't overdo it, though. Too much of this rich French food can give you nightmares."

"I won't. I don't like nightmares, so shove off."

Wassermann had cornered Bergen and Elizabeth at their table in the restaurant of the Hôtel de France, just as they were preparing to consume a chicken casserole. He bent down and boldly sniffed the various dishes. Then he dropped into a chair uninvited and pointed to a chicken leg. "I wouldn't refuse that," he said, reaching for it and starting to gnaw.

Elizabeth eyed him with some amusement. "Who are you and what's your claim to fame?"

"Me?" said Wassermann, chewing. "I'm indispensable, that's what."

"But not to us," Bergen told him in a faintly menacing voice.

"That's what you say," Wassermann retorted brightly. "How about the charming young lady?"

Elizabeth smiled at him. "I'm not particularly charming and I'm well out of my teens. Also, if it's of any interest to you, I'm no lady."

Wassermann grinned back at her. "Just my type."

The restaurant was only moderately full. German soldiers sat at six of the twenty tables, most of them in pairs, though Bergen was the only one with a female companion. Another six tables were occupied by elderly French diners, a rather morose-looking bunch who ate and drank in comparative silence. A blank-faced waiter hovered in the background.

Bergen whipped his plate out of range just as Wassermann

made another assault on it. "Why not concentrate on some-one else—Schmidt's clerk, for instance. He's over there in the corner."

"Waste of time," Wassermann said tersely. He fetched himself a glass from the next table and filled it from the bottle beside Bergen, which contained a dry but full-bodied Fleurie the color of fresh blood. "We can forget about him —Monsieur Charles Schmidt has thrown in the sponge. When he isn't stuffing his guts—like now, with the professor —he sticks pins in a model of Captain Hein and prays."

"What about Magnus? Is he working on Schmidt?"

"And how!" Wassermann managed to purloin another piece from Bergen's plate, this time a wing. "Magnus is taking Schmidt for all he can get—regional specialties, vintage champagne and old brandy. He doesn't seem to have any other ambitions."

"He hasn't," Elizabeth said lightly. "I know him pretty well. He likes his little pleasures but he doesn't like exerting himself."

"Really?" Wassermann leered at her. "Are you speaking from personal experience?"

Bergen leaned forward. "You say Schmidt spends his time praying. Any idea what he prays for?"

"Salvation, probably. And the safety of his municipal water tower."

"Why that?"

"I managed to feed him the idea via his chief clerk. It isn't so improbable, either. Only this afternoon I was over at the gun position, watching that fire-eater Runge. He glared in the direction of the water tower and said something like, 'It'll have to go—in the way—spoils our field of fire.'"

"Sounds plausible," Bergen said thoughtfully. He pushed his plate toward Wassermann. "Help yourself."

Wassermann did so. With extreme deliberation he picked out the best piece of meat, an inch-thick slice of breast.

Elizabeth raised her eyebrows. "Is he always like this?"
"No," said Bergen, "not always, thank God. It doesn't
happen very often in our outfit, but oftener with him than
most."
"It's like I told you," Wassermann said, still chewing. "I'm
indispensable, and that gives me an itch to find out whether
other people are expendable."
"Is Bert indispensable too?" Elizabeth asked in a mildly
teasing tone.
"No idea," said Wassermann.
"How do you plan to find out?" Elizabeth paused. "So
you don't know that either. What about you, Bert—dead
silence from you too?"
"For the moment," Bergen said dismissively. "Give me a
little time and I may show you."
"Think of something," Wassermann urged him, reaching
for the Fleurie, "and be quick about it. We don't have much
time. Or are you hoping for a miracle—you of all people?"

"Here I am at last!" Sergeant Arm announced, flourishing
his bottle of brandy. "The answer to a maiden's prayer."
"You!" the *Frau Doktor* exclaimed shrilly. She recoiled.
"What do you want?"
Arm advanced on her. "Nothing that isn't there for the
taking." He loomed over her, his breath reeking of brandy.
Frau Dr. Werner-Weilheim was sitting in the conservatory
workroom, wrapped in nocturnal solitude, fully dressed
but with skirt hitched up and blouse unbuttoned against the
warmth of the balmy summer night. She had been sorting
through notes and sketches in an attempt to compile a sort
of inventory, but the heat made it hard to concentrate. She
lifted the hand that had been resting on her thigh and placed
it on the table. Arm deposited his bottle beside it.
"I asked you once before," she said sternly. "What do you
want?"

"Nothing you don't want yourself."

"And what," she said in an exasperated voice, "is that supposed to mean?"

"Come off it, darling!" Arm produced two tumblers from his trouser pockets and slopped some cognac into them. One of them he pushed toward her and the other he drained. She stared at him for some seconds, utterly mystified. Arm gave her an encouraging nod. "After all, I'm a man and you're a woman—a whole lot of woman at that."

"What?" The *Frau Doktor* leaped to her feet so energetically that her chair went flying. "You can't be normal!"

"Depends what you mean, sweetheart." Arm perched on the desk and grinned drunkenly at her. "I like my fun. You mightn't think so to look at me, but it's true. And as for normal . . . I'm normal enough in my own way, not that I've any objection to doing it upside down in a hammock if that's what a lady wants, so if you've got any kinky requests. . . ."

"You swine!" gasped the *Frau Doktor*, shrinking back against the wall. "You unutterable pig!"

"Pigs are good at it, darling. So am I."

"How dare you flaunt your sexual prowess at me!" she hissed. "You're mad if you think I'm interested. I know your kind!"

"Not well enough, from the sound of it. What puzzles me is why not. Now that I take a closer look at you. . . ."

"Keep your filthy paws off me! Not an inch nearer or I'll scream!"

"If it gives you a kick, sweetie pie, scream your head off." Fueled with alcohol, Arm was thoroughly enjoying the situation. "Don't worry, no one'll hear you. We're all alone, just the two of us."

She gave a groan. "Do you intend to rape me?"

"Why, do you like the idea?" Arm took a fortifying swig, this time straight from the bottle. "All right, if you insist. At least it'll be a new experience. To be honest, rape isn't really my specialty. Generally speaking I'm more in favor of combined operations—pulling together, if you like."

"Get out, you boor!" spluttered the *Frau Doktor*. "What do you take me for? I wouldn't stoop so low!"

"Don't underestimate me, darling." Arm's face clouded briefly as he surveyed the ample figure plastered against the wooden partition. "I've got class, in case you didn't know. You wouldn't be the first to find out. There was a countess, and a parson's daughter, and the wife of the garrison commander back home in Germany. Like me to produce some references? No, better find out for yourself."

The *Frau Doktor* stared at him, trying desperately to quell the sudden flicker of desire that had set her body trembling. She stared first at his sinewy face with its air of all-conquering assurance, then at his chest, which bulged like a gorilla's, and finally at his tight-fitting trousers. "I despise you!" she hissed.

"Said the actress to the bishop as she lay down and spread her legs." Arm smiled broadly. "Don't worry, darling, I'm well hung. Let's get down to business."

He slid off the desk, picked up the full glass of cognac and lurched toward her. He stood over her without touching her. A moment later he put out his left hand and lightly spanned her throat with his fingers. They glided up to her chin and fondled it. She felt completely paralyzed.

Using his right hand, Arm put the glass to her lips, which opened mechanically. Cognac flowed into her. The *Frau Doktor* drank with face flushed and eyes closed. She choked, gagged, and went on drinking.

"You revolt me!" she said hoarsely, pressing against him. The empty glass fell to the floor and smashed. "I detest you!"

Her legs thrashed wildly as he picked her up bodily, clasped her to his broad chest and dragged her with him to the desk where the plans and drawings of the church lay scattered. He threw her onto it and himself on top of her,

sought her mouth, found it and forced it open, simultaneously kneading her thighs. She clamped them together in a
desperate show of resistance which soon subsided.

"No, no!" she cried, writhing beneath him and clawing
his back. She arched her body against him, but only succeeded in adopting a more convenient position. "No, no!"

"Yes, yes!" he said.

"You mustn't," she moaned. She lapsed into his urgent
rhythm, wound her arms and legs around the body on top of
her. "No, not that!" Her fingers buried themselves in his
tunic. Her accusing cries dwindled and were succeeded by
jerky sighs. "I didn't want you to," she gasped.

"Like hell you didn't!" roared Arm, and came.

He rolled off but lay close to her on the desk, his hands
continuing to roam her body. She snuggled against him.
The desk threatened to collapse beneath their combined
weight as she straddled him.

"You see," Arm said, gratified. "You enjoyed it."

"Yes, yes!" she agreed in a rapturous whisper.

"I told you so," he said, reaching for her again. "You're
quite something yourself. . . . Shall I carry on?"

"To all eternity!" she moaned. Inhaled deeply, then added,
"We've found each other at last. This is a momentous hour!"

Professor Magnus was tottering a little as he left the
Hôtel de France. Captain Schmidt escorted him to the entrance, where the two men said a cordial and noisy farewell.

"It was a great pleasure, Professor."

"The pleasure was all mine," Magnus declared. "A delightful evening, truly delightful."

"That's *la belle France* for you." Schmidt shook the professor's hand for the third time. "I trust you'll join me again
before long."

"Far be it from me to disappoint you, Captain Schmidt
—by all means let's meet again."

Magnus walked off, chuckling to himself. He sauntered unsteadily along the Rue Saint-Martin in the direction of the château. Then he paused and looked up, deep in thought, at the church silhouetted darkly against the night sky. A light was still burning in the tower.

"Yes, that's *la belle France* for you," said a voice behind him.

Magnus spun around. "Oh, it's you, Bergen." He gave a brief chuckle. "Aren't you taking your duties a trifle too seriously?"

"I don't want to lose you," Bergen said. "I might miss a lot of fun if I did. That's why you're under escort."

"Escort or surveillance—call it what you will, young man. All that interests me is, on whose orders?"

"Why ask?" Bergen strolled placidly along beside the professor. "A man doesn't always have to wait for an order before he does something, does he? You should know the answer to that one."

Magnus paused for a moment as though to catch his breath. Their route led uphill now. "Is that meant to be a warning, Bergen?"

"On the contrary, Professor. I'm prodding you."

"To do what?"

"A thorough job."

"In what respect?"

"Come on, you've a pretty shrewd idea what goes on here. This place is suffering from an epidemic of megalomania, and you know it. The master race is drunk with victory. The results could be catastrophic—in fact they're bad enough as is. Men have died here for no good reason. I've been watching you. To judge by some of your reactions, you're prepared to do something about it. Okay, I'll help you assemble the evidence you need."

"You're expecting a great deal, my friend. You're also very young, not that I envy your youth. In thirty years'

time you may understand me, but not before. Who knows?
Perhaps you'll even remember me as a courageous man."

"Courageous? Because you've recognized that chromium-
plated neo-Teutonic werewolf in the tower for what he is?
Because you've poked fun at him? Is that what you call
courage?"

"It's positively foolhardy by present-day standards," said
Magnus. "Fun too, of course."

"You mean you don't intend to take direct action? Not
even if I produce a mass of evidence? Not even if the *Frau
Doktor* gives you covering fire, backed up by Elizabeth
Erdmann? What about the so-called dictates of conscience,
Professor, or is that animal extinct too?"

The professor called another halt. He was panting now,
doubtless because of the gradient and his recent intake of
alcohol. He put out a tremulous hand and gripped Bergen's
arm, hard.

"Don't talk to me about those women! The girl has
neither wit nor morals—not that I begrudge her their lack.
The *Frau Doktor* displays her own version of both, but not
consistently. Given half a chance, even she kicks over the
traces. They say she actually copulated with her *Reichsleiter*
just behind the Führer's back, during a Party Day film
show."

"You make her sound quite human. A promising sign,
wouldn't you say?"

"Promising?" Magnus breathed heavily. "You find it
promising that human beings should behave like animals at
the first opportunity?"

"It may not be promising, but it does present a challenge
—at least to those who haven't entirely forgotten what a
conscience is, or could be."

"My dear young man, what's all this poppycock about
conscience? Anyone would think you were born yesterday.
But then, so was I in some ways. I fought in the fourteen-

eighteen war and even wrote a book about it. Remarque wrote a better one, but its message was much the same as mine. During the Weimar Republic I was all for reconciliation and international amity, human rights, democracy and brotherhood, world peace—you name it, I supported it. They were going to make me vice-chancellor of a university and give me an honorary American doctorate. Then Adolf Hitler came along. His henchmen arrested me and beat me up—a process they referred to as appealing to my conscience. Finally, out of the goodness of their hearts, they relegated me to an academic backwater."

"And now," Bergen cut in, "you're a broken reed. You don't want to know any more. You suffer from ulcers and shortness of breath. You let yourself be terrorized by a woman like the *Frau Doktor* and end by licking the boots of a man like Captain Hein, who enjoys that sort of thing."

"No, never that!" Magnus exclaimed. He sounded suddenly sober. He recoiled a step, then another. The moon illuminated his face—it was ashen pale. "You can't accuse me of that. I abominate the man!"

"But he tickles your sense of humor too," Bergen said. "A couple of laughs—that's all you want out of life, isn't it? They thrashed you like a dog and you can't believe you're capable of showing your teeth effectively anymore. You can, though. You can expose the man and get rid of him, with my help. It'll take two of us. One person's unsupported evidence would never be enough."

"You speak as though we live in a sane, well-ordered world. Even among the advanced civilizations, mass murderers can pass themselves off as statesmen and get away with it." The professor continued to trudge uphill, wheezing. "As for us, my dear boy, we're caught in a spider web of injustice, enmeshed by the laws currently in force. What's more, we're living in what has officially been proclaimed a heroic age. What do you propose to do about that?"

"I see," Bergen said implacably. "So when it comes down to it you're just a tired old man. You've given up. A little cynicism, a little veiled sarcasm—that's all you're capable of."

"What about you?" The professor's tone was indulgent. "An inexperienced young man with a streak of incorrigible idealism. And yet, my boy, we're two of a kind—first cousins once removed, if only you knew."

"I despise weaklings!" Bergen spat out the words provocatively. "I despise people who are too tired and apathetic to act. A man like Hitler could never have existed, let alone come to power, if it hadn't been for cultured, refined, sophisticated individuals like you, Professor. And when, with some distaste but little hesitation, you kissed his feet, he booted you in the face."

"How splendidly self-assured you are!" Magnus might have been talking to himself. Raising his voice, he went on: "However, let's wait and see who accomplishes more, you in your way or I in mine. Who knows, you could be in for a big surprise."

Minor escalation

Captain Hein and Sergeant Runge.
Place: a track bordering the gun position.
Time: one morning on a sunny day in early autumn.

HEIN: Sergeant, I'm extremely displeased. The efficiency of this battery is going downhill fast. Morale has hit rock bottom. Have you given any thought to what I said about methods of improving our combat readiness?

RUNGE: Yes, sir. I suggest a night exercise. A mock attack on the gun position carried out with live ammunition. Staged and performed by me personally.

HEIN: Excellent, excellent! Precisely in line with my own thinking and just what I hoped you'd say. The creation of a realistic battle situation! Of course, I could never officially propose such a plan or order you to carry it out.

RUNGE: That goes without saying, sir.

HEIN: I was right about you, Sergeant—you're born officer material. Carry on, and let me see some results as soon as you can.

Sergeant Runge and Lieutenant Minder.
Place: the officers' billet overlooking the gun position.
Time: fifteen minutes later.

RUNGE (*confidentially*): It won't be long now.

MINDER (*with characteristic caution*): What won't be?

RUNGE: We can expect an attack on the gun position any time—maybe tonight, even. It looks ninety-nine percent certain.

MINDER: An attack, did you say? Who?

RUNGE: Well, saboteurs or something similar. We'd better be ready for them when they come. Just to be on the safe side, what about drawing up a list of likely targets— places the enemy would be bound to use? Take the water tower. We could knock that down to begin with.

MINDER: With Captain Hein's blessing?

RUNGE: Better ask him yourself if you think it's advisable, but I know what he'll say in advance. He'll tell you to use your own initiative.

MINDER (*eagerly*): I'm prepared to, but how?

Second Lieutenant Helmreich and Corporal Bergen.
Place: Battery HQ. The communications center in the château cellars.
Time: an hour later.

HELMREICH: It isn't that I'm trying to talk you into any-thing, Bergen, but. . . .

BERGEN: Don't mind me, Lieutenant. Keep trying.

HELMREICH: I'm not asking you to divulge confidential information. I'd simply appreciate a little chat. To be quite honest, I'm worried.

BERGEN: That's understandable. We've all got reason to be worried, Lieutenant. Anything special?

HELMREICH: There's a move afoot to destroy the water tower. Ostensible reason: the possibility of an attack on the gun position by saboteurs. In the very near future, too. Do you know any details? Have you heard anything—overheard, I mean? Any phone calls on the subject?

BERGEN (*cautiously*): There may have been.

HELMRICH (*extremely confidential*): You see, it's like this. If we knock down the water tower we're bound to upset the town and the town commandant. If we don't, we may have trouble with Captain Hein. And that, in my book, adds up to a very awkward situation.

BERGEN: I see your problem, Lieutenant, but there are ways around it. For instance, if it really became necessary to knock something down, I'd locate the source of the attack and plaster it good and proper. It wouldn't necessarily be the water tower, either.

HELMREICH (*urgently*): Bergen, do you know something definite or are you stringing me along? I have to know —there may be lives at stake.

BERGEN: That's nothing new in this place, Lieutenant, or hadn't you noticed? Corpses seem to be an integral part of the scene. They have to be the right ones, of course.

Ex-Gunner, now Corporal, Schubert and Corporal Bergen.
Place: the canteen, temporarily made available for use as a junior ranks' dining hall and recreation room.
Time: the midday break.

Lunch consists of pea soup and smoked bacon, a filling repast normally reserved for days when action is imminent.

Thickly coated with grease, the soup is being spooned up in almost unbroken silence. A half liter of red wine per man stands nearby.

Bergen and Schubert are seated next to each other, apparently by chance. Choosing a secluded corner, Bergen has kept the place beside him free until Schubert's arrival. Now they are lunching elbow to elbow.

SCHUBERT (*after a lengthy silence, almost choking with embarrassment*): Can I be frank with you?

BERGEN (*dryly*): If you insist, who am I to stop you?

SCHUBERT: I'd like to ask you something.

BERGEN: Carry on.

SCHUBERT (*intensely*): Is it bad to love someone?

BERGEN: Not necessarily. It can be sometimes, though—very bad. It all depends.

SCHUBERT: Perhaps love isn't the right word. Perhaps I mean devotion.

BERGEN: To Captain Hein?

SCHUBERT: Yes. Do you think it's awful?

BERGEN: Not at all—not if the feeling's genuine on both sides. I don't begrudge anyone anything, least of all you. If you like someone you like to see them happy.

SCHUBERT (*confidingly*): I'm not unhappy, Bert, believe me. I'm a little confused sometimes, but only because I'm so happy. Everything will work itself out in time. We're still getting to know each other.

BERGEN: If that means it's all talk and no action, glad to hear it. Perhaps that's as far as you'll get. Anyway, what do you discuss apart from your emotions? Heard anything about the water tower and when it's due to be clobbered?

SCHUBERT: I don't pay any attention to that sort of thing.

BERGEN: You ought to.

SCHUBERT: No, really, Bert. We only talk about big things— human relationships and so on.

BERGEN: Oh, sure, why not, except that everyone has his own ideas on the subject of humanity. Let's play at being human, said the wolf to the lamb as he tore it limb from limb.

Corporal Bergen and Elizabeth Erdmann.
Place: the conservatory workroom.
Time: early afternoon.

ELIZABETH (*expertly patting her hair and clothing into place*): You were a mile off just now. What's eating you?

BERGEN: You're still eager to get hold of that picture, aren't you—the one that's supposed to be a Fragonard?

ELIZABETH (*hopefully*): Why, planning to make me a present of it?

BERGEN: I don't give presents, you ought to know that by now.

ELIZABETH: All right, so you expect something in return.

BERGEN: Maybe.

ELIZABETH: You've had just about everything I have to offer. What more do you want?

BERGEN: You know Johannes Schubert?

ELIZABETH (*casually*): By sight. I've bumped into him a couple of times since Hein's dinner party. Attractive-looking boy, even if he is wet behind the ears. Why, do you want me to teach him the facts of life? He looks pretty feeble to me. You really think I could do something with him?

BERGEN: Perhaps. You might even earn yourself a Fragonard.

ELIZABETH: Is that a firm offer?

BERGEN: Firm as you'll ever get.

ELIZABETH: Any strings attached?

BERGEN: Johannes is my friend, Elizabeth. He doesn't realize it, exactly, but he seems to like the idea of a normal friendship without knowing what it really entails. And that, sweetheart, is my problem and your assignment.

ELIZABETH: What do you want me to do with him?

BERGEN: Just this, to begin with. Take an interest in him. Try and adapt yourself to him—he badly needs some female companionship. I'll make sure you get the opportunity.

ELIZABETH: But what am I supposed to do, exactly—take him by the hand and make a man of him?

BERGEN: Man or mouse, one of the two. All I want to know for the moment is, can he or can't he? I'm getting curious, and it's worth something to me to find out.

Corporal Bergen and Sergeant Major Krüger.
Place: the orderly room.
Time: late afternoon of the same day.

Krüger is ensconced behind his desk. Bergen clicks his heels and receives permission to approach.

KRÜGER (*grinning broadly*): Know what you remind me of? Someone who browns his pants the whole time and blames the smell on other people. Who are you trying to impress?

BERGEN: I don't know what people have been saying about me, Sergeant Major, but if you want my verdict on the latest developments in this place, here it is: The way things are shaping, someone could get killed.

KRÜGER: Killed? We're at war, man! Plenty of people get killed in wars and so could you. So if you've got any information for me, spit it out. If not, stop hinting that you have. And remember this: If you do know something and keep quiet about it, and I find out you have, I'll jump on you so hard your brains will pop out your asshole like toothpaste. All right, man, what's it all about? Let's have it.

BERGEN: If I were you, Sergeant Major, I'd relieve Schubert

of his duties with Captain Hein immediately. Then I'd
send Sergeant Runge on leave, preferably today. Sergeant Arm too.

KRÜGER (*after a lengthy pause, hoarsely but striving to keep
his voice down*): Either you know a damn sight too
much, you s.o.b., or you've got an overactive imagination. You could be in trouble either way. Man, if anyone's ripe for leave, you are!

"How did he die?" asked Captain Hein. "In battle?"

"No," Professor Magnus replied. He sounded regretful,
but the trace of hesitancy in his voice left room for hope.
"He wasn't killed in battle, though he was gravely wounded
on three occasions. In the right arm, to begin with, not that
it made much difference to him because he was partly left-
handed."

"Really?" Hein exclaimed, pleasantly surprised. "So am I.
I generally use my left hand when dressing, also for shaving
and turning the pages of a book—when I have time to read
one."

"What a coincidence!" Hein and the professor, comfortably installed in the banquet chamber, were already on
their third bottle. "Charles Louis' sword arm was his left, so
the injury to his right arm didn't affect him unduly. However, he also sustained internal injuries in the lower part of
the body when his horse was shot from under him. The
beast rolled on him in its death throes. His sexual powers
were almost totally destroyed, but I don't suppose he minded
much."

"Why should he have?" said Hein. "Men who are dedi-
cated heart and soul to a life of heroic endeavor need no
distractions of that sort. They're ruled by one thing only—a
striving for supreme soldierly perfection."

"I've no doubt you're right." Magnus hunched in his big
chair, staring at the empty champagne glass in front of him.

"In fact, you seem to have hit on the logical explanation. The duke's third wound would appear to confirm this. It was a head injury, probably inflicted with a blunt instrument. I'll show you the duke's helmet sometime, if I may. There's a deep depression just above the left temple, also two perforations little more than the size of a pea. Any ordinary man would have died, but Charles Louis paid little heed."

"Because he considered it beneath him to do otherwise!"

"Certainly—you could put it that way. He fought on regardless of his grave injury, and won the day. When they set up his banner, he collapsed. He plunged into the thick of the fray some minutes later, only to collapse once more, dazed by agonizing pains in the head. After the battle they brought him to the place where his ancestors traditionally retired to die—this château. He sat here for weeks, sinking slowly but refusing to accept the inevitable."

"Where did he spend his last days?"

"In the tower chamber—that much seems certain."

"But where exactly?"

"In the precise center of the room. At least, one assumes so."

"Follow me, please," Hein said solemnly, and rose.

Magnus rose too. Feeling the need to fortify himself, he refilled his glass and drained it hurriedly before tottering after the captain. They crossed the square bedroom, walked along the narrow whitewashed passage and ascended the steps to the tower chamber.

Here Hein paused in front of a high-backed chair which dominated the center of the room. The four lofty windows, one for each cardinal point, seemed to stare deep into the starry night. "From here," Hein said, "a man could feel he overlooked the universe—that the world lay at his feet. The same thought must have occurred to Charles Louis."

"Everything points in that direction." Magnus ambled slowly around the central chair, where Hein now sat enthroned. "I've never seen this room before, but it's almost exactly as I imagined it."

"I'm not surprised," Hein said, sinking back with his eyes closed. "The chair and its setting are worthy of the man himself."

Magnus nodded. "The north window symbolized his prospects of total victory. It faced Paris, where the kings of the time resided, rulers by birthright but infinitely less deserving of supreme power than our duke. In the east, three hundred feet or more below him, lay the town—the domain of the underling. It is still there."

"You echo my own thoughts, Professor."

"In the west, the church—final resting place of his ancestors, its tower like a finger raised in admonition, indicating the path of duty. Seated here in his chair, the duke must have been aware of this symbolism. It also appears that he came to believe in the higher purpose of death—his death and that of his ancestors. Seeking fresh reserves of strength, he gazed southward, through the fourth window."

"Toward the present site of our gun position, you mean?"

"What met his dimming eyes in those days was an expanse of meadow, pasture and forest, rolling hills and winding valleys. No doubt he saw in them the great battlefield of nature, for he recognized the inevitability of the endless struggle to which every mortal creature has been destined by the universal spirit. He died as he had lived, with the composure proper to a great and gallant man."

"And was carried to his tomb from here?"

"To be absolutely precise—no, not straight to his tomb." Magnus leaned on the back of the ducal chair. "It's probable that they first conveyed his body to the château cellars."

"Whatever they did," said Hein, "we can no doubt assume that they did it with due reverence."

"I'm sure we can." Magnus walked to the west window and beckoned to Hein to join him. "Down there at the entrance to the château, almost exactly where your car now stands, Captain, they set up a tent of the size and shape favored by contemporary generals when encamped with their armies. This one was of heavy black velvet."

"And Charles Louis lay in state beneath it?"

"Perhaps it would be more apt to say his coffin did. The casket was already closed and the duke's sword lay on top of it. Whether he himself reposed inside I do not know—not yet, but I'm determined to plumb the mystery surrounding his death. I trust that I can count on your assistance."

"You can indeed, Professor—to the hilt."

"The coffin appears to have been transferred to the church at midnight on a Saturday—the precise hour and day of his birth. It was carried by eight pallbearers, among them four seasoned commanders of elite regiments—mostly cavalry, one assumes. Behind it, walking alone, came the French king, followed at a distance by the mightiest men in France. No women were permitted to attend."

"No women?"

"On instructions from the duke himself. Seated in that chair—the chair in which he died, scorning a conventional death bed—he summoned his pages and ensigns and dictated every detail of the ceremony. First, the death march from the château to the church, performed by the remnants of his soldiers arrayed in three ranks, flaring torches held high, drums beating out a muffled, insistent, compelling rhythm. Tum ta-ta tum, ta-ta-ta-ta tum."

Hein joined Magnus in a reprise: "Tum ta-ta tum, ta-ta-ta-ta tum!"

They stopped. Abruptly, the stillness of the night exploded. Broad tongues of flame rent the sky.

From the south, where the gun position lay, a rapid series of detonations burst upon their ears.

Sergeant Runge had selected one of the evacuated houses overlooking the gun emplacements as a base of operations for his morale-boosting exercise—one with a balcony, a feature to which he attached special tactical importance.

Here, working unseen under cover of darkness, Runge had deposited twelve hand grenades taken from captured French stocks and a machine gun of British manufacture. He also brought along his own submachine gun and three full magazines.

With the tacit approval of Captain Hein, Runge had set the operation for midnight. A margin of thirty minutes either way was allowed in case of need or expediency, but the sergeant was already in position by 11 P.M.

He began by laying out the grenades in a neat row on the balcony, near the wall. He opened the balcony doors wide, having prudently remembered to oil their hinges on a previous tour of inspection, and wedged them open with some books that had been left behind in the house. Not that he was aware of it, they happened to be by Romain Rolland, that tireless advocate of Franco-German friendship.

Runge's next step was to set up the British machine gun on a table which he had also placed in readiness. He did so deftly and with extreme care. The balcony parapet proved to be conveniently low. The gun position was immediately to his front and well within view.

That done, Runge picked up his loaded submachine gun and left it just inside the door, also open, which led to the landing. He propped it lovingly against the wall and arranged the two spare magazines beside it.

Runge retired to the passage and lit a cigarette, cupping it in the hollow of his hand with the expertise of an old soldier. For the last time, he carefully ran over the essential features of the premises which he had chosen as an operational base and from which he intended to conduct the separate phases of his operation—with live ammunition.

1. The balcony. From here, saboteurs lob grenades at the gun position. Assumption: A skilled grenade thrower with plenty of range is hard to detect.

2. *The room immediately inside the balcony door. From here, saboteurs spray the gun position with machine-gun fire, but only briefly. Muzzle flashes readily detectable by chance observer. Hence, care essential.*
3. *Landing and ground floor of house, garden immediately to rear backing on open countryside. Here, simulated pursuit of enemy executed as a one-man operation. Generous bursts of submachine-gun fire and further use of hand grenades envisaged.*

Having devised this watertight scheme, Runge could hardly wait to put it into effect. He went to the machine gun and voluptuously traversed the field of fire once more, then leaned against the balcony, gazing ruminatively into the night with keen eyes that transformed it into day. A chorus of strangled snores rose from the tents housing the gun crews.

He peered across at the officers' billet, where slivers of subdued light showed through chinks in the blackout. The hairdresser's assistant was probably back at work. Either that, or Minder and Helmreich were drinking the night away.

Runge's eyes turned to the tower. It was brightly lit in defiance of blackout regulations and seemed to shine like a symbol of warning and encouragement combined.

He glanced at his watch for the tenth time. It had luminous figures and a sweep hand and could be used as a stopwatch. There were twenty minutes to go till midnight. Twenty minutes too many.

"Let's go," Runge muttered, squaring his shoulders. He couldn't wait any longer.

The first six grenades, which all exploded within the space of thirty seconds, meant little more to Runge than an entertaining game—albeit a game which only an experienced professional like himself could afford to play. His range was considerable and he threw with almost pinpoint accuracy.

Two grenades he lobbed so that they landed near the predictor but behind it, where they would do least damage.

Two more he placed between Guns 1 and 2, 3 and 4, but at a safe distance from the crew tents and stacked ammunition. The last pair of grenades in the first series exploded in the immediate vicinity of the other ranks' latrine. Pandemonium enveloped the tents of the duty crews, issued from the huts lining the field and spread to the aircraft spotters. "Alert!" they shouted. "Alert! Ground attack in progress!" The babble of cries and whine of sirens was music to Runge's ears.

Then, with gratifying speed, Lieutenant Minder's voice rang out. "Gun position under ground attack!" he bellowed. "Load with armor-piercing and prepare to open fire!"

Sergeant Runge gave an approving nod. Minder was reacting correctly. He really seemed to have done his homework. It was clear he was making preparations to bombard the water tower, as Runge had calculated, thus diverting the battery's firepower from Runge and concentrating it on a more suitable target. The exercise promised to be completely successful.

Runge lobbed his next series of grenades with the dexterity of a master craftsman. Four of them straddled the gun position so as to contain the men who were crawling around inside the perimeter. Two more burst near the officers' billet as a reminder to its occupants to keep on their toes in the future.

Somewhere, someone gave a yelp of pain. Runge smiled grimly as he settled himself behind his machine gun. He emptied the first magazine without a single stoppage, two or three feet above the heads of the human ants swarming across the turf. They ducked and raced for cover or flung themsevles to the ground and tried to burrow their way into it.

Runge enjoyed the spectacle so hugely that he yielded to temptation. He inserted another magazine in his smoothly functioning machine gun—fed it until it was ready to spit death if so required.

And death, in answer to his challenge, spat back.

* * *

Lieutenant Minder, who was prepared for Runge's pyro-technics, reacted with speed and assurance. He had brooded so intensely about the sergeant's veiled hints that he went to bed with his pants on and dreamed constantly of the water tower.

When the moment came, he had only to pull on his boots, grab his uniform tunic and steel helmet, and rush outside. The men of Battery No. 3 resembled nothing so much as a flock of wildly bleating sheep alarmed by wolves. It was just as he expected.

"One man wounded!" someone called.

"Leave him!" he called back. He had a pretty fair idea that the grenades were not being lobbed into the position at random but skillfully distributed around it. That meant there was no immediate danger, which in turn meant that the water tower was fair game.

"Probable source of enemy attack: the water tower!" he announced.

Second Lieutenant Helmreich, steel-helmeted but still in his nightshirt, came pounding up to Minder on the double.

"No, no!" he gasped. "They're attacking from three o'clock, not the water tower. I distinctly saw the muzzle flash of a machine gun in the second house along!"

Minder turned on him. "Shut up, you fool, and get out of the line of fire!" He turned and addressed the gun crews. "Target: water tower. Fire at will! Knock the damned thing down!"

Which they did.

Meanwhile, exploiting every available scrap of cover, Second Lieutenant Helmreich crawled with weasellike speed to one of the light antiaircraft guns.

There he found a gunner waiting despondently for orders. The man stared at Helmreich as he crawled swiftly toward him with his bare buttocks gleaming in the moonlight.

"Why the hell don't you open fire?" Helmreich croaked, panting hard.

"What at, sir? The heavies can deal with the water tower on their own. What's the point of wasting ammo?"

"But the enemy's over on the right, man! Over there in the white house with the big balcony."

"Are you sure?"

"Of course I'm sure!" screamed Helmreich. "Plaster it with all you've got!"

"Your responsibility, sir?"

"My orders, you imbecile! Get those twin barrels trained on the dump and keep firing till it goes up in smoke. Fill it full of holes!"

Which he did.

Captain Hein appeared on the scene two minutes later. Order had been restored and the gun position looked virtually unscathed. "Ground attack repelled, sir," Minder reported. "Water tower destroyed in the process."

"Was that necessary?" Hein inquired smoothly. The moon, which was high now, illumined his face with great clarity. It registered no emotion whatsoever. "But then, I suppose you must have had your reasons."

"It was unavoidable, sir," Minder said. "A large number of hand grenades were lobbed into the gun position, almost certainly from there."

"Any casualties?"

"Two wounded," Minder told him briskly. "One with a couple of splinters in the leg. Second Lieutenant Helmreich has a flesh wound in the left buttock."

"Anything else to report?"

Minder hesitated for a moment. "One man killed, I'm afraid."

"Who?"

"Sergeant Runge. One of our machine gunners shot him up in the second house on the right. Concentrated fire."

"Bring him to me," Hein commanded. His voice vibrated like glass.

Sergeant Runge was placed on a tabletop and borne toward the battery commander by four gunners. They deposited their burden on the ground at Hein's feet, close beside the predictor.

Runge lay there in the combined beams of several flash lamps, a symphony in scarlet. Blood had poured down his face, was adhering to his hands, oozing from his uniform. The bullets had riddled him like a sieve, but his lips seemed to curve in a triumphant smile.

Minder said in a low voice: "Helmreich really couldn't have foreseen this when he opened fire on the house."

Captain Hein went down on his knees. He bent over the sergeant and clasped the lifeless head to his chest. "Runge, my dear Runge," he murmured. "You too, you too. . . ." In a groan, he added: "My God, the things I have to endure!"

Interim Report No. 6

Speculations
on the subject of Frau Dr. Werner-Weilheim,
as seen from widely varying angles.

1. Tino Hiller, former NCO:
"Well, I mean—what am I supposed to say? One day, or rather one night, they clicked. And how!

"No reason why anybody should have been particularly surprised. There are plenty of ill-assorted couples in the world, so why not Arm and the *Frau Doktor?*

"This much I do know: It wasn't long before they became inseparable. They seemed to spend every spare moment together. You'd come across them in the conservatory, or up against a tree in the grounds, or in a truck Arm lined with mattresses. They were even spotted in the church, bedded down between a couple of tombs.

"They were welcome to each other."

2. Elizabeth (née) Erdmann, formerly secretary to Professor Magnus:

"The Werner-Weilheim woman was a real bitch. That wasn't my term for her—it came from Professor Magnus, though he did qualify it. 'A first-class bitch' were his actual words.

"I still find it hard to imagine any man taking an interest in her. She was very fleshy, with a tremendous ass, and she stank of sweat. Some people find that attractive, so I've heard. Butchers, maybe, or stableboys. Sergeant Arm certainly did.

"Apart from that, you've got to remember that demand was far in excess of supply. The three girls in the brothel had their hands full. That fat profiteer Softer kept them working overtime, so you could hardly blame them for turning in substandard performances. There was supposed to be another half dozen girls on the game down in D., also working under contract, but the competition for me was pretty heavy, too. It could have been terrific if I'd wanted it that way.

"I ask you: How could ten or twelve girls cater to a hundred and fifty randy antiaircraft gunners, not to mention the town major's office staff, the guards from two local POW camps, and a lot of youngsters from various infantry units stationed in the vicinity? It was asking too much.

"But about that bitch Werner-Weilheim. The only man who was anything like a match for her was Krüger, the battery sergeant major, so she settled for the next best thing—*i.e.*, Sergeant Arm. She drove him around the bend, not that he was sane in the first place."

3. Alfons Arm, now the proprietor of a gas station at Gelsenkirchen:

"Was I a Casanova? My lips are sealed, friend—after all, it wouldn't be fair to the ladies. How could I help it if they all went for me? One was a very well-educated person—she even knew Hitler to speak to. They said she'd done it with a Nazi big shot, but I doubt it. I had to laugh when I saw his picture. A fat-assed s.o.b., he was, with eyes like a pig. Not a fine figure of a man like me.

"Well, if you really want the truth I don't mind dropping a

few hints. This much I can tell you: Everything went like a bomb—one look, a quick squeeze of the hand, and we were away. Fate, that's what it was. "Was she crazy about me? I should say so! You couldn't blame her. I was something to see in those days. Like one of these pop singers, only with more muscle and less hair. As soon as the lady in question came within arm's reach—if you'll pardon the pun—I said to myself: It can't hurt to have a go. It didn't, either. There's many a good tune played on an old fiddle, and she knew every one in the book.

"It has to be love with me, though, otherwise I don't enjoy it properly. So love it was. What's more, it lasted. Taking her all around, she was quite a woman."

Views on the subject of a hero's death
recorded by Professor Magnus,
first at the age of twenty,
then forty years later.
Taken from jottings found among his personal effects.

At twenty:
"All that matters is to give life the higher meaning which alone can make it worth living. The prime requirement is an absolute readiness to sacrifice oneself—for one's country, family and home, for kaiser and Reich, and, last but not least, for one's fellow men. Good, edifying and noble causes, all of them worth fighting and, if necessary, dying for. Man's capacity for decision, in that respect as in others, is what redeems him from a permanently animal stage of evolution.
"Man—the martyr and warrior!"

Forty years later, immediately prior to the events
described here. Like the foregoing passage, this one
was taken from the professor's personal diary:
"All that matters, I suppose, is to cope with life as best one can and survive for as long as possible. The prime requirement is to insulate oneself quite deliberately against the stupefying opiates dispensed by those in power. Whatever terms they

operate with, whether 'beloved country' or 'sacred fatherland,' 'eternal nationhood' or 'Thousand-Year Reich,' 'kaiser' or 'Führer,' one must bear in mind that none of them is worth dying for.

"We should try to live meaningfully. But for what or whom? For an animal that needs our help? For a child doomed to perish at the hands of his fellow men? For a woman? A book? A tree? I've no idea.

"Man—a reptile from the cradle to the grave. No sooner begotten than he crawls to meet his end. We are born to suffer and die. . . ."

*Assertions
made by ex-Captain Minder,
now managing director of a hotel chain.*

"I wouldn't deny that things happened then which seem pretty incredible today. It's all a question of personal experience. Nobody can give a plausible explanation of what really went on unless he can claim to have been there at the time.

"I can certainly make such a claim.

"It so happens that I succeeded Captain Hein at D. after he met his death in such regrettable circumstances.

"Actually, I as good as took over from him on the night our gun position was attacked. There'd been some gross errors of judgment, but I managed to get a grip on things just in time.

"Whatever reservations I may have had about the late Captain Hein, he was never an out-and-out Nazi. He used current jargon, but so did a lot of people—that doesn't prove a thing. It all depended what you thought, deep down inside. We found a book by Nietzsche among his belongings but nobody ever saw him read it. He occasionally said 'Heil Hitler,' too, but he didn't raise his right hand—or, if he did, waved his glove in a sarcastic sort of way.

"Where that delicate subject was concerned, I adopted much the same policy."

7

Death, Too, Calls for Celebration

"Now we're in real trouble," declared Sergeant Arm. "How are you going to dig us out this time?"

Krüger brushed the question aside. "None of your goddamn business."

"I beg your pardon! The only reason I asked is because the *Frau Doktor* suggested it. She's really worried about Captain Hein."

"None of her goddamn business either."

Krüger seemed wholly unperturbed. He fixed his two early morning visitors, Arm and Softer, with a quizzical eye and sat back in his chair, evidently waiting for something. A minute passed in silence.

At last Softer spoke. "Well," he said cautiously, "does that mean you've had enough of him? Hein's a hot potato. I wouldn't blame you for dropping him."

"If that's a dig at the battery commander," Arm said, turning on the portly quartermaster sergeant, "cut it out!"

"Get stuffed," Softer retorted. "Lucky for you we're pals or I'd really give you a piece of my mind. You keep your brains in your jockstrap, Arm, that's your trouble. What you need is a quick kick in the crotch—it might clear your head." Arm bellowed. "How dare you speak to me like that, you fat bastard! Krüger, tell him to watch his tongue."

"Let him be," Krüger said. "If Softer's got some ideas on the subject I'd like to hear them. Well, Softer?"

"Personally," Softer said, speaking with great deliberation, "I don't give a damn who does what around here, but enough's enough."

"Is that another dig at Captain Hein?" Arm demanded swiftly. "The captain's a gentleman and an officer. We ought to back him all the way. It isn't just me who says that, either. Other people say the same—well-educated people with a lot of clout."

Krüger preserved an unbroken silence but glanced encouragingly at Softer, who said, "As far as I'm concerned you can fuck the *Frau Doktor* for as long as she likes it— permanently, if you like, and welcome—but tell her to keep her nose out of our business."

"Cut it out!" trumpeted Arm. "You're talking about a lady."

"If you say so." Softer shrugged elaborately. "All right, so she's driving you out of your mind—I don't give a fart. It's the possible damage to our setup that worries me."

"Keep on like that," Arm said menacingly, "and I'll knock your teeth down your throat."

"Pull yourself together," Krüger broke in. "We're in a tricky spot. Your spare-time activities have nothing to do with it. All right, Softer, carry on."

"The captain," Softer said, cautiously but still grinning, "may be a hero, and all that. . . ."

"He is!" snapped Arm.

"Watch that loose screw," Softer told him amiably, "it might fall out if you don't keep your trap shut. Okay, if it's any consolation I admit it: The captain's a hero. Plenty of people think so, which means he's got connections. But all the connections in the world won't keep him fireproof forever if soldiers fall out of windows and get shot every other week. It's giving the place a bad name. That's why we've got to protect ourselves."

"By selling him out, you mean?" barked Arm.

"We can't afford to go on this way, Arm. I'd sooner have Minder, even if he is a gutless wonder. At least he'd toe the line. We wouldn't have these problems with him in charge—we could go our own sweet way without any backlash."

"You've got to be joking!" Arm looked horrified. He turned beseechingly to Krüger. "Are you going to stand for this?"

"He's talking sense," Krüger said. "Except that it isn't the whole story."

"Look, Krüger, I'm on your side," Arm proclaimed. "You can count on me all the way—you know that. As for the *Frau Doktor*, she's a hundred percent behind Captain Hein. I figure that gives us something to work on."

"Maybe," Krüger conceded. He seemed to ponder for a moment. "I'm thinking."

"Of a way to get us out of this stinking mess?" Softer's tone was dubious. "It's got to stop sometime, hasn't it?"

"The only thing that matters is the battery—my battery," Krüger said firmly. "If I do save Hein's neck, it'll only be as a final favor to my old pal Siegfried Runge. We did come from the same stable, after all. We both helped put this outfit on the map—in our own way."

Arm and Softer realized that, to Krüger, this was the salient point. They sat there in expectant silence.

Some time passed before Softer said, "You don't think too much has happened already?"

"Like what?"

"Well, Runge's dead and a couple of men wounded. The

general theory is that Runge brought it on himself. With Hein's say-so, if nothing more."

"That's a dirty rumor!" Arm interjected vigorously. "The *Frau Doktor* thinks so too."

"What makes her so sure?" asked Softer. "Anyway, why are you so determined to swallow everything she dishes up? Far be it from me to speak ill of the dead, but last night's performance couldn't have been Runge's personal inspiration. He was too deep in with Hein for that—meaning, of course, he was too good a soldier. Runge never did anything without an insurance policy from higher up."

"There's no proof the captain knew a thing about it," said Arm. "Aren't I right, Krüger?"

"Stop wasting time, the two of you," Krüger told them wearily. "You still haven't caught on, have you? We're all in the same boat, and anybody who jumps gets drowned."

"Good for you!" Arm slapped his thigh. "Well said!"

"What have you dreamed up this time, you bastard?" Softer asked.

Krüger grinned at him. "I've checked through all the available evidence, and here's the picture as I see it. Early last night, saboteurs—probably operating at section strength —systematically infiltrated the edge of the gun position. They laid out a quantity of hand grenades and set up a machine gun. Then they waited, smoking French cigarettes, until the right moment came along, shortly before midnight."

"You really believe that?" Softer asked.

"No," Krüger replied airily, "but what's the difference? It doesn't matter who believes what, just as long as I can produce some solid evidence—which I can. It all adds up, my friends. From their base in the house which was destroyed later on, the saboteurs launched a well-planned attack on our gun position. They lobbed grenades and shot off two magazines of ammo from a British Bren. And that was when our old pal Runge went into action."

Softer registered discreet amusement. "How are you going to prove all this?"

"Easy!" Arm broke in. "It's clear as daylight. Our boys reacted the way they'd been taught by the captain. Ground-defense Plan No. 1: an immediate counterattack, using all available firepower. Runge led the counterattack and bought it in the process, worse luck."

"That's it, more or less," Krüger confirmed without hesitation. "He picked up his tommy gun, which he always kept handy, and charged in the likely direction of the enemy —with a total disregard for personal danger, as they say in the citations. He cornered the saboteurs, exchanged shots with them, and was killed. Not by the enemy, but by a premature burst of covering fire from his own side."

"If anyone's to blame for the poor bastard's death," growled Arm, "it's that stupid Helmreich."

"The question is," Softer said, frowning, "did anyone apart from Runge set eyes on these so-called saboteurs? You'd better find an answer to that one if you want to clear the mess up properly."

"Don't worry," Krüger told him. "I never do things by halves. It so happens I've found a gunner who was out of bounds at the time in question—in other words, he left the battery area without permission because he had a date with some prostitute or other. That was just before the balloon went up. After intensive questioning by me, he'll be able to state on oath that he saw a number of shadowy figures escaping. Half a dozen or so."

"Christ, that's good enough!" Sergeant Arm heaved a sigh of relief. "I must tell the *Frau Doktor* right away. She'll be tickled pink. Everything was on the level after all, so that puts her hero in the clear."

But Softer asked, after Arm had hurried off: "Are you really sure you can pull it off again? I can't help wondering about a couple of things. For instance, can we count on our hero in the tower, and what will Minder write in his report?"

"You got it wrong, chum," Krüger told him simply. "Our hero has to count on me, not the other way around. As for Minder, I'll make sure he knows what to write."

"No less than I expected of you, Sergeant Major." Hein tapped the report which Krüger had jointly drafted with Minder at his behest. "An admirable piece of work."

"So you approve it in every detail, sir?"

"I'm even prepared to endorse it."

"And I can have a free hand if it becomes necessary to make a few internal rearrangements—transfer a couple of men, for instance?"

"Do anything that has to be done, Sergeant Major. You can count on my fullest support."

Captain Hein was standing between the central windows in the banquet chamber. He was in full uniform, his hands sheathed in silver-gray leather, his peaked cap tilted infinitesimally over one eye in a way which lent him an almost daredevil appearance. The uniform sat smooth and tight on his body like a second skin—his real skin.

"Thanks to your exemplary spadework, my dear Krüger," he said, "there seems to be no reason why we shouldn't bury Runge in a fitting manner—no man deserves it more. We'll lay on a modified form of state funeral."

Krüger's jaw dropped. "State funeral?"

"Full military honors, anyway. Catafalque, vigil, funeral procession, volleys at the graveside, et cetera, et cetera. I'll organize it personally, with your assistance."

"Forgive me, sir, but after all that's happened— well, I'd advise against making too much fuss."

"Krüger," Hein said sternly, "you have your sphere of responsibility and I have mine. Kindly leave such things to me. After all, Runge was as much your comrade-in-arms as mine."

"The pick of the bunch," Krüger said promptly. "On the

other hand, knowing him as I did, I don't think he'd have gone for a lot of pomp and ceremony. He'd have preferred a simple, dignified funeral."

"Possibly," said Hein, sounding faintly annoyed. "Under certain circumstances, however, a man can become a symbolic figure. We must take that into account."

"But haven't we kicked up enough dust already?"

"Be so good as to spare me your more vulgar turns of phrase!" Hein put his hands on his hips. "Such remarks are out of place in a situation like this."

"A situation which won't be too easy to handle, sir. One house riddled with machine-gun fire, one municipal water tower destroyed, one man killed and two wounded. We have to find a convincing explanation for all those things and sweep them under the carpet, fast."

"Deal with it!" Hein commanded with mounting displeasure. "You do your part and I'll do mine. First, a plausible explanation for the damaged house—very well, it was shot up during hand-to-hand fighting; second, the demolished water tower—essential if we were to clear our field of fire; third, the two minor casualties—they received prompt medical attention and will be awarded the wound badge in bronze. As for our fallen comrade, I shall take responsibility for him—in fact I insist on doing so without interference from you!"

"Might I inquire exactly what you propose, sir?"

"I've only just begun to work out the details." Hein's gaze seemed to rove across some distant horizon. "To start with, however, his body must be laid out in the church, in front of the altar."

"Impossible!" Krüger blurted out.

"The word 'impossible,'" Hein said sharply, "does not form part of my vocabulary. You should know that."

"I'm sorry, sir. All I meant was, the church is Catholic and Runge was a Lutheran. What's more, he was a staunch nationalist and Socialist, not to say National Socialist. He'd seem out of place, lying there surrounded by French aristocrats."

"Krüger," Hein said, his patience wearing thin, "you seem either unable or unwilling to follow my train of thought. Why?"

"Because I'm a practical man, sir."

"I fully appreciate that, but try for once to comprehend my attitude. Higher values are at stake here, Krüger, timeless and transcendental values such as heroism and the recognition it deserves. You must either grasp that or trust me implicitly, which amounts to the same thing. If you're unable to do either, you're against me. Is that what you're implying?"

"Of course not, sir," said Krüger, but there was a faint note of menace in his voice. "All I care about is my—I mean, our—battery. How to protect its reputation, that's *all* I'm concerned with."

"In defiance of me, if necessary?"

"Never, sir! I can't imagine you doing anything to harm the battery."

Captain Hein leaned against the wall and folded his arms. "I hope, for both our sakes, Krüger, that there'll never be any serious misunderstanding between us. If you should ever feel tempted to withdraw your allegiance from me—not that I can believe you would—the consequences would be simply catastrophic. You understand what I'm trying to say?"

"Not quite."

The captain stared long and hard at his sergeant major. A minute went by. Then he said, "Since you don't seem averse to a discussion of hypothetical differences between us, I'll gladly give you my views on the subject. To repeat, if it has ever occurred to you to make trouble for me. . . ."

"Pardon me, sir, but I never even considered the possibility."

"Just a theory, Krüger—a sort of war game. So you've never even considered it. Very well, but suppose a day came when you did. Suppose you tried to get rid of me. Several methods suggest themselves. Like you, I know them all. What do you think would happen? Would I throw in the sponge—even, to take an extreme case, submit to arrest? Of course not—I should fight like a lion! But even if you succeeded in eliminating me—and I wouldn't put it past you—I should drag you all down to destruction with me. You know what total war means, Krüger. Well, that is precisely what you can expect from me. My end would mean the end of Battery No. 3—my battery and yours."

Krüger did not hesitate for an instant. "Full military honors it is, sir. All the same, the church is out. I suggest we display the body in front of it under a black awning. Softer can produce some material that'll look like velvet. Battery funds will cover the necessary expenses, including black crape armbands for all men on parade. As far as the grave goes, I suggest a choice spot in the grounds—say in the middle of the flower bed bordering the terrace, under that old silver fir."

"Agreed," said Hein. His voice was cool again, as though nothing important had occurred. "I don't propose to bury him without due ceremony, but I'm prepared to accept your recommendations. Attendance will be restricted to what might be described as an intimate circle, limited in number but worthy of the occasion."

"Very good, sir," Krüger said promptly. "Your instructions will be followed to the letter. If you like, I could even arrange for a party of war correspondents and cameramen to attend. They might include it in their next newsreel."

"Why not?" said Hein. "It can't hurt the people on the home front to see how we pay our respects to a fallen comrade."

* * *

"Excuse me, sir," Bergen inquired politely, "but could I speak to the CO?" He was visiting regimental headquarters, ostensibly for the purpose of checking the direct line from Battery No. 3. "It's important. Personal, too."

"Anybody can say that." The orderly officer, a hippopotamus of a man, made a routine gesture of dismissal. "Everyone around here thinks he's vital to the war effort. How come it's personal?"

"My name's Bergen. I'm distantly related to Colonel Rheinemann-Bergen."

The orderly officer belched unashamedly and patted his stomach. "That's different—if it's true. And if you're not too distantly related."

It was true, Bergen assured him. Their relationship was close, if not intimate. The colonel was a sort of uncle. The orderly officer heaved himself to his feet and waddled off.

A few minutes later Bergen found himself face-to-face with the CO. Although deeply embedded in an armchair, Rheinemann-Bergen remained an imposing and paternal figure. He waved Bergen into a chair beside his own.

"Well," he inquired wearily, "and what species of Bergen are you, Corporal?"

"One of the Hamburg Bergens," he was told. "My father's a county court judge."

"Dear old Adolf?" The colonel gave a rather strained laugh. "Fancy toting that name around for the past seven years! I bet he hasn't lived it down yet, eh?"

"Father can't help his name but he finds it embarrassing. He may even find it distressing, for all I know." Bergen eyed the colonel curiously. "Still, I suppose it's a common complaint these days. Plenty of people are suffering through no fault of their own."

The colonel, his attention captured, sat up and pressed a button on the desk at his elbow, staring at his visitor. He looked even more imposing than before. An orderly appeared and was dispatched for a bottle of Château Lafite. The colonel did not speak while the glasses were being filled. Then he raised his own to the corporal. They both drank.

"Well," he said at last, "how's your father faring these days?"

"As well as can be expected."

"So he's still in the land of the living," the colonel observed dryly. "For a man with his political views, that's saying a good deal. Or has he also bowed down before the cross —the crooked cross, I should say? No, I'll wager he hasn't! Tell me, do you take after him?"

"In a lot of ways."

"That's bad, or could be." The colonel smiled sympathetically. "And you're serving in my regiment?"

"In Battery No. 3, Group No. 1."

"Is that why you're here?" The colonel sounded a trifle uneasy. "Well, you certainly belong to the most successful unit in my bunch, if not the whole of Ack-Ack Command."

"You could call it that," Bergen said cautiously. "I'd use a different description myself—if I was asked."

"But I'm not asking you!" exclaimed the colonel. "What's more, I trust you haven't come here in the hope of badgering me into personal comments on the subject of your battery. If you're here to pay a family call, I couldn't be more delighted. Your father and I always got on well in our very different capacities, he as a conscientious public servant, I as a conscientious soldier. Let's drink to old times."

They drank, but Bergen was off again before they had put their glasses down. "Do you really know what's happening in your regiment, Uncle? I hope you don't mind me calling you that, incidentally. If it would ease your mind in any way, I'd be glad to tell you. For instance, have you any idea what goes on in Battery No. 3?"

"Some idea," said the colonel. He sank back with an air of fatigue. "I know as much as I want to know."

"So you're aware of the murderous charade that took place last night?"

"I've just received a detailed memorandum on the subject. Very plausible at first glance. Plenty of corroborative evidence. Any reason why I shouldn't accept the report as it stands?"

"Men are dying in Battery No. 3. Quite apart from that, it's run by people who don't allow their subordinates to live with even a minimum of human dignity."

"That, my dear boy," said the colonel, draining his glass and sinking still farther into the armchair so that his massive frame seemed to dwindle, "is your view of the situation. Others see it in quite another light. It may not appear so at the moment, but we're at war, and war has an unfortunate habit of killing people—inflicting casualties, I should have said."

"And you take this killing for granted, like the activities in a slaughterhouse?"

"Of course not. Casualties are regretted, also recorded with extreme care, but there's no practical way of preventing them. Not at present, nor at any point in the foreseeable future. Of course, if the time ever comes. . . ."

"So till then, Uncle, the murderers get a blank check. Till then they're licensed to hunt their fellow men. The open season opens whenever they say so. Criminals, madmen and perverts are officially encouraged to believe they're the saviors of their country."

"My God," said the colonel, "I almost envy you for being so breathtakingly young. You're also a carbon copy of your father, but that I don't envy you. You've a lot to learn."

"Who from?" Bergen demanded provocatively.

"Not from me. I can only offer you the modest fruits of my experience. For instance, a realization that the innocent always suffer with the guilty under any system. Or again, that death is the fertilizer of heroism. Doesn't that convince you?"

"It makes me want to puke."

"Your father would be proud to hear you say so, I'm sure." The colonel had almost disappeared into his chair. "Well, it's only what I'd expect from cousin Adolf, but coming from you it saddens me. You're obviously deficient in a sober, realistic acceptance of the inevitable."

"In that case," Bergen said, rising, "I might as well go."

The colonel nodded. "Yes, but before you do, consider this—something trivial by your standards but not unimportant to me: I'm a soldier, plain and simple, and I'm determined to remain one. I despise bullying and persecution of all kinds—in fact I abhor it—but there's nothing I can do to prevent it. Not at present."

"I feel sorry for you, Uncle."

"By all means feel sorry," the colonel said wearily. He raised his glass. "I could even understand it if you felt an urge to despise me. On the other hand, don't be too quick to admire your father for contrast's sake alone. The devil's playing football with us, my boy—all of us. Whichever way we bounce, we all get booted in the end."

Sergeant Major Krüger treated the quartermaster sergeant to a comradely smile. "Softer, old pal, I think it's time we organized another little party. One or two of the boys need a tonic, and quick."

"What sort of tonic?" Softer asked, kneading his pudgy hands together eagerly. "Who are you planning to put the heat on this time?"

"You, for a start."

Softer frowned. "If that's a joke it isn't up to your usual standard. Why pick on me? You know you can count on me any time. I'm your right-hand man."

"You're turning into a fat pig," Krüger told him amiably, "a fat, bloated, gluttonous pig masquerading as a soldier. All you care about is making money."

"Why not?" Softer refused to take umbrage. "I do my

stuff, don't I? I deliver the goods, even when they run to a burial tent complete with German eagle—silver on a black background. It cost me a fortune, but then I'd do anything for you. You only have to wiggle your little finger."

"Just lately, Softer, I've had to wiggle it twice before you come up to scratch. You're getting sluggish because you eat too much. Your brain's going soft because you're pickling it in alcohol. Added to that, you've been overdoing it at the recreation center. Things can't go on like this. You're starting to lose sight of the only thing that matters, and that is, you can't feather your nest in peace unless our system runs like clockwork."

"Doesn't it?"

"No, and if you can't see that it only goes to show how useless you've become."

Softer was visibly wounded. "You'd better tell me what you mean."

"We had a good bunch of senior NCO's once—guts, initiative, team spirit. Well, now they're turning into a rabble. All that interests you is cashing in, and damn little of your takings find their way into battery funds. Also, I have to swallow the fact that you're in cahoots with a railwayman who amuses himself by fumbling with children in the park. As for Forstmann, he's cunt-struck. He spends all his spare time with a French prostitute—yesterday I even had to dig him out of the brothel in working hours. Runge's dead and Moll's turning into a pimp's bookkeeper. But the worst of the lot, in my opinion, is Arm."

"So it's true the *Frau Doktor*'s got him where she wants him?"

"Softer, that question proves your brains are scrambled. Not only has she got him where she wants him, which is halfway up her backside, but he's starting to feel at home there. He already sounds like a gramophone record of the bitch."

"Hence the little get-together you mentioned." Softer swore he had never been more on his toes, never more alert to the battery's interests. For one of Krüger's associates, any less solemn profession of loyalty would have spelled commercial ruin. Krüger's threats were not to be taken lightly. "Okay, we'll make it a real orgy. Leave it to me."

The party took place on the evening of the same day. Everyone privileged to attend had first to drain a tin mug brimming with Softer's "special," which consisted of one-third grain spirit, one-third *framboise* and one-third kirsch— a colorless concoction also known as a flag-waver.

They were already swaying when Krüger summoned them to gather around and commanded beer glasses to be charged with Black Forest raspberry brandy. "This," he proclaimed, "was Siegfried Runge's favorite drink, so let's have one in honor of his memory. He's still down in the cellar, wrapped in a tarp, but tomorrow he'll be on display outside the church, just the way we'd all like to be—just the way the captain wants it. To Runge!"

Krüger and Softer drained their glasses at a single draft. The rest followed suit, but more slowly.

"My friends," said Krüger, happily surveying the faces around him and noting that they were already somewhat the worse for wear, "the late Siegfried Runge was a cheerful man, as we all know. He wouldn't have wanted to cast a blight on the proceedings. That's why, tomorrow or the day after, we're going to celebrate his funeral the way he'd have wanted—with a monumental bender. Party games too, including the League of Nations."

"Who's in for it this time?" Softer inquired gleefully.

"Bergen," announced Krüger. "Neumann and Hiller will see he knows his stuff."

"I certainly will," Neumann said. "I only hope Hiller pulls his weight. League of Nations, eh? How many countries?"

"At least fifty," Krüger told him. "Runge was a real expert—he had nearly eighty at his fingertips. The only one who ever gave him any competition was Arm here."

Arm shuffled his feet modestly. "All the same, I usually came off second best. Runge could always come up with three or four more delegates than I could—Oriental ones included."

"Right," said Krüger, "let's have another in memory of the one and only Siegfried Runge."

"Runge was a real man," Softer said. "Hung like a bull, he was, and knew what to do with it."

"So do I," Arm muttered heavily.

"Go on," said Softer, "you aren't in the same league."

"Don't you believe it!" Arm leaped to the defense of his manhood. "The *Frau Doktor* could tell you different. She doesn't have any complaints."

Softer winked at the others. "Maybe she's easier satisfied than most. Maybe she's the sort who comes before she's gone."

"You're absolutely wrong," Arm assured him, leaden-tongued. Softer poured him a tumblerful of schnapps which he drained with a noise like water vanishing down a drain. "She's hot stuff, that woman."

Prompted by a nod from Krüger, Softer continued to needle Arm. "Anybody could say that."

"But I'm not anybody," growled Arm. "It's the gospel truth—she's the hottest thing since Cleopatra."

"Can you prove it?" Krüger asked mildly.

"I don't have to. I know my onions, and if I say she's hot stuff, she's hot stuff."

"Just saying so isn't good enough," Softer persisted. "We want proof."

Arm gave a hoarse laugh. "What are you after, a quick piece? You'd just love that, wouldn't you!"

"Out of the question, of course." Krüger looked meaning-fully at Softer, who refilled the glasses, this time with

hundred-proof vodka left over from the Polish campaign.
"Our friend's right, Softer. No offense meant, but you
wouldn't be impartial enough. I suggest someone like Moll
here."

The paymaster sergeant started at the sound of his name.
"What am I supposed to do?"

"Test the *Frau Doktor*'s bath water," Softer explained.
"See if it's as hot as Arm says."

"What the hell are you talking about?" Arm demanded
scornfully. "She doesn't open her legs for all and sundry."

"Do you mind!" Moll protested drunkenly. "I'm not all
and sundry."

"No," Arm said, "but you aren't me."

"Anyway," sneered Softer, "why make difficulties? What's
the matter—frightened of the truth?"

"He's trying to wriggle out of it," said Kaminski.

Arm drew himself up with an effort. "I'm not trying to
get out of anything, friend. I appreciate a joke as much as
the next man, but just between you and me, the *Frau Doktor*
isn't just hot stuff—she's refined too. How do you expect me
to get her into bed with Moll?"

Krüger stroked his jaw. "It'd need careful planning, of
course."

"To quote Captain Hein," said Softer, grinning at Krüger,
" 'impossible' isn't part of our vocabulary. We ought to be
able to swing it somehow."

"If only," said Krüger, "to back up the statements made
by our friend here. Alfons Arm is a man of his word. He
doesn't deserve to be mistrusted."

"No, I goddamn well don't," Arm said belligerently. "I'm
not going to have people doubting what I say."

"But you won't let them check for themselves?" Softer
persisted.

"I can't very well, not without trouble. What do you
think, Krüger?"

"Well," Krüger mused, "there are ways. Switching horses in midstream, for instance. An old CO of mine tried it in pitch darkness with a little help from me, and it came off. Just as long as you don't chicken out at the last minute. . . ."

"Me chicken out? Not on your life!" Arm stared around him with fuddled defiance. "I don't give much for Moll's chances, that's all. I doubt if he's up to it."

"What!" exclaimed Moll, on a hiccup. "Thass a challenge!"

"Are you going to take him up on it?" demanded Softer.

"A hunrapercent!" the paymaster sergeant replied, just before he slid under the table. "A hunrapercent," he repeated from the floor.

"Moll's game," Krüger said. "How about you, Arm?"

"Let him try." Arm sounded grimly determined. "Choirs of angels, that's what he'll hear. The *Frau Doktor*'ll swallow him whole and spit out the pieces."

Elizabeth Erdmann detached herself from Bergen with a sigh. "Is that the best you can do?"

"Thanks a lot," Bergen said, rolling over on his back. "You've got a talent for making a man feel ten feet tall."

"Oh, Bert, why won't you try and understand?" Elizabeth blinked dreamily at the masked lamp that cast a dim glow over her bed. "You've no reason to feel offended. There's nothing the matter with your virility. It's just that it isn't enough for me, your being a man and nothing more. I need something else."

"Like what?" Bergen stared up at the glass roof of the conservatory. Its framework was barely visible now, and the trees towering above it had become dense, ill-defined shadows. "You expect me to turn into Prince Charming, or something?"

"What gets me down is the feeling of emptiness, afterward." She spoke in a low murmur. "We give each other pleasure, I know, but the spell doesn't last."

"The spell? Come off it, girl, we don't live in an age of enchantment."

"Anyone would think you'd lost faith in everything."

"I really give that impression?" Bergen sounded pleased. "Maybe it's a sign of progress. Skepticism can be an asset in this place."

Elizabeth sighed again. "Damn the war," she said. "It's spoiled nearly all the men I know. They try and live faster and harder, just in case they miss something before they're snuffed out. We're no different, Bert. Most people have forgotten what it means to be tender. Most but not all, thank God."

"Not all?" Bergen asked sharply. "So you've found an exception. If my guess is right, I was the one who recommended him. Is it Johannes?"

"What if it is?"

Bergen sat up and looked at her with a trace of surprise. "I bribed you to take an interest in him and now you're volunteering to do it for free."

"Why not?" she said. "You pointed him out to me so I took a closer look. Thanks to you, I've had a chance to talk to him. Do you know what I've discovered, Bert? He's got the markings of everything a woman loves. Absolute devotion, real tenderness. . . ."

Bergen hooted with laughter. "You're welcome to him, but only on the terms agreed on."

"I couldn't care less about terms."

"I could. Pardon me for reminding you, but I made you a firm proposition. What's more, you were pretty emphatic about what you wanted."

"Forget about it."

"Like hell I will." Bergen gave her an affectionate pat on the shoulder. "I'll deliver Johannes to your door the first chance I get, but I insist on paying the fee we agreed on."

"The Fragonard?"

He nodded. "I've already got a local artist to produce a copy, same size and style. Fake a couple of bullet holes and Hein'll never spot the difference. We'll swap them just as soon as we can." There was a pause. "Or aren't you interested anymore?"

"Not as much as I was," she said. Sensing he was suspicious, she added, "Please try to understand, Bert. I've a feeling that Johannes could mean a lot to me. However our relationship develops, I don't want to devalue it in advance by putting a price on it."

"Come on, Elizabeth, who do you think you're kidding? You don't have to pretend with me—we know each other too well. No need to act noble. Be absolutely honest—why aren't you excited about the picture? Don't you think it's worth the effort, and if not why not?"

"All right," she said, reluctantly. "It's Magnus. He's behaving as if he hadn't located the Fragonard, but he knows damn well where it is. He's already made some notes on it."

"Let him. Goering isn't interested in the professor's notes. He wants the painting."

"In that case, why all the delay?"

"It's obvious. Magnus is deliberately marking time. He likes it here and he wants to spin out his stay. The place has other features that interest him far more than the Fragonard. You can have it—with Johannes Schubert thrown in."

"But you reserve the right to decide when and where? What do you hope to get out of it—some kind of perverted pleasure? Well, I warn you, don't take your kicks at my expense."

"If we handle things the right way, sweetheart, you won't lose and neither will I."

Battery Sergeant Major Krüger saluted in the gloom. "A very good evening to you, Professor."

"And a very good evening to you, Sergeant Major."

Magnus had retired to his favorite haunt, a stone bench beneath and a little behind the church. Facing it was a low wall, and beyond that the ground fell away steeply to the town of D., which lay bathed in gentle moonlight at the professor's feet. Imaginable in the far distance were Paris and the Louvre, of which Magnus had yet to become curator. For the moment, he had to content himself with the funerary church of the Dukes of Orléans.

"Well, Professor," Krüger said smoothly, joining him on the bench, "and what little scheme are you hatching this time?"

"Scheme? You sound as if you distrust me."

"I'm afraid I do." Krüger leaned toward Magnus confidentially. He indicated the church. "These canned corpses of yours—I'd have thought they kept you busy enough, but apparently they don't. You seem to be developing outside interests."

"And you disapprove?"

"Yes," Krüger said flatly. "It isn't that I begrudge you a little fun—you can tell how generous I am from the amount of wine I keep you supplied with. It's the principle of the thing that matters."

"What do you mean?"

"I'll tell you. First, there's your stamping ground—this bone yard. As far as I'm concerned you can do anything you like there. You can dig up your corpses and auction them off or melt them down for soap. That's your business. On the other hand, Professor, there's my stamping ground—Battery HQ, the gun position and the men who man them. In other words, Battery No. 3. The battery's my outfit and I'm the one who makes it tick the way I want. You follow?"

"Not altogether, Sergeant Major." Professor Magnus spoke with quiet courtesy, keeping his head averted. "Particularly as I'm not aware of having intruded on your sphere of command."

"Look, Professor," Krüger said, "I've got a broad back. I let people get away with murder but I do draw the line somewhere, and that's when I spot somebody trying to take me for a village idiot in uniform."

"I'd never dream of such a thing," Magnus assured him with a mixture of entreaty and alarm. "I beg you to believe that, Sergeant Major. I'm a professional civilian, don't forget. It's over twenty years since I was in the army and I've probably forgotten the rules. No doubt you'll refresh my memory."

"Happy to, if it's really necessary." Krüger's tone was indulgent. "Okay, let's assume you've forgotten what a sphere of command is. The man in charge has a special responsibility for everyone and everything inside it. I'm responsible, among other things, for keeping my men fed and watered, you're responsible for sniffing around inside this church; I'm responsible for battery discipline, you're responsible for keeping your team in line. . . ."

"Ah, I'm beginning to understand. You're trying to hold me responsible for the conduct of my female assistants."

"I'm not holding you responsible, Professor—you *are* responsible! Horizontal activities are all right with me as long as people don't carry them too far. Indirect interference in my sphere of command, let alone direct meddling, is something else. That's where I put my foot down, hard."

"I suppose you're referring to the *Frau Doktor*. My dear sir, that lady is a law unto herself."

"You're still responsible for her."

"Officially, yes, but the lines of demarcation overlap, as it were. Of course I can tell her what I want done in the way of work. As to what goes on inside her head, whom she sleeps with, whom she influences and by whom she allows herself to be influenced—those are matters outside my jurisdiction."

"That's the whole snag, Professor. You're applying civilian rules to a military setup, and it won't do. In my unit, I supervise all the things you've just mentioned. Know what my usual policy is? Keep the men so busy they don't have time to step out of line."

"You have an enviable knack of simplifying every problem, Sergeant Major. My own sphere of operations is far more complex, nor is it confined to the church. It also extends to the château and the gun position, where we expect to find still more relics of the past."

"What? You mean you're thinking of branching out?"

"I've no wish to, but I feel it incumbent on me." The professor spoke pensively, apologetically. "In particular where the château is concerned. Great men used to retire there to die."

"Once upon a time, maybe. We're there now, and we're alive."

"Ah, yes, you're living there—but where, exactly? The suite occupied by Captain Hein used once to be a retreat for dying dukes, gravely wounded, suffering from fatal diseases, lapsing into senile decay. . . . The very stones reek of death."

Krüger looked unimpressed. "That's all right with me, I'm billeted two floors down."

"I know, I know—probably in the rooms that housed the attendants of the dying—the nurses, the moppers of sweat and launderers of soiled bed linen, the removers of vomited blood, of pus, urine and buckets of excrement. . . . Also lodged there were the murderers—the physicians, servants and secretaries whose function it was to cut short the agonies of the moribund and thus save the rulers of the day a great deal of trouble and expense. It was their politically constructive task to ensure a timely and uncontested succession to the dukedom, and they earned their fees in a variety of ways."

Krüger eyed Magnus apprehensively. "Is that the kind of crap you've been feeding Captain Hein?"

"What you choose to describe as crap, Sergeant Major, happens to consist of authentic historical facts. I could quote you many more. For example, the cellar where your quartermaster sergeant stores perishable foodstuffs such as butter, sausage and cheese was once used as a morgue. Embalmers worked in the room which now serves you as a canteen, possibly on the very table where you and your comrades eat your meals. Intestines and vital organs were removed and emptied, brains extracted from the skull, lungs, liver, kidneys and heart replaced by a filling of hot dry sand; a viscous, rapidly setting substance was prepared in a caldron and pumped into the arteries. You should take a closer look at the floor there—it still bears traces."

"What if it does?" Krüger strove to appear unmoved. "Who are you trying to impress? The war hadn't been going more than a couple of days when I came across piles of bodies in a Polish forest. Horrible, really horrible, I don't mind telling you. Twenty-four hours later one of my men came staggering toward me with no head on his shoulders. The blood was spurting from his neck in a fountain but he kept going for a few steps before he keeled over."

"I understand," said Professor Magnus, bowing his grizzled head. "My knowledge of history pales beside your experience of the present-day world, is that what you mean?"

Krüger had completely recovered his poise. "All I'm saying is, stay off my turf and make sure those women do the same. As for your little chats with Captain Hein, I keep my ear pretty close to the ground and I don't like what I hear."

"You probably overestimate me," Magnus said. "Which means you probably underestimate Captain Hein."

"I don't much care either way. The main thing is, keep strictly out of my business. I'd hate to have to teach you and your lady friends a lesson."

"No need," Magnus said. He sat up and cocked his head, listening. Quietly, he added: "Not now."

He could see lights moving rapidly toward them from the château, the faint and flickering flames of five candles stuck in a silver candelabrum. It was carried by Johannes Schubert, and behind him, wrapped in the ducal cloak, strode Hein. The night sky hung over them like a star-spangled awning as they headed for the church and disappeared inside.

"What the hell's going on?" Krüger demanded with perceptible irritation. "Did you put the captain up to this, Professor?"

"My dear Sergeant Major," Magnus protested, "I'm no magician. Even my imagination has its limits."

"But what's going on?" Krüger sounded uneasy.

"The captain appears to be searching for his personal identity. Whatever he understands by that activity, it might be inadvisable to disturb him while he's at it."

"At what? I asked you a question, Professor."

Magnus did not reply. His exultant smile was invisible in the gloom, but there was a wheezing sound as his breathing quickened abruptly.

"Listen," Krüger said with quiet menace, "if you've sent him over the edge I'll blast you with every gun I've got. I'll have you out of that greenhouse so fast your feet won't touch ground—I need it for the transportation section as it is. I'll kick you out of the church and use it as a storeroom. Military requirements come first. Is that clear enough for you?"

"Quite clear, Sergeant Major, but why not wait and see how things turn out? There may come a time when you'll be glad of my cooperation—my testimony, even. Remember that."

"My ship's come home," Gunner Wassermann announced, busily throwing his things together. "I'm walking out of here with only a couple of scars to show for it."

"Going on leave?" Bergen asked.

"Transferred!" Wassermann exclaimed triumphantly. "I've been biding my time for months, but it was worth it. My system paid off at last."

"What about Krüger?"

"If anybody knows the score, it's that man. He got my number the first time he laid eyes on me."

Bergen registered no surprise as he watched Wassermann pack his belongings with gleeful haste.

"So you're washing your hands of Battery No. 3," Bergen said.

"Yes, and good riddance."

"What's it costing you?"

"Costing me? That sounds like sour grapes. I bet you'd come with me if you could."

"Where to?"

"They gave me a choice. Either another combat unit or a home posting near Berlin, as an instructor at a vehicle maintenance school. I didn't take long to make up my mind."

"Why the sudden generosity to you, of all people?"

"Because I'm a shit-hot mechanic. That's what Krüger told me with his usual courtesy and charm. He went on to say that an expert of my caliber deserves an assignment worthy of his talents."

"Arm is letting you go, just like that?"

"He doesn't have any option. There's nothing he wouldn't sacrifice for the sake of the *Frau Doktor*, not to mention her hero upstairs. Krüger was gambling on that."

"But why, for God's sake?"

"Because I sounded off at the psychological moment, that's why. I dropped a hint to Captain Schmidt's chief clerk that Runge was gunning for the water tower—that he couldn't wait to knock it down. Which meant, in practice, that he must have had Hein's approval. That's my passport to Berlin."

"It all sounds too easy." Bergen looked skeptical. "I can't believe it, knowing Krüger."

"Oh, he covered his tracks. I had to swear an affidavit to the effect that I never said anything to anybody about the possibility of future damage to the water tower."

"And if someone swears different?"

"They're wrong. It's all down in black and white, just in case. Krüger knows how to handle these things. By the time they contact me in Berlin the whole incident won't be worth shit."

"So you're running out on me—leaving me stranded?"

Wassermann shouldered his pack and picked up the suitcase. "Not stranded," he said with an easy grin. "In your element, more like. You want to clean this place up? Fair enough, do it on your own. I don't plan to be one of the casualties. If you're really set on making trouble, make it and welcome. I've had enough."

"Don't you want to know what happens?"

"To be frank, pal, I'm not that interested—not anymore. This place is a rat's nest, and the quicker I'm out of it the happier I'll be. I'm not thirsting for blood, my own or anybody else's. So long."

"I'm cold." Captain Hein, stiffly seated in his high-backed chair, shivered. "I feel as if my blood had turned to ice water."

His personal orderly and confidant, Johannes Schubert, was standing in the center of the great banquet hall. A variety of emotions jostled one another in the young man's face—helplessness and eagerness to please, devotion and concern. Hein was dressed only in a billowing white nightshirt, unbuttoned to reveal the crisp golden curls on his chest. His face shone with an almost phosphorescent pallor.

"I'm in pain," the captain announced, extending his hands. "I feel limp. My blood is cold, but it throbs in my veins. There's a buzzing in my head. A film seems to cover my eyes, thick and growing thicker every moment. I can hardly see you, Johannes. Come closer."

Schubert went to Hein and spontaneously clasped his hands. The captain surrendered them without demur. They were sticky with sweat.

"Is there anything I can do, sir?" Schubert asked.

"I have a fever," Hein said. A tremor ran through his body. "Kindly open another bottle of champagne and put out one of the large glasses."

"Shall I fetch your dressing gown?"

"No, Johannes. The dressing gown is too thin—not warm enough. I need something to soak up the sweat. Ah, these waves of fever! I was wounded several times, you know— once in a peculiarly frightful way. Some of the doctors suggested that I was no longer a man. How ludicrous! I live a fuller life than anyone I know. Pass me the ducal robe. Wrap me in it."

Johannes Schubert tugged the heavy purple-and-silver cloak from the stand on which it hung, arranged it around Hein's shoulders as he sat there motionless, draped it around his body, drew it with tender concern across his hero's thighs and knees.

"Stand behind me, Johannes. Place your hands on my chest and let them lie there, quite still. Don't breathe on me, though, and remember—no possessiveness! Just your soft, feather-light touch on my heart. It does me so much good. There, stay like that."

Standing behind the captain's chair with his arms about him and his hands resting lightly on his chest, Johannes Schubert froze. Seconds passed, but they might have been hours charged with hushed and vibrant intimacy. It was like a process of mutual inhalation.

At last Hein said, "That did me good, Johannes. I feel better now. Bring me the mirror hanging on the wall of my bedroom. I have an urge to inspect myself."

Schubert swiftly opened one of the numerous bottles which always nestled among blocks of ice in a large silver bucket. He placed it in front of Hein together with a large crystal glass, which he filled. Then he brought the long wall mirror from the bedroom. Hein looked into the mirror, hesitantly at first, then with mounting interest. His image assumed gratifying dimensions as he drew himself erect. Carefully, he got to his feet and struck a pose, feeling like the incarnation of a historical painting. The ducal robe gleamed opulently in the candlelight.

"Is it really me?" he asked.

"Yes, sir."

The captain nodded at his reflection. He gazed into his own eyes and said, with an inclination of the head: "Greatness is unthinkable without sacrifice. Loyalty entails self-denial. Fulfillment means a readiness to risk all. Can you see that now, Johannes?"

"Yes, sir," Schubert breathed, "I can."

"Prop the mirror against the wall so that it reflects me full length. Then stand beside me." Schubert did so. Karl Ludwig Hein put out his arm and drew Schubert close, until both of them were reflected in the long glass.

"What do you see?"

"The two of us, sir."

"Precisely, Johannes, you see us both. What you do not see is death—death which peers so constantly over our shoulders and has hounded me all my life. It wasn't only the death of a dog that darkened my early days, Johannes—dogs are short-lived in any case. A friend died in these arms of mine —a boyhood friend whom I loved. I risked death to drag him from the rocks of a mountain torrent. He vomited blood and water before he choked and died. Then, in the first few days of the war, a brother officer was blown to pieces beside me. His brains spattered my face, his lifeblood gushed over my hands—these hands, Johannes, which now lie in yours. They were steeped in blood to the wrist."

"But you survived!" Schubert cried ecstatically. "That must mean something, otherwise there'd be no point in living. Everything in our world must have a meaning of some kind."

"I wish to see the duke's tomb, Johannes." Captain Hein drew himself up. He swayed, but only for a moment, then pulled the ducal robe more closely around his shoulders. "Light me!"

Schubert picked up the nearest candlestick and preceded Hein down the winding staircase. They emerged from the main portal of the château and walked across the rutted lawns to the church. The shadowy figures of Magnus and Krüger swam into Hein's field of vision, but he ignored them and strode on.

Schubert flung open the double doors. Hein passed ceremoniously inside and walked up the aisle to the coffin which was standing just in front of the main altar. Here he lingered. The candles cast only a feeble light in the large vaulted nave. Shadows swarmed around them.

Hein said, "Hold the light as high as you can, Johannes. I want no shadows to obscure my view." The words came with an effort. His face glistened with sweat and he was breathing heavily. "Wherever I am, I must have clarity, crystalline clarity."

He swayed a little as he spoke but recovered himself swiftly and stood there stiff as a ramrod, willing his body into immobility. Only then did he bend over the coffin, an elongated metal box, plain but imposing. Its sole adornment was an inscription which seemed to shed a magic glow. Magnus had traced the characters and numerals in white chalk, ostensibly to obtain a clear photographic record. Charles Louis' monogram stood out distinctly, together with his dates of birth and death. A bare thirty years separated the two.

"A truly great man," Hein said, deeply affected.

Using the knuckle of his right forefinger, Hein tapped the coffin lid as though beating out the first four notes of Beethoven's Fifth Symphony. He repeated the tattoo three times.

"It sounds hollow," he said.

Schubert was at a loss to comment, but Hein had already straightened up with a jerk. "Of course," he went on triumphantly, "Charles Louis has severed his links with mortality. He belongs to the inviolable, the unattainable."

"A legend," Schubert observed cautiously.

"A phenomenon!" the captain amended. His voice sank to a whisper. "Incomprehensible, like so many things in life. But then, nothing is more incomprehensible than man—man the warrior."

Hein bowed before the duke's coffin. He bowed low, so low that he began to sway like a tree bending before a gale. A moment later he tottered and fell forward onto the coffin, arms outspread and body limp with fatigue.

His open mouth caressed the cold, dusty, timeworn metal. Almost inaudibly, he murmured, "Oh God, my God, the torments you ask us to endure!"

These, according to Professor Magnus, were reputed to be the dying duke's last words.

Johannes Schubert trembled.

Interim Report No. 7

Statements
made by General, formerly Colonel, Rheinemann-Bergen
*   (ret.),*
author of a noted military manual available
in all West German army libraries and entitled
"Anti-aircraft Artillery Under Ground Attack."

". . . only too delighted to put my views on record, especially at this juncture, when people are beginning to see things in a clearer light. This trend has been confirmed by a Federal President of particular merit. I don't mean Herr H., although, in retrospect, one must grant that even he cherished a modicum of goodwill from his angle. No. I'm referring to Herr L., who has acknowledged that the German soldier of those days was only fighting for his fatherland, not Hitler. . . .

". . . and so our ranks—I'm talking about combat units—

contained virtually no Nazis whatsoever, or, at most, a mere handful of Nazi-contaminated individuals, all of whom we treated with the utmost contempt. . . .

". . . no need, I imagine, to point out that exceptions and misfits occur in every army in the world . . . even the Americans, as recent events have shown . . . after all, it would be unfair to brand every American soldier with equal responsibility for . . . deserving, instead, of our heartfelt sympathy and understanding . . . not to mention the atrocities perpetrated by certain Soviet servicemen. . . . And again, consider those murderers on the other side of the Wall. . . .

". . . many avowed opponents of Hitler in our ranks, of whom I can justly claim to have been one. When in conversation with brother officers known to and trusted by me, I almost invariably —and from a very early stage—referred to him as 'the Bohemian Corporal.' I later described him as 'that madman up top.' I can supply you with depositions to that effect.

". . . had, of course, to proceed with extreme caution, even where close relations were concerned . . . as, for instance, in the case of my cousin's son. . . .

". . . I told him: 'I'm a soldier, Bert—no more but certainly no less, and we soldiers have a duty to do everything militarily possible to defend our country. . . .'

". . . over his head, I'm afraid, certainly at that stage . . . could have been a form of youthful idealism, lack of realism— you know the sort of thing. . . ."

Comments
made by Professor Magnus
relating to the funerary church at D.
Taken from contemporary notes
made available by his widow.

Entry No. 17:
"A straightforward assignment, certainly at first glance. Prospects of success good. Potential difficulties capable of elimination.

"The *Frau Doktor* perseveres, employing her own inimitable methods. One new feature: She has actually taken to sleeping with a sergeant, doubtless as a means of winning him over in the interests of our research here. Well, she seldom hides her light under a bushel when her own conception of 'higher values' is at stake. Not even the *Reichsleiter* escaped her clutches. She might be said never to have shrunk from anything or anyone when it mattered to her.

"That woman certainly knows the meaning of total commitment!"

Entry No. 23:

"Then there's Captain Hein, the war hero. A figure straight out of a fairy tale—a military fairy tale.

"Just like Duke Charles Louis. He was generally known as Philippe Eugène. Charles and Louis were only his fifth and sixth names respectively, but to please the captain I've upgraded them to match his own. An outstanding success!

"Am continuing to weave my tangled web. Great fun. It delights Captain Hein and entertains me no end. A mishmash of chronicles, romances, legends and pure fiction. Am gleaning as much personal information about Hein as I possibly can, then knitting it together into a pseudohistorical figure which fits him like a glove—Saville Row could do no better. He reacts with Pavlovian predictability. To borrow his own terminology, I'm on target!"

Entry No. 31:

"Am now devising a 'burial layout' for the captain's delectation, solely to whet his increasing interest in the church. The details imaginary but effective.

"The ground plan of the church is cruciform. I have put the number of persons buried there at 140, distributed as follows:

"Eight bodies immediately beneath the altar and accessible via a flight of marble steps behind it: dukes regnant;

"Twelve bodies in the left transept: their spouses;

"Twelve bodies in the right transept: prominent statesmen belonging to the Orléans family;

"Thirty-six bodies left and right of the main aisle, toward the front: their wives, aides and henchmen, also princes of the Church, diplomats, bailiffs and stewards;

"Seventy-one bodies left and right of the main aisle but toward the rear of the church, juxtaposed and superimposed: more trusty noblemen, priests and soldiers, also a court poet. Only one out of more than a hundred, which should teach poets not to overrate their importance—a vain warning, no doubt!

"Total: 139.

"No. 140, situated immediately in front of the altar, is the coffin of our hero, Charles Louis. It may be simply an anonymous casket left there by chance during some military campaign or other. Probably empty."

Entry No. 35:
"If I have been rash enough to underestimate anyone in Battery No. 3, that person is Sergeant Major Krüger. His shrewdness and self-assurance are startling. Little chance of hoodwinking him.

"Krüger made his attitude plain last night—so plain that it almost took my breath away. Not a man to antagonize, I realize that now.

"I was still being taken to task by him when Captain Hein stalked past us dressed in the 'ducal' robe, escorted by that young orderly of his. We followed.

"While we were standing in the shadows at the back of the church, Hein appeared to be smitten by some form of fit. He fell on top of the coffin and lay there embracing it. I gripped Krüger by the arm, but all he said was, 'Quite a sight, eh? Anyone'd think he was queer for coffins. . . .'

"Well, why not, if it amuses the man?'"

*Further information
of a personal nature
supplied by Elizabeth (née) Erdmann,
now married to her fourth husband,
a respected export-import dealer based in the Cologne area.*

"War's a state of emergency, and that applies to the emotions as well. I could tell you plenty if I wanted to. So could a lot of other women, only they prefer to keep quiet. So do I, these days.

"Plenty of strings to my bow? That's an understatement— any girl could take her pick providing she was in the right job. Nurses, switchboard operators, clerical staff, and so on. Never a dull moment.

"It wasn't just a question of opportunity. There was something else involved—something typically feminine: We were sorry for the poor boys. All they wanted to do was forget the war, and we helped them.

"The sad thing was, the 'first' night so often turned out to be the last. No less than three of my boyfriends were killed in action. Two died in Russia and the other went down in the Atlantic—he was in submarines. They were all unofficially engaged to me, so I like to think they didn't die unconsoled.

"I was anything but a beginner when I arrived in D. The ratio of men to women must have been about fifty to one. I could have had my pick, but I was still naïve enough to long for something special, the big thrill, the once-in-a-lifetime experience. . . .

"All right, I admit it. Johannes Schubert was the one. He was so pure and unspoiled, so unsophisticated and full of romantic dreams. He was the only one I felt really attracted to. I loved him.

"It was frightful, what happened to him, but it wasn't my fault. . . ."

Question: What about the Fragonard in the banquet chamber?

Answer: That's completely beside the point.

Question: How much do you know about Schubert's death?

Answer: Nothing! Nothing for certain. It shocked me more than I can say, but I wasn't involved. Other people knew far more than I did. Better ask them.

Question: Can you suggest anyone?

Answer: Bergen, if he's still alive—and if he's willing to talk. He was at the bottom of it all.

Remarks
made by ex-Lieutenant Seifert-Blanker,
formerly adjutant of Group No. 1, No. 317 Regt, AA Command,
now employed as the general representative
of a U.S. automobile company in West Germany.

"Really, my dear fellow, not that tired old tale, I beg you! It's ridiculous to try and cast me as a sworn enemy of the late Captain Hein.

"On the contrary, we worked admirably together. My only duty was to promote the interests of our unit, and Captain Hein was a member of that unit.

"That's why it so absurd to claim that he and I were at loggerheads, ostensibly because he was appointed to command Battery No. 3 over my head. There were also some who said that his Knight's Cross should really have gone to me. They may have been right, but I never begrudged him the decoration.

"Nor, as others seem to have assumed, did I plant Corporal Bergen in Battery No. 3 with instructions to make a nuisance of himself.

"Hein was an extremely able commander. As such, he enjoyed my regard and admiration. Not that I was blinded by his undoubted merits. I recognized his personal failings at an early stage and did my best to draw the appropriate military conclusions—I repeat, military. Mark that word. Just in case you're unaware of it, the soldier's world has no room for emotions of a private or personal nature. I certainly had none."

8

On the Value of Human Life and the Function of Supply and Demand

"This funeral ceremony for Sergeant Runge," announced Krüger, "—it's all set up."

"Every last detail?" Hein demanded. An ethereal glow seemed to play about the captain's brow. His steel helmet was clamped beneath his left arm.

"Everything's going according to plan, sir."

"Have the men from the propaganda company turned up?"

"Yes, sir. A camera crew, two still photographers and a war artist. I've impressed on them that this is a private ceremony. They've promised to respect the fact and not call attention to themselves."

"Very good," said Hein. He raised his voice and called, "Schubert!"

Schubert appeared, carrying a sheaf of roses which had been left in Hein's washbasin until the last moment to conserve their freshness. There were twenty-three radiant red blooms, one for each year of the late gunnery sergeant's life.

"Let's go," said the captain, after a brief glance at his

watch. Carefully, he lowered the steel helmet onto his head. "1130 hours," he added. "The ceremony can begin."

11:30 A.M.: The battery commander, escorted by his orderly and the battery sergeant major, leaves his quarters, descends the château staircase, and emerges into the open. He pauses for a moment and looks around keenly, then proceeds to his command car, which stands waiting a yard from the bottom step. Hood, sides and trunk are swathed in black crape. Corporal Kaminski sits rigidly behind the wheel.

11:35 A.M.: Captain Hein climbs in but remains on his feet beside the driver, statuesquely erect. Krüger sits immediately behind him with Schubert on his left. Hein gives the windshield a sharp slap with the flat of his left hand. The car moves off at a walking pace, as prescribed, in the direction of the church. Distance: two hundred yards.

11:38 A.M.: Lieutenant Minder, also following instructions to the letter, issues the requisite commands: "Atten—shun! Slope—arms! Present—arms!" Then, with drawn sword, he hurries up to the battery commander, dips his blade, and reports, "Escort present and correct, sir!"

The captain acknowledges this information with a perfunctory salute, then vaults lightly from his car and proceeds to inspect the escort. It is a platoon-strength body of men comprising three NCO's and twenty-four gunners, the most that can be spared from Battery HQ and the gun position without imperiling the unit's combat readiness, which naturally takes precedence over all other considerations. Hein passes along the ranks with measured tread, solemnly, stiffly, as if staring through a succession of blank windows.

11:45 A.M.: Captain Hein, escorted by Lieutenant Minder, completes his inspection. He halts abruptly, turns, pauses for a moment or two, and sets off again, this time toward the black awning beneath which the dead warrior reposes in an oak coffin, stained black. This, like the wreaths issued to all participants, has been ordered by Krüger and paid for out of brothel takings, alias battery funds.

Posted around the coffin are four of the dead man's comrades-in-arms, Sergeants Arm and Moll in front and two gun-position bombardiers behind. Hein takes up his post facing them. He looks neither at the coffin nor at the wooden faces of the men surrounding it, merely raises his hand to his helmet and keeps it there for almost a minute—ample time in which to take some excellent publicity pictures.

11:50 A.M.: Captain Hein inclines his head toward the coffin, draws himself up and intones, "Senior Gunnery Sergeant Siegfried Runge, gallant friend and comrade, we shall never forget you!"

These words, which appear verbatim in Krüger's typed schedule, are the prearranged signal for the pallbearers to convey the coffin to the grave. Donning their slings, the four raise the oak box to hip height and stand ready to move off.

"We will now," says Hein, "pay our last respects."

11:55 A.M.: The coffin is borne with solemn tread— Krüger has already rehearsed this procedure at least a dozen times—to the open grave. The route, barely fifty yards long, is strewn to a width of ten feet with fir branches. The three hostesses from Softer's recreation center have seen to this under his personal supervision.

Accompanied by Krüger and Schubert, Captain Hein re-enters his command car. The escort slow-marches in its wake. The men from the propaganda company are beside themselves with delight. One of the photographers secures a more effective camera angle by slithering into the grave itself, but the mourners appear unconscious of him and his clicking, whirring, scribbling colleagues.

Down below in the town of D., as though to order, a church bell tolls.

12:00: "Now!" says Captain Hein.

The pallbearers put down the coffin. The escort re-forms. Lieutenant Minder's voice rings out in a series of commands, then:

"Fire!"

A volley from twenty-seven rifles crashes heavenward above the fields of France. Promptly, from the gun position, a second volley echoes the first. The double report is repeated three times.

According to plan, the men left behind at the gun position have been privileged to take part in the ceremony from afar. They stand there among the guns, also at platoon strength, waiting for the crucial moment. Hein's idea, Krüger's organization. Both men enjoy the result.

"My good and gallant friend!" cries Hein. "You have trodden the path which each of us may one day have to tread. You have become an example to us all. No matter that you died on foreign soil. Your fatherland is here and everywhere. Farewell, and rest in peace!"

The sergeant's coffin is lowered into the hole with a dull thud. A burial party swiftly shovels earth on top and tamps it down until all that remains is a smooth red mound. On this, at Hein's bidding, Corporal Schubert lays the twenty-three roses. The captain gives a last salute.

Finis.

"We've fed and watered the propaganda boys," Krüger informed Hein. "Roast chicken and beer."

"Good," said Hein, carefully combing his silky white-blond hair. The steel helmet had left it in some disarray.

"They have a request, sir. They'd like to reconstruct the battery's defense against ground attack by enemy saboteurs."

"In broad daylight? But it took place at night."

"They say they can get around that with filters and other gadgets. It'll look like midnight by the time they're through. I've issued them with three cans of gasoline for making the necessary flames and smoke."

"Very good," Hein said absently. He had walked to one of the tower windows and was gazing down at Runge's grave, which lay to the east, overlooking D. "Anything else?"

"Yes, sir. Your presence at the gun position would. . . ."

"Surely that's not essential?"

"Not essential, sir, but desirable. If you aren't there, Lieutenant Minder may find his way into one of the newsreel shots, not to mention Second Lieutenant Helmreich."

"My car," Hein commanded with split-second decision.

"Ready and waiting, sir."

Hein nodded approvingly, donned his cap and trotted downstairs. Accompanied by Krüger, he drove to the gun position.

Minder started to report but Hein silenced him with a curt gesture.

"Carry on, men!" bellowed Krüger, acting as the captain's mouthpiece. "You can do better than that!"

The propaganda team was led by a bespectacled sergeant major. "Good to have you here, Captain," he said happily. "It'll give the proceedings a bit more class. Please stand near one of the guns and leave the rest to us."

Hein gave no sign of having heard, well aware that there was bound to be a gun in the background wherever he stood. He merely nodded at Krüger, and Krüger, in obedience to his unerring instinct, sang out, "Second Lieutenant Helmreich, report to the battery commander at once!"

Helmreich scurried up like a frightened rabbit. He strove to produce an impeccable salute but failed to convince. There was something ineradicably civilian about his bearing.

"What are you, of all people, doing here?" Hein inquired sharply.

"I'm sorry, sir, but this reconstruction isn't quite accurate. You see, I was on the spot at the time. . . ."

"Isn't Runge enough for you?" Hein demanded with icy calm. "Who do you plan to slaughter this time?"

"I'm sorry, sir, but. . . ."

"Remove yourself," snapped Hein, "this instant!"

Second Lieutenant Helmreich set off at a crouching run toward the officers' billet and disappeared inside. Minder grinned broadly, as did some of the men in his immediate vicinity.

Krüger took command. "Clear the field of fire," he yelled, "—for the camera!" He directed a comradely smile at the newsreel sergeant major. "Okay, make it snappy but give us the full treatment."

"Leave it to me," the propaganda man told him gratefully, and proceeded to deploy his minions. "Concentrate on the captain, boys. Come on, let's hit the public where it hurts!"

A close-up of Hein, then another. Then another, followed by a medium shot. Hein, his gaze piercingly heroic as ever, in the foreground. Just beyond him a gun crew leaping to man their gun, traversing the barrel, grimly determined yet laughing as they went about their lethal business. Finally, a long shot showing the gun position in a state of antlike activity.

Next, various details. A machine gunner crouching expectantly, a hand squeezing the trigger, flames leaping from the ruined house, dense clouds of smoke spreading until they dominated the scene. No doubt about it—this was *total* war.

"Are we doing all right?" asked Krüger, standing close behind the captain so as not to be left out of the picture. "How does it look?"

"Not bad at all," said the newsreel sergeant major. "There's something missing, though. Not enough pep."

"How do you mean?"

"More noise would help."

Hein suddenly came to life. "Load with armor-piercing."

"Pardon me, sir," said Lieutenant Minder, "I must have misunderstood. Did you say armor-piercing?"

"I did," Hein replied calmly. "Three rounds apiece for guns Nos. 1 and 2. That ought to be enough, I think."

"Terrific!" exclaimed the newsreel man. "Just the ticket! Now we can really go to town."

"You, Herr Minder, will take command of No. 2 Gun," Hein continued. "Your target will again be the water tower."

"But it's little more than a ruin, sir."

"In that case, you need have no hesitation in clearing the horizon of what remains. I shall assume personal command of No. 1 Gun."

"But...."

"You're holding us up, Minder." Hein's tone brooked no opposition. "Our friends in the propaganda company have a duty to keep the German public informed—fully informed."

"Thanks, Captain," said the newsreel sergeant major. "It's great to meet someone who understands our problems. You won't regret this." He ordered his cameraman into a foxhole not far from the house in which Runge had died. It was already pockmarked with bullet holes.

"Hang on," Krüger whispered to him, "not that one. If I know the captain, he's got something else up his sleeve. You're in for the fireworks display you've been dreaming about for years."

The sergeant major's spectacles glinted. "If you're right," he said, "I'll turn him into a national hero overnight. All depends what he supplies in the way of material, of course."

Meanwhile, Hein had stalked over to No. 1 Gun. "Armor-piercing," he decreed. "Three rounds rapid fire."

The gun commander didn't bat an eyelid. "Yes, sir," he said. "What target?"

"The officers' billet," said Hein.

The gun commander followed his instructions without a moment's hesitation. "Range two hundred," he said. "On target?"

"On target," echoed the gun layer, but ventured to ask: "What shall I aim for—front door, ground floor, first floor?"

"Start with the roof," said Hein. "Carry on."

"Fire!" shouted the gun commander.

The first shell ripped open the roof of the officers' quarters. A gaping hole six feet in diameter appeared in the tiles. The next shot pulverized the right-hand side of the roof, the third and final round destroyed what was left. Smoke began to rise from the rafters and tongues of flame darted forth. One of the gable ends collapsed with a crash.

Out of the house, on all fours, liberally coated with ceiling plaster, crawled a figure in officer's uniform: Second Lieutenant Helmreich. Nobody paid any attention to him.

Captain Hein's voice rang clear across the gun position. "Your turn, Minder!"

And Minder, with the aid of an equally efficient gun commander, battered the remnants of the municipal water tower until all that had ever obstructed the battery's field of fire was razed to the ground.

The newsreel sergeant major gave a moan of delight. "Unique, absolutely unique! Got it all in the can, boys?"

They had. Beautiful stuff, every last foot of it.

Major escalation

Lieutenant Minder and Sergeant Major Krüger.
Place: Battery No. 3 orderly room, on the ground floor of the château.
Time: early afternoon on the morrow of Runge's funeral.

Krüger is leafing through some files as Minder enters.

MINDER (*urgently*): What's wrong, for God's sake?
KRÜGER (*ingenuously*): What should be wrong, Lieutenant?
MINDER: This place is falling apart at the seams, can't you see?
KRÜGER: Not at my end it isn't—not at Battery HQ. I hope the same goes for your bunch at the gun position. Nothing wrong there, is there?

Minder approaches, plants both hands on Krüger's desk and leans forward confidentially. Krüger sits back with an expectant air.

MINDER: There was a two-hour operational exercise planned for this morning but the captain never turned up. This afternoon's training schedule listed a full turnout for arms drill but the captain didn't put in an appearance again. Why not?

KRÜGER: That's his business, isn't it?

MINDER: Krüger, what's the matter with him?

KRÜGER: Nothing that I know of, Lieutenant.

MINDER: Is he sick?

KRÜGER: I'm no doctor. Better ask the MO.

MINDER: Jesus Christ Almighty, won't anything jolt you out of your goddamned complacency? How far have things got to go before you sit up and take notice? First a mock alert with fatal results—very well, accidents do happen. But then that pompous bloody funeral. . . . Megalomania, I tell you—pure and unadulterated megalomania. And finally, to cap it all, this pointless popping off in broad daylight, right into the middle of a building occupied by an officer. Helmreich might have been killed!

KRÜGER: May I set the record straight, Lieutenant? The incident you refer to was a demonstration arranged for the benefit of a visiting propaganda team. No shells were fired into the middle of the officers' billet. Only the roof was destroyed. Second Lieutenant Helmreich happened to be on the ground floor at the time, so you can hardly say his life was in danger.

MINDER: I beg to differ.

KRÜGER: Have you put your views in writing? Has Second Lieutenant Helmreich made a written report at your suggestion? If so, sir—and I find it hard to believe—

don't forget to go through proper channels, will you?
Reports and complaints have to be submitted to Battery
HQ, which means to Captain Hein via me.

MINDER: Who are you working for, Krüger?

KRÜGER: No one in particular, Lieutenant. Just the battery—
yours and mine.

Bert Bergen and Elizabeth Erdmann.
Place: the conservatory workroom.
Time: late afternoon of the same day.

Enter Bergen, brandishing a thick roll of brittle canvas.
He slaps it down in the middle of the desk, shoves everything
else aside, and unrolls it to reveal the Fragonard. Elizabeth
Erdmann stares at the painting open-mouthed.

ELIZABETH: How did you manage it?

BERGEN: It was a breeze. I swapped it for my fifth-rate copy
during the funeral. There was nobody in the château
except me. I was on switchboard duty.

ELIZABETH: At last!

She gazes with dreamy delight at the valuable canvas. Her
eyes, as Bergen is pleased to note, have taken on an acquisi-
tive gleam.

BERGEN: Know what? You're going to arrange a bang-up
dinner for two. I'll supply all you need, and that includes the pick of the captain's cellar. Chablis with the
fish, a good Burgundy—say Nuits-Saint-Georges '33—
with the meat, and a jeroboam of champagne afterward.

ELIZABETH: But not here in this greenhouse. The *Frau Doktor*
has staked a permanent claim to it after dark. She likes
to be alone with Arm.

BERGEN: I know. Don't worry, she can have the place to
herself. The professor has a dinner engagement at the
Hôtel de France and I've cleared the bailiff's apartment

for you—no one'll disturb you for hours. Softer, Kaminski and Forstmann have gone to Paris with the three usual tenants.

ELIZABETH: What about Johannes?

BERGEN: He'll come, unless I'm very wrong. Seems to me he doesn't have much choice. The youngster needs straightening out, and that's where you come in.

Johannes Schubert and Karl Ludwig Hein.
Place: the tower chamber.
Time: dusk.

Captain Hein is leaning against the embrasure of the north window, staring toward Paris and beyond. The picture in his mind's eye is of Germany.

Cradled against his chest like a child in need of protection is a small-bore rifle, all steel-blue metal and gleaming wood. Abruptly, he glances down at Runge's grave.

Corporal Schubert is standing behind him, motionless as ever, bewilderment struggling with a dogged endeavor to grasp what is happening. He begins to tremble.

The captain raises his rifle, takes swift and unerring aim, and fires. He smiles with relief and leans back against the embrasure.

HEIN: There was a bird on Runge's grave.

SCHUBERT: Singing?

HEIN: It sang, certainly. It also left droppings, and that I refuse to tolerate.

Schubert relapses into dismayed silence. He retreats a step—two steps—as though on the verge of flight. Then he freezes again, a prey to some emotion he cannot identify. His face has gone very pale.

He watches Hein raise the rifle a second time and, after aiming for a split second, pump the magazine empty. The captain's hands caress his gun as if it were a woman.

HEIN: It was a dog that time.

SCHUBERT: A dog?

HEIN: Yes, some flea-bitten mongrel or other. It was heading for the grave.

SCHUBERT: But. . . .

HEIN: To squat or lift its leg—why else? Mongrels know no better, the disgusting creatures. They even sniff each other's bottoms!

SCHUBERT: But to shoot an animal down, just like that? Just because it does what it has to do—because it can't help itself? I don't understand. I simply don't understand. . . .

Hein lowers his rifle. He walks over to Schubert and puts his arms around him, drawing him close.

HEIN: You've much to learn, Johannes, but never fear—I'll be patient with you. Don't move! Don't put your arms around me. Stand quite still. Give no indication of your feelings for me—not a sign, however instinctive. Control yourself. Stay motionless. Let yourself drift along like a man on the breast of an endless river.

Quite suddenly, Hein breaks free, thrusting Schubert away from him. Schubert staggers backward, collides with the opposite wall, and slides to the floor.

Hein leaps onto the low sill of the north window and spreads his arms wide. His eyes seem to glow in the dimness.

HEIN: Nothing can extinguish me, Johannes! Whatever the challenge, whatever the abyss that confronts me, nothing destroys my equilibrium. Perfect poise, mental and physical. If there is a higher purpose in life, tell me!

Schubert scrambles to his feet in utter terror and rushes blindly from the room.

* * *

Frau Dr. Werner-Weilheim and—in quick succession—Sergeants Arm and Moll.
Place: the conservatory.
Time: early evening of the same day.

Sergeant Arm, flourishing a bottle of mellow Cognac Otard, approaches his lady with a possessive air. She stares at him expectantly.

FRAU DR. W-W: In a hurry again?
ARM: I always am, with you. Any objections?
FRAU DR. W-W: Of course not. I love it.

Arm clasps her in a bearlike embrace, kneads her shoulders, back and buttocks. She starts to pant heavily, a fact he notes with satisfaction.

FRAU DR. W-W: But you're even more impetuous than usual, sweetheart. Won't you have something to eat or drink first?
ARM (*snorting with feigned impatience*): You're the only meal I want. Get ready, and switch the light out—I'm feeling romantic tonight. Be with you in two minutes. Got to shake hands with the man I enlisted with.

Frau Dr. Werner-Weilheim retires to her room, disrobes swiftly, turns out the light and lies down on her bed.
Arm opens the door for Moll, who has been eavesdropping avidly.

ARM (*whispering*): Just a few grunts and groans, otherwise keep your trap shut. Stick to business.
MOLL: Don't worry, I'm not a beginner.

Minutes pass. Arm squints into the darkness, listening. He hears a cry of sensual pleasure, followed at once by an outraged bellow. The light goes on abruptly.

FRAU DR. W-W: You pig! You filthy beast! Get out of here!

Sergeant Moll flees through the door, not forgetting to express his appreciation. "Lovely piece!" he mutters swiftly as he flits past.

Arm stands in the doorway, relishing the situation. The Frau Doktor launches herself at him and tries to claw his face.

ARM: Calm down, baby, you passed with flying colors.

FRAU DR. W-W: How dare you do such a thing to me, a representative of German womanhood! You'll regret this, you brute—you'll regret it as long as you live!

Bergen and Schubert.
Place: the junior ranks' quarters, Château D.
Time: as above.

Bergen is lying on his bunk fully dressed, staring at the ceiling. He does not move except to glance at his watch from time to time.

Enter Schubert like a frightened deer. He pauses in front of Bergen, then drops onto the neighboring mattress with a groan.

SCHUBERT: I need help, Bert.

BERGEN: You look all in. When did you last eat?

SCHUBERT: Breakfast—or was it lunch? I can't remember exactly. Does it matter?

BERGEN: You're a growing lad—you need feeding. Well, Uncle Bert has a treat for you. You're invited to supper by Elizabeth.

SCHUBERT: But the captain may need me.

BERGEN: Later. I wangled you this invitation and you're going to accept it. Fortify yourself—I don't know exactly what for, but time will tell.

SCHUBERT: Why do you do all these things for me?

BERGEN: Let's say it's because I'm a friend of yours. And

please don't think I'm trying to corrupt you. There are
plenty of things worse than having dinner with a girl.

SCHUBERT (*pensively*): He fired at two living creatures in
cold blood. First a bird, then a dog.

BERGEN: He's pulled the trigger on human beings before
now. And hit them. It's all part of the job.

SCHUBERT: It was horrible—I can't describe it any other way.
I love animals and birds.

BERGEN: Save some love for your own kind. I'd start with
the female sex if I were you. Nothing changes your ideas
like a girl, if only for a few minutes. Okay, shove off.
She's waiting for you.

Arm, Moll and Krüger.
Place: the ground-floor canteen, Château D.
Time: evening.

*Krüger is discovered sitting alone. He has cleared the can-
teen of staff and customers by the simple expedient of giving
them all local passes until midnight. His expression conveys
enjoyment of the total silence that surrounds him.*

*He drinks a Munich beer and smokes a Dutch cigar, listen-
ing intently for untoward sounds. He has pulled off his boots
and propped his feet, in their gray army-issue socks, on the
white cloth which adorns the senior NCO's table.*

*Krüger looks unusually placid. He smiles to himself, evi-
dently waiting for something. Time goes on, but still he
shows no sign of impatience.*

*At last, Arm storms in with Moll at his heels. Both ser-
geants are extremely agitated. They can hardly contain themselves as they click their heels at Krüger, who eyes them
coolly.*

ARM: A complete fuck-up, Krüger, and it's all the fault of
this numbskull here!

MOLL: Easy, pal! I did my stuff.

ARM: Like hell you did! You didn't go to it right away, like she's used to with me. I knew you'd screw the whole thing up.

MOLL: I tried a little finesse—I'm a gentleman, not a billy goat. She spotted the subtle difference.

ARM: And kicked you out. Chewed your balls off and tried to mark me for life afterward. She'll have her revenge, you mark my words. "You'll regret this forever"— that's what she told me.

KRÜGER: Fine. So everything went according to plan.

ARM (*staring at him in disbelief*): How do you mean? She's boiling mad. It's curtains for all of us, not just me.

MOLL (*reminiscently*): She wasn't bad, all things considered. Not first class, though. Not what I'd been led to expect.

ARM (*furiously*): Shut up, you lousy amateur! Stick to jerking off in the future—it's all you're capable of. All you've done is spoil a damn good lay. I'll never forgive you for that.

KRÜGER (*pacifically*): Have a sense of proportion, both of you. Things went wrong, but only from a limited angle. Generally speaking, they couldn't be better.

ARM: You don't know the *Frau Doktor*.

KRÜGER: She doesn't know me, you mean. This outfit is a closed shop, and now she realizes it. We've finally spiked the old bitch's guns, thanks to you two. What do you say we celebrate with a couple of snorts?

Bergen and Magnus.
Place: the restaurant of the Hôtel de France in D.
Time: late the same evening, after dinner.

MAGNUS: Why do you keep spying on me?

BERGEN: To find out what you really think.

MAGNUS: I thought I'd made that clear. What more can I say?

BERGEN: You already said plenty, Professor, but I suspect you kept quiet about plenty more. You didn't want to whet my curiosity too much. Unfortunately for you, I'm the inquisitive type.

Professor Magnus sniffs the brandy which has just been set before him, accompanied by a café *filtre. He stares into space with narrowed eyes. A lock of ice-gray hair falls onto his brow.*

MAGNUS: All this badgering—it only irritates and depresses me. Why not leave me to my own little world? I've no wish to trespass on yours. History is all I know and care about. I've made a study of the subject.

BERGEN: Yes, and I can imagine what conclusion you've come to. Everything stinks—everything and everyone, isn't that it?

MAGNUS: A jaundiced view of life for one so young. I suppose you feel you're at the mercy of forces which operate like cosmic vacuum cleaners. You're right, but who taught you?

BERGEN: People like you, Professor. I've watched you at work on one of your tombs up there in the church, full of professional enthusiasm and personal contempt. Why, could you smell the rot? Could you smell the decay and corruption that defeats every age, including our own? Massive walls, lead coffins, engraved plaques—great men have always tried to cheat the passage of time but they never succeeded.

MAGNUS: Quite right, my boy, none of it's worth a fig. A hollow laugh, perhaps, but nothing more.

It was midnight.

Captain Hein stood on the threshold of the tower chamber, surveying the entire world through its four windows. He knew that, whatever its location and claims to beauty, every region and country in that world was fundamentally a battlefield. Its sole destiny was to provide an arena for seed-time and harvest, life and death, the superimposition of one layer of ashes upon another, the spreading of human manure. Some had to die so that others might live.

Hein leaned against the doorframe, drained of energy. Tears sprang to his eyes. He groaned and gazed up at the stars.

He had draped the ducal robe around his shoulders and pulled it tight over his chest, which rose and fell with a quick, erratic rhythm. He was cold, but his face burned beneath the film of sweat that glistened in the light of the full moon. His head ached. He pressed both hands to his temples and massaged them with circular movements. Panting, he clenched his fists and beat a harsh tattoo on his forehead as though to clear his brain of the thoughts that oppressed him.

Suddenly he froze, listening. "Who's there?" he called. "Is that you, Johannes?"

"No," came a voice from the darkened banquet chamber, "it's me—Bergen." There was a sound of slowly approaching footsteps.

"I didn't send for you," Hein said curtly. He straightened up with an effort. "I'm expecting Schubert, no one else."

"Schubert," said Bergen, "is otherwise engaged."

Hein brusquely dismissed the remark with a twitch of the hand. He looked exhausted. "If that's an insinuation, forget it. I'm not interested in obscene gossip."

"But, Captain, isn't it just possible that your idea of obscenity may be an integral part of human nature? It depends on your point of view, surely."

"I refuse to accept that."

"Lots of people have tried to dictate what's acceptable and what isn't, but no one lasted long in the role of Almighty God."

Hein sank back against the doorframe, almost as if he were trying to evade a blow. "I didn't send for you," he repeated.

"I thought you might need me, since Schubert's detained. Wouldn't it interest you to know what's keeping him—or rather, who's keeping him?"

Karl Ludwig Hein swung around abruptly and reeled across the tower chamber. He slammed into the narrow strip of wall between two windows, grazing his forehead and leaving a smudge of whitewash on the shoulder of his purple cloak. He gave a little cry, like a hurt child.

"I'm accustomed to being alone," he said in a flat voice. He might have been speaking to himself.

"We all have to get used to that sometime, Captain. I'm afraid we don't have any option."

"Loneliness," Hein went on, still to himself, "—loneliness is the price of life, the final and inescapable account each of us has to settle sooner or later. Every day brings another farewell—to a friend, a cherished hope, a brief moment of beauty. No one mourns our passing."

"Isn't that because we mourn no one in return—not even a man like Runge?"

"Runge made a sacrifice," Hein said, "one of the sacrifices which must always be made when a man resolves to find himself. Life entails death, true, but death begets life—it's the inexorable cycle of creation. What finer flower bed than a grave, after all? Besides, there was a valid military reason for Runge's death. From a soldier's point of view, it was the perfect way to go."

"I know how it happened," Bergen said. "I overheard some of your phone conversations with Sergeant Runge, and not by accident. You talked him into shooting up the gun position and he got killed in the process."

"No, no, Bergen, you're wrong. I never urged him— there was no need. I merely refrained from dissuading him."

"Doesn't that amount to the same thing?"

"Certainly not. You find it impossible to think in military

terms. I don't hold it against you, but one thing you must believe: I'd sacrifice my right arm if it would bring him back."

"What about a boy like Schubert, Captain? What would you sacrifice for him?"

Hein, clinging to the window embrasure, stared down at the darkened grounds. Quietly, he said, "For a friend? My life, if he deserved it."

"Fortunately for you, I don't think he does—not by your standards."

Hein straightened up and pulled the soiled cloak tighter around his shoulders with a swift, tremulous movement.

"Where is he?"

"In the battery brothel, Captain."

"No," Hein said. He laughed with an effort. "No, Bergen, I don't believe you. Nothing could be more alien to my world, and Johannes Schubert is part of that world. Anyone can make a mistake. Anyone can succumb to temptation in a moment of weakness, but Johannes would never demean himself that way—I'd stake my life on it."

"A losing bet, Captain." Bergen strove to sound matter-of-fact. "I didn't say he was in bed with one of the regulars. They're in Paris on a sort of company picnic and I doubt if they'll be back before reveille."

"And meantime? Well? Out with it, since you're obviously burning to tell me."

"Meantime he's having a cozy evening with the Erdmann girl."

"That bitch? Did you put her up to it?"

"Even if I did, Captain, the main thing is, she invited him and he accepted. He didn't back out because he couldn't— because he didn't want to."

"I don't believe it. I can't believe it."

"Would you like a conducted tour, Captain?"

"That won't be necessary," Hein said, trying strenuously to conceal his uneasiness. "The mere fact that you ask such a question betrays how little you know either me or Schubert. Mutual distrust plays no part in our relationship. Our word alone suffices."

"Then ask him what he's been up to. I'll dig him out for you."

"Johannes keeps nothing from me. He tells me everything."

"You don't want to know, do you?"

"That," Hein said gravely, "is a remark I shall choose to ignore. I have never ducked the truth in my life."

"In that case I'll get the boy so you can ask him yourself. It shouldn't take longer than ten minutes to tidy him up."

Johannes Schubert reported to the tower chamber fifteen minutes later. Captain Hein did not appear to have moved a muscle in the interim. He was still standing in the window embrasure, statuelike.

"There you are at last," he said. "I expected you earlier."

Schubert flushed scarlet. "I didn't realize, sir. No one told me."

"Well, you're here now. That's the important thing."

"But where has he been in the meantime?" Bergen put in. "That's important too, wouldn't you say, Captain?"

"Is it important, Johannes?" Hein asked. "Does any importance attach to it—in comparison with the relationship that exists between us?"

"Even I wouldn't attach much importance to what's happened," Bergen said, "but happened it has. And with Elizabeth Erdmann." He turned to Schubert. "Isn't that right, Johannes?"

"You don't have to reply," Hein said hurriedly, with a note of warning. "You're answerable to me alone, and then only if I deem it right or necessary."

Schubert, standing between them, clasped his hands together like a choirboy at prayer. Hoarsely, he said, "I don't know what I'm supposed to say. I don't have any sense of guilt."

"Good enough," Hein said, as though that settled the matter.

Bergen shook his head. "Nothing wrong with a clear conscience, Captain, but what's it worth? Perhaps he can't recognize when he's guilty in the eyes of those who count. You've been to bed with her, Johannes, haven't you?"

"No!" groaned Hein.

"What if it's true, Captain?"

"Then he's lost—finished! But I still don't believe it. Johannes, tell me I'm right to believe in the existence of absolute and unblemished purity!"

Schubert hung his head. "I think I'm in love with her."

"He means he went to bed with her," Bergen said stubbornly.

Johannes Schubert gazed at his battery commander, entreating forgiveness. He found himself looking into a face of granite. "Is it really so bad?"

"You actually copulated with this woman?"

"It all seemed so natural. . . ."

Hein blanched. "In that case, you and I are finished. Forever."

"I never dreamed that I'd. . . ."

"So much the worse!" Hein bellowed the words like a beast in pain. "You're incapable of thought—incapable of thinking as I do, totally insensitive to higher things. You're just another uninhibited, instinct-ridden creature—one of the lower orders of humanity. Contemptible, worthless!"

"But, Captain," Bergen said, ostensibly trying to pacify him, "the boy only did what comes naturally. Who doesn't?"

"Silence!" barked Hein. "Get out of here at once—you too, Schubert. You have no place in my world, so leave it!"

He pointed at Schubert, right arm at full length and face averted as though he could not endure the sight of him.

"Go," he said in a choking voice. "I never wish to see you again."

A few moments later Captain Hein had the tower chamber to himself again. He stood alone in the wavering candlelight, hugging the ducal robe about him. The darkness behind him sucked up his shadow.

He felt infinitely tired, so tired that he could scarcely keep his feet, but he fought for poise, self-control, composure. Movement returned to his face, which rearranged itself into a frozen smile.

He reached for the candelabrum which stood on the table in front of him and picked it up in his right hand, simultaneously adjusting the ducal robe with his left.

Slowly and sedately at first, then faster and ever faster, he strode through the banquet chamber, down the winding staircase, down the château steps, across the terrace and into the park, where he made for the church. The cloak billowed out behind him like a banner.

Reaching the doors of the church, Hein drew back his foot and kicked them open. They swung inward and struck the massive stonework with a crash. The nave reverberated like a mighty gong.

Resolutely, with the candelabrum held high, he stalked toward the altar—or, more precisely, toward the bulky metal coffin that stood before it. He deposited the candelabrum on it and looked around. To his right, seated on one of the altar steps, he saw a figure.

Hein recognized Magnus. He gave an exclamation of surprise and pleasure.

"Professor! What are you doing here at this hour?"

"I've been waiting for you," Magnus said without moving. "For several nights, as a matter of fact. Ever since the first time you came. I was sure you'd put in another appearance."

"I came—I couldn't help myself. I had to be here."

Quietly, he added, "Where else could I have gone at a time like this?"

"What time is that?"

"The moment of truth," said Hein. He joined Magnus on the altar steps, separated from him by the coffin. "You could liken my situation to that of a man who claws at the ground in an earthquake, knowing that it will either swallow him or bear him up—casting himself on its mercy. And now I find you here too, beside the coffin of our duke."

"His coffin," Magnus said, "but not his final resting place."

"Do you know for certain, or are you still guessing?"

"His coffin is empty, and I know why."

"So you've found out what really happened! Tell me, was he buried with his comrades on the battlefield, or did some malicious enemy carry off his body and destroy it?"

"Neither." Professor Magnus stared into the candlelight with narrowed eyes. "He rotted to death, in a manner of speaking."

Hein looked incredulous. "He what?"

"He died of creeping decay."

"Poison, you mean?"

"In the initial phase, ulcers covered his abdominal region. His lymph glands swelled. Next came inflammation of the tonsils, loss of hair and running eyes. Then his skin erupted in a mass of purulent sores. His spinal cord softened, his brain shriveled. He ended his days as a putrescent vegetable."

"But what had happened to him?" Hein cried in torment. "What disease had attacked him?"

"It destroyed him utterly," Magnus pursued. "His legs were the first to fail—he couldn't walk, let alone ride a horse. Two servants had to lift him from his night commode. Then his hands and arms went. They had to feed him like a little child. He became bald and toothless. His tongue swelled until he could no longer articulate."

"My God," Hein groaned to himself. "Why did it all happen—who was to blame?"

"His ravaged brain deteriorated steadily. He stank of sweat and pus, urine and excrement."

"But why—why?"

"He was suffering from syphilis, then incurable and known as the French pox. Charles Louis contracted it on campaign, no doubt from one or more of the camp whores who crossed his path—and there were few he failed to sample."

"No!" screamed Hein. "No, not that!"

"Putrefaction was so far advanced when he died that his physicians had no choice but to cremate his body. And that, Captain, is why this coffin contains nothing but stale air."

Hein rose from the altar steps and rushed off into the darkness without casting another glance at the empty sarcophagus. Shadows engulfed him like a boundless sea from which there could be no return.

Interim Report No. 8

Comments
made by Frau Dr. Werner-Weilheim
with special reference to
the function of women in wartime.

"As a member of the professor's team, I was kept busy with research work—not, of course, that it prevented me from taking an active interest in the troops' welfare. Quite irrespective of rank or appointment, needless to say. Our fundamentally democratic attitude shone through clearly, even in those dark days.

"For example, I mixed socially with a signalman named Bergen, likewise a number of the more senior NCO's with whom we came in contact. I received no thanks in the first instance and became the victim of distressing rumors in the second, but no matter—one has to take these things in one's stride.

"Be that as it may, the atmosphere in D. was generally—indeed, predominantly—harmonious. The local town Commandant, Captain Schmidt, displayed a touching eagerness to please, and Second Lieutenant Helmreich of Battery No. 3, an extremely nice young man, lent me his wholehearted support. Lieutenant Minder, too, made consistent efforts to fulfill the wishes of his battery commander, Captain Hein, who was a wholly exceptional person. A war hero, a man of honor, a gentleman and philosopher.

"Even today, I shudder when I recall his tragic end."

Particulars
supplied by ex-Quartermaster Sergeant Alois Softer
in response to questions about his wartime activities.

"What more do you want to know? I expect you've already been given the lowdown on my recreation center—not brothel, as some people used to call it. That only leaves the question of my stores—not loot, if you don't mind.

"To begin with, my real job was to keep battery morale in peak condition. Ask yourself this, and be quite honest: What three things make a tired soldier sit up and take notice? I'll tell you. Decent grub, a few beers, and a piece of the other.

"In practice, that meant keeping the boys supplied with canned food, liquor, perfume, panties, bras and stockings, gloves, blouses, lace, et cetera. . . . I stocked the lot and sold everything at rock-bottom prices.

"Know the secret of my success? I was always two jumps ahead of the opposition. Even in Poland when the guns were still going off I managed to save various shops from being burned or looted for no good reason. I did the same in France too, except that my system got more efficient the farther we advanced. After the shooting stopped I went in immediately and made some clever deals with French shopkeepers and dealers. It was all legal and aboveboard, mind you—in fact you could call me the founder of the Common Market.

"The upshot was, I could offer our boys various selections for dispatching to their loved ones back home. At cost, more or less. For example:

"*Selection A:* for gray-haired mums and grannies. Contents: three kinds of sweet liqueur, namely, Cointreau, Chartreuse (yellow or green according to choice), and Crème de Menthe (green or white); Brittany lace or Chinese silk, sufficient for one dress; nougat from the Rhône Valley or almond cakes from Provence. Cost: RM50.

"*Selection B:* specially designed for girlfriends and fiancées, also sisters. Wives too, of course. Contents: one complete set of underwear, all colors including black; three bottles of perfume; two lipsticks, mascara complete with brush, nail polish, et cetera, et cetera. A real winner! Cost: likewise RM50.

"I also provided special assortments for fathers, brothers and male friends, with the emphasis on champagne or red wine. Then there were designer dresses and women's shoes made to order, crocodile handbags, stoles in any fur from rabbit to mink, buffalo-hide bottles, Benny Goodman records, a full range of French letters—anything a man or woman could want, and no item over RM100.

"As for transporting the stuff back home, I had two trucks from Arm's haulage company working a regular shuttle service, also a goods train permanently reserved for me by a railwayman who owed me a favor. . . ."

Further explanations
given by Elizabeth (née) Erdmann.

"I was very young at the time. I'm not excusing myself, simply trying to explain a couple of things. For instance, my emotions, or whatever you choose to call them. I know the Werner-Weilheim woman had some uncomplimentary names for me—easy lay, and so on. That was rich, coming from her!

"Still, who cares, if she got a kick out of it? Not that she got much of a kick out of anything, poor old cow. I bet she thought of the war effort even when she was lying on her back with her legs open. Yes, Krüger sneaked Moll into her bed with Arm's help—I know it for a fact. We laughed ourselves sick, especially as there wasn't much to laugh about in those days.

"It was all the professor's fault. Stirring things up was his favorite hobby. He played people off against each other—me

314   HERO IN THE TOWER

against the *Frau Doktor*, her against Krüger, Krüger against
Bergen, Krüger and Bergen against Hein. It was his idea of fun.
"To top it all, he swiped the Fragonard from me. Thanked
me for having 'rescued' the picture and promised he'd keep it
safe. He said he'd hand it over in due course, but he never did.
There was a funny side to it, I grant you."

*Uncorrected notes for an expert opinion
drafted by Colonel Alfons Piepenbrink (ret.),
official historian to Antiaircraft Command.*

"Like other units in Corps I-IX, Battery No. 3 displayed
military virtues of the highest order, certainly during the campaigns in Poland and France, and also—up to, say, winter, '41—
during the Russian campaign. Thereafter, the effects of dilu-
tion, expansion and replacement were such as to impair the
quality of the antiaircraft corps to which it belonged.

"There were wide variations between the regiments comprising that corps, principally, no doubt, because their commanders
did not enjoy the same standard of training and had not been
selected with equal care. Some were short on combat experience
and lacked the iron determination proper to their level of
command.

"The real problem was that these antiaircraft units only came
into being after 1933, being recruited from artillery formations
belonging to the former *Reichswehr*. They contained substantial numbers of officers drawn from semi- or para-military
organizations such as the police. Finally, the ratio of regular
to reserve officers varied widely between individual units and
worsened as the war progressed.

"Thus, whether in ground combat or in numbers of enemy
aircraft shot down, almost all the really outstanding individual
successes were scored by highly trained regulars with genuine
guts and initiative—Hein, for example.

"The latter officer, who was equally successful in a ground
and antiaircraft role, soon became not only a personification of
true heroism but a target for ruthless attacks by the enemy. It
was not long before our erstwhile foes assigned teams of Resist-

ance saboteurs to hunt him down, exploiting every opportunity to destroy this living symbol of German military valor. "Only this can account for what ultimately occurred."

Felix Sandner,
wartime member of a propaganda company,
now a senior cameraman with the West German TV network.

"What's wrong? What are you beefing about? Faked pictures? Mock fires concocted out of cans of gasoline? Buildings shot up in broad daylight and filtered to look like the small hours? So what?

"Man, like where have you been for the last hundred years? Didn't your mother ever tell you the facts of life? A movie camera isn't a Bible you swear on—it's a gadget for recording what you want it to.

"A cameraman shoots what he's told to shoot. The director decides what goes in front of the lens. You can splice it all together in the cutting room—corpses, eyeballs, atomic explosions, girls' tits—the lot. They've been doing it for decades. Look at *Hiroshima, Mon Amour.* . . ."

Question: Did you know Captain Hein?

Answer: I shot him a couple of times. He was just another assignment.

Question: So he didn't make any particular impression on you?

Answer: Why should he? Most of those death-or-glory boys were like peas in a pod, basically. So much for so-called heroes. . . .

9

Prussian Roulette—Final Phase

Next day dawned crystal clear. The French sky took on a positively Prussian shade of blue. The birds flew high and filled the air with their song.

The first lavatory to flush in Château D. made itself heard at an early hour. The sound came from the top floor, where Captain Hein had his quarters. Krüger registered its source and was awake in a flash. His nose for trouble told him that particular vigilance would be advisable today. He killed a few minutes by personally shooing his men into the grounds for an early morning workout.

After shaving and imbibing his usual half tumbler of crème de menthe, he made his way upstairs. It did not surprise him to find Hein fully dressed. The captain was standing, bright as a button and patently sober, in the center of the tower chamber. The morning light seemed to ripple over his erect figure.

"There you are at last," Hein said.

Krüger clicked his heels. "I hope I'm not too late, sir."

Hein smiled grimly. "So do I, Sergeant Major. We've let

things slide lately. The situation has caught up with us. Neglect always does."

"We'll straighten it out, sir," Krüger assured him. "You only have to say what needs to be done and how you want it done. Also why, preferably."

Hein raised his hand in an admonitory gesture. His voice was as clear and incisive as if it had never been frayed with alcohol. "I'm a generous man, as you know—generous to a fault—but my generosity has been disgracefully abused and exploited."

"Not by me, sir."

"If it had, you wouldn't be standing where you are now. I'm not reproaching you personally, Krüger. On the other hand, I'm bound to say that reprehensible things have been permitted to happen in the sphere of command for which I hold you accountable—things which are absolutely alien to my nature."

"Slipups, sir, that's all. Nothing serious."

"Don't playact with me, Sergeant Major. I know your game—in fact I deliberately take it into account. No cooperation without the occasional concession, eh? Well, it's a system that cuts both ways, certainly where we're concerned."

"It could break down altogether if things get really rough."

"What do you mean?" Hein demanded. "Are you threatening me?"

"I wouldn't put it that way, sir," Krüger said quickly. "All the same, things being like they are. . . ."

"Oh, and how is that?" Hein laughed aloud, his voice even frostier than his face. His hands knotted themselves into fists. "I thought I'd already made your position clear. Allow me to sum it up for you. You not only help to establish a brothel on military premises but take your cut as well—on behalf of battery funds, naturally. Arm is running a haulage business in which you also have a share—again for the benefit of battery funds. Softer's mail-order firm is thriving—yet another source of considerable profit to you or battery funds, whichever. Did you really imagine that I was ignorant of these things?"

"Whatever's going on and whatever you choose to call it, sir, it's all for the good of Battery No. 3."

"Which I command."

"Of course."

"Which I command and shall continue to command at least for as long as it takes to bring you and your cronies to justice, should I so decide. I could break each and every one of you—or don't you think I'm equal to the task?"

Krüger stiffened his back. "What do you expect me to do, sir—this time?"

"Corporal Schubert has been a great disappointment to me —I might almost say, a crushing disappointment. He has deceived me, abused my trust, gone behind my back, betrayed our common ideals."

"I see," Krüger said impassively. "In other words, sir, as far as you're concerned, he's dead."

Captain Hein did not appear to have heard. "So much for my views on the subject. Now it's up to you. Knowing you as I do, I'm sure you'll devise an effective and permanent solution of some kind."

"With the emphasis on permanent, sir?"

"Effective action on your part might help me overlook several other matters. Any suggestions?"

"Well, the first thing might be to promote him."

"Promote him? My dear Krüger, what on earth are you driving at?"

"As an NCO, Schubert would be part of my immediate circle—a member of the club, so to speak. That way we'd be in a position to strong-arm him a little—prod him into doing the right thing."

"Not bad," mused Hein, "not bad at all."

"Quite apart from that, sir, promoting him would spike a few people's guns if anything happened to cause misunderstandings outside the battery."

"Excellent!" Hein treated Krüger to an amiably conspiratorial smile. "You can be ingenious when you try—and you're trying now, eh? I knew you wouldn't disappoint me."

"A permanent solution. . . ." Krüger meditated for a moment. "I suppose there's no alternative?"

Hein buried his face in his hands as though the light hurt his eyes. Tonelessly, he said, "Krüger, we're at war. We both realize it and we've always been prepared to act accordingly. Ultimately, there are only two choices open to any subordinate of mine. Either he's one hundred percent for me—in other words, us—or he's against me and the men under my command. In the first instance he's a welcome addition to our ranks, in the second he's a foreign body and must be eliminated."

"By me."

"It might be more apt to say, by methods of your devising. You have my express approval. Is that plain enough?"

"Then I don't have any choice."

"For me or against me—remember? It has to be done, and done thoroughly. We owe it to ourselves."

Krüger nodded. "Leave it to me."

"Good," Hein said, rubbing his hands. "Another thing, Sergeant Major—one that will no doubt gladden your heart. Tell that witch doctor Magnus and his harpies to go to hell."

"You mean I can dump them on Captain Schmidt?"

"If you wish."

"It'll be a pleasure," Krüger said grimly. "What's more, it'll pep up one or two of the weaker brethren, in view of what's got to happen to Schubert."

"I see we understand each other," said Hein. "Not that I had any doubt of it."

* * *

Krüger was sitting at his desk, seemingly deep in thought, when Softer entered the orderly room. The battery sergeant major had breakfasted in the interim off a half dozen eggs scrambled with cream and poured over a slice of lightly fried ham the thickness of his little finger.

"Here are the latest returns," Softer announced. "We're making a nice fat profit, according to the figures. Carry on this way and battery funds'll be competing with the Bank of France. We could retire tomorrow if we wanted to."

"And desert the captain?"

Softer could not suppress a chuckle. "Where does he come in? By the time I really got started here I was already making ten times a captain's pay. Now it's more like a hundred times. What's Hein got that could possibly interest us?"

"Information, most of it about you. If he wanted to, Hein could have you transferred to a punishment battalion or haul you in front of a court-martial. Profiteering, persistent misappropriation of government property, embezzlement of army funds, repeated and successful attempts to convert captured supplies to your own use. . . ."

"Hold it!" Softer squirmed like a cornered rat. "What are you hinting at?"

"I'm not hinting," Krüger said menacingly, "I'm drawing your attention to a few facts. Hein could crucify us all if he wanted to."

"But not after all that's happened, surely?" Softer protested. "He's got Runge on his conscience, to begin with. He blew up the municipal water tower and flattened two houses. He's also responsible for getting at least two men wounded, quite apart from the fact that he's shot a number of animals including the mayor's dog—and the mayor's a personal friend of the town commandant."

"Balls! You won't find anything about dogs in army regulations."

"Yes, but this dog was being taken for a walk by the mayor's niece, and she was accompanied by the railwayman who takes care of our transport problems. That puts us under an obligation, I figure."

"Bring him here," Krüger said firmly.

"What are you going to do?"

"Teach him a lesson. Both of you."

"Take it easy, Krüger old chum! The man's important to me and my business interests, which means you and battery funds as well. It'll cost us something if you don't treat him right."

"Jesus Christ, you sound more like a Yiddisher shopkeeper every day. You can't see beyond your own nose. Well, let me tell you this: You aren't the brains of this outfit, you're the asshole. And don't come moaning to me about short-term expenses. I'm thinking of the long term, which is all that matters. Damn well find that man and wheel him in here."

The railwayman was ushered in, a scrawny little runt with watery eyes, an outsize nose and a voice of surprising volume. A reassuring nod from Softer confirmed his faith in the righteousness of his cause.

"A dog's been shot," he said plaintively.

"A dog?" echoed Krüger. "We ran over a couple of dogs during the Polish campaign—squashed them flat under the tracks. We mowed down a couple more during the French campaign, one with a tommy gun because he got on our nerves and the other with a hand grenade. Blown to bits, he was."

"Yes, Sergeant Major, but this dog was a lovely golden retriever—sort of. The mayor was very attached to it."

"Sanctimonious bastard!"

"Pardon?" The railwayman looked puzzled. "Did you say bastard? Who were you referring to?"

"You."

"But why?"

"Because you're trying to take the heat off yourself. You're trying to gloss over your own kinky little hobbies by dropping our battery commander in the shit on account of some lousy mongrel, in the hope that we'll overlook your filthy behavior with children."

"Don't say that!" exclaimed the man, thoroughly shaken. "You've got me wrong. I'm the fatherly type—I love kids. You can't reproach me for that, surely, not when I've done so much to promote better relations with the French? Added to that, I've done a lot for the welfare of your men. Softer, here, can confirm that."

Softer nodded.

"But he won't," snapped Krüger.

"Look, Sergeant Major," the railwayman said uneasily, "I've been misjudged. All I ever did was put my arm around the child, very gently."

"Balls, people have seen you at it. I can produce witnesses —plenty of them, if you're interested."

"But Softer. . . ."

"Softer needs his head examined too," said Krüger. "Go on, let him in on it."

"Well," Softer told his business associate, rather reluctantly, "it's like this: no dog, no child—are you with me?"

"Not quite," whined the railwayman. "Could you be more specific?"

"Nothing happened," Softer explained. "Neither one thing nor the other. It's the only way of keeping our welfare organization in business."

"Otherwise," amplified Krüger, "in plain language, I'll have you summarily arrested for indecent assault on a minor. Get the idea?"

The man gave a lugubrious nod. "The mayor's dog got

mixed up in some target practice and was fatally wounded. Captain Hein had nothing to do with it. Right so far?"

"Yes," Krüger said contemptuously. "And now, you dirty old man, move it in double-quick time."

"What's this League of Nations game?" Bergen asked Tino Hiller. "It sounds ridiculous. Nobody but a cretin could have dreamed it up in the first place."

Hiller shrugged. "It's just a game. They play it often."

"Do you enjoy it?"

"No, but I don't beef about it either. There's no point. Most of them think it's the height of entertainment."

"But you don't?"

"I'm one of the minority, like you. We're outvoted, so we might as well surrender."

"Without a fight?"

"Look, Bert, standards are low around here. If you want to make out you have to adapt yourself to the lowest common denominator."

In accordance with Krüger's instructions relating to the next session of the NCO's social club, they were rehearsing the gibberish which constituted the essential humor of the game. Players were obliged to imagine an international conference attended by delegates from every country in the world. It was a point of honor to be able to name at least thirty such delegates in the prescribed manner. Experienced players could enumerate fifty, and an acknowledged master like Arm, who was closely rivaled by Softer, had sixty or more names at his fingertips.

"All right, Bert, give me the name of the delegate from Switzerland."

"Herr Fuckimucki," Bergen said reluctantly.

"Sweden?"

"Count Clapcocksen."

"Italy?"

"Signor Stinka di Finga."

"You see, you can do it if you try. Don't forget, though, thirty names are the absolute minimum. You have to drink a schnapps for every one you miss, and our friends will be itching to see you under the table. Especially tonight, when there's bound to be a real bender in honor of your pal Schubert."

"Poor bastard. What's he done to deserve a party?"

"He's being promoted, didn't you know? That's what it's all about. They've got a whole program planned—the League of Nations thing is only one item. There'll also be songs from Neumann and dirty stories from Arm."

"They turn my stomach, the bunch of them." Bergen winced.

"Puke in private," Hiller advised. "God help you if they really work you over. Give them a single chance to take offense and they'll do you in. You wouldn't want it to come to that, would you?"

They were lying side by side on the one patch of ground that had not been entirely ravaged by gun tractors. Grass and flowers surrounded them. They stared up at the sky past the sharp outlines of a blue-green fir. There were very few clouds to be seen. Everything looked provocatively peaceful.

"Tino," said Bergen, "what's the reason for it all? Was it bound to happen, with a superman like Hitler in charge, or is it simply war that brings out the worst in people—turns them into a herd of guzzling, boozing, fornicating swine?"

"I wouldn't dwell on it too much if I were you," Hiller said. "Brooding dulls the brain, and dull brains aren't an aid to survival in this outfit."

Bergen shook his head. "An outfit commanded by a hero—and what a hero! Hein's got a few flaws, sure, but they're all part of a hero's equipment. Then there's Krüger, a shit-hot military practitioner who regards the battery as his life's work and personal property. Finally there are these, docile

creatures who call themselves NCO's and drive the men like
cattle. What a ghastly combination!"

"Accept it, Bert. Play it cool—it's the only way to stay
healthy." Tino Hiller stretched and yawned. "Okay, back to
the gospel according to Krüger. What are the names of the
Polish and Bulgarian delegates?"

"Pullmypudski and Havitoff. Oh, shit, it's too goddamn
asinine for words! Count me out."

"You'd better fit in or they'll cut you down to size—or
try to. Nobody can afford to complain, and that includes
you."

"Where's the captain?" asked Lieutenant Minder.

The question was addressed by field telephone to Battery
Sergeant Major Krüger. The answer came back pat.

"The captain's busy."

"But I have to speak to him urgently about our training
schedule."

"Nothing the matter with our training schedule, is there?"
Krüger spoke in a tone of polite inquiry.

"The trouble is," Minder said confidentially, "there hasn't
been a decision about who's to succeed Sergeant Runge. I
can't run the show properly unless I get some definite instructions on the subject."

"Why not?" Krüger demanded. "I thought you were
carrying on as usual. In other words, the way Captain Hein
likes it."

"But I'm not certain what that is."

"If you can't find out for yourself, Lieutenant, I'm sure
the captain'll let you know."

"In that case, may I speak to him?"

"Sorry," Krüger said. "The captain left instructions that
he wasn't to be disturbed."

Hein was sitting alone in his tower, heroically imbibing
champagne which he was obliged to pour for himself. He

passed the time by playing Wagner records—the "Ride of the Valkyries," "Siegfried's Rhine Journey" and the funeral march from the *Twilght of the Gods.*

Then came Leander, with "Davon geht die Welt nicht unter!" followed—three times in succession—by "Ich weiss, es wird einmal ein Wunder geschehn!"

Finally, an interminable repetition of melodies from *The Merry Widow,* an operetta known to have found favor with Adolf Hitler, the Führer and Supreme Commander. Likewise with Captain Hein.

"Sir," panted Lieutenant Minder, robbed of breath by his rapid climb and a sense of audacity at having penetrated the tower chamber unbidden, "it's about a successor for Sergeant Runge."

Hein listened idly to a Lehár waltz. "Runge has no legitimate successor. He's irreplaceable."

Minder hastened to agree. "Of course, sir. However, there seem to be two gunnery NCO's who might serve as a stopgap. Bombardier Kreuzer of No. 2 gun and Bombardier Vishinsky of the predictor crew."

"Kreuzer's breath smells," declared the captain, "which probably means he's sick. As for Vishinsky, he can't even clear the high-jump bar at one meter thirty-five."

"I was only thinking. . . ."

"Well, don't!" snapped Hein. He rose and stalked across the tower chamber, swayed for a moment but recovered himself immediately. In a clear, incisive voice, he proclaimed: "This battery is an extension of myself. No man could have a more faithful friend or implacable enemy than me. There can be only one decision in my unit—for me or against me. Have you made up your mind yet?"

"But of course, sir. My loyalty to you naturally takes precedence over everything else."

"Very good," said Hein.

"In that case, sir, what are your orders?"

"Prepare to move out."

"Pardon?" said Minder.

"Are you deaf? I said prepare to move out."

The lieutenant's jaw dropped. Hein's order meant that all tents must be struck, all equipment assembled, all quarters vacated. Stored ammunition had to be loaded into trucks, guns and range finders prepared for the road. Finally, the men themselves had to stand to in full marching order, ready to repel an imaginary attack. It was a gigantic piece of bullshit, Minder reflected, the latest and most outrageous example of Heinian despotism.

"But. . . ."

The battery commander cut him short. "Kindly do as I say, promptly and without hesitation. Only failures use the word 'but.' You follow me?"

"League of Nations it is," said Krüger, leaning comfortably back in his orderly-room chair. He surveyed Bergen with interest. "All right, let's see how much you've learned. Tell me the name of the delegate from China."

Bergen knew what it was: Prince Wankinahankee—or was that the one from Hawaii? Subtlety counted little with his fellow NCO's, who hailed newly devised names with delight. For instance, Tino Hiller had thought up an Oriental delegate whose name, freely pronounced with a strong rustic accent, sounded like Fark U Nu. Bergen had found it hard to raise a smile.

"I haven't got that far," he replied cautiously. "I've only learned the European ones so far—about thirty of them."

"Unfortunate," commented Krüger. He sounded almost hurt. "Looks as if you don't go for our party games. Too childish for you, is that it?"

"Not at all, Sergeant Major. I imagine they're specially designed to foster team spirit among the members of your club."

"A club that doesn't appeal to you, eh? You're always

giving us the cold shoulder. Aren't we good enough for you?"

"Don't get me wrong, Sergeant Major," Bergen said, as politely as he could manage. "I'm quite prepared to take part in your entertainments and I'm doing my best to develop an appreciation of them, but everything takes time."

Krüger's eyes narrowed. "Sometimes, like now, I get the nasty feeling you're a born troublemaker—a malcontent. Added to that, you've got brains, which means you're on the lookout for pickings. Who or what are you planning to pocket this time?"

Krüger had to wait for an answer. He did so with patient deliberation, keeping his eyes fixed on Bergen like a gigantic cat watching a mouse. They did not waver even when the telephone rang.

It was Lieutenant Seifert Blanker, the Group adjutant:

GROUP ADJUTANT: Krüger? I've just received a communi-
cation from your unit, signed by the battery commander. It contains a request—or suggestion—that Lance
Bombardier Schubert be promoted to bombardier forth-
with. It's headed "Most Urgent." Rather unusual,
wouldn't you say?

KRÜGER: Not coming from Captain Hein, sir, as I'm sure
there's no need for me to point out. The promotion is
for meritorious conduct. Captain Hein wants it confirmed at once.

GROUP ADJUTANT: But it isn't standard procedure.

KRÜGER: To Captain Hein, standard procedure means his
own way of fighting the war. Just in case any snags
cropped up, he instructed me to put in a direct call from
him to the Group commander. Will that be necessary?

GROUP ADJUTANT: Very well, very well. If you want the
promotion confirmed as urgently as all that, take it as
read.

KRÜGER: Thank you, sir. Anything else?

GROUP ADJUTANT: Yes, as a matter of fact there is. Only a
minor point, I trust. Is it true that Captain Hein has
issued a unit movement order?

KRÜGER: May I inquire how you heard, sir? Did somebody
contact Group HQ direct, without going through the
battery commander? Lieutenant Minder, say?

GROUP ADJUTANT: That's quite immaterial. What matters is
whether such an order has been given or not. No movement order has been issued by us, nor are we planning
to issue one in the immediate future. If it's true, it's
bound to cause a lot of unnecessary fuss. If I were to
inform the Group commander. . . .

KRÜGER: I wouldn't do that, sir. It's simply a unit exercise for
special training purposes. The battery commander bears
sole responsibility.

GROUP ADJUTANT: Very well, that's all right. I'm relying on
the accuracy of your information, mark you. On your
head be it. Good-bye.

"They're all the same," growled Krüger, slamming the
receiver back on its hook, "—all of them! Why should you
want to be different, Bergen? What do you hope to achieve
in the long run? Belong to our outfit—whether you want to
or not—and you have to live by the book. There are some
rules you can't get around, but that still leaves plenty of
scope for a smart boy like you."

"I'm ready to obey the rules," Bergen said. "It isn't me
I'm worried about."

"Schubert, is it? Why, have you got a crush on the boy?
You wouldn't be the first—not that it's any news to you. Or
is it just that you don't want him upgraded?"

"Why should I mind?"

"Because he'll be taking over the battery signals section
instead of you. I know you were earmarked for the job,
but circumstances rule you out. Is that what's eating you?"

Bergen knit his brow. He tried to gauge the drift of

Krüger's remarks but failed, so he preserved an impassive silence.

"Know what?" Krüger said gaily. "You look as if you could use a change."

"What kind of change?"

"No need to ask, I was going to tell you anyway. You're a trained signaler. Okay, check every foot of field telephone cable between here and Captain Schmidt's office. Then check the lines to Group and Regimental HQ. That ought to keep you busy for the next few hours."

"You want me out of the way?"

"For your own good. I've a hunch you may do something stupid and I want to make sure you don't get the chance. I've got a soft spot for you, but it certainly won't last unless you show a bit of appreciation."

"What are you planning to do with Schubert?"

Krüger looked unusually placid, and his voice had the dark and gentle cadence of a funeral address. "Every tree gets the ax sometime. The only question is, when?"

"What's the matter?" Elizabeth propped herself on one elbow and stared down at Johannes Schubert, who was lying beside her fully dressed. She sounded puzzled and uneasy. "Is it the daylight that's bothering you?"

"I don't know," he said dully. "I feel as if everything's closing in on me."

"You too?" she said, raising her eyebrows.

"Everything and everyone," he repeated in a gloomy voice. "I feel as if I'm being hunted, ganged up on, driven into a corner. There's a noose around my neck and it's getting tighter all the time. I can hardly breathe."

They were lying on Elizabeth's bed in the conservatory, surrounded by partition walls. Orange light flooded them as the early autumn sun began to set. They clung to each other, but his hands were stiff and hers soon went limp.

"You don't love me," she said tormentedly.

"I do!"

"Then why not show it?"

"It's so difficult," he stammered. "I want to, really I do, but I can't. It's this place. Everything's getting me down, Elizabeth. What can I do?"

"You poor baby," she said, almost dispassionately. "You're all the same at heart. What's a girl to do—feel sorry for you or despise you? I wish to God I knew."

"Hi there!" called one of the military policemen—Konz or Kator—from some distance away. His Hitler salute degenerated into a friendly wave.

Krüger was standing with Arm outside the tented transportation workshop on the grounds, inspecting a vehicle which had been stolen from a neighboring unit the previous night. "Cover that thing up," he told Arm.

"Think that's why they've come?" Arm asked nervously, jerking a thumb at his lastest acquisition, a jeep-style BMW. "They aren't usually that quick on the draw."

"I'll check," was all Krüger said. He went to meet the two MP's, who looked more than ever like twins. "Long time no see!" he called jovially. "Must be at least a week. Don't tell me the schnapps has held out this long?"

Konz—or Kator—smiled. "We never make pigs of ourselves, not with high-quality stuff like yours. We make it last."

Krüger smiled back. "But a few reinforcements wouldn't be refused, eh?"

They exchanged handshakes, grins and nods. Their relationship might have been described as connivance at first sight.

"Well," said Krüger, "what is it this time?"

"To be honest," said the MP with the slightly more substantial sausages of flesh on his neck, "we just dropped by to tell you we'll be dropping by tomorrow afternoon. About 1400 hours, if it's okay with you."

"Why?"

"To check on a couple of things," said the other MP. "Somebody's made a complaint. In my opinion it isn't worth the paper it's written on, but we've got to look into it. Public indecency, and so on."

"I see," Krüger said with complete outward calm. "They probably say we're running a brothel here. Well, it's a barefaced lie."

"I took that for granted," one of the MP's observed, rather ambiguously.

"Even if you were running such an establishment," added the other, "it isn't expressly permitted but it isn't expressly forbidden either. In other words, it's none of our business."

"That's all right then," said Krüger. "In that case, just drop by tomorrow and load up with a few dozen of the best."

"You're a pal." Konz—or Kator—slapped Krüger on the back, and both MP's grinned warmly. "Unfortunately, there's something else— the fly in the ointment, you might call it. Complaints about a brothel are all wind and piss, like I said, but there's a complication."

"What is it?"

"Well, the charge doesn't refer to an establishment proper. It mentions an individual, female, nationality French, first name Marie-Antoinette, surname unknown. She's alleged to have presented her unclothed posterior to a German lady and uttered the customary invitation. I'm afraid we'll have to check."

"I know who's at the bottom of this," growled Krüger. "It's that bitch Werner-Weilheim. She's been stirring things up ever since she got here, but she won't do it much longer. The whole thing's a heap of horseshit, my friends. You really want to stick your noses in it?"

The two MP's laughed in unison. "No question of wanting to, pal," said one of them. "We've got to. Not before 1400 hours tomorrow, though."

* * *

"It's time for a cleanup," Krüger told Arm, who was staring at him dubiously. "What's more, you're the man for the job. It's your turn, Arm—you owe me a few favors."

Arm licked his lips. "Were those two here about me? You mean to say they traced the vehicle to me?"

"Of course," Krüger assured him brazenly, "and no wonder, the ham-fisted way you do things. Don't worry, though —I managed to dig you out. Not for the first time."

"Thank God for that!" Arm heaved a sigh of relief. "I've got enough on my mind as it is, thanks to that woman. She's after my blood—foaming at the mouth, she is. She'd bite my balls off given half a chance. That's love for you!"

"We're getting rid of her," Krüger announced with sovereign self-assurance, "her and the rest of her bunch, by arrangement with Captain Hein. We simply point out that this is a theater of war and tell them to get lost, quick. Bingo!"

"You think it'll work?" Arm asked, hope dawning. "Man, would that be a load off my mind!"

Krüger nodded confidently. "The lady can beef as much as she likes—she won't get anywhere. Leave it to me, Alfons. You'll be sitting pretty before you know it. But don't think I'm doing it for the sake of your bonny blue eyes, because I'm not."

Arm shrugged. "Nothing's free with you, not even a bullet in the back."

"Now that you mention it, chum, it's time for another game of Prussian roulette. In honor of the latest addition to our club."

Arm temporarily forgot his personal tribulations at the thought of Schubert's promotion. "That lily-livered, underdeveloped s.o.b.! His balls haven't dropped yet, and Hein promotes him! It's abnormal, that's what it is. Something ought to be done about it."

"You never said a truer word," agreed Krüger. "This

time we'll play the game with live ammunition, and you're going to arrange it."

"Me?" The word was a yelp of disbelief. Arm began to stammer. "But, Krüger, you've never asked me to do such a thing before. . . ."

"There's always a first time."

"But why me?"

"Why not?"

"You're fooling me, just saying it to see how I react." Arm paused. "Aren't you?"

"Stop bleating. I meant what I said."

"Couldn't I offer you something instead—my haulage business, say, or a piece of it? A big piece, if you like. Say fifty percent for you—I mean, battery funds. What do you say?"

"It's worth discussing," said Krüger. "A fifty-percent interest for battery funds, eh? I might accept that, but nothing barred. Not just a share in current takings—vehicles, spares and fuel as well. Also, I'd need some kind of guarantee."

"Done! What was that about a guarantee?"

"We've got to go whole hog—we don't have any choice, not with Hein putting the screws on. If we want a free hand in future we'll have to make a thorough job of it. That's where the Prussian roulette comes in. There are only two people we can't trust a hundred percent. Know who I mean?"

Arm nodded. "That tricky bastard Bergen, for one. He doesn't belong in our club. The same goes for Tino Hiller. He may know all there is to know about the guts of a five-ton truck, but he'd be more at home having tea with the vicar than swapping beers with the boys."

"Bergen's otherwise engaged," Krüger said. "He won't disturb us—I've taken care of that. As for Hiller, he's going to have the privilege of playing Prussian roulette for once.

With your gun, which you'll have loaded in advance. How about that for an idea?"

Arm's low whistle conveyed infinite relief. "It might work! Hiller's dumb enough to join in rather than risk being called a killjoy."

"So give him the wink and be subtle about it. Tell him he'd better play if he doesn't want to look like a horse's ass."

"Ladies and gentlemen," said Softer, gleefully surveying the assembled members of the historical research team, "time's up. This is the end of the line. All change!"

Professor Magnus returned his gaze with equanimity. "Every comedian is his own best audience, Herr Softer. You appear to be enjoying yourself."

"You can say that again." Softer put his hands on his pear-shaped hips. "It'll be a pleasure to show you the door. I volunteered for the job."

"Can you be more specific?" Magnus inquired, still without rancor.

"Certainly I can. You're civilians, ladies and gentlemen. You happen to be smack in the middle of an operational zone. For various important military reasons, not to mention your own safety, we've got to clear the area at once. In other words, shove off."

"Where to, may I ask?"

"Anywhere you like. There's plenty of accommodation downtown. Apply to the town major—he'll take care of you."

"Mad," said Professor Magnus, turning on his heel, "but not without method."

Elizabeth, who was standing motionless in the background, said, "May I make a comment too?"

"No," Softer told her sharply. "Keep out of this, you amateur tart. Girls like you belong in hotel bars. You upset the regular trade."

"Just one moment, Herr Softer!" Frau Dr. Werner-Weilheim squared her shoulders. "Administrative matters are my responsibility alone. As far as I'm concerned, neither you nor any other NCO, not even Herr Krüger, has any authority to remove us. I wish to speak to the battery commander in person."

"Tough luck, he's busy."

"Nevertheless, I insist on speaking to him at once."

"Who the hell do you think you are?" Softer chuckled to himself for a moment, then suppressed his hilarity and said quietly, "You seem to forget, *Frau Doktor*—the captain's a war hero."

"I know," she shrilled, bosom heaving, "I know! He's also a man of honor, a gentleman of the old school and a creative personality."

"Too true," said Softer. "A perfect description, but you obviously don't know what it means from your angle. You're a big disappointment to the captain, *Frau Doktor*. He thought you were a pure and unsullied specimen of German womanhood, and what showed up instead? A female like all the rest—ready to drop her drawers the first chance she gets and none too choosy about who she does it with. You can't expect the captain to tolerate that kind of behavior—it turns his stomach."

"You swine!" hissed the *Frau Doktor*. "How dare you slander me to the captain behind my back, set him against me, drag my name in the mud, trample on the dignity of my sex? Don't worry, you'll suffer for this!"

Softer retreated a step for safety's sake. "Can it, you old bitch. I'm out of your class."

"Silence!" she screamed. "You'll regret every word you've just said. I'll have you court-martialed, you and all your cronies, Arm and Krüger included."

"You wouldn't be the first to try," Softer retorted. "The fact remains, you're on your way out. Being generous, I'll

give you half an hour to get clear of the place—well, let's
make it forty-five minutes. If you aren't gone by then I'll
have you thrown out."

"Today," Krüger said briskly, "we're happy to welcome a
new member, the one and only Bombardier Schubert. I hope
he appreciates what it means to join the club."
Johannes Schubert strove to conceal his bewilderment.
"I'll try to."
"So he doesn't know the ropes yet," said Krüger. "Never
mind, he'll learn soon enough. Let's kick off with a toast—
two fingers of the best all around."
They drank with a kind of reverence. The first man to
finish was privileged to call the tune. He could request the
others to sing scatological songs in unison, demand solo performances for individual members, or inaugurate the traditional League of Nations game. This time, however, Krüger
seemed reluctant to waste time on such diversions. After a
number of swift glances at his watch, he suddenly cleared
his throat.
"Right, let's get down to business. A game of Prussian
roulette in honor of our new member."
So saying, he slammed his 8-mm automatic on the table.
The gun had a conspicuously pale wooden butt, and
Schubert, schooled by Bergen in advance, took careful note
of it. Sergeant Moll's brand-new 8-mm followed, then three
assorted pistols belonging to Softer, Forstmann and Kaminski. Softer, grinning happily, shoved the guns across to
Schubert.
"That makes five," said Krüger. "There's one missing."
"Where's yours, Hiller?" called Arm.
Tino Hiller pulled Arm's 8-mm automatic from his pocket
and put it with the rest. His hand hovered over the gun as if
it hurt him to remove it, but he eventually did so to a chorus
of cheerful laughter.

"Fire away," Krüger exhorted the new member. "That is, unless you've filled your pants already."

Deliberately, Johannes Schubert put out his hand and grasped the pistol with the pale wooden butt—Krüger's. He pulled it toward him and examined it with apparent indecision, then put the muzzle to his head.

"Whoa!" called Krüger. "No bet! It's against the rules to inspect a gun first. They'll have to be shuffled again. Neumann, you're a neutral observer—you do it."

Neumann did a thorough job. He strewed the guns across the tabletop, stirred them, piled them up, knocked them down, and switched them from hand to hand like a cardsharp.

Krüger, whose eyes remained almost shut throughout these proceedings, might have been dozing. Arm could scarcely contain his excitement and rocked from side to side. Schubert gazed spellbound at Neumann's busy hands and the guns he was pushing around the table, particularly the three 8-mm pistols—one with a pale wooden butt, one new-looking and one smeared with oil—which belonged to Krüger, Moll and Arm respectively.

As he did so, Bergen's advice echoed through his head. Play safe, Bergen had said. Subordinates usually acted under orders from their superiors, so the probability was that the loaded gun—if it existed at all—had been loaded by order of Krüger. That made his own gun the best bet. On the other hand, was it a double bluff? Who could weigh the probabilities in Battery No. 3?

On impulse Schubert reached for the third 8-mm—the oil-smeared automatic which belonged to Arm and had been introduced into the game by Tino Hiller. He put it to his forehead, keeping his eyes fixed on Krüger, who was leaning back with an expectant air. Schubert even thought he detected an encouraging wink. "Carry on," said Krüger, and the others watched him intently.

He must fit in with the rest, Schubert told himself. He must show these men how much he trusted them because he was one of them, or wanted to be. He had no alternative.

And so, with the automatic Arm had lent Hiller aimed between his eyes, he pulled the trigger. There was a flash, a half-muffled report, a fountain of blood, and he slumped headfirst into the litter of guns and bottles. His lips moved in a last effort to speak, but all that emerged was a bubbling, dying whisper, so faint as to be almost inaudible, "Why . . . I only loved . . . so why. . . ."

Then he lay still.

"He's gone," Corporal Neumann said knowledgeably. "Nothing to be done."

Krüger leaped to his feet with the rapidity of a startled predator. "God damn it! he cried accusingly. "That's carrying things too far!" He glared at his faithful minions, who had shrunk away from the horror on the table and were plastered against the walls. "How did it happen? Who did it —who's responsible?"

Nobody spoke. The NCO's stared at their sergeant major, not the dead man. The fear in their eyes was mingled with confidence. Confidence in Krüger.

"Right," said Krüger. "Whose gun was loaded?"

"Not mine, to begin with," Sergeant Arm said promptly. "I lent it to Hiller so he could play, but there wasn't anything in the chamber."

Krüger turned to Hiller with a look of unbounded astonishment. The others followed suit.

"Well, Hiller? What's your version?"

Hiller shook his head numbly. "It's true I borrowed the gun from Sergeant Arm, but I passed it on just as it was. I can swear to that."

"And I," Arm declared loudly, "can swear there wasn't a round in it when I handed it over. I checked in advance."

"In that case, Hiller, you're in for it." Krüger extended

his right arm and advanced on Hiller until his forefinger prodded Hiller's tunic in the region of his heart. "If it's true, you'll be court-martialed, and that could mean a short walk on a cold morning."

Tino Hiller went very pale and shook his head again. He tried to speak but failed.

Krüger abruptly withdrew his hand. "The fact remains, you're a member of the club. You've done your bit for Battery No. 3, and that counts for something. We don't leave a pal in the lurch, not in this outfit. Right?"

The others promptly nodded, one and all. There was even a murmur of approbation, and the usually taciturn Kaminski boomed a ritual response, "Right!"

Krüger rewarded him with an appreciative smile.

"Okay, carping at each other won't get us anywhere. Let's concentrate on the facts instead."

"What facts?" Arm inquired eagerly.

"Fact number one, Schubert's a goner. His death has been officially confirmed by the NCO i/c battery medical section, and nobody's going to bring him back to life. Fact number two, it'd be crazy to compromise a fellow NCO with a fine record. That leaves one alternative. It was an accident. The poor devil was cleaning his gun, took a round up the barrel, and pulled the trigger by mistake. It happens every other day."

"Let's get it down in writing," suggested Softer, looking as smug as a cream-fed cat.

The others, apart from Hiller, nodded again. They were infinitely relived by this renewed justification of their faith in Krüger. "Yes," they chorused, "that's the way it was."

"Right," said Krüger. "We'll continue this session at the recreation center, but tone it down. We're in mourning, sort of. Neumann will stay with the late lamented to clear up the mess and give any unwelcome visitors the brush-off."

"It'll be a pleasure," Neumann assured him.

"Hiller," pursued Krüger, "comes with me for a concentrated briefing. The rest of you clear out fast. See you at the recreation center in half an hour's time."

Bert Bergen did not reappear at Battery HQ until just before midnight. He paused in the doorway of the canteen and stared at the long, tarpaulin-covered shape that lay on the table, guarded by Neumann.

"So it's true," he said quietly.

"Shove off," Neumann called. "This place is off limits. Strictly no admittance. Krüger's orders."

Bergen gave no sign of having heard. He slowly came closer and halted beside the table. "So you actually got him, you bloody murderers."

"I wouldn't talk like that if I were you, pal, not even in your sleep." Neumann's tone was quite friendly.

"Why, are you planning to rub me out like this poor, gullible kid?" Bergen shook his head grimly. "Schubert bought it just because somebody didn't want to set eyes on him again—somebody whose wish is your command. Executioners, that's what you've turned into."

"Come off it, Bergen, you're talking bullshit—dangerous bullshit at that. I'll forget you ever said it." Neumann looked worried now. "It was an accident, that's all."

"While cleaning a gun?"

"Right the first time! How did you guess?"

"I'm getting wise to your methods. Everything's wrapped up, I suppose. Plenty of witnesses, all telling precisely the same story. . . ."

"It's all wrapped up and tied with pink ribbon," Neumann assured him. "Like you said, he was accidentally killed while cleaning a gun. I saw the whole thing, but the star witness is your pal Tino Hiller."

"Hiller?" Bergen heard himself ask incredulously.

"I bet that surprises you, doesn't it? Krüger's got all the details down in writing. And now shove off."

There was a long silence. Then Bergen said, "I'd like to see him."

"Tough titty," snapped Neumann, stepping between him and the head of the table. "No can do. I'd need Krüger's permission, and when he hears you've come barging in here...."

"Get out of my way," Bergen said quietly.

"Why make trouble for me?" Neumann entreated. "There isn't much to see, so you might as well save yourself a shock. Viewing bodies is morbid, if you want my opinion. You ought to bury people quick and remember them the way they were—the way you liked them best."

Bergen shoved Neumann vigorously aside. He bent over the body and raised the tarpaulin, then stared down at the thing that had once been Johannes Schubert's face, a boyish face radiant with almost classical beauty. It was thickly encrusted with blood from a gaping wound in the back of the head, where the bullet had emerged.

Bergen dropped the tarpulin, turned on his heel and walked out. He was weeping dry-eyed.

Candles were burning in the banquet hall—all the candles Hein could muster. Stuck in a variety of candlesticks, silver, gilt and brass, they were arrayed on the table, along the walls, on the floor, on chairs, on the sideboard. They flickered fitfully in the draft that carried from the four open windows of the tower chamber.

Hein stood amid the clusters of light dressed in a long white nightgown. The ducal robe lay trampled at his feet. He refilled his glass and, with a gesture of revulsion, flung the empty bottle at the wall. It smashed. He poured some champagne down his throat and dropped his glass as well, then stamped on it till his bare feet bled. His set white face was streaming with sweat.

He swayed, trampling the ducal robe once more and

bloodying its opulent folds. On the verge of losing his balance, he staggered to the table and gripped the polished edge, recovered himself quickly and stood there breathing hard with his mouth agape. He strained every nerve as he peered into the chain of dancing lights and beyond them at the ominous shadows near the door. A pair of eyes seemed to glint at him from their depths.

"Is that you, Bergen?" he called.

"Yes," Bergen said.

Hein nodded. "I'm glad you've come. At least there's one man in this unit whose sincerity I can rely on." He sank down behind the table, but only to reach into the bucketful of ice beneath it and reappear with another bottle in his hand. He brandished it like a weapon, then smashed the neck against the table edge, took a new glass from the ranks facing him, filled it, drained it, and ground it to splinters.

Dully, he said, "When will they cease, Bergen, these everlasting, agonizing demands on me? The things people expect of me—the things they compel me to do! I aspire to greatness and they stifle me with their vile trivialities. I offer them loyalty and they betray me in return. I love them, only to have my feelings trampled underfoot. My God, what a world!"

He leaned across the table, supporting himself on his palms. "And yet, Bergen, despite everything, the world is a place of ordeal, of total and unlimited commitment. I've always known it, but the realization haunts me—torments me. I've never been able to comprehend why others don't realize it too. I've tried—desperately—to impress it on all who have ever been close to me. I begged them, entreated them, went down on my knees to them as the angel did to the Lord before he destroyed Sodom and Gomorrah."

Hein slumped forward onto the table, scattering bottles and glasses. Champagne gushed across the tabletop and dripped to the floor like blood. The liquid beat a fast and furious tattoo which dwindled until silence claimed the room once more.

Soaked in champagne and sweat, Hein drew himself up. He stood straight, spread his arms and let them fall. For minutes he stared into nothingness, seemingly oblivious of Bergen's presence.

At last he said, slowly and painfully, "Everything must take its course, I suppose. I grasped the higher meaning, the true purpose of human existence, and tried to fulfill it. Those who resist, who fail to recognize their true destiny, who are incapable of identifying their allotted goal in life, must be compelled! We must compel them into greatness, loyalty and love, even if they perish in the process."

With swelling chest and contorted face, Hein grasped the end of the refectory table and heaved. His cheeks turned purple and the breath rasped in his throat as he raised it to shoulder height, arms trembling, then tipped it sideways. Several hundred pounds of solid oak crashed onto the chairs, smashing them and sending candlesticks cascading to the floor. Wax splashed everywhere and flames licked at the tapestries on the wall. Hein laughed harshly at the sight.

He strode through his bedroom and along the narrow passage leading to the tower chamber, ran up the steps and, negotiating the great chair in the center of the room, made for the north window.

Once there, he leaped onto the parapet and landed with his legs spread, balancing like a gymnast. He steadied himself briefly against the window embrasure, then stood erect and unsupported, gazing into the distance.

"Death," said Karl Ludwig Hein, "holds no terrors for me!"

Involuntarily, Bergen moved closer to the captain until he was standing just behind him. Then he kicked him, abruptly but hard, in the buttocks.

Hein screamed and grabbed the window frame, but the worm-eaten wood disintegrated.

Robbed of his hold, he plunged into the abyss and landed with a muffled thud on the flagstones at the foot of the tower. He lay there inert, much as a soldier named Schulz had done not many weeks before.

"That," Bergen muttered to himself before leaving, "was unavoidable. I couldn't help myself."

He walked back along the passage, crossed the bedroom and reentered the banquet chamber. The tapestry-hung walls were aflame.

Other flames licked avidly over the upturned table, darted across the carpets, engulfed the ancestral portraits, soared to meet the timbered ceiling, desiccated by centuries of existence.

Bergen picked his way skillfully and safely across the burning room. He ran downstairs and, without encountering anyone, reached the junior ranks' dormitory. Sneaking through the darkness, he lay down on his bunk.

Two minutes later he heard a babble of cries. He smiled and said nothing.

"The château's on fire!" someone shouted, shaking him. "The whole place is going up!"

Bergen rolled over on his bunk. "Who cares?" he said.

Extracts
from a statement made by Major Born (ret.),
formerly of the Judge Advocate General's department.

". . . investigated it all in the fullest detail. I emphatically reject any unfounded suspicions and imputations—emphatically!

". . . can only confirm what I discovered and put on record at the time . . . scrupulous objectivity and attention to detail, eager only to serve the ends of justice. . . . I still stand by my findings. They were as follows:

"Schulz, a gunner, fell from a window while cleaning the same;

"Runge, a sergeant, was killed in action while attempting to repel enemy saboteurs;

"Schubert, a bombardier newly promoted on his battery commander's recommendation for services above and beyond the call of duty, wounded himself fatally while cleaning a service automatic;

"finally, Captain Hein, a victim of circumstance. Fire broke out in the dilapidated top story of the old château where he was stationed, rousing him from his bed. He must have tried to call for help from a window in the tower chamber, but the frame he was holding disintegrated and he fell. He broke his neck and died instantly.

"Such are the facts."

Edited version
of a funeral oration
delivered in honor of Captain Hein
by his regimental commander, Colonel Rheinemann-Bergen.

". . . And so we bid farewell to a comrade of whom it can truly be said: We shall not see his like again. All in all, he was a heroic personality who has carved himself a niche in the halls of eternity. Let us endeavor to keep that thought constantly before us.

"Our late lamented comrade set standards which will be binding on us from this day forth. He sacrificed himself to the last, staunchly and steadfastly, in the hope of a better tomorrow for Germany and mankind in general.

"Standing here beside his grave, we pay tribute to his greatness of mind, his gallantry, his unique power of decision, his soldierly spirit, his iron will. Here was a man who spent his entire life in readiness to make sacrifices—sacrifices for Germany, his fatherland, his world. No one who died as he did can have died in vain, comrades, or the history of that world would lose its meaning.

"But meaningless it cannot be, comrades, nor will it be as long as there are still Germans who retain a proud awareness of their nationhood—and they are a breed of men whom nothing can destroy. What—I ask myself and you—can give greater hope for the future than that?"